Southern Fried Monster

J. Oliver Glasgow

DEDICATION

Dedicated to P.C.

I wrote these funny words about fear long before you helped me realize the truth that had somehow always been right behind them...

... and that ultimately freed me.

Maybe our own hidden truth *is* the monster that creeps up behind us just waiting for us to club it over the head, cook it up and eat it?

CONTENTS

1.

Once upon a time in a town not so very far away from here and on a day not so very long ago, there was an unassuming guy with the unassuming name of Guy that became the most powerful person on the face of the planet. Many years before this wholly remarkable transformation (it was wholly remarkable because the process of transforming into the most powerful person on the face of the planet did not actually transform Guy's unassuming nature – well, not really all *that* much) he attended an unassuming high school making plans for his very nearly wholly unremarkable life.

"So as you can see from this chart, with your parent's excellent background and your," here the guidance counselor, Dr. Maria Isabella Consuelo Aufvedersane, paused and looked over her glasses while she fished around in the thesaurus of her mind for the best (and most delicate) word to describe Guy's unassuming academic record, "suitable grade-point average, you should be able to get into pretty much any area college after you graduate next year and follow in their footsteps. And from my most pleasant conversations with them, I understand that they are very interested in whatever it is that you want out of life," and then she added with only the slightest drop of voice as if she were a used car saleswoman making an obligatory legal disclaimer, "as long as it is a career from the wide and generous list they have arranged for you."

Guy looked briefly at Dr. Aufvedersane's torso, her breasts were pressed together by the vest that completed the three-piece ensemble and yet still allowed for an exposure that was perhaps a little too racy for her conservative position of responsibility as it could be worn with or without a blouse – and on this present date she had chosen sans instead of con.

His present thoughts of his friends' mixed analogy that she was both hot and weird filled his head in these intermediating moments. They thought she was hot for, well, obvious reasons. But they did not think she was weird because she was an attractive Hispanic woman with a last name that was clearly an English transliteration for a German word. No, they thought she was weird for the overly personal way she seemed to acquaint herself with their parents' desires for their lovely children's futures.

The immediate need for reply dispelled his present panoply of thoughts like the autumnal wind dispels the fog from San Francisco Bay as he answered flatly, "As long as it is Aerospace Physics or Industrial Real-Estate Law."

"Well, it's only natural that they would want you to follow in their footsteps. The Sayonara's," then thinking better of it she corrected herself, "Dotty and Frank, only want what's best for their little Guy."

Guy was not amused at the double-dimples that formed on the corners of her Latino mouth as she concluded her thought. Nor was he amused at her cute replacement of the name Guy for the word guy – it was a pun he was more than used to.

In fact he was rarely amused at all.

No, in this moment he was more concerned that his friends thought *him* weird.

They did not think he was weird because he was a plain-looking White Anglo Saxon Agnostic with a last name that was clearly an English transliteration for a Japanese word. They did not think he was weird because he was remarkably unassuming. No, they thought he was weird for the very thing he was about to reveal to Dr. Aufvedersane.

"I want to be a chef."

The fact that the guidance counselor had actually laughed out loud at him was one of those stinging events that still brought the blood to his cheeks upon the mere passing of the thought even eighteen months later as he was getting ready to leave for college. Everyone has had one of those moments. Most everyone can recall a time after potty training when they thought they had this whole self-control thing licked only to find that a little pressure in just the wrong way made for an awkward walk to a fresh change of clothes. The slightest breeze of such a memory can bring near-agonizing warmth to the face, even in an empty room – even while doing something as trivial as reading a book.

And now as Guy prepared to leave for college, that remembered moment echoed in his mind bringing with it the inevitable elevator-drop in his stomach.

She had fucking laughed at him!

He had purposed in his heart at that very moment to show them all how wrong they were. He would become the greatest chef in the world. People would come from far and wide to sample his culinary delights, nearly addicted with their appetites for all dishes Guy.

Unfortunately, Mommy and Daddy Sayonara did not quite share the same dream. As Guy was packing the final items in his duffel bag and preparing to take it out to the already overstuffed GMC Pacer, Dotty spoke to him from her motherly perch on the corner of his bed. "Please be reasonable, Guy."

Shoving a T-shirt into the duffel bag to punctuate his consternation, "I am being reasonable, Mom. I just really know what I want to be. I know what will make me happy."

It was Frank's turn to try. "Son, no one knows what will make them happy before they are forty. Hell, even then it's a grab-bag chance to get it right." At this Dotty shot him a disapproving look that suggested he had better tread lightly. The kid was fair game, but she would not tolerate any collateral damage from this little fracas. Tempering his words and facial attitude slightly to make up for the misstep he continued, "That is to say, give it some time."

"What your father is trying to say is that you needn't declare a major until your junior year. So just take general studies until then. Give yourself time to discover what you would be most happy doing."

Stuffing in some underwear, the force of his hand doing the screaming because it was inappropriate to do so with his voice to his parents, "I am doing what would make me most happy doing."

Ok, so the grammar was a little rough, but you can't have everything when you are eighteen and standing your ground for the very first time.

"What your mother means is that you can *think* about declaring anything you want for the next two years."

Guy concluded, "…just as long as it is one of the two things on your list for me."

His parents were tag-teaming this one. So he guessed it would be his mother's turn next.

"There. Now that we all have that straightened out – Frank, be a dear and take Guy's last bag out to the car."

Right on cue.

Guy let it go. Well, at least verbally let it go, for now. He said his goodbyes and climbed in, scrunching up next to all his stuff, and with a wave, drove away while his mother cried and his father busied himself with wrapping a manly arm around her and pulling her in close doing the Dad thing.

As soon as Guy got to college he declared his major in culinary and promptly signed up for an overloaded schedule of basic courses and some classes specific to his chosen curriculum. To keep the additional costs off his dad's credit card and thus avoiding unwanted entanglement, he arranged for small student loans to quietly pay for the additional classes.

The plan had worked flawlessly. So now, some two years later, just after starting his junior year, he stared at the phone in his dorm room. His parents had moved on in life and were now busy remembering what it was all about before children. All they needed from Guy was the occasional call or visit, the end-of-term report cards, and the odd request for additional money to know that all was well on the Guy-front.

The reason Guy was now staring at his phone was that it was already past the appointed date to declare a major. This was the moment where he picked up the phone and made that much-dreaded and much-procrastinated call to his parents to let them in on his little secret that he was now two years away from graduating with a full culinary degree.

But it was his passion. Well, it is difficult to say that Guy was actually ever really passionate about anything. But in this one thing he was very nearly almost passionate.

"It can't be all that difficult," he said to the phone. "I will simply pick up the receiver, dial the ten numbers, and talk to my parents.

"It is simply that simple."

But it wasn't simply that simple, really. He knew what was coming. He had known it since the time that they had told him what was coming only two years before this moment.

Guy wondered, as he stared at the touch pad full of numbers, exactly why they still called it *dialing*. He supposed that it was maybe a little too politically incorrect to say that you would "touch somebody up" or "I will touch your number sometime". And so another piece of just-past-modern lingo would be grandfathered into our society, leaving future generations to wonder what it is all about.

He picked up the receiver. It felt strangely heavy in his hand. He could imagine that even the phone was cognizant of the weight this moment held for him. As he dialed their number in what seemed like slow motion, the receiver seemed to grow even heavier with every tone.

At first he thought about maybe coming up with a phone-receiver-diet for his fall Nutrition Class project. Perhaps he could help overweight phone receivers shed those unwanted pounds. But as the tones played in his ear he found himself wondering if the tones were perfect thirds or diatonic steps apart. One thing was certain - whoever the tone engineer was for the phone company, he or she had managed to come up with their own new tonality.

Next up, Guy's Sonata Number 1 in the key of touchtone.

He held the receiver to his ear as its heaviness continued to increase and listened as the relays clicked – connecting his call. Eventually he heard the familiar ring of his parents' phone. Even their ring had a chipper buoyancy to it.

Guy had never really had a chipper buoyancy to him - especially not now.

"Hello?" came Dotty's wholly optimistic interrogative.

"Hi, Mom."

"Oh, hi Guy! How are you doing pumpkin?"

Pumpkin pie would be nice right about now – just the right amount of allspice and some cool whipped topping on top, just a dollop. Guy's immediate thoughts returned as he answered, "Oh, I am fine. Just fine. I have some information for you and Dad."

"Fantastic. I will get your father. Hold on," and before Guy had a chance to foreshadow the bad news or prepare her for the coming train wreck in any way, shape, form, or fashion, he heard her hand muffle the receiver and yell through the house, "Frankie? It's our Guy on the phone. He is about to make his big announcement."

Guy's stomach lollopped as he heard the barely audible reply yelled back from another room. He thought it rather sounded like, "Get otter tea by the station." But he realized it was probably more like, "I'll pick up the other extension."

A moment later there was a cheerful click followed by his father's confident and booming voice, "Guy, my man! How are you doing big fella?"

Guy had never really ever been confident, booming, or big.

"I guess I am doing pretty ok, actually."

"So what's the big news?" Dotty asked.

They were tag-teaming already. This was not going to go well.

The moment had come. Funny how when you have two years to prepare for something bad that you can almost put it completely out of your mind. But more often than one would predict, it pops into your brain bringing that feeling that a term paper is due the next day and by way of procrastination has not really been started yet.

Guy had that feeling now.

No time like the present. Guy said flatly, "I am going to be a chef."

There. The deed was done. It is finished. No more spooky jerks as he remembered the coming express train in the middle of the night. And amazingly, his receiver was back to a svelte nine ounces in his hand.

But his moment of glory was fleeting - gloria brevis.

"Son, we have been over and over this and…"

"And nothing, Pop," Guy cut in. He had never really ever called Frank Pop before, so it came out sounding forced, terse. But he continued bravely, "I have found something that I like to do and I am going to stick with it."

Dotty reasoned, "You can cook any time you want Guy. But a thing is different when it is your living. You enjoy it now because you haven't really had any demand to do it."

"Actually I have been taking the classes for two years now – and I am doing quite well for my half-way point through the major."

"What?" came Frank's angry drill sergeant impersonation.

"I have been working on a culinary major for two years now," Guy said with a *case closed* finality to his voice.

"But Guy, we have seen all your grades and know how much all the courses have cost us," Dotty said with a *case re-opened* authority in hers.

Guy explained how he had managed to take the class-load without their knowledge and told them about the student loans.

"Ok, just because you made a bone-headed mistake and committed yourself to a few years of debt after you graduate doesn't mean that you are an indentured slave to your present course. You can simply switch to something reasonable," Frank interjected.

This was his parent's version of good-cop/bad-cop – only in their case it always came across as bad-cop/bad-cop.

Guy wanted a donut.

"You both just don't understand. This is my life. I am an adult. I want to do this one thing for myself."

There was a pregnant pause on the phone. Guy was able to hear cross-talk softly in the background. It sounded like somewhere a young Mexican boy was telling his Mexican parents that he had decided to become an INS officer and they were trying to talk him out of it, but Guy couldn't be really sure because the whole thing was in Spanish.

"Well, you told me this was going to happen, Frank."

"It is a good thing we prepared for this, Dotty."

Guy knew this was bad. They had started to talk to each other as if he wasn't in the conversation.

"What are we going to do?" Dotty asked.

"I suppose you need to go ahead and tell him the plan," Frank said in a Teflon way.

"Ok, Guy," his mom said now clearly addressing him, "We are going to cut you off."

The real impact of this statement did not hit Guy all at once. It had no immediate registration with the depth of its import. But he picked up enough to elicit a response. "What?"

That's our hero. Swuft, as they say in the South.

"What your mother is trying to say to you is that as long as you want to 'do this one thing for yourself', then you will do this one thing *by* yourself," Frank stated.

"What?"

"We are cutting you off, pumpkin. We are not going to fund your delusional fantasy." Then Dotty added, "It's what our pastor calls *tough love.*"

This was bad. His mother was now using catch phrases. If the Industrial Real-Estate attorney was using clichés, he was in trouble.

"All I am asking for…" he began to debate.

"…is a chance to prove yourself, and we are going to give you that chance. As of this moment, you are financially on your own." his father said, ending the debate as well as the call. Both parents hung up as if on cue.

Guy looked at the receiver as he placed it back in its cradle and began to lay out his strategy. The fall semester was bought and paid-for. He also already had his books and dorm room which came with a meal ticket and parking permit. Then for the last eighteen months, he would need to take out grants and student loans. But there were lots of students on the buy-now-pray-later program. There was no shame in that.

So all he really needed was consumable supplies to get him as far along as possible.

He reached over to his nightstand and pulled out his wallet. Rifling through its contents he found a credit card and a department store card that were in his parents' names. Guy would have to act fast if he was going to beat them to the punch, knowing full well they would probably call in to cancel the cards as soon as they thought to do so. This would mean an immediate shopping trip was in order.

Now, some of the most monumental lapses in judgment in all of history have occurred when college students go on a free-for-all shopping spree with mom and dad's credit cards. And this was certainly no exception.

Six hours and six shopping cartfuls later, his half of the dorm room was filled to the brim with six hundred dollars' worth of consumable supplies – everything a growing college-boy needs. The place looked like it was fortified to survive an alien invasion.

The only problem was that Guy was six years too early for that. Well, that and the fact that these types of supplies don't seem to last very long in a dormitory. And so, a short six weeks later, pretty much everything was gone.

The next two years were relatively uneventful, save for the two times he got laid. And one of those didn't even really count because it was with the college bike (you know the joke – everyone got to ride) at a frat's open-invite kegger. If you can't get lucky there, then you can't get lucky. But other than these more than typical college events, there was the discovery of the dry rub. Now *that* was eventful.

Six months after the "talk" with his parents, Guy was in his dorm room working on a mid-term project. Spring break was coming up the next week and Dex, his far more than unassuming roommate was packing for the inevitable road trip to Daytona, Florida.

"You should come with us."

"Nah. You know my money is tight. I can't afford it." Guy went back to working on his list of ingredients.

Dex leaned over his now quite stuffed suitcase and said in a most beguiling way, "You know, Guy, you don't *have* to live like this."

"What do you mean?"

"I mean you could have plenty of money if you wanted."

"How?"

"All you have to do is change your major to communications or political science and I would be willing to bet that Dotty and Frank would drop you a cool 2k to get you through the rest of the year."

Guy was beginning to get a little annoyed. It wasn't bad enough that Dex had looks and a future going for him – he also had that certain "X" factor. Everyone wanted to be his friend. And to top it all off, he never looked like he had to try very hard to accomplish anything he wanted. But worse than all of this put together, he was presently interrupting Guy while he was putting the finishing touches on some research for a new dry rub. It was his mid-term culinary grade and the ingredients list was nearly complete.

"I told you Dex. My cooking is everything to me."

"But you said yourself you aren't really good at it. All you have managed is a C average."

"C+," Guy corrected.

"Ok, C+. That is your *major*. You should be acing that stuff."

Guy didn't want to admit his roommate was right.

"Look, you haven't lost a lot of time. You have most of the groundwork done. Just switch your major to something pre-law and you can hump-it with a slightly larger class-load. Hell, I am on the five-year plan myself. We can graduate together, do a quick three-year law degree and open our own firm. Maybe we can even get into politics and shape the world's future from conversations in bars or strip clubs. It will be fun! Dotty even said she would help us get it all started."

At the mention of his mother's first name, Guy heard an imaginary record scratch to a halt. Everyone stopped dancing. Life froze.

"She did, did she?"

"Yup."

"And just when did you speak to my mother?"

"Just this morning," Dex said. Guy was beginning to see red as his roomie continued, "I was telling her how hard things were going for you – that you were having to skip the annual fling in spring."

Dex went back to packing as if there had been nothing wrong with his talking to the enemy. As Guy wrote down the last ingredient for the rub, a thought occurred to him. "And how much did she offer you if you succeeded in talking me into the change?"

Dex answered matter-of-factly, "A matching 2k. Just think about it, buddy, we could be blowing $4,000 in Daytona next week!"

Guy let a few moments pass while he watched in disbelief as his friend continued to pack. At length Guy said with morose, "I could never sell out a friend for $2,000."

Without batting an eye, Dex replied as he continued to pack, "Then on second thought, maybe law isn't the right field for you." Stopping his packing for a moment, he looked over the mess and said with an air of discovery, "Hey, how do you feel about math? I hear that once you get past astral physics, the degree program isn't that hard. Granted you will probably need at least another semester or two on that program, but I am sure your folks won't mind."

In the social mores of our society, it is simply not permitted for a young man in college to storm out of a room, slam a door, or cry. But Guy crumpled up his mid-term project list, stuffed it in his jeans pocket, and did all three of the prohibited things in that order.

In his anger, he walked across campus to the culinary labs. There he pulled the crumpled list from his pocket and began yanking ingredients off the shelf in order, following his own instructions carefully. Within a matter of moments he had a large mixing bowl filled with six of the seven ingredients he had written down.

Now, in college culinary work, it is every student's responsibility to provide their own ingredients for each semester. The purchase list for this particular semester had all but bankrupted Guy. The bowl in which he now worked contained more than $50 in raw ingredients – far more than he was even worth at the moment. And this is why the action he was about to take was such a huge tragedy. For while his eyes were still filling with bitter tears and his anger at the moment was causing his hand to shake a little, he grabbed up not one container but two off the shelf above his workspace and dumped them in the middle of his work.

Grabbing them up quickly he managed to keep the contents of one, the baking powder, mostly in its container. But the other one, the dill, expelled nearly all of its contents right in the middle of the dry rub.

It wasn't even the right ingredient. No chef in his or her right mind would add dill to the other six ingredients he had chosen. It was more than completely wrong. But Guy was not a chef in his right mind. Looking at the catastrophe, and already swaying from the ever increasing pressures this melodrama was placing on his shoulders, he went ahead and completely snapped.

Guy stood there and absentmindedly stirred the concoction for what seemed like a matter of moments to him but turned out to be hours. Looking at the designs the spoon was making in the dry rub, he realized that this was the end. There was no more money and this project was due the next day. He had blown it completely.

There came a time when his own fatigue and hunger caused him to stop his stirring and he had to face reality. He would get an F for his mid-term, give into his folks, and go on vacation the next week in Daytona. He supposed in the end, it wasn't really so bad selling out to yourself if you ultimately became wealthy and fat.

In an almost comical last-ditch effort to save his now dying dream, he wetted his finger and stuck it square in the middle of the dry rub. Lifting it up to his still-optimistically hopeful tongue he expected that he would wretch and vomit out the remnants of his all but gone lunch in a perfect metaphor for the remnants of his all but gone ambitions.

The tip of his finger plunged smack in his mouth, and as he relaxed from his guarded stance, he allowed his brain to compute what his tongue was already singing in jubilant revelation. The stuff was not horrible. The stuff was not even mediocre. It certainly wasn't C+, and in fact it was simply amazing.

The look on his professor's face the next day in class was one of sheer astonishment. The heavens opened up and the angels sang, "Halleluiah!" as he tasted the most amazing thing he had encountered in over twenty years of teaching.

"This is the most amazing thing I have encountered in over thirty years of teaching," Dr. Misanthrope said. He liked to exaggerate his own tenure as an educator – well, downright lie about it actually. "I know I told you kids that dry rubs would always taste bad alone, that they would be bitter or coarse. It is when they are applied to the meat and the meat is cooked that they work their magic. But here, Mr. Sayonara has really shown us *something*. This is truly amazing stuff."

As he made his way to the next student's bowl he announced, "A+, 100, congratulations Mr. Sayonara. I look forward to the second half of your grade this semester as you apply it to all the meats on your list. It should be quite *something*."

Other students crowded in around him and began tasting the concoction. All of them sang its praises and Guy lived out his first Warholian fifteen minutes of fame. But glory is fleeting - gloria brevis, and all that. As he launched into the second half of his semester, Guy ran into the chef's equivalent of writer's block. One might call it dry rub block.

Meat after meat – fish, beef, chicken, et al, all of them cooked in a variety of ways seemed to be immune to the glory of the rub. For one reason or another it just didn't work. The dry rub became the perfect metaphor for Guy, himself. It promised a lot, had a great amount of potential, looked good on paper, but in reality was ok, just ok. It was so-so. Not too bad, actually – well, not really. And so with every disappointment bringing a D or a C upon the tasting, Guy managed to escape his junior year with a C+ average.

All potentiality, no real delivery – aye, there's the rub.

Thus, one year later, Guy Sayonara graduated with a C. He walked the stage knowing absolutely not a soul in the audience. Even Dex had left, going to Europe for one last summer blow-out before he plunged into his own last year of college. Guy strolled the stage in mortar board and robe, shook the hands of his dean and of his president, accepted the scroll with the red ribbon wrapped snuggly around it, and walked off into a life full of potential and bursting at the seams with debt.

He had no idea that in four short years, he would become the most powerful man in the world. But for now, he was just an unassuming guy with the unassuming name of Guy.

2.

There is a largely unknown psychological secret about success. It is largely unknown because it is profitable to keep it unknown. And profit begets greed.

If one traces the motivations to *action* they would find a plethora of root causes for all the effects in the world. There are all sorts of stimuli that explain why we do the things that we do. Love is a good one. So is hate. And there are even causes for the things we *don't* do, like apathy and laziness. But probably the most interesting among these catalysts is greed.

Greed is intriguing because it can be a mouse or it can be a lion. In its smallest apparition, it might cause one to work a little harder on the job. In its enormity it can change the mind and soul of a person, and what they once feared they will now desire to possess, even to own.

And so it may be greed that has prevented the world from finding out one of the simplest and smallest of psychological secrets. It is small, and yet in and of itself, it may have put a number of clinically trained psychologists' kids through college. This cash cow to the shrinks is the fact that depression very nearly always follows success.

This is nothing new. It has happened from the beginning of time and is even captured very clearly in ancient writings like the Bible. Elijah, after achieving a massive victory for which he fought for some seven years against that hussy, Jezebel, celebrated by retreating to a cave and praying for his life to end. He felt isolation, fear, loneliness, and angst.

They didn't have Disney World back then.

"Elijah of God, you've just called down fire from heaven and thwarted Jezebel and the priests of Baal! Now what are you going to do?"

"I guess I will crawl into a cave and die."

But in this simple story we learn that depression is an almost automatic response to success. The larger the success, the larger the depression can be. In fact, one might even consider depression as the little light on the dashboard that tells you that you have been successful – that your job is done.

In Elijah's case, the cure was just as simple as the problem. God told him to go out into a neighboring country and find his replacement named Elisha. It was a simple task, but the mere activity of *doing* a simple task will most often rescue us from our depression. Just *do* something. The solution is *in* the doing, making ourselves busy with another task.

Now, not all depression is the result of success. It is a fairly complicated thing, actually. But in Guy's case, the depression that came on him after graduation was extremely easy to diagnose. A good shrink would have stretched it out for at least six months had Guy not been so broke and so in debt. So he retreated to a cave. He hocked the few items he had left, cashed in all the bonds he had been given through the years for birthdays and such, made everything he could liquid, and rented an apartment.

He had chosen Huntsville, Alabama for his new home because the Department of Defense had been successful lately, due in large part to the heightened state of global terrorism, but mostly because there were people in high places making large, sweeping decisions, driven mostly by greed. Huntsville is an engineering town and whenever the DOD is successful, Huntsville is successful. And where there are a lot of newly hired engineers, there are a lot of newly opened restaurants.

All the new chef jobs seemed to be in Huntsville, Alabama. And so, Guy was in Huntsville, Alabama. The only problem was that coming off of the huge success, taking on the world and graduating with a degree in culinary, he had crawled into his newly rented cave and was in the process of asking for his very life to end.

In a world swirling around him rife with greed and success, Guy was depressed. Go figure.

There were some shining moments, as most depression in most cases is not complete depression for most people. He did actually like his apartment a little. It was a one-bedroom on the ground floor, second door from the left-hand side when you stood in the parking lot and looked to the rising sun. His back door slid open onto a nice little concrete patio that was perfect for grilling out in the moderate climes of northern Alabama.

The patio even had a little wrought-iron fence wrapped around it. Apparently the previous renter had either a little extra money or was extremely adept at welding, and had somehow convinced the landlord to allow him or her to set it up. The low step-over black railing broken up by the odd pair of rather tall poniards of staggered height seemed a little out of place, but the gothic look added to its overall charm for a twenty-two year-old graduate out in the world for the first time.

And Guy was even fond of the neighbor one door down past the breezeway that cut all the way through the building. Calvin was a construction worker in his mid-thirties with jet-black hair and a perpetual two-day stubble that added that certain panache to his pork-chop mustache. He was one of those southern boys that didn't realize that the mullet haircut had been out of vogue for years. Well, actually, it had never really ever been *in* vogue. But it had been popular with the NASCAR set for a while.

His neighbor, Calvin, always seen with his inevitable side-kick, a can of beer, would walk up to Guy's open patio and speak on southern platitudes until the mosquitoes of the evening chased them both in for the night. He didn't seem to have much ambition in life, but Guy found some comfort in the thought that for some people, this was enough to be happy - just working and living.

Best of all, Calvin had a jet-ski that he would ride wide-open on Guntersville Lake or in the Tennessee River on the weekends. It was a short drive to the sun, fun and beer. Guy was blown away by the jet-ski. He hoped to acquire one someday.

"Hell, man. Maybe you should just go and buy one," Calvin suggested in his gravelly voice ladled with a solid southern accent. Guy always wanted to suggest that Calvin clear his throat, but he was afraid it would be rude to bring it up. "They have all those instant credit things going all the time. Hell, that's the way I bought mine."

"No, Cal. I think I want to pay off some debt, make it big, and then buy one with cash," then squinting to the side from his four-dollar lawn chair in the mid-day sun he added, "At least that's my plan, anyway."

"Heh, well at the rate you're flying, that should be within a century or two. Just wake me up when it's time to zoom," he said as he began to head back to his own apartment. Calvin's sidekick was now a sad and lonely empty aluminum can and he wanted to take it back to introduce it to a bunch of others so it could have some company in the recycling bin while he recruited a new fresh, young sidekick to take its place.

"I have an interview tomorrow!" Guy called out to Calvin's nonchalant backside in a vain effort to regain some stature in his neighbor's eye.

"Good luck with that," Calvin called back without really looking, holding the empty beer can up high in the air in a mock salute.

As was his usual custom, Guy reached down on his right and picked up a handful of pea-gravel from the side of the patio and began throwing pebbles one at a time at the base of the grill where he was cooking some of the last hamburger meat he had in his refrigerator. He spoke to the grill as the pebbles pinged and ticked off its base, "Ah, Calvin is right. Who am I kidding? I have been here for weeks, been on countless interviews, and haven't even been offered a spot as a Sous-Chef."

The next morning had brought a somewhat renewed optimism with the dew of the Tennessee Valley. Even though this was indeed Alabama, Huntsville was snuggled into Monte Sano Mountain where the basin floor north of the Tennessee River was considered all part of it. Guy woke up actually embracing the day. It seemed to be basted in opportunity.

He only nicked himself two times due to nerves while shaving. And then managed to calm himself a little as he cooked his own breakfast. He even managed to remember not to put his good shirt on until *after* he had brushed his teeth, which meant that he had avoided splattering it and cussing at the misfortune of having to where his second-best.

All was set. He hopped in his car and drove the short trip down to Governor's Drive in time to be a good fifteen minutes early.

The Mongolian-style restaurant was new to these parts, but Huntsville was a rather metropolitan town despite its fixed position as the "Heart of Dixie". Usually these places did better in more progressive communities. But the owner had felt that the timing was right for this rather diverse market.

Things had not been the same there since the German rocket scientists had chosen that spot to call home after they defected near the end of World War II. Redstone Arsenal had become the home of the Marshall Space-flight Center, and whether the rest of the public was aware of it or not, the Huntsville Operational Space-flight Center or HOSC had been the real center of control for all the missions from Gemini through the first half of the shuttle flights.

Thus all of Huntsville became a town where you were either an engineer or you were working in an industry that fed, clothed, or otherwise took care of engineers. Germans lived next door to Indians. Indians lived next door to Greeks. Sprinkle in a few Americans cut right out of a Norman Rockwell painting, simmer for four or five decades and you end up with a clean and happy environment of diversity and tolerance.

Oh, there was the occasional KKK rally held that would make the Six O'clock News, but that was really on the fringe and mostly a thing of the past.

So all kinds of experiments worked there that might fall flat on their collective fannies in other southern towns or cities. And Wayne Avarice was one entrepreneur that felt the time was right for the Mongol horde to invade the Rocket City.

"This will be his fifth restaurant in Huntsville," a gentleman sitting next to Guy in the lobby said without introduction, "I think it's really cool the way these millionaires operate. I bet you could strip him of ever last dime he had, drop him off in any town in America with nothing but the clothes on his back, and two years later he would be rich again. That's the way it works, you know."

Guy had always been a little leery of total strangers that could strike up conversations with other total strangers, especially when they started it in the middle of a thought like this man had. And now he was facing that awkward moment where he would either have to reply in kind or pretend to ignore this person. This was the opposite of what he had in mind to be doing right now. He should be mentally preparing for the challenge ahead, not wasting time talking to this total git who was probably his competition for the morning.

"Yep," he said cheerfully enough. But then Guy realized his blunder. He had elected to say yep instead of just plain yes or yeah. Yep is a word fraught with obligation to continue one's thoughts. John Wayne never said yep without adding an, "I don't mind if I do," or a, "not unless we head them off first," at the end of it.

Sitting in the rather sterile waiting room of the rather nicely located office suite across from Big Spring Park, Guy thought it was good that he was very quite near the progressive Mental Health Center. He would need their care if his thoughts went much further awry from normality.

"I suppose you are right," he continued. But then realized he had made an even greater gaff. He had created a sentence that begged for a name, any name to put at the end of it. And he couldn't just say, "man". That went out with the seventies. So Guy let his sentence lilt in the air to suggest he needed an introduction. Might as well plunge all the way in – in for a penny, in for a pound.

"Joe."

"Ah, Joe," he finished after being given the answer.

"Joe Calamari," Joe said as he extended a hand to shake Guy's.

"Nice to meet you. Guy. Guy Sayonara."

Guy wondered why men always felt compelled to say at least one of their names twice during introduction. He figured deep down inside that it was somehow Sean Connery's fault in some vague way.

"Sayonara, interesting name for a chef. You're here for the chef position, right?"

"That's me. Are you here for that as well?"

Joe smiled with confidence (maybe a little too much confidence) as he said, "Oh yes. That is why I am here. Say, didn't you recently apply for that new Italian place over on Airport Road?"

Guy was a little surprised. "Yeah. How did you know?"

"Small town. As big as it gets, Huntspatch is nothing more than a small town."

Guy was desperate to bring an end to this conversation. He needed to get in his zone. He needed to psych himself up. This was his big chance and he had a really good feeling about it. The buffet of life was opening up in front of him and he was the first in line. To attempt to bring a close, he raised his eyebrows in his best impression of a harmless cowboy and said with finality, "I guess you're right."

The two of them sat there in silence for a moment. Guy had noticed the secretary looking at Joe with familiar glances. It was like they were in on something and he wasn't. A clock on the wall was ticking and Guy's nerves felt raw each tick. He just knew at any moment a buzzer would sound and he would be told he was next, please step into Mr. Avarice's office.

"In fact," Joe continued. Guy wondered how people could seemingly pause conversations and then just continue at any time in the future.

Guy found it a great strain trying to buffer partial conversations so that he could follow thoughts when the person finally decided to complete their sentence. He was still waiting for Mrs. Warlock to finish her sentence from fifth grade. During a quiet reading session, she had startled the class with her sudden shrill announcement, "Now students I want you to listen to me. This is very important." All the kids stopped reading and looked up at her with innocent expectation. "It is very important for you to remember that when you read you should always…"

That is where she had just dropped off and never really finished her thought. Guy had wondered why all the kids were ok with this. It was like they were all in on something and he wasn't. Still to this day some eleven years later, Guy's mind was saving that little fragment, waiting for it to be completed - someday.

No one back then had really ever explained the impact or symptoms of being addicted to prescription diazepam, or how some certain young teachers were addicted to it because their husbands had talked them into joining a circle of swinger friends and that wife-swapping was beginning to take its toll on her so much so that she was seeking shelter in a pill bottle. All Guy knew was that Mrs. Warlock looked really hot in a mini-skirt.

Joe's sentence continued to flow as Guy was pondering the deeper meaning of his past, "In fact, you've applied at a number of places – mostly owned by the Braseltons, Oxenstiens, and the d'Pestos."

Now Guy was really intrigued. "Wow. What is it? Have I got a camera following me around?"

"Nah. It's just a small town. All these owners know each other. They compare notes. You can't interview with one without interviewing with them all. Chefs are sort of like trading cards. They play a little game where they trade out and talk about fresh meat."

Guy was a little disgusted. "And I'm fresh meat."

"Well, I wouldn't say fresh any more. Seems like you have been out on the counter now for a few weeks. More like a little gamy if anything," Joe said in a joking voice. He even added a little, friendly titter of a laugh at the end – very convincing as harmless fun.

But Guy's world collapsed like a flan in a cupboard. He was just about ready to give in to his despair and seek refuge in his cave until evicted for lack of rent. If this man was telling the truth, he didn't have a prayer of a chance.

But Guy screwed up his courage to the sticking place with the recollection that this Bozo *was* his competition and this was probably just a mind game to throw him off his plan - probably.

"Well, you say what you will. I rather fancy my chances."

The words were no sooner out of his mouth than Guy realized how nervous he was. The only time he used the word fancy was to describe some elaborate decoration or outfit. And what was worse? He had actually used the word "rather" as well. He quickly reminded himself to get a grip.

Just then the door to the inner-sanctum, the holy of holies, the office of Mr. Avarice opened up and the secretary cleared her throat as the previous applicant left with a big smile on her face. Joe leaned over and whispered to Guy, "That's Tara Smucker. She will be stiff competition. She's *easy*. But she has a pretty good gig at d'Pesto's Barbeque Pit out on Winchester Road. So Old Man Wayne would probably have to come up with more than he's willing to part with to have her."

Guy would have felt suddenly alone, but it was now his turn. He had come in just after the easy chick and right before the asshole sitting on his left now whispering in his ear with the breath of the mouthwash-impaired. Guy wondered if it would be more politically correct to consider Joe as toothbrush-challenged.

Tara had no more than crossed the threshold of the sanctuary that was this office where one gets interviewed, than the secretary said, "Mr. Avarice will see you now, Mr. Calamari."

But Guy's brain had not caught up with his ears and had subsequently sent a message to his body to get up before everything fell into phase. He stood up *with* Joe when the realization sunk in that it was not he that had been summoned. The blood flushed to his face as he quickly sat back down, more embarrassed than angry that he had been apparently skipped.

The mind is a funny occupier of time. While waiting for his now interrupted turn, Guy learned that there were twenty-seven squares of carpet that made up the sandpaper design that hid dirt so well between cleanings. He knew the maker of the clock on the wall and noticed how the first letter in the name stretched around to the nine and that the last letter just touched the three, its sagging characters in between making for a smile on its face. And he had finally realized that the secretary reminded him of the second daughter on the old TV show Petticoat Junction. Guy wasn't sure, but he thought her name had a Joe in it as well. This all reminded him of Joe in the office stealing his interview and quite likely his job.

The blood returned to his face – but this time it was anger more than faux pas.

Again by surprise, the door to the maker-of-his-future opened. This time the man himself was standing full in the threshold stopping Joe for one last handshake. Guy was not quite sure, but he could have sworn he heard the words, "Sounds perfect, Joe. We will see you on Monday."

To say Guy was devastated would be an understatement. But to his surprise he heard Wayne the millionaire entrepreneur say, "Come on in, Guy. I've saved the best for last."

Joe laughed heartily as he passed by and shook Guy's hand saying, "Nice to meet you Guy. It would be good to have you as my Sous sometime."

Guy wanted to say something curt, something cutting. He wanted to leave this prick bleeding in his own blood and spittle. Reaching as deep into the darkest regions of his brain as he could, Guy conjured up the most treacherous of incantations and opened his mouth as he spake, "Thanks. You too."

Guy was not all that dark, as it turns out. But he thought it was a good dig.

Smiling big for the new boss Guy stepped across the lobby painfully self-aware of every single position of every single aspect of his body and how it would be interpreted by his future employer.

He was not dark, but he was certainly thoroughly disturbed.

Stepping into the main office, Mr. Avarice offered, "Please, have a seat."

"Thanks. And thanks for the opportunity to speak about the chef position," Guy said as he sat down in a fairly large, dark red, winged back chair. He took a moment to notice that whatever budget was spared on decorating the outer office was blown on this display of power and wealth inside.

"Not at all. I have looked forward to meeting you since I looked at your resume," Mr. Avarice said as he sat down behind the ornate mahogany desk.

Guy was first cognizant of feeling at a slight disadvantage as Mr. Avarice seemed to leer down at him from a throne of judgment. But then he realized that it was just a feeling because first of all his chair was purposefully built lower to the ground and secondly because Mr. Avarice's advantage was much greater than slight. He owned the *whole* fucking place. It didn't really matter how people *felt* about it.

"So, tell me a little about yourself, Guy."

The nerves were probably at their worst right before he began an interview. This fear was far greater than any he had experienced in his life. This time it wasn't an alien in a B movie, it wasn't a campfire story late at night, and it wasn't even a loose stray dog in the neighborhood chasing him as he ran to the ice cream truck for help. This time it actually meant something. This time it was his dream on the line and a dinner waiting to be bought at the grocery store that mattered most.

And all of it rested on how well he answered a few questions.

Funny, isn't it? How you can prepare for something for years, pay more money than you have to be taught, go into debt proving your dedication to a supposition, do everything right, spend your blood sweat and tears for trials and successes along the way, and in the end it all boils down to how well you do in answering a few questions from a complete and total stranger that has no idea what you have gone through to be where you are? At least that is what Guy *thought* it all came down to. But he was wrong again, wasn't he?

"Well, I have been passionate…"

Guy's voice cracked. He sounded like a prepubescent boy trying on the lower octave for the first time. He cleared his voice and began again.

"I have always been passionate about cooking. I…"

Mr. Avarice interrupted, "I see here that you attended that school down in Atlanta. You graduated, did you not?" He was no longer paying attention to Guy but was now busy thumbing through his two page resume. Guy had needed to stretch a few sentences and use a fairly large font on the word processor to get two pages out of his life.

"Yes, sir. That is correct."

This was bad. Guy had barely finished his first sentence and had already lost control of the interview.

"I don't suppose you ever met the Herefords while you were in Atlanta."

Not wanting to say no too quickly, Guy made faces that he hoped would be interpreted that the name sounded familiar and that he just might have spent a summer on the Riviera with the clan Hereford as he said a very slow, "No."

He was about to say something else when Mr. Avarice said, "Shame. I went to college with Bennie. He was my roommate. You can never underestimate the help you will get later in life from someone like a good college roommate."

"No, sir."

There was an awkward silence for a moment. Guy took this to mean it was his turn to continue. "So, I spent years working on a large variety of recipes and preparing techniques. I am particularly proud…"

"Did you ever meet the Tannenbaums?"

"Umm, no," Guy answered honestly.

"That's a shame. Very connected, that family. You would do well to meet up with them should you ever go back."

"I'll try to keep that in mind. Also, I developed a rub that I am particularly fond of," Guy said as he tried to force the conversation back into a more interview-like mode.

Setting his resume down, Mr. Avarice said, "Guy…"

"Yes, sir?"

"First of all, let's dispense with the sirs and misters. You can call me Wayne. May I call you Guy?"

"Sure," Guy looked for the comfort to say it and finding none, said it anyway, "Wayne."

It was as uncomfortable coming out of his mouth as he felt wearing the last outfit his mother picked out at a department store. With shame he realized that had only been four years ago. His face showed it, too. So Wayne smiled a genuine smile to put him at ease.

"You know, Guy. I am a successful man. I didn't get that being a bad judge of character. Mongolian Barbeque is not French cuisine at its finest. It's five sweaty men standing around a hot flat surface scraping dishes of mixed veggies and meat with long poles, then scraping the contents off in a bowl to hand back to the waiting customer. Hardly Cordon Bleu."

"Sure, but I think that my rub…"

"I have heard about your rub. I look forward to you perfecting it someday. But let me shoot straight with you. Every restaurant owner in Huntsville knows you or about you. You simply are not in the circle and you don't have the right stuff to break into the circle," then looking as if he realized it was a tad too severe, he amended, "well, at least not yet.

"I have hired Joe to be the chef, but I didn't want to just turn you out. I have a position in one of my restaurants on North Parkway."

"A Sous Chef job," Guy said, his voice dripping with disappointment and surly conclusion.

"Oh heavens no!" Wayne corrected. Guy's hopes raised a little until Wayne continued, "We couldn't possibly start you that high up. But our chef there needs a number three food prep. Now, it doesn't pay a lot, but we could probably start you out with a salary of 16k. Of course that would not include any over time, but it would be a good foot in the door and it would give you a chance to learn some of the reality of the business."

"Reality?"

"It's been our experience that college students might as well learn astral physics or criminal justice rather than culinary. They would be just as prepared as the culinary grads. That's reality."

"I'm sorry, Mr. Avarice - Wayne. But I believe I have a brighter future than that."

Not meaning at all to sound as sarcastic as it came out, Wayne said, "Good, then you've decided to give up this whole chef thing. Very good for you."

"That's not really what I meant. I mean I am going to make it someday. And you and all your friends will not determine my future."

"Guy, this is *me* talking to you. I am loaded from knowing this business. I know what people want. It is not Guy Sayonara, college graduate." As severe as his words were, his voice and mannerisms actually projected a sense of caring as if Wayne were trying to talk a friend down off a ledge. "Now if a line job is beneath you, then I suggest that you are not really prepared for the restaurant gig. At any rate, I have some more business to attend to and I will leave the line job open until you land on your feet."

Guy wanted to get angry. He wanted to hate this pompous twit. He thought that money and power made people stupid and he swore that he would never be like that when he finally made it. Well, except that he would rain down retribution on all those that tried to stop him on the way up. But beside that, he would try to be benevolent.

Everyone thinks of themselves as the good-guy in life – even Ghingas Khan.

Giving his best Mongol attitude, Guy stood and said, "Thank you for your time. But this won't be the last you hear of me."

"I look forward to it," Wayne said as he looked back down at his desk and began preparation for his next appointment.

Guy showed himself out and after saying goodbye to the pretty secretary, drove home, changed into some shorts, went out on his wrought-iron surrounded patio and began to throw little pebbles at the base of his grill.

Ping.

Tick.

3.

>_You have just entered the << Southern Nights >> chat room.
Local time is currently August 14, 8:38 pm CST.

Benvolio: I don't care what anyone else says, Belladona27 is right.
Tarkus: 4ll y0u p30pl3 d0 1s b4bbl3!
Belladona27: thanks ben. at least there is one person sticking up for me.
Jennfer19: she has no idea what she is talking about.
GuyChef: anyone seen hotlawdex?
Shivagit: stop all the l33t-speak Tark. This is a grownup chat room.
Lambie22: GUY! Welcome back to chaos!
Benvolio: she does! i think she is really onto somethinge here.
Tarkus: ,,|,, y0u, B3nv0l10. W3 w1ll c0ncqu3r3 y0u!
Tinkerhell: hey guy! how is hunstvilee? missed ya! ;-)

Lambie22 whispers to you: I hate it when Tink uses cutesy words with you...
You whisper to Lambie22: really now...
Lambie22 whispers to you: she thinks she can flirt with you.
You whisper to Lambie22: well, dex isn't on. that's all.

Junglejim: lay off Bell, Jenn. she is intitled to her opinion
Belladona27: it just seems possible to me, that's all
Lambie22: haven't seen dex all night, babe. but its good to see you again.
GuyChef: huntzville sux. but i did manage to get my bot running again! ;-)

Tarkus: y0u w1ll b3 pwn3d by m3!
Benvolio: probable, is more like it.
Lambie22: sorry to hear it, guy. what's wrong?
GuyChef: just job stuff

Lambie22 whispers to you: well she knows that dex is hers and you are mine.
You whisper to Lambie22: all yours babe.

Jennfer19: i will NOT lay off. Bell could not be any more wrong!
Shivagit: i hate it when these l33t t33ns are up past their bedtimes...
Jennfer19: she's crazy!

Tinkerhell whispers to you: so how ya been, sweety?
You whisper to Tinkerhell: not bad, and you?

Shivagit: if he used the word pwned, you know what is coming next...
GuyChef: what's possible, bell?

Lambie22 whispers to you: you haven't been on for so long! i have missed you. ;-)
You whisper to Lambie22: missed you too. been having trouble getting settled in.
Tinkerhell whispers to you: really missing you, stud.
You whisper to Tinkerhell: oh really? well drive on down to huntsville!

Shivagit: i can just hear it coming...
Benvolio: stfu Jenn.
Tarkus: 4ll y0ur b4s3 4r3 b3l0ng t0 us!
Junglejim: maybe a little disturbed but not crazy! :-)
Shivagit: damn! was that predictible or what? Tarkus, leave us the fuck alone!
Belladona: you know Gilligan's Island, Guy?
Tarkus: y0ur p3tty w0rds m34n n0th1ng t0 us!
GuyChef: yup
Shivagit: where's a room monitor when you need one.
Jennfer19: she's nuts, don't listen to her!
GuyChef: 7 strandeed castaways.
Benvolio: the more i think about it, the more right bell is.

Lambie22 whispers to you: i wish it wasn't so far away from here. i would like to spend some time with you... alone.
You whisper to Lambie22: that would be good. but you know you don't like to syber.
Tinkerhell whispers to you: i might just do that (drive down). i may get a bonus this month.
You whisper to Tinkerhell: just don't let dex or Lamb find out.

Jennfer19: ingore Tark, and he will go away Shiv.
Junglejim: haha, ben.
Tarkus: "ingore" haha... someone needs a dicktionary! muhahaha!
Belladona: well, my theory is that the only hetrosexuals there were the Howells.
Jennfer19: (*stops up ears and sings, lalalalalala*)
Benvolio: seems perfectly reasonable to me.
GuyChef: so you have Gilligan and the Skipper, Mary Anne and Ginger...
Junglejim: I can get into that.

Lambie22 whispers to you: yah. I'm not like that syberslut, tink.
You whisper to Lambie22: oh, i don't know. i think she doesn't like it. at least that is what dex tells me.

Jennfer19: fuckoff, tark.
<< Tarkus has left the room >>
Belladona: right so far guy.
GuyChef: but what about the professor?
Benvolio: which pair, Junglejim?
Jennfer19: I cant believe you heathens! augh!

Lambie22 whispers to you: if i liked it, would you log on more often?
You whisper to Lambie22: it would be a consideration, i s'pose.

Tinkerhell whispers to you: they know nothing. our little secret.
<< Hotlawdex has entered the room >>
Tinkerhell whispers to you: besides, the secret part makes me so...
You whisper to Tinkerhell: yes? so what...?
Tinkerhell whispers to you: umm... how does one say it?

You whisper to Hotlawdex: hey man.
Hotlawdex: whispers to you: hey bro. wuzzup?

Belladona: the professor was a cellabate.
Junglejim: the twin muffs, you fool! i aint no fag.
Shivagit: celebate, celebate, drool to the music!
Jennfer: lol, Shiv
Tinkerhell: haha, shiv.

You whisper to Hotlawdex: enjoy europe?
Hotlawdex: whispers to you: absolute. enjoy alabama? (hahaha)
You whisper to Hotlawdex: yeah. don't rub it in.
Hotlawdex: whispers to you: how is the rub thing going?
You whisper to Tinkerhell: wet?
Tinkerhell whispers to you: purrrrrrrr... that's it.
You whisper to Tinkerhell: i love it when you purr in my ear.

You whisper to Hotlawdex: i need your help, but hold on a sec. let
me handle something...
Hotlawdex: whispers to you: Lamb getting jiggy wit ya already?
You whisper to Hotlawdex: you know it!

Jennfer29: reprobates, one and all!
Belladona: lol

Lambie22 whispers to you: i'm not very good at it. i can't type with
one hand.
Lambie22 whispers to you: hell, i can't even type with 2!

Shivagit: wow! Tark left!
Jennfer19: all it takes is a woman's touch.

Tinkerhell: may i IM you? i am always afraid i will send a message
to general chat when we whisper.
Benvolio: uh-oh... someone getting a little whisper action from
Tink...
Tinkerhell whispers to you: ah hell!
Lambie22 whispers to you: haha?
You whisper to Lambie22: sorry. was trying to type with one hand.
Lambie22 whispers to you: lol. i am so glad you belong all to me.
You whisper to Lambie22: you know it, babe.

Shivagit: or you just got lucky or he got bored or both.
Shivagit: hey jenn... would you please IM me?

You whisper to Tinkerhell: don't worry about it. no one will figure it out.
Lambie22 whispers to you: see, dex hasn't been on one minute and she is already going at it.

Jennfer19: sure thing, hun.
Benvolio: ooo... Jenn and Shiv sittin in a tree.
Junglejim: k*i*s*s*i*n*g

You whisper to Lambie22: horny bitch.
You whisper to Tinkerhell: horny bitch.
Lambie22 whispers to you: you said it!
Tinkerhell whispers to you: you said it!

You whisper to Hotlawdex: hahahahahahahaha
Hotlawdex: whispers to you: what's so funny?
You whisper to Hotlawdex: you woulda had to have been there... but these chicks on the inet are funny.
Hotlawdex: whispers to you: heh. you know it. got one IM'ing me right now.
You whisper to Hotlawdex: go figure.

Belladona: they must be gone. Jenn isn't having a shitfit over you spelling out kissing.
Junglejim: she is probly just jealous because she wanted mary anne to herself...
Benvolio: kinky.

Hotlawdex: whispers to you: so what help do you need?
You whisper to Hotlawdex: got an interview tomorrow.
Hotlawdex: whispers to you: at a restaurant?
You whisper to Hotlawdex: no, at a DOD firm. didn't your father know someone at ANI TramTek?
Hotlawdex: whispers to you: you know it... only my godfather.
You whisper to Hotlawdex: well, i am interviewing for a techwriter job... just to make ends meet until i can land a chef gig.
Hotlawdex: whispers to you: dotty will be happy to hear that!
You whisper to Hotlawdex: not a WORD to my parents!
Hotlawdex: whispers to you: you got it, man.

Belladona: well i gotta go. big day tomorrow.
Junglejim: nite, Bell

Benvolio: g'night, Bell.

Hotlawdex: whispers to you: yeah... i will have my old man put in a good word for you. but you know...
You whisper to Hotlawdex: yes?
Hotlawdex: whispers to you: they are not the best DOD company... they are kind of a medeocre one at best... maybe no great future there.
You whisper to Hotlawdex: that's cool. it is just to get me some cashflow.

Belladona: we will continue this tomorrow. ttfn. ;-)
<< Belladona has left the room >>
Junglejim: she keeps a room humping...
Benvolio: for sure. well, it's getting about that time for me, too.

Hotlawdex: whispers to you: i should be able to do that. i will see what my dad can do.
You whisper to Hotlawdex: thanks, dex. catch up with you later. gotta go take a cold shower.
Hotlawdex: whispers to you: get some cash and a lapdance will take care of that better for you. :)
You whisper to Hotlawdex: yeah, yeah. whatever. thanks for the help.
Hotlawdex: whispers to you: no prob.

Junglejim: peace, bro.
Benvolio: peace. out.
<< Benvolio has left the room >>

GuyChef: well, i am going to punchout. big day tomorrow.
Hotlawdex: good luck with that!
Lambie22: good night, guy! come back soon! (*cries*)
Tinkerhall: nite, guy! snuggle good in bed and dream of me!
Lambie22 whispers to you: grrr!

>_You have left the << Southern Nights >> chat room.

>_You have just entered the << Southern Nights >> chat room.
Local time is currently August 28, 9:42 pm CST.

Belladona27: that's the way I see it.

Jennfer19: not so sure about that.

GuyChef: what's the topic today?

Lambie22: GUY! how are you?

Benvolio: bell was about to ask us all a question about an old TV show again.

Tinkerhell: hey guy!

Benvolio: go ahead, bell.

Hotlawdex: hey Guy, how did your first week go?

Belladona27: ok, gay or straight? – the entire cast of F-Troop.

GuyChef: The actors or the characters?

Belladona27: the characters

Benvolio: gay

Junglejim: gay

Jennfer19:straight, what about the captain and wrangler jane?

Shivagit: gay

Lambie22: wasn't wrangler jane called the "Post Mistress"?

Belladona27: lol – Mistress of the "Post"

Benvolio: lol

Junglejim: hehe

Lambie22: ok, so she was a bi-SMB

Tinkerhell: even the indians?

Hotlawdex: gay

GuyChef: what about the sergeant and the corporal?

Benvolio: gay

Junglejim: gay

Jennfer19: liberace gay

Shivagit: gay

Lambie22: gay

GuyChef: et too, lambie?

Lambie22: et me

Junglejim: not yet…

Jennfer19: lol

You whisper to Hotlawdex: can I IM you?

Hotlawdex: whispers to you: sure!

GuyChef: howdy.

Hotlawdex: whazzup, bro?

GuyChef: thanks for your help, the first week was pretty cool!

Hotlawdex: glad to help. dad was happy to recommend ya.

GuyChef: they have me on a pretty easy project for now. all i have to do is attend meetings, take notes and write down things into nice sentences. then i have to put everything in the form of template.
Hotlawdex: and it pays well?
GuyChef: unbelievably well!
Hotlawdex:good work if you can get it!
GuyChef: so well in fact, that i think i can have my loans paid off in a few years!
Hotlawdex: wow! that is groovy! so how much?
GuyChef: you remember how much i hoped to make as a chef starting out?
Hotlawdex: yeah...
GuyChef: double it.
Hotlawdex: wow! so you are buying the tickets to florida?
GuyChef: not so fast, retard. i need to get caught up on a few things. but i took my first paycheck today and stocked the kitchen and bar!
Hotlawdex: nice weekend ahead for you!
GuyChef: aye.
Hotlawdex: not so cool ahead here...
GuyChef: why not?
Hotlawdex: i start law school on Monday. i have to start drying myself out so i can be conscious my first day!
GuyChef: lol - good luck with that!
Hotlawdex: i will need it.

>_You have left the << Southern Nights >> chat room.

>_You have just entered the << Southern Nights >> chat room.
Local time is currently May 12, 10:03 pm CST.

Hotlawdex: straight to IM, eh?
GuyChef: well, we are leaving for Navarre Beach tomorrow, i didn't want to get caught up in the usual silly stuff out in Southern Nights.
Hotlawdex: they do get a little silly, but we knew most of them in high school. hard to walk away...
GuyChef: so do you have everything ready on your end?
Hotlawdex: yup. i even talked to the two girls and they are still going.
GuyChef: i am not really excited about the blind date...

Hotlawdex: look, i am a year away from graduating law, you are an upwardly mobile corp tech writer... its time we had a few flings with girls that are looking for such!

GuyChef: i'll just look at this as another spring break, then.

Hotlawdex: don't be so morose! this will be a good, adult, relaxing time!

GuyChef: and a time to celebrate.

Hotlawdex: celebrate? what?

GuyChef: i got a promotion today!

Hotlawdex: fantastic! what's the position?

GuyChef: i am now tech writer manager and also got my security lvl 2.

Hotlawdex: wow! that's cool!

GuyChef: not really. its so low, i can even talk about it here. but i will be involved in some more interesting projects than the chrome flange one i just rolled off.

Hotlawdex: chrome flanges are pretty cool!

GuyChef: lol - riiiiiight.

Hotlawdex: so you will need to cook us up a HUGE steak dinner on the grill to celebrate!

GuyChef: probably not... i have sorta become a vegetarian.

Hotlawdex: what?!

GuyChef: yeah, my heart is just not really in cooking any more. but i will mix up some veggies on the grill if you like.

Hotlawdex: that sounds cool! plus there are a few good restaurants nearby the rental house on the beach.

GuyChef: ok. i will see you in opelika at 4:00 pm CST. you have my cell if you get lost.

Hotlawdex: won't happen. i know the road to opelike like i know the back of my hand.

GuyChef: good.

Hotlawdex: that's in indiana, right?

GuyChef: very funny.

Hotlawdex: see ya tomorrow, bro!

GuyChef: ttfn.

>_You have left the << Southern Nights >> chat room.

>_You have just entered the << Southern Nights >> chat room.
Local time is currently April 29, 8:03 pm CST.

GuyChef: congratulations, you old schmuck!

Hotlawdex: thanks you old ditz!

GuyChef: so it's all official?

Hotlawdex: well, i still have a few paper chases left, but yeah.. i will graduate for sure. all the hard stuff is done.

GuyChef: ok, i will need to get you to represent me some time.

Hotlawdex: for what? i have lost track of your position, but you must have a whole team of lawyers working for you by now.

GuyChef: nah. just security 3 now. but i am working on some cool stuff.

Hotlawdex: like?

GuyChef: can't really go into details. but it involves working with sub-venders.

Hotlawdex: ah, you are working for the navy now...

GuyChef: no you dolt. i take a large secret project and figure out how to break it down into sub-parts. then we divvy those out to vendors in such a way that none of them will be able to figure out what the whole is.

Hotlawdex: you were never very good at figuring out what the hole is.

GuyChef: that's why i am not becoming a lawyer and you are!

Hotlawdex: lol

GuyChef: ;-)

Hotlawdex: you are a twerp.

GuyChef: yeah, but at least i am not a legal twerp!

Hotlawdex: well, i won't be either until i pass the bar.

GuyChef: i have every confidence you will with flying colors.

Hotlawdex: <-- fingers are crossed.

GuyChef: talked to gina-tinkerhell lately?

Hotlawdex: no, we had a falling out.

GuyChef: sorry to hear that. what happened? you to have been pretty tight since navarre.

Hotlawdex: i am alergic to cheating

GuyChef: youch!

Hotlawdex: and with someone i know here in atlanta. it was a bad scene.

GuyChef: yipes! and i still like her cousin. that could get awkward.

Hotlawdex: nah. is Kallie-Lambie still in mississippi?

GuyChef: aye. she is. tupelo. not too far from huntsville. we hook up from time to time.

Hotlawdex: well don't feel weird on my account.

GuyChef: i want you to think about the words you just said... hehe.

Hotlawdex: ok. so feel weird.

GuyChef: get used to it, you are going into law after all.

Hotlawdex: watchout or i will sue ya!

GuyChef: but i will say that there is something special about Kallie.

Hotlawdex: wedding bells soon?

GuyChef: not sure... she feels that i should have stayed "true to myself"

Hotlawdex: you mean and stay a chef?

GuyChef: yeah. she thinks everyone should find their "core" and stay there.

Hotlawdex: good thing my core is getting drunk and fooling around.

GuyChef: yep, you are in your core, dex.

Hotlawdex: i sense the inner struggle inside you, Father.

GuyChef: you do not know the POWER of the DOD-side, Luke.

Hotlawdex: lol

GuyChef: i gotta turn in. big day tomorrow. but we need to get together and party after your graduation.

Hotlawdex: you know it, dawg.

GuyChef: them are fightin' words!

Hotlawdex: hehe, ok so you are not a dawg.

GuyChef: thanks, i would hate to have to sue you for defamation of character!

Hotlawdex: what character?

GuyChef: touche'.

Hotlawdex: one thing is for sure, though...

GuyChef: Whazzat?

Hotlawdex: The world is becoming our place now!

GuyChef: You know it! I just feel like we have finally arrived!

Hotlawdex: see ya bro.

GuyChef: out.

>_You have left the << Southern Nights >> chat room.

4.

And then... the aliens landed.

Anyone that didn't have Mrs. Owens for a fourth grade teacher might easily miss out on how the Earth could handily be conquered by an initial alien force of three. But Guy was fortunate. He had Mrs. Owens as a fourth grade teacher.

Just about every boy and maybe even some of the girls had a crush on her. She was just that kind of woman. Simple, elegant, she embodied all the wholesomeness of a good *Fun with Dick and Jane* reading book with the vivacious curves of a sixties' playmate. She was one of those women that could be all things to all people and yet have the creative insight to capture the individual's learning imagination as well as the heart.

Guy remembered continually the lesson near the beginning of fourth grade when she opened all the children's minds to logic and reasoning for the very first time. In that sterile and cold institutional classroom made cheerful only by the standard issue food pyramid (which Guy noticed had changed many times over the decades – so much for standards) and the obligatory health and science posters, Mrs. Owens wove her magic with a simple proposition to the class of jello-minded simpletons.

"We are going to play a game," she had started innocently enough. "In this game we are going to use our imaginations. Let's pretend that this school was going to come to each and every one of you and give you $10,000.00 a day for a full month." This offer naturally elicited squeals of excitement from the whole class. She certainly had their attention.

"Now, let's say for the sake of argument that this school was then going to give you a choice. You could take the $10,000.00 a day and keep it, or you could receive a penny on the first day and double it each day after for the same thirty one days." This counteroffer then brought forth an equal number of groans from all. There was absolutely no way that any of these financial geniuses would pass up $10,000.00 a day for a paltry penny a day even if you did promise to double it.

Then she had the class take out their pencils and, through multiplication, figure out that ten thousand times 31 is 310,000. Then she had them multiply one penny times two. The two cents paled in comparison to their brilliant stack of $310,000. Even doubling it for a full week, they only got to 64 cents.

The class began to congratulate themselves for obviously making a fine and rather brilliant financial decision. It was perfectly clear to all that the United States should simply turn over all fiscal responsibilities to this class of 19 scholars.

"But, for the sake of diligence we should be thorough and complete the exercise," she coached. Without realizing it, they had all been exposed to words like argument, diligence, and exercise in ways they had never thought of before. With some agony, they trudged on holding their number 2 pencils precariously between tiring fingers and scratched out with some effort the next set of numbers.

By the end of their second week, they were only up to $81.92. Looking over their rows of numbers that were neat for some and maybe not-so-neat for others, they collectively congratulated themselves for proving how smart they all were. They could clearly retire now to the polo club and nurse their aching fingers after putting in a good month's work.

"We're not finished quite yet," was the gentle instruction that brought forth even more consternation than before. The class was becoming collectively more confident in their abilities to make early decisions and less confident in this mad woman's desires to inflict pain and suffering on their writing digits. But they still lacked the gravitas to completely overthrow her. So they trudged on with the next row of numbers. "Keep your hand on the plow and don't look back," she had encouraged though none caught the Biblical allusion.

By the end of their calculated third week, they were at $10,485.76. Some of them had to grudgingly concede that they were up to a number higher than the original $10,000 in the first offer. But it was little Mary Margaret that was the first to point out that this was the entire sum of the Plan B so far and that by this point Plan A would be up to $210,000. There was much relief on all their faces when Mrs. Owens conceded this point to Mary Margaret followed by a growing boiling of contempt as she gave the instruction to press on.

Nearly all the students were coming to the conclusion that the school board had slipped in their screening process, and had somehow allowed a sadistic loony to make her way through the system and was now going to subject them all to a full school year of unnecessary pain and torture.

"Let's continue."

Some students temporarily held their pencils in their left hand while they began shaking their right hands in clear protest, trying desperately for the sympathy spin. They looked like columns of one-winged turkeys trying fruitlessly to slip the surly bonds of the laminated classroom floor. She stoically stared them down. They were very nearly ready for mutiny. They could feel the impetus growing but were still a few steps shy from possessing the HMS Owens.

This time around as they ciphered their forth row of numbers, they noticed the process was taking much longer. For many of them the popular thought was that it was taking longer because they had simply been at this torturous work for a very long time and they were becoming tired. But for a precious few (of which unfortunately Guy was not one) the idea was dawning that it was taking longer due to the rather large numbers at play. By the end of this forth column of numbers, they were at $1,342,177.28.

Staring in stunned disbelief, they began to feel for the first time in their short existence how devastating it was to have absolute confidence in an incorrect conclusion. Mrs. Owens, undaunted by the slackness in their previously bright and shiny faces suggested with a question, "And are we finished yet?"

The entire class was definitely finished. Their world had been rocked by how wrong they had all been. And yet this demon-lady was now asking for more. It would be simply rubbing salt in the wounds. But eventually the brighter of the students realized that they were only at day 28. There were three more in the month of thirty-one days.

Some had to turn their paper over for the final computations. Others had to get a whole new sheet of clean white paper with neat blue lines across and double, thin red lines running down the left side. At least for these, the wide open space seemed to provide a refreshing energy where their numbers could roam free without so much crowding. A new piece of paper was often all the elbow-room needed for creation to flow. It was the New World of thought where the Lewises and Clarks of creative imagination could explore, yet not without risk to life and limb.

At the end of their investigative trip, the class arrived at $10,737,418.24 and Mrs. Owens had cemented her position as the final authority of all things unknown but soon to be explained.

"The quick, the sloppy, the children that do not think things all the way through will be content with their $310,000 while the patient, the neat, the children that use math as a finely honed instrument will rule those with their $10,737,418.24.

"Now let me ask a question to each and every one of you." And they all knew she was, too. She was speaking to each and every mind as they began to bud in new ways. They could feel it in their souls. Each one was becoming aware of something new stirring in them. Each jello-minded simpleton was beginning to feel the warm light of reason and logic shine on their fertile soil as they all learned a lesson that none of them would forget for as long as they lived. "Which group do you want to belong to?"

After some discussion, it was decided that they all wanted to belong to the ten million dollar club.

"Then you will have to master math, science, reading, history, and all the other subjects you will encounter in your journey through life. It doesn't stop when you graduate. It just becomes a more personal journey. But it is a journey that will never end. It just sometimes takes momentary pauses while we enjoy what we know for a while."

And so it came as no great shock to any and all of Mrs. Owens's pupils down through the generations that three aliens could easily up-end the whole of the planet Earth.

The Ggelvring were not from the planet Ggelve. For some strange reason, people of Earth always think this to be the rule. That is, unless they look to their own planet where humans come from Earth. No, Ggelvring come from a planet that would be extremely difficult to pronounce in any human dialect because their aural communication is derived from a flap of open skin on what we might call a neck. Many of their sounds come across as clicks, pops, and sputters. It just so happens that Ggelvring is one of those sounds that easily translates.

It is one of the few concepts from their planet that translates at all. These were not your usual Science Fiction fare. The fact that they were bipedal may be about where any similarity ends visually as well. Many scientists found it much easier to simply not attempt to compare them to us at all.

Their greenish grey bodies splotched with the occasional spatter of yellow veins radiating out from little hubs all over actually looked more like two rather long ten-inch PVC pipes bent in zig-zags and joined at each zig. So from each large and solid cloven foot, their round and stout legs grew up without shape to backward jointed knees that provided extra stability. From there, the nearly perfect cylinders moved toward their first juncture at the crotch where once they joined to form what we might call hips they immediately split again in diagonal lines moving away from each other to zagging points where they sharply bend back again towards one another to join once more at what we might call shoulders. Here they split sharply back out to form appendages we might equate to arms complete with double-jointed elbows that allow for completely free movement in all directions.

The effect of this design could remind one rather easily of one chromosome threatening to split in a fit of mitosis and meiosis. From front on, they looked a little like two letter Xs stacked on top of each other made out of green, grey, and yellow PVC pipe. What we would call the chest area was therefore an open diamond that was completely empty, an opening one could clearly see through.

There were even more distinguishing features as their organs we would equate to eyes (for they had two as well) grew as stalks from what we might call shoulders. They were completely independent and could look in all directions at once. But when they focused on a single subject together they gained the added bonus of depth perception provided by the stereography.

The head, which was not really a head per se, grew from the Y formed in the shoulders before they bent back down to form arms. A neck with the same diameter as the rest of the PVC stuck straight up to a triangular head which was shaped rather like that of a Praying (Preying) Mantis insect. Void of the need for eyes or mouth, the large triangular shape was simply a center for nerve clusters, cooling, a location for one center of the creatures' consciousness, and showcased a single black spot that looked a little like a shallow orifice in the upper middle of the flat surface one might call a face. The other location for its consciousness existed in the left side of the chest branch for the Ggelvring that happened to be right-handed.

Many scholars of the fifteenth century calculated that the human consciousness resided in the heart. It was modern medicine that first made the mistake of assigning this home of thought to the brain. It would be several more centuries before the human race caught up to the rest of the universe in understanding.

The Ggelvring right hand (for those that were right-handed) was a massive and sharp snapping claw much like a lobster's and acted like a pair of gardening sheers or hedge clippers – 'nuff said. The left hand was a set of six extremely flexible and lithe, tightly wrapped coils that formed long and limber fingers. These could independently move in all directions for any purpose, but could act in unison to completely surround, grip, and with supreme strength control an object of nearly any shape.

The purpose of this configuration was to allow for the most efficient form of hunting and gaining nutrients in an act that we might equate to eating. The Ggelvring only liked to hunt creatures that posed a threat to them. They would identify the area of the creature that housed its control center (what we might consider a brain) and grip that area with their left hand while neatly slicing it off with the right. They would then lift the extracted mass to the flap of loose skin on their necks and drain by suction all the nutrients from it.

In the Ggelvring religion and philosophy, they would never consider ending a life. It was beyond their ability to tolerate such cruelty. But their threshold for defining a sentient life-form was a concept shared by most interplanetary species. If a species was capable of reaching such a conclusion that life should not be taken, then there must be intelligence, a conscience, ergo a soul. But if a species attacked or showed signs of violence, then clearly it fell into the other category of life form – food. And being without a soul, the religion of the Ggelvring permitted the guilt-free pleasure of feeding upon the food at will.

But beyond that, their religion also incorporated their concept of sex, or activity for the purpose of reproduction – which was imminently pleasurable to the Ggelvring.

The only way for the Ggelvring to multiply at all was asexually. When a Ggelvring is hunting for food, there is the risk of injury. This risk triggers a feeling of euphoria that is quite pleasurable to them for when they are injured in any way, the process of replication begins. Like our starfish and other examples on Earth, any portion of a Ggelvring can spawn a completely new Ggelvring. But ideally a single injury will cause a string of events to occur.

First their consciousness which can switch back and forth between their triangular head and their left chest pipe (for right-handed Ggelvring, it would be the right chest pipe for lefties) actually splits and is stored temporarily in both. Then the two places where the pipes join at the shoulders and hips split apart and the two pipes fall on the ground supported by a foot and a hand each – looking rather like the letter M for a moment. The head goes with the claw in all cases for it can better defend the large target (the black dot on the face). Nearly immediately the other halves of the body grow out from it like TV antennae from the hip and shoulder. The two in the middle join to form the other half of the chest while the outside rays form the arm and leg.

The coil finger side grows another head and both halves right themselves nearly in unison in a matter of seconds. The rush and euphoria is extreme for the Ggelvring as the side that kept the head is considered in their heuristic the parent and the side that grew a head as the child.

The head always stays with the first generation of a new Ggelvring, but they have no concept of generational hierarchies. So there are no Grandparents as it were. There are just parent and child relationships. Occasionally a lefty and a righty will live together to provide companionship one for another and in these cases they may act as joint guardians for the child – suggesting which life choices to make.

But a child is born with full knowledge and therefore does not require rearing as we know it. The mere fact that there are lefties and righties is interpreted by some as proof positive that there is a God, while others believe it was just a random chance happening that is explained by further random mutations.

Those that believe in God believe that It had four arms and legs, two of each kind, and that It split in two different directions, the force of which formed the two main continent masses on their planet, the name of which we cannot pronounce but in written form would translate something like Ggel-Ta.

Krel was a Ggelvring whose parents had high hopes. Its birth parent (a righty) had wanted it to go into planetary management while its life partner, a lefty, had wanted Krel to go into rhythmic enunciation (a form of entertainment that was quite profitable to Ggelvring).

But Krel had shunned its parents, opting instead for a dream of going into space colonization. It just knew that its future was there. Krel would be the greatest colonizer of all time. Plus Krel had an unnatural desire to multiply. Not just the once permitted by law for all settled planets, but as many times as it desired. Krel saw a future where it would be the seed parent for an entire civilization of planet managers and rhythmic enunciators.

The only problem was that Krel was only so-so, average. It was quite almost something really special in the Space Colonization Corps Academy. But it only got Cs and C+s on its tests. The professors thought that Krel had so much potential but they just couldn't see Krel really making it. It was all potentiality and very little realization. It was ok – just ok.

And so, Krel left the support structure of its parents and struck out on its own path in the SCC, accepting a job as the third wave colonizing a rather insignificant planet in a rather insignificant solar system.

"Third wave," Krel sputtered to itself in its quarters. "I won't be the seed, I will be simply the cleanup crew. But at least it is better than tech writing." Krel looked dejectedly at the floating mirror projection and added halfway due to an over-developed sense of conscience, "Nothing personal to tech-writers mind you... There are some that are extremely professional and for them, it is a complete career full of reward. But for some..."

A friend of its roommate from the academy had offered Krel a job as a tech writer to make some credits and have a life rather than to take a position of third wave, but Krel had turned it down. It would rather try to work its way up through the ranks than become a sellout.

Leaning back in the cool, slick surfaces of its quarters, Krell apathetically flexed one of its coiled fingers against a button on its projection unit switching it to an outside view. It watched the screen flicker into focus as the first wave, an officer named Brel, launched in the landing craft. From their vantage over the lower pole on approach, they had collectively agreed to start their assault from the tips of two continents closest to the frozen polar land mass and work their way towards the equator.

This would mean that the second wave would start on the smaller of the two continents after the first had some time on the larger of the two. Mathematically they predicted that Krel could begin its assault on what was leftover of the area near the gulf of the continent just past the equator on the other side. There were smaller groupings of animals there that would be perfect for cleanup leaving the larger land masses for the primary and secondary waves.

Krel mulled the details of the assignment over in its mind while watching Brel's descent – first a blaze of orange followed by a frosty blue as the tiny craft's resistance mobility fields forced it to glide gracefully down along the particles of space matter that acted as conductors for the movement of light. This was another determining factor of the evolutionary stage of life on a planet.

Most animals could understand the relationship between light, matter and energy. That was easy. Many had figured out that energy somehow equated to mass and light, or that light equated to energy and mass. Even most animals that were considered food and therefore not intelligent life could manage to artificially light their habitats with energy and mass or combine mass and light for energy used in heating. But sentient life forms could then make the jump, the leap to the idea that mass is derived from energy and light.

This then was the real beginning that separated life from food for most species of the known galaxy. It was a life form being able to take the step beyond these basic equations and understanding that light, energy and mass were simply instantiations of the same core thing – much like solid, liquid and gas are three principle states of a common element. This core entity then could be manipulated in the transference and balance between the three instantiations to accomplish such useful things as faster than light travel, clean energy, and a really, really cool orange and blue glow to spacecraft as it maneuvers into the atmosphere of a planet full of food.

The Ggelvring had studied this particular planet full of food for some time. With every contact, the animals (food) would attack. There was a possibility that sentient life existed, but the larger animals that possessed rudimentary modes of combustible mobility and fission energy would strike out in violent aggression.

So it was decided that the blue planet would be colonized, first consuming the upright animals that posed the greatest possible threat. Replication would be easy there – no question about it. Then after that food had been exhausted, a zoological survey would be made of any further expansion before the mother-ship returned and the planet converted into a stable ecosystem for the Ggelvring.

Krel's tendrils tapped nervously at the console while it watched the now light blue speck move down and out of sight near the farthest point on the tip of the rather large continent. It would have to wait and watch the progress for at least twenty to thirty rotations of this blue ball with the wispy white clouds until it would get its turn. Switching the monitor to its target, Krel wondered what it was like to be there right now. What would it be like to be among these animals as the clean efficiency that was Ggelvring colonization began?

Staring with dreams of procreation at the smaller continent on the other side of the globe from their present position stretching out from the equator to the cooler climes of the distant pole, Krel traced its finger over the curve of the coastline that formed a gulf that reached down to a large peninsula. It would begin its third wave there at the heart of that region, just above the coastline by what seemed only fractars from this vantage point, but was in truth really a stretch of what must be hundreds of sectars.

He thought about the bipedal food. It couldn't help but think that it must be very impressive to be there with them. The Ggelvring would move and grow with such rapid elegance that the creatures, if they had consciousness at all, would surely be impressed.

Krel leaned back, resting comfortably in the knowledge that these animals had no such capacity for sentience. It would sleep well tonight with the guiltless knowledge that all was working in the universe exactly the way God had intended.

5.

Looking out off the southern point of Cape Agulhas, Daniel Guedbye watched as the Atlantic and the Indian Ocean played with each other like two titan toddlers crashing Tonka toy trucks making explosive noises with their immature mouths all the while. The tawny grass reaching out into the craggy rocks that in turn extended out into the watery foray reminded him of the way his people had reached and fought their way into this future of freedom.

He liked it here - the brazen wilderness and isolation of it all, the feeling of really being at the end of the Earth. This was the southernmost point of the huge continent where for decades, nay centuries, the minority majority had struggled to free themselves from the oppression of a relative handful of imperialists. And here, he had always *felt* free. Even way back in his youth when he was born in time to know of Nelson Mandela in the present and feel the bitter bite of Apartheid, he could come here to escape.

Daniel always imagined the white and red banded lighthouse to be a beacon of hope that would pull all of Africa into a future of liberation and release. The pervasive salt mist that you could feel in your breath was the livable discomfort that all would have to endure while they lowered their heads and pressed on to the brave new horizon.

And how fitting was it that the lighthouse was now a museum - that the epic struggle would now be embodied in an antiquated metaphor? As Daniel stood on the very spot that only five centuries earlier had baffled Portuguese Navigators as their compasses showed no variation between magnetic and true north, he pondered for a moment at the fact that there is today a 24° variation west, as the magnetic poles are constantly moving. Time brings many changes – some bad and some good.

The sidearm at his hip and the rifle weighing solid and heavy in his hands were just as much evidence of these changes as the badge on his chest worn with pride. Where only a few decades earlier he had been the oppressed majority, now he was bringing the security of law and order to the brave new land. And it had been no picnic at the beach, that one thing is certain. When emancipation had finally reached these shores like the crashing waves that now played before him, his people did not understand it.

Daniel remembered his first day on the job when he had to arrest a fellow liberated. The hardened and dirty old man had heard through the news on the street that they were all free and had subsequently decided to take his first ride on the bus. He had never been able to afford such an extravagance – and now that they were all *free*, in his mind he would not have to pay for anything anymore. To this weathered old soul, freedom would bring him food, clothing, and a palace to live in – all of it free for that was what freedom was all about.

It was Daniel's unfortunate assignment to be the one to calm the public calamity and disorderly conduct by arresting the man and booking him, thereby ironically taking away the freedom for which they had all fought so hard. He wanted to explain things to the old man, to make him understand that freedom wasn't free and that he would have to work now just like all the other free people. He wanted to help him earn the new future not wanting to deny that the old fellow had already paid his dues and then some. But his boss had made it clear that they had no time for such luxuries. There was far too much disorder to be weeded out for them to fight the war one person at a time – free or otherwise.

Now looking out into the salt spray towards Antarctica, Daniel wondered about the old man. He wondered if he had survived his two years in prison for inciting a riot. And most of all, he wondered what his first collar now felt towards him. Would each convict spend their time in incarceration thinking to their own rehabilitation or would they feed on the growing bitterness, all the while throwing mental darts at posters of Daniel Guedbye?

Reaching down and picking up one of the dark shards of rock, Daniel threw it with all his pent up frustrations and anger at the unfortunate circumstances that this present darkness had thrown upon us all. And as he released the shard, he felt the frustration release with it and he watched with satisfaction as the seas hungrily gobbled it all up. Allowing a momentary shudder and a momentary sigh, he felt the wave of peace wash over him and gobble up all the inner turmoil.

He drew in a long cleansing breath and released it as he wondered if any of us were ever really truly free.

Just then, just there as one chapter in his life was coming to a close and another one beginning, something caught the corner of his eye. Up in the air where the few seabirds that were braving the currents were soaring, something moved in a distinctly different pattern. It was not dipping and ebbing with the streams of air like the avian friends were as they watched for little fish that would make easy sustenance, but it was after the same thing in the end.

Daniel followed the speck as it rapidly grew and made minor arching changes to its trajectories. Almost instinctively he surmised that this was something from the heavens. He had seen enough science fiction movies to know what a meteor would look like. But as it approached he became aware of an intelligence as it made the corrections of an incoming airliner on approach.

Immediately he grabbed for the microphone clipped to his epaulet and called in an emergency code to headquarters giving his location and a request for backup. But two more things were on his mind. First he wondered what the official code was for a space ship and second he realized that backup would not get here for another fifteen minutes. And by the looks of it, it was a good bet that the object hurdling towards him would beat that by a good fourteen minutes and forty-five seconds.

He decided to use the code that closest fit the situation, "Headquarters," he said in his beautifully clipped English accent, "Headquarters, this is officer 514 with a 10-34. We have a situation here and I am requesting backup – just east of the lighthouse museum. We will need assistance." Then thinking one better, he added, "Make that a 10-70, might as well get the fire lads out here as well."

"10-4, assistance and backup en route."

All the time, the object was growing and for all intents looked as if it were going to hit the very ground where Daniel stood. But just at the end, he witnessed a film of blue envelope the arrowhead of a capsule and heard a warm hum as it gracefully yet swiftly slowed and alighted on the peat between him and the lighthouse off in the distance. As steam wafted from the dark and smooth grey surface it gave the impression of extreme heat, but Daniel could just swear that if he placed his hand flat on the surface, it would feel cool to the touch.

As he cautiously approached, he knew what this was. He also knew the score. There would be others here in a while, but in the universe of cosmic first contact, that would be an eternity. He couldn't very well ask the visitors to take a number and be seated. And so it would fall on him to be the ambassador for all of mankind. *"And why not him?"* he reasoned. He certainly knew at the core all the good and the bad that the Earth had to offer. And what more fitting place where the most beautiful landscape on the planet had witnessed through the ages the greatest tragedies of man's greedy raveling as well as his finest triumphs of manumission. *"And why shouldn't it be someone that had witnessed both?"*

Just then a seam appeared on the side of the craft. This was it, he thought. This was the moment of truth. Daniel took a moment to straighten his uniform. Looking down at his front he made sure that the hem of his shirt buttons lined up with the clasp and fly of his slacks. Then glancing at his feet he noticed that the black leather looked a little scuffed.

He quickly took turns standing on one foot and then the other as he buffed the tops of his shoes on the calves of his slacks. They looked a little better, but then again it was one final ironic metaphor for the condition of this planet. It was worn and scuffed a little but overall it was looking better than it had in the past.

"You can do this, old man. Just get a grip," he said to himself. And the result from his own encouragement was a snap in stature as he stood at his tallest and proudest.

The seam opened with a soft hum that suggested centuries of technology where engineers worked in concert with artisans to make moving parts perform in perfect harmony. This was no B movie alien - that was for damn sure!

The portal opened into a graceful ramp. Daniel stared into the dark void. It was only about thirty feet away or so, but he could not make out what was happening inside save for some shifting in the shadows. That was when it happened. The wide-eyed bewilderment that the innocence of youth embraced began to give way to the suspicion of maturity. As Daniel watched the movement inside, he became aware of a rushing adrenaline wave coursing through his veins. His heartbeat doubled and then trebled as he began to question his own anticipation.

What if this was a threat?

He felt his grip on his rifle tighten in preparation. He even glanced down to check the bolt. All was set. With a casual motion, he slid his thumb over the safety.

Click.

But what threat could come from such a craft? There couldn't be many – that is unless they were tiny. And then what would they do? Bite his ankles?

Daniel checked his growing emotions and reigned in the onslaught of terror. In the end he decided to just keep his wits about him and be prepared for anything.

Now he was beginning to wonder if he was the best person to do this after all. Perhaps he *should* wait for backup to get here.

Just then the shifting shape was no longer a mystery. It unfolded itself as it stretched out of the craft in front of him. As it extended to its full twelve feet in height, the fear returned. Daniel was nearly shocked to immobility as his eyes took it all in - the green-grey color, the yellow splotches, the odd shape of piping, the huge cloven and substantial feet, the bizarre shape of the head with only one eye, and the lack of a target as the chest was an open diamond. But most of all, he was agape at the huge scissor like claw on the right hand that threatened again and again with snapping clicks.

It looked like the alien had also taken its safety off.

Daniel raised his rifle to his shoulder and sighted the big black dot in the middle of the head with the grace and calm of experience. He would be able to fell the frail creature with ease. One shot from the 35mm and that dot in the middle of the triangle would be as empty as the diamond in its chest.

In a commanding voice, Daniel shouted out, "Let's take it nice and easy fellow. No need to start things off wrong between us." But what he did not understand was that he had already started things off wrong. The threat of his loaded and ready weapon as well as his easily readable emissions, Daniel had shown the Ggelvring all it needed to legally, morally, and spiritually know to hunt with impunity.

But now Brel would need to be injured to make its glory complete. So it began to follow standard protocol and procedures – just like in the simulators and training seminars back home.

Daniel saw the beast stretch back and let out a frightening and guttural wail from its opening on its neck. The flapping skin sputtered and slapped in wet spasms as the horrible sound echoed even louder than the crashing waves nearby. It sounded deep and fierce like the roar of a lion and elephant combined. The terror in Daniel was total and complete.

Then the alien took a rather heavy step forward with its left foot and the ground in front of him thundered with the force. The alien combined with this, a swinging snap of its massive and mighty claw.

Being able to take absolutely no more of this turn of events, Daniel felt the practiced and professional pressure increase in his index finger. His breathing became as calm as a quiet lake and he concentrated on the shot after the shot like a bowler thinks about the follow-through of a good pitch in cricket. Daniel visualized the hole that would become of the dot, and increased the pressure on the metal.

Before the alien could take the second step, the trigger pulled and the crack of the cap being fired splintered through the otherwise serene sound of the ocean's music. Daniel watched the hole made perfect by his skill. The alien took a full step back and as if in slow motion the joint at the shoulder and the one at the hip separated. In horror he watched as the whole bloody thing fell in two pieces on the ground.

The two halves looked like two rather large letter M's standing side by side. The ocean wind blew and whistled through the scene of carnage and the graying clouds offered a fitting pall as they glided effortlessly over the area. Daniel felt the chill of the approaching storm – in more ways than one.

How would he be able to explain to the Earth that the alien had landed and before it could say, "Take me to your leader," he had literally blown it in two? But anyone else in his position would have done the same thing, wouldn't they?

In the aftermath, Daniel had not even lowered his sights. He had just left his rifle in the ready position. The bolt had already been reset and another round readied. The grass moved in the wind like an imitation of the waves down below. And Daniel measured the meaning of life, and of death — of beginnings and endings.

Just then, one of the M's started to move. He watched in cautious silence as the two top joints of the M sprouted pipes in V's. Before he knew it, the damn thing had righted itself and was joined by a twin beside!

All of a sudden, the tables had been shifted. It was no longer mono e mono.

As Daniel braced for another defending shot, he watched as one of the creatures began to run off towards the lighthouse museum. Now he had a quandary. If these things were indeed hostile, should he save the people or himself?

As a trained officer he realized that he would not be able to do the former unless he first took care of the latter. Taking aim at the remaining creature that was now screaming and charging towards him, he squeezed off another expert round.

The alien divided again. Only this time, Daniel would not contemplate the meaning of life. He began emptying round after round into the M's as hard and as fast as he could. To his shock and dread, the alien regenerated and doubled with each blow matching the speed of regeneration to that of his aggression.

Being exhausted of rounds for his rifle, Daniel backpedaled with increasing speed across the open grass. He reached blindly for his sidearm and brought the revolver up expertly using both hands to brace the recoil. In what was becoming a hopeless ballet of violence and battle, he fired off round after round. Each time the alien divided, one half would run off in a different direction towards towns, villages, and cities. But one kept driving for him with fierce intensity.

Daniel knew this was going to go badly for him. But with the gumption that saw him through decades of oppression and frustration, he continued to fight. He would never, never, never give up.

It was only a moment or two later that he became aware of the hollow click, click, click the empty revolver was making with each impotent trigger pull. The blood rushing in his ears masked the sounds of reality as he was barely aware of his own scream in the fray.

The creature was fully on him now and as the gun continued to make its harmless clicking sound, Daniel felt the long coils of the alien's left hand wrap around his head. He kept firing and screaming the whole way as the huge claw came down around his neck.

Daniel Guedbye felt a slight pinch around the nape of his neck as he was thrust into the inky black void and the flying feeling of freedom.

Brel raised the head of the creature up to its intake flap at its neck and formed a perfect seal around the spouting base. It barely had to pull with any suction as it felt the nutrients, warm and satisfying, drain down into its digestive systems. It was beyond a doubt the best food it had ever tasted. Then came the thrill that what lay ahead was meal after meal as Brel did what came completely natural to it.

It would be able to feed and breed without end for quite a while. Already some nineteen or twenty of its progeny were making their way to their own glory. To be honest, it had lost count in all the euphoria of the moment.

Brel took a moment to report back to the mother ship that the landing had been a success and that the second wave could probably begin as planned. It would communicate back later with further details.

Everyone on the ship was exceedingly pleased – all, that is except Krel. That should have been *it* down there. This should have been *Krel's* big day. But it guessed that it had to be patient. If it was going to realize its own dream, it would have to give it time. Besides, its own landing would only be a few revolutions of this tiny blue planet away.

What is it like then to be there in the world when a really big story breaks? People saw the beginning of 9-11 as a momentary interruption to their favorite morning news show. They were sipping on their coffee watching the perky newswoman interviewing a chef about their latest dry rub for the football tailgating parties when their attention was jarred with the story that some nut had flown a small airplane into the World Trade Center.

When you see that first news clip of a bombing or a kidnapping or a run-away bride, there is no way of measuring the expectant result on your life. It is difficult to tell if this will be a discarded bit of trivial happenstance, or grow into fodder for coffee klatch conversation for weeks to come. The really big stories start out small – like an incorrect assessment that a small single engine plane has smashed into the World Trade Center.

Some people may have dismissed that as "those nutty New Yorkers are at it again!" or "Probably some pissed off Red Socks fan." They may not realize that as they drove to work, the story that would not leave them alone as they tried to flip radio stations to find some good Tom Petty music, maybe Free Falling, would turn into an event that would eventually liberate 50 million people in two different countries while the rest of the world looked on and tried to determine whether or not this was a good thing.

And so, small insignificant stories about a woman that is a vegetable and has a husband that wants to pull the plug captures the world's attention and yet starts out as some small announcement by some newsperson with perfect hair as we drink our coffee and say, "Hey, that's really something. Would you look at that?"

This day was no different. As the world woke up, different media outlets that were trying to prove themselves to be truly world in scope rather than just about America with the occasional mention of some place like Pakistan thrown in just to keep up appearances, jumped at the news coming from across the Atlantic.

People in Times Square watched monitors as they purchased and consumed their bagels and coffee on their way to a fast-paced day of meaningless shifting of paper stacks. The lady with perfect blonde hair was preempting the perky lady that was interviewing the chef that had just gotten out of prison for embezzlement and yet could whip up a mean salad. As they watch on, few are aware at just how often news-people say the word "now" when they are live and unscripted. But some have suspected that the word "now" has come to replace the word "umm" in speech training communication classes.

The blonde said, "And this just in from South Africa. There has been a disturbance in several towns and villages where unexplained events are unfolding. Now, the local authorities were not available for comment, but early reports are claiming that some sort of skirmish is ongoing. Now, the local government has announced that it is investigating several corroborated reports that it may be terrorist related as there have been deaths. Now, we are getting reports that there has been violence, but that it seems to be widespread and sparse. Now, contacts at the UN have told us that they do not believe that it is a coordinated effort, but that relief will more than likely be necessary and are calling for all nations to pitch in with the effort to help out local authorities as soon as the problem is better understood. Back to you Tracy."

The camera came back to a somewhat caught off guard Tracy, the perky woman interviewer who was turned awkwardly towards a monitor showing the blonde's image as if they are looking face to face – all for the benefit of the audience at home for all they really saw was a green rectangle. Tracy asked the pre-scripted question trying to look like she thought of it on the spot and as if she had been following the story being reported rather than arguing with the makeup artist about the shade of blush that was being used. "So has the Republican White House said anything about how they are going to deal with this new threat to stability?"

"Now, we do know from our White House correspondent that there has not been an announcement yet as the events are unfolding. But we do know from the past that one of the reasons for the current disapproval numbers is the perceived slowness with which this administration responds to crises."

The perky lady turns back to the camera and speaks directly to the coffee drinking and bagel eating masses, "And we will be following this story as it unfolds as you stay tuned to the network you can trust to give you in-depth information when world events break out. We will be back just after this."

Most everyone dismissed it as probably some dumb-ass freedom fighter pulling together a ragtag army and killing a few thousand more Africans to make some point. As long as they got to their stack of waiting papers and began their shifting, what did they care? Others even thought it was probably some rabid Red Socks fan trying to screw things up again.

Who knows?

It was only later that day that the first video started to be shown. People watched in horror as they ordered their deli sandwiches made with thinly sliced and lean meat. The images were jumpy and blurry at first. They saw something that looked a little like clay animation stick figures prance across city streets. From a distance it was hard to judge shape and size, but it looked as if they were savagely killing many people.

One of the twenty second news clips that was being shown in a virtual loop was a jarring scene where one could just barely make out a creature holding something up to its neck like a head and then throwing it down as it moved towards the cameraman and the scene breaks into the scrambling lines of a broken camera.

For most people that watched in the delis, they thought it rather a shame what was happening to those poor people down in Africa and how things would change after the next election.

But by that evening, just eight short hours later, people around the Earth started to get the impression that this was more than just a good story that would last until the Sunday morning news talk shows had their say about it. By that evening, there was video of helicopters spraying fields of aliens with bullets and their multiplying into swarms of thousands. There were reports of whole cities being evacuated and border military being made ready.

By that evening in the states, a mere twenty hours after the first encounter, this was no longer a Cessna being flown into the World Trade Center by a rabid Red Socks fan. This was the whole of the twin towers falling and the world realizing that something significant was transforming before their very eyes.

Wives looked at husbands with worried looks, wanting desperately for a returning look of comfort and security that everything was going to be all right. But husbands were not looking back with comfort. Husbands were looking back with a look of loss and worry. It would not be easy to tuck their children in bed tonight and retire to the boudoir for a short session of pin the tail on the donkey before the late night talk shows came on.

There was no doubt about it. Things were decidedly fucked up.

No one got to see who won the myriad of different reality programs that night. On all channels the world watched as the collective militaries of Namibia, Botswana, and Mozambique took turns making the Ggelvring the winner of the largest, whiz-bang reality show of them all. Zimbabwe didn't even try. The executive order was given for evacuation north into Zambia or Northern Mozambique. But the bulk of their fighting forces were being deployed to secure the route from the current administration offices and homes to adjacent airports as they fled the country.

Ironically it was Zimbabwe that took the longest to be infiltrated and conquered. Without the organized use of force, the Ggelvring were completely reliant on local skirmishes for procreation – a small piece of rather useful trivia that evaded a world now lusting for war and defense by violent intervention.

The Ggelvring moved with blinding speed and within hours had even mastered pretty much all forms of transportation left behind by the fleeing food that suited their purpose.

It was the first sleepless night the world had ever shared.

6.

By day two of the alien invasion most of the networks had eerie graphics that read "Alien Invasion – Day 2". Nearly everyone went back to work while governments around the globe urged optimism and a continuation to normal day to day Gross National Product. News reports were full of insider information on top-secret strategies and how there was great confidence that the next technique would surely work.

But in the southern half of Africa it was impossible for news outlets to spread calm faster than the Ggelvring were spreading fear and death.

Most of the fastest growth was centered in and around diamond mines and guerrilla militant headquarters. It was here where defense and aggressive offense were mainstays that the savage butchery would spawn so many alien vermin that the jungle began to look like a large basement floor teaming with rodents. Sophisticated arrays of weapons meant to thwart lines of thieves and enemies only hastened the inevitable demise of all humans that had the misfortune of being in that certain geographic disposition.

The most horrific failure though came in the Democratic Republic of the Congo where close ties to several major world powers and large defense purses used for the absolute opposite thing from defense afforded a nice arsenal of completely uncalled for power. The General of the armed forces had been sitting on several thermobaric devices and had been itching for a legitimate reason to employ them.

The weapons create a huge pressure wave which effectively sucks the air out of the lungs of anyone unfortunate enough to be within range. But there is nothing new to these devices and by the time of the alien invasion, they had already been used extensively by Russian forces during the battle for Grozny in Chechnya.

But before Congo used them, a Pentagon attaché had convinced the General that a thermobaric would be totally the wrong ordinance to use in this situation. Instead, he strongly suggested that a more conventional fuel-air weapon be tried since the aliens were not infesting caves, but were covering open ground in massive herds at high rates of speed.

"You mean like a Daisy Cutter?" the large black General asked looking the full part of Macarthur complete with corncob pipe and aviator sun glasses.

"Well, actually no. The Daisy Cutter isn't precisely a fuel-air device. And world opinion may be a little negative to its use at the current time – since Afghanistan, if you know what I mean." James Navarone of the United States carefully corrected.

Leaning over his cool steel desk resting his weight on two massive fists, James believed the General's stern expression became even sterner (if that was possible). "I don't really give a great big diddly-fuck what the world opinion may or may not be at this moment, Mr. Navarone. I have an enemy front of aliens moving into my country and conventional weapons have so far proven useless against them. I want the biggest ball of fire and smoke we can produce shy of making my own country glow in the dark and I need it fast because, to be honest, I would prefer it if the smoldering field were Zambia's mess to clean up and not the Republic's."

"Well, there is also the small fact that you currently don't have any at your disposal, but we did sell you some FA units seven years ago that will nearly match their footprint," James offered.

"How big is the footprint?"

"1k," James said flatly conveying that the bomb would clear at least 1,000 feet of land (or more than three football fields) killing everything within its radius.

The General smiled. This would indeed be a good day.

Sitting back comfortably in his oversized black leather chair, he looked to his field commander and gave the order. Then looking back to Mr. Navarone he asked with a smile, "Feel like a chopper ride to the front, Jimmy?"

James Navarone, never one to miss an opportunity, gratefully accepted the General's offer and after acquiring the specific location and time the General had in mind (just south of the Zambian border, in three hours) told the General that he would meet him outside headquarters at the field car after he stopped by his own office to pick up his jacket. It was a believable ploy that bought him just enough time to make yet another £10k from his contact at the British news agency – yet another wanting to appear global in scope. There would be an amazing coincidental meeting as the live news chopper would just happen to be in the area at the time of the big show.

The General wouldn't mind. James knew that he loved the publicity and would actually slap him on the back afterward and ask, "Why didn't *you* think of that?" with a big belly laugh. Mr. Navarone smiled to himself with confidence as he thought upon this and climbed in the jump-seat behind the large General. The field car spun out towards the nearby dusty landing strip while all the occupants save James held onto their hats. James didn't have a hat so he held onto his toupee.

Two hours later, the British news agency had already procured all the revenue for exclusive feeds from as many agencies as possible. The ones that really counted were in the United States where the schmucks were known to pay a bundle even if all the competitors were showing the same thing – actually, especially if all the competitors were showing the same thing. It was free market economy at its best. Pay £10k, make $100k.

Do the math. News is big business, baby.

"We now interrupt this program to bring you a late-breaking update," news people around the globe said with a palpable enthusiasm. Within minutes, the world was briefed on the military plan to strike at the aliens. Each network had their own retired general or major explaining what the FA ordinance was, how large the explosion was likely be, and what world markets were currently selling them to any interested buyers.

And we wonder why we have problems with terrorists!

The graphics were slick and some networks had actually figured out the timing and coordinated product placements and last minute commercial breaks as the aircraft neared what was now being termed Ground Zero. They spent $100k and made millions.

Money makes the world news go round.

They all were told to point to a place on the map that looked like the southern region of the Democratic Republic of the Congo. This was James's only stipulation to the media. But the actual mission was taking them all rather deep into Zambian territory. The lush green was mixed with the beige tufts of open terrain as the world watched the helicopters gathering in the pale blue sky. Wisps of white clouds painting thin streaks behind the large bomber moving into view over the horizon.

They say that one of the last great surges of the world markets were massive up-sales in the products featured as the news people with perfect hair asked everyone to stay tuned for the big moment just after this commercial break. But they needn't have asked. No one was moving one inch. Everyone watched so intently, for so long, that after the big event the water-tables in all the major cities dropped by at least twelve feet due to the simultaneous flush. After spending the night awake together, the world had now gone to the bathroom together. Too much closeness may not be a good thing.

Coming back from commercials, the tension was once again swiftly pulled taught like the strings of a guitar. Any more tension and the darn things would start popping. People nearly held their breath as they saw from the air the approaching line of what looked to be scores of aliens. One retired commentator from Texas that had been brought back out of a forced retirement to disseminate a calming servility to the masses said, "It looks like the herds on my Pappy's back 40."

Several channels added commentary about the growing outcry from the animal rights activists. They were upset at the lack of respect for the invading aliens and that we should find a way to understand their aggression and maybe learn to live in harmony with each other.

All the time that the gibbering nonsense the talking heads are paid to come up with on the spot streamed over the audio, people around the globe witnessed the tightening suspense as the bomber was approaching the awaiting helicopters at about the same rate as the herds down below. The immovable object was once again playing with the irresistible force and the world hung in the balance between.

And then all went quiet as the bomb was released. All the bets were made, the teller windows were closed. The gate had been called, and the trumpets had sounded. Now there was nothing to do but watch.

The bomb looked like such a fragile thing. It dipped and bobbed with wind pockets and corrections as it plummeted unerringly at the approaching front. The extreme zoom lens, held stable by the gyroscopic technology used to first get men into space, gave the slight vibration look of aliasing that added to the mounting strain on the collectively jangled nerves of the viewers. But the camera never left it. It traced it down while the split-screen second camera stayed on the unflinching line of approaching grey-green stick figures.

Just at the last moment, the camera pulled out showing the last few hundred yards of flight. The audience was robbed of seeing the impact as the fuel was dispersed to a large area above the ground in a matter of milliseconds and ignited by the explosion. There was one brilliant flash and then a concussive vacuum of cloud and debris – all eerily without sound. The sound and shockwave came seconds later as the mushroom cloud began to rise off the jungle floor. The helicopters rocked gently on the wave.

After a moment of clearing, the helicopters began to move in. As the wind was moderate but constant that day, the clouds soon cleared as commentators were explaining what the world would very likely see. News directors are so afraid that if there is silence for too long on the air that the public will switch channels to watch re-runs on some other station. You have to keep the sound coming, even if you aren't really saying anything.

But the audience didn't need the interpretation. They could discern for themselves. The steam and smoke from splintered and charred trunks of trees arose from the dry brown dirt floor of the crater. All was motionless save for the clearing smoke. But the human mind is not easily convinced. It was as if the world collectively didn't believe it. And so there were fleeting seconds where the camera just scanned the twisted and gnarled landscape below. But as if from some cosmic synchronicity, the cheers began in virtually every corner at the same time. Bars and living rooms alike were filled with high-fives and cries of elation.

Many people were filled with the satisfaction that they had been right all along – this really *was* somebody else's problem and someone else would figure out a solution somewhere.

But in nearly every location, it was the small unnoticed observer refusing to take their eyes off the screen that had first caught sight of it. There was motion under the vapor. It was slight at first, barely perceivable. But all it took was their cautiously but clearly uttered command to the rest of the group to, "Look," usually joined with a gesture of an outstretched arm and pointing finger to turn the cheers of jubilance into a stifled discomfort and shift in mood.

As the billions of pairs of eyes re-fixed and focused on the landscape, they all began to see it too. There was a movement in the crumbs of dirt. It began to ungulate and sway as long tubular structures grew out of the mottled ground like a freakish Chia landscape. It rather resembled those eighth grade science movies where crystal growth is filmed in extreme fast motion using stop frame animation.

But there were no tricks to the camera here, kiddo. This was real. This was a living nightmare.

A sobered world looked on as the jungle floor righted itself and began brushing off the dirt. Then as the new teaming masses of not scores but tens of thousands gathered their thoughts, they restarted their migration to the north. But this time, flanks of numbers too large to count splintered off to the east and to the west.

All of a sudden this wasn't somebody else's problem anymore and someone else wasn't going to figure out a solution somewhere.

That's when it began. That's when the world markets that had been reticent to declare the African markets as closed first admitted that there was a serious problem. For one thing, diamonds would most certainly be closed from Africa, thereby spiking the price of the large cache in Australia. It is quite nearly impossible to understand exactly what kind of effect something like this has on the world markets. But needless to say, this was the shot heard round the world.

All the businesses that relied wholly on this market began to ask Wall Street for a twenty day moratorium on trade. If the world began calling in debt markers, whole industries would be made bankrupt. With this request, the monetary ratios for all currencies to African currencies became wildly inflated.

A handful of millionaires were born in that moment, but an innumerable amount of rich people became destitute overnight. Wealth like matter is finite, but unlike matter wealth can be made. Unfortunately it cannot be made completely in a vacuum.

Watching over the new masses of Ggelvring as they relentlessly moved out and away from the Republic's failed experiment Brel communicated back to the mother ship, "Everything is going very well. The food is fighting with such vigor that our plans can be pushed up quite a bit."

"How much do you think the time-tables should shift?" the flight commander asked.

"Well," Brel said as he cleaned the spray from its latest kill from its torso and looking to the north through the jungle to Rwanda, "we should hit the equator with the next revolution of the planet. I think we are well passed the livestock's ability for fissionable explosions. They have surprisingly not employed them yet, but it is a probability given their proven inhospitable temperament. But even if they did, they would have to use so many of the devices that they would render the planet unlivable," then Brel added for effect, "for *them*."

Ggelvring have a slightly different concept of humor from the human species (think French – Jerry Lewis would have been big on their planet... *very* big), but this last punched the right buttons and the ship's crew erupted in what we might consider flapping and sputtering noises, but that they felt to be a most pleasurable sensation much akin to laughter.

Brel waited the appropriate length of time to let the slapping sounds subside and then he continued, "It is true that the immediate blast site of such an attack would break us down to an atomic level, but for all of our forces at the perimeter, it would simply be a larger catalyst for expansion. So, in short, I think the landing party at the far tip of the neighboring continent can begin when the terminating line reaches daybreak there on the next revolution."

"Very good. We will prepare the landing party."

Krel heard all of this from its quarters and nearly tittered with delight. Its day was coming and the area north of the gulf would be the beginning of its budding. It looked on at the viewing screen with shiny black orbs resting easily on the shoulder stalks. In not so long a time now, it would feed beyond its sensibilities in a growth lust. Sure it would be just cleaning up the lower east coast of that smaller, less significant continent, but it would be *its* mark on this tiny blue marble spinning gracefully in the black space.

And it would only be the beginning of the career that would prove all its dissenters wrong – once and for all.

Back on planet-side, Brel took a moment to survey the fruit of its progeny and was deeply satisfied. It was good to work. It was good to do a good job with its own claw. The campaign was going well and one of these days after its retirement, an entire planet of Ggelvring would pay homage to Brel's likeness in every walk of life in perpetuity. This would be its planet – the planet Brel. That was the reward for being the best in its work-stream.

As the front began to leave Brel as it expanded in an arch to the north, it realized that the time for contemplation was now passing and it hurried to catch back up with the feeding frenzy moving into nearby villages.

The news media running endless loops of the day's carnage in the United States was tucking an uneasy nation into bed at the end of Day 2. Dads watched from their armchairs and moms from their settees as the anchor-people began showing news of a slightly different sort. The public was beginning to clamor for the United States to get involved. Once again, the world somehow managed to portray America as the bad-guy for not having solved this problem by now.

What was worse? The person-in-the-street interviews showed that even Americans were wondering why the US had not solved the problem yet. This then was immediately picked up by news channels that actually were global in scope and shown to a public hungry to blame. By midnight EST, the world's reaction to the apparent apathy of America had driven the value of the dollar down by three cents in relative value. This may not sound like a lot, but the economic effects continued to grow as they rippled through the markets. Very soon now, institutions would be forced to begin calling in markers and demanding payment of immediate debt in order to make up the difference.

Vera Foreman kissed Alfred, her husband of forty-two years on the cheek the morning of the fourth day of the alien invasion. Alfred's meaty hands were holding the fork and knife at slight angles as he hurriedly chewed the mouthful of scrambled eggs and summer sausage. The warm and yellow rays of the morning light streamed through the sunny window sheers of the kitchen in steep angles, colliding with the counter tops and appliances in a brilliance that announced the jubilant day.

They had made Ft. Wayne their home for thirty-eight of those years and this kitchen had seen four children grow to maturity and fly the nest. They had looked to the brave new future, they had joined in fear at the news of race riots, they had celebrated when Alfred had become the first African-American to reach the position of shop manager at the plant, and they had cried at the untimely death of their third child as she brought into the world their granddaughter as she simultaneously departed from it.

But this morning, the slanted rays had brought a perfect cheer to this, Alfred's last day of hard work. For today was his sixty-fifth birthday, and there was a big fat pension waiting for him at the closing whistle. The plant would shut down a few minutes early as the vice president flew in to give him his gold watch.

The thought of that, the taste of the food, and the warmth of the kiss from Vera was more than enough to curl the corners of his mouth up in a chomping bow as he continued to think upon his good fortune.

The watch was really it though. Something so insignificant, something he could easily buy for $59.00 at any jewelry store, and yet it was the single thought that would help him on with his shoes on some mornings when his feet were swollen. It was the watch that would make some lonely afternoons at the drill-press pass by just a little bit faster. And he would get to shake the hand of the vice president of the company – himself!

"Can you just imagine?" he would say to Vera as they watched yet another summer evening setting sun dip over the roofs of the houses across the street. "The vice president himself will fly all the way out here and hand *me* the watch."

Vera would pat his knee with pride as the man that had been a bulwark to her for decades, a shelter from the storms stuck out his chest with pride and sighed in his relaxation. His shoes would make the click-clop sound on the wood surface of the porch as he guided the swing, much like he had guided their lives, at just the right tempo for her and with a strength that brought to her a gentle security.

And today was the day. Today was Alfred Forman's day at last.

"Do you think those alien things will make it any farther?" she asked as she scraped a few remnants of egg onto his plate, his appetite seemed better than it had in quite some time. That would mean a romantic session was probably in store for them that evening, but even the comfort in that thought was not enough to dispel the distress in her mind. She was watching the morning news on the small counter TV even though he had made it clear he wanted nothing to do with the news on this particular day. And with the distress she felt from the stories she watched, she needed to hear it from his voice. She needed to know one more time that everything was going to be ok.

"Those things can't swim," he said in a quiet confidence of a sing-song lilt. "If they could, they wouldn't be heading north so far." This seemed to make a great deal of common sense to her, and she was already feeling some better when he continued, "And when they get to the north? Where are they going to go? The governments can just blast some bridges and at a certain point, they will hit ocean, or sea or river. Someone will figure all of that out soon."

"Well, it sure is a shame about all those other folk over there. The reports are just gruesome, Alfred."

Finishing off the last bite of breakfast, Alfred Foreman folded his morning crossword up (as was his usual custom), sipped a last sip of coffee from the cup while holding his tie with his free hand, wiped his mouth before he would even dare think of kissing his beloved, and said, "Vera, I don't want you watching that mess today. It will only make you worry. Why don't you go find a nice dress in town and get ready for a dinner out on this special night?"

And she smiled, and hugged, and kissed, and felt so much better.

He really did look dapper in his tie. It would stand out on the shop floor — that was for certain. *"And why not?"* she thought, *"My man should have his day to stand out."*

And with one last kiss and a volley of "I love you," he was gone out the door with a spring in his step she hadn't seen in nearly twenty years.

Alfred pulled into the parking lot and into the special space saved for him near the front door, his blue Pontiac sidling gracefully into the parking place. Stepping out of the car, he made his way through the front door to what he knew would be a ballyhoo of cheers and slaps on the back. But as he crossed the threshold, only one person was there to greet him. None of his team, none of his employees was there, only the HR lady that he would see once a year to go over his pension, benefits, and tax withholdings.

"Mr. Foreman, I'm so glad to see you on this special day. Congratulations!"

"Thanks, Penny." Then looking past her, he shook her enthusiastically outstretched hand as he asked, "And where is everyone else?" The sing-song lilt was still there, but it only barely covered the doubt that was hidden underneath.

"Your retirement is certainly a special event. Before we begin your last day, won't you please join me in my office?"

Her handshake had already been converted into a shepherding gesture. If she had been alone, she would have looked rather like a game show model showing off a new washing machine.

"Alright, Penny. I imagine there may be a few forms to fill out."

As they entered her office, Alfred made himself comfortable in the large chair set up for visitors as she made her way around the desk to her chair behind. Normally, he would feel some trepidation and nervousness here. There was always the thought in the back of his mind that he was about to hear some bad news like he was fired or he was going to manage lay-offs. This was the office you would hear such things. Even in his annual review, he would feel skittish hoping that they didn't lower the boom in some unsuspected way.

But no such thoughts were in his mind today. What were they going to do? Fire him on his last day before retirement? The thought of it made him chuckle a little.

"I'm glad to see you are in the spirit. This is a big day for all of us. We sure are going to miss you Alfred."

"I would like to say I'm going to miss this place, but I'm not," Alfred said sternly, but then he softened into his teddy bear self and said, "Now the *people* I will miss," and then with the stern expression, "But not the place."

She smiled at his wit and charm. Then she straightened herself up and became business. HR people have that knack. They can be human one minute and HR the next. It is one of the most frightening things in the universe to witness. Alfred felt a sudden chill as the outlandish paranoia returned, no matter how unfounded.

"Alfred, do you remember article 39 of the company by-laws?"

"Remember it, I helped the union draft it when we needed to settle that dispute back in the recession of '92."

"Right, you really stepped up and saved the company that day. We probably wouldn't be here today if it had not been for you."

Then looking curious Alfred asked, "But what does that have to do with me today? All that clause was about was how the company could shelter itself from bankruptcy should some unforeseen financial devastation fall upon it by calling for a cessation to all benefits."

Alfred's voice trailed off. A look of stunned shock fell upon his face like the sudden curtain at the end of Act 2. Then starring at her he continued the rest of the clause, "in whole or in part."

"That's correct Alfred. You helped us draft that so we could calm our creditors and still save face with the union."

"But the company isn't in any financial devastation…" he lilted, hoping against hope to end this silly nightmare before it began.

"Actually, we just had three of our five largest markets close to us yesterday and the overnight investments we make in order to fund certain ongoing projects like pensions is now being required to keep all the plants operational. Alfred, we are spending our capital on expense. We will not get that money back."

"Which means…" Alfred said in a leading way. If the axe was going to fall, he didn't want this bitch dillydallying about it. He wanted it to fall in a clean chop.

"Which means we had to make the decision to either disband the pension fund or close some plants."

"Had," he repeated her past tense verb to make a point.

"Had. The decision has been made. We have elected to exercise article 39 in part. We really had no choice after the alien invasion began in the southern tip of Chile this morning."

"What did you say?"

"They have landed in Chile, haven't you been watching the news today?"

Alfred was momentarily distracted but he couldn't dwell on yet another promise to Vera that looked to be broken. He returned to the more immediate issue in front of him, "Never mind that, you made your decision and you selected me as the lucky man."

"Alfred, I wouldn't call it lucky. I would say that it is a huge sacrifice that you and others are going to make to see that all of these men and women have a future."

Standing up, he slapped his hands down on her desk in an uncharacteristic fit of rage as he said, "And what about my future? What about my past?

Didn't you just say that I single-handedly saved the company in '92? And what thanks do I get? You turning me out into the cold? I think not!"

"Alfred, calm down," she coached.

"I will not calm down, I will leave this place right now, go to my lawyer's, and sue this company for every penny," he said, quite oblivious of the pun on her name.

Penny said, "If you leave before 5:00 PM this evening, you will have abandoned your post and as you well know you will not be eligible for the other retirement benefits which include your medical coverage for life for you and Vera."

His blood was boiling. Alfred was a trapped animal. He was living in an impossible world facing impossible barriers. There was nowhere for his anger to run, nowhere for it to fly.

After several moments of just standing there, Penny broke the silence with direction to, "Go to your team. Work the day. All this will blow over in time and your pension may be repaid. Don't make things worse on yourself than they already are. Think of Vera, Alfred. And besides, Vice President Gordon will be here near five for your ceremony. That will at least be something."

It was there that Alfred found the motivation he needed to spend a day operating floor equipment in his tie and wait for the precious moment of the five o'clock whistle to sound. For it was in that perfect moment when the whole staff gathered around, speeches were made, hands were shook, and the watch was given, that the whistle blow signified that Alfred Charleston Foreman was well and truly retired from the Triple-A Machinery Company of Ft. Wayne, Indiana.

Holding the watch in his left hand he faced the employees all chanting his name and calling for a speech. When they had all quieted down, Alfred said, "I have only one thing to say on this auspicious occasion. For thirty-eight years I have let my hands do the talking for me on this floor."

There were several calls of "Hear here," and "I know that's right."

Then Alfred said, "And I'm not about to break form now." And with that he hauled off and punched Vice President Gordon in the nose so hard that it split open revealing cartilage and gore.

And as he walked off the floor he shouted back over his shoulder, "And you can take *that* to the bank and get me my pension. You will be hearing from my lawyers." And then the door opened, and then the door closed, and no one at the Triple-A Machinery Company ever heard from Alfred Charleston Foreman again.

Within seven more days, Brel's invasion was spreading into Asia Minor, Europe, and points further east and north. The second wave was cresting, bridging the gap from South America to North spurred on by the ultra-violent corrupt governments and cartels. And as market after market fell, Wall

Street finally did close to prevent utter ruin. Rich people had long since converted as much of their wealth as they could into gold and joined the mass exodus from the cities to the shelter of caves where they could be found.

So far it looked like nothing would stop the encroachment of the aliens. Even the few small nukes that were attempted proved to make matters far worse than they had been. Even though the center of the blast seemed to destroy the aliens completely, it also destroyed all other life as well. And the alien population at the perimeter seemed to feed on the radiation. It created a macro version of fission in the creatures, splitting them time and time again.

As productivity waned due to the crippling fear shared by humans around the globe, governments began to feel the bind of reduced or even non-existent tax revenue and in many cases simply folded completely.

7.

Dex was waking up to a different world every day. Sure he had passed the bar. Sure he had landed a job at a prestigious firm (thanks, dear old Dad!). Sure he had his choice of women. But that didn't stop the fear that happened every morning.

As he woke up in his sleek Buckhead condominium in Atlanta, the louvered bars of light across the blonde hardwood floors pointed the way through his California chic décor to the bathroom that held for him all the horrors of the new world. It was not the alien invasion that brought Dex trepidation. The second wave of those tubes of chaos had moved west once out of Mexico and the first wave in southern Europe had moved east and north into the Ukraine and surrounding areas. It looked like the eastern half of the US, and all points immediately north and east were safe.

For those of you that play Risk, Greenland and Iceland were extremely safe properties at the moment – or so it would seem.

As he stood beside the bed and stretched in his designer pajamas, he moved slowly to the chamber of horrors. Life wasn't really that bad. Most of his day was phenomenal. Nice car, nice work, nice fun – all the things a growing boy needs to stay happy. It was just *this* moment that caused any real trepidation. It was *this* moment he would suppress the rest of the day only to remember it afresh tomorrow morning.

Oh the joy!

Sitting on his throne, he read. The novel was good; it actually took his mind off things for the time it took to finish his business. The two to three pages a day pace was good as well for those novels that he wanted to read, but just never seemed to be able to find the time. It allowed Dex to live the book for a very long time.

Flipping the page and coming to a chapter break, the cool feel of the marble tile on his bare feet brought him back to this reality as he carefully made a mental note of the page he was on, and placed the book carefully back into the magazine rack beside.

Bookmarks were for wusses.

Now came the moment of truth. Now he would have to clean himself up. Leaning forward he took the necessary actions but before discarding the tissue, he took a moment to look. There it was. Just like the day before and the day before that - the bright red smear of oxygenated blood.

Dex couldn't remember everything he had read about colon cancer. All he knew was that bright red comes from arteries and dark red from veins. At least that is what he *thought* he remembered. He also remembered a friend in college shitting blood and after having the melodramatic meltdown, going to the doctor only to find he had a perforated colon from eating too much junk. A condition the doctor didn't seem too concerned about and in a few days, everything was back to normal.

At least that is what he *thought* he remembered.

And in his gripped fear, he finished his business and with the flush began his daily trip into denial that would last at least another twenty-three hours and forty-five minutes. Besides, at the first sign of it, Dex had called his doctor only to find out that he had closed his practice and moved to the mountains of North Georgia. There were so many that had done this that most doctors that stayed behind out of a sense of duty were treating mostly emergency patients, or those with really good connections. Dex had really good connections, but he also had a great case of denial going.

Pretty much everyone left on Earth had a really good case of denial going. For the most part, people seemed to be going through their day to day lives as if nothing were wrong. It was a serious state of shock that permeated the whole globe. But what was one to do? They couldn't all go stark raving mad. So, most people just kept going through the paces in a general apathetic stupor. It was easier for those that had jobs that were still in demand.

"Thank God I'm a lawyer," Dex had assured himself in the mirror. "Even if the whole world is going to chaos," then thinking better of it he corrected, "especially if the whole world is going to chaos, people are going to be suing each other to the bitter end."

For some reason, this thought that was meant to be cheerful did not carry with it the usual afterglow. Dex was seriously scared this time. He was not going to be able to sue God for a new colon. And he certainly didn't think the new visitors gave a rat's ass (no lawyer pun intended). He imagined the end was coming sooner or later by one means or another.

God hadn't created a birth certificate yet that didn't have an expiration date on it.

Dex was just concerned his wasn't too far away. In a way that mimicked nearly all the other humans on the planet, he absently walked over to the telephone that was remarkably still working. As it turns out, there are still some at the phone company that consider the network to be a national asset rather than a stomping ground for their favorite political game of the week and Ma Bell was still on duty.

With the dial tone pleasantly humming in his ear, Dex quietly dialed Guy's number (or "touched Guy up", but that didn't really work for our heterosexually confident Dex).

Ring.

Ring.

Pause. Even the phones were morosely apathetic.

Ring.

Click.

Silence. Nothing was there. It was a big nothing named Guy. Dex could hear him breathing. "Guy?"

Silence. The nothing was still there – more breathing. "Guy, this is Dex."

"Hang on. The report is almost over."

That sounded a bit cryptic, but now Dex could just barely make out the sound of squawky voices in the background. So he hung on a moment.

Guy Sayonara was on his back patio, sitting in his cheap lawn chairs, flicking small rocks at his grill. As they skittered off the metal base in different directions, they joined the small galaxy of pebble bodies scattered around the now-dormant grill.

Tink.

Spock.

Clang.

Tink.

The small radio was tuned to NPR and a report that held his attention long enough for him to momentarily rejoin the world at large and care enough to step out of his haze of insane blandness was just concluding.

"It's NPR," Guy said sliding back into the apathetic fog of defeat.

"Yes, I know."

"It's one of the few stations still broadcasting this early in the morning."

"Yes, Guy. I know."

"You see, all the other channels are having a hard time finding round the clock help."

"Yes, Guy. I know. But I want to talk to you about something far more important.

"It's the money thing," Guy said looking out at the sunrise over the dewy grass courtyard that stretched out between his apartment and the next row that ran just off angle enough to not be completely parallel to his building. It was an angle that would cause all the residents to wonder if the construction workers were following the designs of some tormented architect or if they were merely drunk.

Most people settled on the drunk theory. Why else would all the other apartment buildings comprised of eight apartments each, two stories with an upstairs and downstairs dogtrot through the middle be perfectly parallel except these two?

"Yes Guy, the whole economy is in trouble."

"Trouble?" Guy's voice gave the first hint of not being completely swallowed up in gloom. "Trouble? Hell! It's bleeding right down the crapper."

Dex was stunned by Guy's choice of words. He had wanted to know that there was still a constant in the universe. He had wanted to know that Guy was still plain old Guy. He had wanted to hear the voice of the standard bearer. And here he was, the bearer of the standard, all but telling him his diagnosis as a metaphor for all the world to hear.

"Yeah. Down the crapper," Dex agreed.

"So how are you, Dex?"

There was a long silence. Guy didn't care. He was returning to his stupor. Dex was returning to his denial.

"What was the report about?"

"What?"

"Just now. You made me wait for a moment. 'Hang on,' you said."

"Oh, NPR was just talking about the backwash."

The backwash was a new euphemism the media had given the survivors. In every country, the aliens have killed just enough people to accomplish two things: 1) Keep their company front moving forward at the fastest speed possible with replication and feeding happening at alarming rates, and 2) Demoralize a people so completely that they walked around like veritable zombies, totally incapable of mustering a counter attack.

It was the prevailing belief that these unfortunates, the backwash, were being kept as fresh supplies of nutrients should there be an unexpected new turn or need to retreat. But for those observers still keen enough to formulate halfway intelligible observations, the backwash was by no means a minority. In fact, the majority of the population was staying intact and alive. They were just stunned to a level of productivity that would afford them the ability to merely stay alive.

In the book, *Watership Down* by Richard Adams, the rabbits had a name for this condition. It was called "tharn". A rabbit would go tharn when something had shocked it into a state of not caring anymore, like a car's headlights on the highway.

The whole world had gone tharn. Even those not attacked yet by the front. For most people, happy apathy was the order of the day. The Earth was fast becoming a defeated lot.

"What about the backwash?" Dex asked in an effort to care about something else beyond his bloody ass.

"Well," Guy said as he reached down for a fresh handful of pebbles from beside his patio. The poniards of his irregular wrought iron fence pointed to his feet. The shadow of the taller of a pair closest to him just covered the toe of his left shoe. He was dressed for work even though there was another good hour before he had to leave. "They were observing how interesting it is that in the Middle East, the Jews and the Muslims trace their roots back to the same man, Abraham through different sons."

"Well, actually the Saudis that adopted the Muslim faith," Dex corrected.

"Right. Whatever. Anyway, the Muslims go back through Ishmael and the Jews through Isaac."

"Right…" Dex said in a way that communicated, "So what?"

"Well, they are half-brothers and have been at war with each other for some 4,000 years," Guy said matter-of-factly.

"Right…"

"And all over slightly different understandings of the same God. Ala and Yahweh."

"Right…"

"Well, they all were praying. And Ala/Yahweh did not deliver either of them from their enemy."

"Right…"

"So NPR concluded that Nietzsche was right," Guy concluded.

"That God is dead?" Dex asked.

"Precisely."

There was a long pause. Then Dex observed, "But NPR has been saying that for years. We really need to get you to stop listening to NPR."

"But there isn't anything else to listen to this early. All the other stations sign on around eight or so."

"Oh, yeah." Then thinking that there probably was no harm since they were all going to die anyway Dex added, "Maybe it's not too bad to listen to NPR, just take it with a grain of salt."

"Well, whether or not God is dead, they have stopped killing each other over there."

"Perhaps God is alive and well," Dex thought with a twist of irony but then he realized it was difficult for him to have such faith under the current bloody circumstances. "Well, at least we both have work."

"Sort of."

"What do you mean, sort of?"

"Well, ANI TramTek had to cut everyone back to half pay to make things last as long as they can."

"That is probably pretty wise."

"But the economy is so crazy. Some things are cheap while others are ridiculous."

"Do you have enough money to hang on?" Dex asked with some concern.

"Probably. But things are tight. Good thing I am a vegetarian now. Meat is through the roof at the stores. But I am concerned about ANI."

"Really? Why?"

"Well, you remember once telling me that they were not the best DOD company to work for?"

"The word I used was mediocre."

"Right. Whatever. The thing is this: there are x number of DOD companies in the country. The money from the government really doesn't mean much anymore and there certainly isn't a lot of tax revenue with the west coast getting eaten alive. So, all the DOD companies are asking employees to basically work for free or with half pay while they all bid on the remaining new contracts being issued from the government."

"And what are those?"

"Come up with a way to kill the aliens. But the problem is that even if someone came up with a way to kill them, the government really couldn't give them anything of value until the whole world economy righted itself anyway. So every contract is like getting work on speculation and even if you are successful, you may never see any money at all."

"So the only slightest chance of any meaningful future…"

"Would be working for one of the few companies that actually has a shot at a contract."

"And ANI is mediocre."

Tink.

Tick.

P'ting.

Dex wanted this call to cheer him up. It had failed. He wouldn't feel better until he was bartering for something valuable in order to evict a bunch of deadbeats in downtown Atlanta later that day.

"Well, Guy. I wish the best of luck."

"Look around, Dex. The best of luck don't mean very much right now."

Looking for some way to make Guy feel better so that he could feel better, "Well, maybe something will turn up. Fate often has a way of just tripping into your life from time to time."

Tink.

Tock.

"Well, goodbye, Guy. Take care."

"Dex, it's always good to talk to you. Somehow you make me feel a little better about my life each time. I mean, we had our differences back in college, but I never felt like I didn't have someone at least routing for me."

"Where Guy goes, so goes the world. We have to keep you going, man. Things will pick up soon. I guarantee it."

"Good as the word of a lawyer?" Guy inquired.

"Good as the word of a friend." Dex assured.

They hung up and Guy went to work. Showing up early didn't really help much. Guy's boss was on the war path trying to get final figures in for the big DOD proposal that would make sure they all had a living – if you could call this a living.

If Dex was going to make good on his word it certainly was not going to be this day. But as it turned out, the events that transpired a mere week later proved Dex to be a friend of his word beyond the preponderance of evidence and, yea, even beyond the shadow of any reasonable doubt.

8.

You are flying over the desert floor, following a road in the safe comfort of an ultra-sleek helicopter. The cool air-conditioned breeze blows gently on your face while the yellow sand and orange rock bathe hot in the mid-day sun below. Your wistful shadow glides over the bumpy terrain darting in and out of the sudden changes to the landscape. Only insects can find shelter in the short shadows of cactus and scrub from the boiling and arid heat that shimmers off the basin floor. The tar looks like it is virtually melting between the gravel that paved this lonely stretch, miles from anywhere in all directions.

Just up there you see it for the first time, a minivan carrying a happy family from Las Vegas to Los Angeles. They are making the Las-y trek singing tunes from their favorite animated movies as they make their way to the theme park where they will meet the characters in real life! The road unwinds out in front of you like some sidewinder crossing the valley of death. Nothing but blind curves ahead as the minivan peeks in and out of cliff formations as the desert floor deepens.

You decide to zoom ahead and leave this merry jaunt. Picking up speed and gaining altitude, you fly over the minivan with increasing speed, feeling the comfortable pull of the Earth as you safely glide over the family below. You pass unnoticed by the happy band as you make a straight line over the jagged terrain that will force the Earth-bound pistons to negotiate via long curves.

You no sooner clear the first small mesa range when you see it. The bridge ahead has collapsed into the ravine below. The drop is severe as you suddenly realize that the minivan filled with the hopes and dreams of a future generation will fall hundreds of feet to the small river below. All will be lost. Everyone in the minivan will die. The smallest daughter will never have the chance to be afraid of the human in a mouse costume while mom and dad coax her to pose for a picture she will one day show her fiancé.

Realizing that the curve before was too severe to allow for a visual warning the only chance the hapless family has is you. Shouting orders at the pilot, you direct her to go back fast. Perhaps you can head them off at the proverbial pass. But as it takes what seems an eternity for her to hear your command, understand it, and begin to turn around, you already know that it is too late. There is no hope for the van but to once again become enshrined in the museum of artifacts that proved Newton correct.

You decide that Newton was a real jerk for falling asleep under an apple tree to begin with.

The chopper eventually manages to turn around, but you feel as if you are in molasses – sticky and gooey as the rotors groan against the strain. Slicing through the heat of the day you shoot your way back with all haste. But you know that hope against hope, you will be there to do nothing but witness the plunge. You are simply too far away.

What do you feel in that moment? What would you do to save a family that is about to meet their collective end? How far would you take your deal with God or the Devil or whomever it is that you reach out to in times of distress?

You make your bargain and hope for the best. Actually you hope that the worst will happen not in your sight for to you it is a foregone conclusion that the worst will come. There is absolutely no way around it. Sometimes shit just happens.

But as you approach the faulty bridge fully expecting carnage, there is none to be seen. You clear the ledge and look down the ravine. No van. No family. No daughter that will never be afraid of the human in a mouse costume.

Curious, you give an order to the pilot and she follows the road ahead, staying slow and low to ensure that you don't miss a single thing. It takes an eternity to make the slow curve to the right. But clearing the cliff that sticks out like a finger blocking your investigation, up on the right you see it.

Still ahead of you in the shimmering waves, a tire has blown out on the minivan. You can see Dad get out as he begins to curse at the tire, kicking and screaming all the while. He doesn't know if he can change it with the spare that he neglected to check before leaving and the nearest station is more than thirty miles in either direction. Sweat immediately begins to dampen his back as he rubs his forehead with his forearm. What on Earth did he possibly do to deserve this misfortune?

And the whole while he is fussing and cussing at his ill-fated luck, you are rejoicing and shouting with happiness and glee. The family will not die. You will not have to witness it. And most of all, you will not have to carry the burden that you were powerless to stop it.

That is how we are and that is how God is. God is in a helicopter. He can see beyond the mountains and the cliffs. He knows what will befall us should we continue on our reckless path. Sometimes He allows events to unfold. But from time to time, the tire on the minivan will blow. It will force us to stop before some even greater calamity falls upon us. And while we stand there in the baking heat of an impossible situation crying at the fact that nobody cares about us, He is up there in a helicopter trading high-fives with all the angels. For you were about to suffer a terrible loss, and instead you suffered a minor inconvenience.

That is how the ways of God are. And that is precisely what happened to Guy.

The curves of Research Park would make for the perfect sports car commercial in 1966. It was the era of cool long before the yuppie gods of urban planning came to town. In that renaissance era when form and function walked hand-in-hand, the city developers cut wide meandering curves through the vacant sloping fields to the west. Trees formed natural breaks between the large rectangular buildings replete with cantilevers galore.

Modern developers would pout at the waste of land. Straight lines in roads are so much more economical than curves. And so much more dull.

Engineers in their eggshell yellow wind breakers and straight-leg slacks smoked Kool or Kent cigarettes before slipping on their suit coats for another day of dreaming the impossible and then making it happen day by day. If you have forgotten the magic of that era, it is easy to catch a glimpse of it. The next time you see a full moon, take a moment not to take it for granted. Imagine being part of a generation that thought it important, yea paramount, to walk on its surface – and then they did it!

That was the generation that built the buildings that Guy's GMC Pacer now negotiated as he drove to work. Here in his world, the buildings have dingy-tiled ceilings and yellowing blinds on the windows. The X-Generation no longer look to the stars but to the battlefield and their bank accounts. City planners see the gracefully curved roads and research the imminent domain laws looking for the right combinations of loop-holes that would allow them to bulldoze the whole lot and put in more sensible straight lines. They could fit another five buildings in – easy.

Long gone are the echoes of Kennedy's voice as he spoke over a crescendo of cheers, "We choose to go to the Moon. We choose to go to the Moon. We choose to go to the Moon in this decade and do the other things, not because they are easy, but because they are hard."

It has been replaced with young men and women saying, "We choose to buy on credit. We choose to live for money. We choose to make the deal happen in this decade, not just because they are easy, but because we can live like they do on the TV shows."

But even those shallower thoughts had past. As Guy drives down the road that Jack built all he really cares about is making the deal happen not to live like the TV people, but simply to live. Pulling into the vast parking lot that once housed the company that created the Lunar Lander out of thin air, Guy's thoughts were on the sequence of sub-contract distribution should his company win one of the precious few DOD contracts to be awarded today.

He walked into the half-empty lobby. Some of the ANI TramTek staff had already gone stark raving loony. Others had simply checked out. But Guy noticed that just barely half of them, or maybe a little bit more than half, had decided to just keep driving through life – almost as if nothing bad was happening at all.

If Guy had been in his right mind; if any of them had been in their right mind, they would have noticed that even though they were still functioning physically the life was already gone. There was an emptiness of doom that veiled the light of life from their eyes. They were simply going through the paces waiting to hear the news of their future. They were waiting for the next moment to come, one moment at a time.

They were waiting to die.

How would you spend your time should you suspect that it was all over but the credits? What would you do if you suspected that things were coming to an unnatural end with a certainty? For all the people that remained at ANI TramTek, they simply continued to go through the paces with a hopeless apathy that must accompany total defeat before the final whistle is blown. The team is down by 67 points and they are at the two minute warning, but the coach is making them finish the game.

They just go through the motions and wait for the final moment to relieve them their purgatory.

Guy walked to his desk. It was a one of the few real offices (some of his work was confidential and required a door to close). Passing by the cube farms he absently said hello to those he saw along the way. Occasionally one would look up as if to ask if he had seen the big game last night, but no one actually asked. There were no more games.

Guy walked into his office, sat down behind his desk, and waited. At 8:30 they would know. At 8:30 the word would be given.

Sitting there staring at the blotter doodles in front of him he remembered for a brief moment what life was like before them. There was a scratchy picture of a chef's hat beside a computer terminal. The hat had an X marked through it with strong, pressing grooves of anger while the terminal was surrounded by the radiating hash marks one sees in comics around gold or money.

There was no doubt about it. Guy had sold out. Things got a little tough and he had been unwilling to risk any more than he had already risked. He had not reflected on the decision he had made before he made it. And he had turned his back on the work that might live on after he has gone.

A soft knock at the door broke his concentration. It was Natalie. "Hey boss, are you coming to the lobby? They are about to make the big announcement and everyone is gathering to watch it on the large TV there."

Looking up at her with hollow sincerity Guy smiled and said, "Yeah. Sure. I will be right there."

Natalie left and Guy looked back at the blotter again, drumming his pencil at it while he stared. He was thinking of nothing and everything all at the same time. With a final stroke of his remaining self, he scratched another deep X through the chef's hat. The lead of his number 2 pencil snapped from the overwhelming pressure and he cursed at it as he stood and left his office behind.

In the lobby, the now growing mass of hopeful remnants were gathering under the large flat panel TV hanging on the wall. The screen showed the joint symbols of the Pentagon and the DOD. The closed circuit cameras at the national briefing room were already on and a podium could be made out behind the overlaid logos.

People were whispering their last words of encouragement as the logos dissolved and the spokeswoman stepped up to the mike.

"Ladies and Gentlemen, thank you for your audience this morning. The following is a list of the DOD contracts that are being awarded. I will announce them in no certain order. There are twenty-five initiatives that are being assigned today. I expect to hear from each company that is listed before COB today. If no word is given, the second on the list will be contacted.

"The initiative awards in no certain order are: Containment and Control awarded to Beecham and Associates, Dallas, Texas. Deterrent awarded to BNJ Enterprises, Modesto, California. Field Communications – Intercept awarded to Bly Technologies, Oak Ridge, Tennessee. Field Communications – Command and Control awarded to Polytel Communications, Slidell, Mississippi..."

One by one the announcements were made. Some in the crowd counted the names to keep track, others held on to something should they faint. Guy was one of the majority that just allowed the sound of her words to wash over him taking no particular interest in the outcome one way or the other.

His decision had been made two years earlier. The scribbles on his blotter were all the evidence required. His end was already written. The only question now was would it come today or maybe in the next week or two. What he did in the meantime was meaningless.

The spokeswoman from the DOD droned on. The twenty-five awards were named and not a single one went to ANI TramTek. Some people cried. Others ran screaming from the building. But most just stood there in a state best described as tharn. They were simply waiting for the approaching headlights to bring an end to the madness.

The company announced the layoffs slightly after 10:00 AM. It turns out that three contracts were handed out in the Huntsville area and ANI TramTek was number seventeen on one of the items. The chances of sixteen other companies passing up the only contract they can get were Slim and None, and Slim left town riding a 1966 sports car, baby.

Eventually security convinced all the hangers-on to go home. There was nothing more to do here. But amazingly, even after the announcement many would go back to their desk and continue to work and even more amazing some would return the next day and stare at the closed doors for hours wondering what it all meant.

Guy drove home in pretty much the same mind as he had coming in this morning. The trees whipped by his Pacer as he drove back down the lazy curves to the straighter angles of Governor's Drive. Heading east he made his way back to the apartment complex that had confounded the blue collar and young professional residents with its perfectly parallel buildings – save one.

Guy arrived at home, opened the front door, slipped off his tie, dropped it on the kitchen counter, and made his way out to his patio through the sliding glass door in the back. The door felt heavy in his hand as if something ominous were about to happen. Still he walked out and sat down in his cheap woven lawn chair in a total state of tharn. Sitting there content to watch the world go by, he began picking up stones and throwing them once again at the base of his grill.

But not a single pebble had the chance to make the "ting" sound. For as the first one hit and landed among its scattered brothers, its satisfying sound was drowned out by the roar of the landing space pod.

The pointed capsule landed not twenty feet in front of Guy and dug a trench thirty feet long as it came to a violent stop just at the apex of the two crooked buildings. Guy wondered if the architects knew that was going to happen and laughed a soft snort at the irony.

Everything about this landing was just as impressive as the one Daniel Guedbye had witnessed. Unfortunately for Krel, the tharn of the surrounding food had rendered them incapable of demonstrating the same emotional shock that was offered to Brel in respect. But that was the price of being the third wave.

All the risk, but none of the glory.

Krel knew that would all change some day. And in the meantime, it had to make a good show of it. Otherwise there would be no threat and thus no procreation.

In some ways, being on the third string may actually be more of a challenge in the long run. It's easy to score a touchdown when the adrenaline is flowing being pumped by the cheers of hundreds and the blast of a fight song from the band. Just try to pull off the same trick on a Tuesday afternoon in an empty stadium surrounded by morons.

Krel realized how good it would have to be. It played its part to the hilt. Every nuance was precisely executed the way they were taught in the academy. As it thundered its hoof in the direction of the food sitting inside the little coral with the black fence around it, Krel knew that the technique was flawless.

But the food didn't move. Well, Krel didn't think that it moved at first. But then it noticed that the food threw something at a metal object in from of it.

P'tink.

This angered Krel. It would really have to turn on the ferocity in order to provoke the food to violence. So Krel decided to let loose a guttural roar. The deafening cry echoed off the oddly non-parallel buildings. Krel took a moment to notice the angles that were just a little off and laugh to itself how backwards these creatures really were.

But still no response. The food just sat there throwing small rocks at that black object.

Skank.

Krel was embarrassed. This food was not screaming in fear. It was not running for the hills. It was just sitting there mocking Krel.

Spok.

That was the last straw. Krel was going to either provoke this creature to violence, or it was going to simply eat it. At this point time was the issue. If Krel didn't score a kill or a split in the next few moments, the SCC would not see it as material worthy for a promotion.

The embarrassment Krel felt coupled with its anger at this apathetic creature that should be filled with terror forced it to run across the open terrain and attack the food with reckless abandon. Jumping over the small fence was no problem at all. Did this puny creature actually think that such a trivial thing would stop the vastly superior Ggelvring? Krel took another moment to be amused at the impudence of the food on this planet.

Deciding to give it one last try, Krel let loose with its mightiest of battle cries.

Guy sat there and looked up at the alien that had nimbly jumped over the wrought iron fence. *"So I guess this is how it all ends,"* he thought to himself. The riddle of the calendar blotter on his desk was being answered on this very morn.

Looking at his grill, for some reason a Bible verse popped into Guy's mind from Vacation Bible School – a summer tradition in the south where children go to church every day for one week hearing stories, making crafts, eating cookies, drinking Kool-Aid, and memorizing verses.

It was from the book of Luke, 20 "But God said to him, 'You fool! This very night your life will be demanded from you. Then who will get what you have prepared for yourself?'

Guy regretted not pursuing his dream to the end. But even that regret was not enough force to budge the immovable object of his tharness. Picking up another pebble, he threw it at the grill.

Tick.

This seemed to agitate the alien that let out another fierce cry. Guy tried to care. But try as he might, there just wasn't any more care left in him. He didn't even flinch as the alien stretched out its coiled fingered towards his head.

Krel was beside itself in anger. This food was making a mockery of it. Krel new the SCC was watching so it decided to make this kill as stunning as possible. Reaching out the tightly coiled fingers of its left hand, Krel prepared its claw for the kill with several aggressive snaps at the air over its head. It took one last forceful step towards this pathetic excuse for food and wanting to make it look really dramatic, it slammed its hoof down hard.

That was when the world started to go funny for Krel. Something happened that was all wrong. For as it brought all its weight to bare on the hoof in order to make for a spectacular display, the flat of the hoof landed on some of the tiny pebbles that the food had been throwing in defiance. The pebbles rolled like marbles under its foot and Krel felt the gravitational pull of this planet yank backwards on its body as inertia joined in on the merry prank. Krel's finely developed equilibrium announced that all was not right in Mudville or whatever this place was called.

The sky became a kooky angle to the ground as its flailing arms circled in fast waves trying to catch something, anything that would prevent the now certain fall backwards. But they found nothing upon which to grasp and all twelve feet of Krel began to fall like a mighty redwood felled on the side of a hill.

Guy watched in stun silence as the monster comically slipped on the pebbles like a banana peel. Buster Keaton couldn't have done a better prat had he tried. It was almost as if the fall were in slow motion. The alien waving its arms trying to right itself only to succumb to the Earth's loving pull in a slow and arching dive backwards.

If there had been a swimming pool there, Guy thought the alien would have made a splash large enough to drench the life guard on the other side.

But there hadn't been a pool, had there? All that was there to meet the back of the alien's triangular head and left breast pipe were the irregularly staggered poniards of the wrought iron fence. They impaled the alien in two different places at precisely the same moment.

Guy sat there and stared as the alien shuddered and then fell silent not ten feet away from his cheap lawn chair. One of the spikes was sticking through the large black dot on the front of the alien's flat face. The other was dripping gore from right in the center of the angle in the pipe that made what would be its left chest area.

Guy blinked.

Years ago a sociologists asked 100 people over the age of ninety, "If you had to do it all over again, what would you do differently?" And although nearly every answer was unique, there were three prevailing themes that seemed to emerge. 1) They would risk more, 2) they would reflect more on what they were doing while they were doing it, and 3) they would do more that would live on after they died.

Here at the feet of one champion of mediocrity was the now Earthly remains of another champion of mediocrity. Through some crazy cosmic collision of irony, they had met in an accident that both provided life to one that was surely dead and death to one that was most assuredly alive. One had risked, and one had played it safe.

In the end, we have to ask if it's better to live with regret than to die with some ill-conceived notion that our choices can actually change how we ultimately view our own lives. We will never know for sure, because the one that could actually answer the question was now lying sprawled at the feet of the one that couldn't, its two centers of consciousness impaled on some ornamental wrought iron that all the neighbors had thought was gaudy and in the poorest of taste.

Maybe the higher lesson here for all of us to learn is that we shouldn't be so quick to criticize how our neighbors decorate their yards.

9.

Guy leaned back in the aluminum frame wrapped in yellow, white and green polystyrene strips that made up his chair and watched as the sun painted a clock across the alien's corpse with the shadows of the black wrought iron points creating a double set of minute hands. He read the time of day from this makeshift sun dial.

Quarter past dead.

Picking up some more stones, Guy was going to begin throwing them at the grill again. But he had become so completely apathetic that he didn't even care about hearing the sound that they made as they bounced to a halt. So he just stared at them in the palm of his hand. They were lifeless and still. Sort of like his newfound friend over there.

Looking at the gruesome gazingstock and its gore as it glistened in the increasing sun, Guy began to remember rudimentary muscle movement from somewhere deep in his subconscious. He could feel almost by instinct his limbs requesting to move in certain ways. It was almost like his muscles had memories since his brain had apparently checked out completely.

Without emotion or thought he stood up in front of the lawn chair. Relaxing his hands which were by his side allowed the lifeless pebbles to fall to the ground, scattered around his feet like boulders at the base of a large rock slide. He stood there for a moment – as still as the pebbles now at rest on the concrete of the patio. Looking at the splayed spectacle that adorned his little fence, he blinked again.

The call to movement was once again received from Guy's muscles. Compelled by nothing more than the absentminded desire to follow their command he quietly shuffled across the patio to the carnage on the other side. There he stood and looked upon the alien's ending. It was quiet. It was still. It was dead.

Without really thinking about his actions any more than a nightshift worker at a drill press doing the same repetitive motion over and over, he reached down and grasped the large head at the angled corners on either side. Then with one fluid motion he pulled it straight up the pole to the top where it stopped as it pressed against the bulbous base of the point. Increasing his force a little bit, the head gave as the base of the point was forced to re-enter what should have been its face had it been human.

As the spike slid through the gaping head-wound, it produced the slimy sucking sound that strawberry Jello makes as it is slurped through a straw by a rude fourth grader in the lunchroom of any school at twelve noon. And as it cleared the back side of the head it made a surprising little pop as the suction yielded to the collapsing exit wound on the other side. Once it was free from the fence's cold embrace, Guy dropped the head down to the side and watched as it lolled around a bit on the end of the shaft that served as its neck.

For a few moments he watched as the gentle rocking motion of the head's shadow became a comical pendulum to the hands of the sun dial. Half past dead. Guy snorted a little laugh out his nose at the thought.

But then the expressionless pallor returned to his face, as Guy reached down and grabbed the left breast-pipe and like the head began to pull it up the fence spike. This time it seemed to skitter and vibrate a little on the way up. He imagined there must be bone inside that was scraping against the metal of the poniard. It yielded a soft scraping sound as it stuttered its way up to the point. The trail of gore that was left behind appeared to not serve as much of a lubricant.

This time it took a little more effort to free the mangled tissue, bone and muscle from the head of the spike. Eventually Guy was able to manage by pushing the tube to the side, thereby stretching what must have been muscle and tendon far enough out to allow the bone to slip around the other side of the spike's base. There was a slightly wet snapping sound as it popped off the spike and came to rest on the side of the little fence.

Guy stepped back assessing the crumpled mass that had been a terrifying alien only a moment earlier. Not much too it actually. He wondered why there had been such a fuss about these things. But the compulsion to move as called for by his muscles returned and would not allow him any more time to daydream.

Reaching down, he grabbed one of the large cloven hooves and began to drag the carcass across his pebble strewn patio towards the sliding glass doors. He found it easier to turn around and lock the hoof under his right arm, dragging the corpse behind him as he went. The arms of the alien began to stretch out behind as the ground's friction pulled against Guy's blank-faced progress. The head of the alien bumped up and down at every irregular shift in the poured concrete. Surprisingly enough, it was not as heavy as it looked.

Guy was expecting something this big to weigh at least 400 lbs. But even though it was more like 200, he was able to manage pulling it without breaking the trance of tharn that still seemed to have him firmly in its grasp.

As he pulled and dragged the alien towards and through the sliding glass door, he became aware of a mild irritation that pierced his blank mind like a spike that thrust through a calm flat surface. For some reason, the alien had stopped following him so obediently and his forward motion had subsequently ceased entirely. Guy tried again to start up his forward motion but again he was stopped as he heard a soft thump from behind. Repeating this attempt over and over to continue his calm and serene pilgrimage was met each time by the same soft catching thump from behind.

Thump, thump, thump.

Eventually he became agitated enough at his inability to forward progress that he turned around to see what was wrong. Grabbing up the alien's leg in a re-grip as he was now facing the corpse, he gave another quick pull towards the interior of his apartment.

Thump.

Guy could now plainly see what the problem was. The alien's other leg had splayed open from the friction of the short journey and its crotch was now wedged against the sliding glass door; the other leg sprawled out along its base outside. Not wanting to admit he really had a problem, Guy tried several more times to just force it through the opening. Each time, the alien's crotch thumped against the base of the door.

Thump, thump... thump.

Not really wanting to rip the door off the track (that would mean he might lose his deposit when he moved out), Guy pushed the alien back out the door by applying pressure on the leg like it was a broom handle and he the night janitor sweeping up a bit. But the corpse was catching on the concrete and the joints of the leg collapsed. The net result was that nothing much happened by way of movement. So Guy fussed a little and dropping the leg, went back outside. This time he grabbed the other leg and pulled it back over the smooth surface of the door in a big circle like someone trying to start an old prop plane by hand. The leg collapsed by the other one as he dropped it over the threshold and onto the carpeted surface of his small living room.

Guy thought about the irony of a dead thing in a living room and snickered a little as he stepped his way across the crumpled form. Turning his back to the alien and grabbing up the two legs, one under each arm like some sort of reverse wheelbarrow, he pulled the alien sliding across the carpet and onto the linoleum of the kitchen beyond.

There Guy took a moment to pause as he leaned against the kitchen counters and looked down at the collection of angular tubes lying on the floor at his feet. He wasn't really sure why his own muscles had called him to drag the beast here, but here it was - a kitchen-floorful of alien.

His muscles apparently were not done with their desired job for they once again interrupted his own desire to just stand there and stare. Turning around, he opened a drawer and found his professional cutlery that was purchased for his chosen career in what seemed like a time hundreds of years earlier. The knives were expensive and each one served its one very specific purpose. Back in college he had spent not one but two semesters perfecting the craft of preparatory butchering.

Now working with what must have been muscular memories of those days, his hands began to trace the form of the corpse on the floor. He could feel the joints and ligaments just below the surface as he absentmindedly learned by feel the physiognomy of this recently diseased creature. After several minutes of such tracing, Guy picked what would be the very best starting point which was just under the right shoulder joint by his best estimation.

The tip of the first blade expertly selected was built for fast piercing and ripping. And the foil did not disappoint. Within seconds he had a nice bloodless incision that crosscut from the upper right shoulder down the left breast tube to the still open wound from the fence. Using a butcher's fork, he pulled back the loose flap of skin and deftly swapped out blades to the sleeker upturned blade used for separating muscle from bone.

Using his fingertip, Guy traced the orange bone to the shoulder joint and found that the two bones from the two chest tubes actually crisscrossed at what should have been the trachea had this been a human. There, they angled out slightly to either side, forming little flying buttresses like an old-time cathedral roof. Quite sturdy, this construction.

Guy traced back down the rounded shoulder bone to the point where the two bones crossed at the neck. The tissue surrounding the bones was a pale pink similar to the color of Pepto Bismal and the tendons were a shiny and translucent milky white. There at the hinge where the two bones crossed, Guy noticed what looked like a small hairline jagged fracture forming in each bone at the juncture. Making an educated guess at how these creatures must split, he took the tip of the new knife he had picked up and traced the jagged little fissure with just the slightest pressure.

The bones snapped with a loud crack and separated like a spring-action lever. The head dragged over with the left shoulder – the side opposite from the massive claw. In that moment, the huge claw snapped shut and the elbow drew in towards Guy's thigh where he had been kneeling. Scrambling up quickly, he grabbed at the counter and steadied himself as he exited the kitchen.

His heart was beating fast. At least that was something un-tharnish to do. He at least was again interested a little in staying alive. But as he stood there waiting for another sudden movement, he realized that it must have been a reflex caused by a sudden tension on the tendon running down the right arm as the tubes pulled apart from one another. Over time, his breathing returned to normal and his curiosity returned to abnormal.

Slowly, Guy returned to his work as he studied the new structure that was exposed by the initial split in the creature. He noted that if the skin had remained intact, the whole of the creature probably would have had enough controlled energy from the snapping of the once-taught tendons to literally spring into two upright pieces. But as it was, with the incision he had so cleanly cut down the right breast pipe, the pale orange bone was sticking out from the pale orange mass of tissue and whitish tendons.

It all looked like a conglomerated mess of yogurts (orange, raspberry, and pineapple) thrusting out from the skin that looks more like a leathery mess of collard and mustard greens. Lunch anyone?

But Guy was well used to the sight of butchery. Two semesters, man. Two semesters.

Going back to his work, he continued to trace down the right breast pipe slicing green-grey skin with yellow splotches exposing more and more of the front side of bone. As he traced behind the knife tip with the index finger of his other hand, Guy noted many such hairline fractures that zig-zagged their way across the bone. "This whole damn thing is built to fall apart," he whispered out loud. The sound of his own voice in the otherwise quiet work added a certain edge to the proceedings.

Finding another whitish tendon stretching from the outside corner joint of the chest, Guy pulled slightly on it exposing that it extended all the way down to the hip joint. Placing the flaying blade precisely under the connection to the side chest joint, he gave a neat plucking motion that severed the tip of the tendon from the bone. There was a loud pop as the tendon snapped and rolled all the way down to the hip like a broken banjo string.

As it whipped down to the base, this popped hard against his thigh cutting through his khakis and slashing his skin. He yelped with the pain that issued forth with the blood. Guy jumped up and grabbed some paper towels. Pressing hard against the cut, he looked down at the open alien on his kitchen floor and said, "I guess I had that coming."

But the cut was not too deep and the bleeding subsided with pressure and time – two things that were not going to help his alien friend at all. Crouching down, Guy slowly pulled back the skin flap on the inside of the left chest pipe. There he saw something that almost looked like the thin white flank of meat one would see on the side of a shark having the color of fish meat but the consistency more of cow. Excited by the discovery, he cut swiftly to free all the interior skin from the flank to see how long it continued up the inside of the diamond-shaped torso.

Eventually he pulled back the skin all the way up the back side to the separated collar bone. Gingerly cutting the top and bottom of the flank, he was able to virtually peel the entire flank out only occasionally having to cut away a filmy tissue that held it in place like a thin skin-sack membrane. Most of the membrane came apart like cobwebs as he pulled; only needing a small cut here and there along the way to continue the extraction.

When he was done, he was rewarded with a long thin flank of white meat. It was about ten inches wide, two inches thick, and an amazing thirty-six inches long. Now that he had the technique down, he was able to very quickly remove the partner flank from the right chest pipe. All in all there was enough meat to equal a good side of beef once the cow bones are removed.

Guy stood there in the kitchen looking at the clean slabs of white meet on his counter. He still had that daydream haze going and happy apathy of an individual living is absolute trauma induced shock. But there was something new stirring in his brain. There seemed to be a purpose that he was missing here. There was something important that he needed to do. But his brain just couldn't quite put its finger on just what it was.

But as he stood there absently flipping the last knife in his hand a thought began to emerge from the dark wings of his subconscious. Slowly it took shape and announced itself as a purpose. This new concept stepped out of the fog of his mind, took center stage and in the spotlight he spoke aloud…

"Dry rub."

Reaching up in the cabinet, Guy pulled down a large bottle of the stuff. He had gotten in the habit of making the occasional batch when he was bored on the weekend and needed something mindless to keep his hands occupied. Now the jar felt solid in his grasp, the cool glass reminding his palms of reality. The cap unscrewed with the familiar scratching sound reminding him of happier times when he pursued his craft with gusto.

He rubbed the herbs and spices into the white flanks of meat on the counter like a well-trained Swiss masseuse. All the while new aromas wafted up from once foreign chemicals introduced to each other like extended branches at a family reunion, strangely attracted to each other. The smells were nearly intoxicating as they fused and merged. Never had his dry rub ever reacted with any meat like this. They were the kissing cousins catching awkward glances over the Coca-Cola cake during desert, both showing subtle signs of being antsy for the chance to run off to the paddle-boats for a private tour of the lake.

Guy immediately draped and folded the huge flanks of well-seasoned meat on a rather large platter and carried it outside to his patio – taking special care to mind the pebbles as he walked. He set the platter down on a small side table beside the grill and opened up the lid. Looking down at the cast-iron grill, Guy's instincts suggested that the open spaces between the heating surfaces were not quite right for the consistency of this meat. So he quickly stepped back inside and fished out a griddle plate he had purchased for just such an occasion.

Guy snapped the griddle plate in place and cranked up the gas to a level sufficient to more fry the steaks than to grill them. Then he sat back and waited for the gauge to show the right temperature reading to begin his more earnest work. Eventually the shimmers and waves coming off the lid announced the approaching moment for Guy with even more accuracy than the little trinket of a temp gauge. Opening the lid to the oversize griddle surface, he realized that the flanks would stretch nearly all the way across the three foot surface. These were some serious lengths of steak!

Once the sizzle of the flanks announced their full contact with the surface of the griddle, he quickly slammed the lid shut. The convection heat was the most important part in the early steps if he wanted to trap in the moisture and juices with a searing action. Stepping back from his work, Guy sat with satisfaction in his rickety garden chair. "Seven minutes per side and then five minutes per side," he reminded himself for steaks this thick.

As he watched and waited for each time juncture, his mind was not on the half mutilated creature still lying on his kitchen floor, his mind was not on telling the world that the creatures could indeed be killed, it wasn't even on the larger question of facing his own fears and conquering them. No, on that fateful day when Guy began his new journey he simply wondered if a human could even eat this as food. He imagined that in a saner world, there would be all kinds of tests. The FDA would never allow anyone to get as far as he had today in a course of time anywhere less than five years. There were far too many bureaucrats whose livelihood depended on preventing people like Guy from doing things like this on days like today.

But there wasn't an FDA any more, was there.

So guy cooked – simply satisfied in the act of the cooking. It really didn't matter to him if it was ever eaten. He was just content in his wundershock – standing there with his spatula and apron he had rummaged out between flips. Staring at the shimmers as they resonated from the grill, Guy became lost in his thoughtless dreams. He didn't even jump when Calvin walked up, holding one of his last cans of cold beer.

"Hey, dude," Calvin rasped without emotion.

"Hey."

"Some weather we've been having lately."

"Yup."

Calvin took a moment to slurp some off the top of his beer, foam clinging to the center of his biker mustache. "I reckon you are grilling something today."

"Not really grilling. More like frying," Guy corrected. At this point they were just standing there watching the shimmers from the heat together. There were small pauses between statements. The pauses of those lost in a world of terror.

"So what's on the menu, Chef?"

Chef. It was a name he hadn't used in quite some time. It felt good to hear it again, actually. During his rummaging trip inside, Guy had found a few party plates that had come with the apartment. Apparently the previous renter was moving to someplace incompatible with mint green and yellow Corel plates. But for Guy it had been a real boon because – hey! Corel! You couldn't break them, that was for dang sure.

Guy looked at Calvin and noted that he was in turn looking at the stack of three Corel plates. "Fillets. I am frying them. Fried fillets," Guy said absently.

"Well, man. You know I haven't eaten in a couple of days and those things smell amazing. Usually I wouldn't ask. But…"

"Sure man. Grab up a plate."

And without giving a second thought to the FDA or morality or health standards, Guy opened the grill and sliced off an end of one of the fillets. The sight was amazing from a culinary standpoint. The steaks were now tan and seared on the outside and white on the inside. The juices that emanated carried with them the distinct aroma of the dry rub. It was enough to bring tears to a Chef's eyes.

Using the fork and knife combination, Guy placed the meat on the plate that Calvin now held with distinct anticipation. "It may just be because I am starving, but this is the most amazing smell I have ever smelled in all my born days," Calvin praised.

"It's nothing really," Guy said with false modesty. "Just some of my special dry rub."

Calvin used the same fork and knife that served the meat to slice off a thin and perfect bite from the end. Guy watched with some detached curiosity wondering if he was about to commit manslaughter. It would be just as well. Another alien was sure to land soon and they would all be dead shortly thereafter. What did it really matter in the current state of things if he poisoned his neighbor in the balance?

He supposed it was too late to consider the ethical ramifications as Calvin used the two prong fork to hold the piece of hot, juicy meat close enough to his lips to pull it in with his teeth veritably slurping it into his mouth. Guy watched with growing anticipation as Calvin mulled the bit over in his mouth. He was waiting for the inevitable – *"Not bad"* or *"Pretty almost ok"* or *"It's pretty alright. It's almost but not quite…"*

It was what he had faced his entire ill-fated career. As Guy waited for the other foot to fall and for Calvin to pronounce his cooking as totally mediocre, he wondered why he had gone down this road to start with. He supposed it was because the whole bloody world had gone mad and he simply needed something to do on a sunny afternoon.

As he was beginning to dish up the inward regrets, Calvin started to make an audible grunting sound. This was followed by silent nods as he closed his eyes. Moving his head side to side, the moans of appreciation became louder and louder. For a moment, Guy thought all the scene needed was a soundtrack of bown-chicka-bown-bown to look like something out of a porno flick. Calvin for all intents and purposes almost looked to be having an orgasm.

Opening his eyes wide, he laid the plate down on the table to get better control in order to cut off another slice. "Man, Guy! This stuff is amazing!"

"Really?" Guy asked in disbelief.

The fork was already in Calvin's mouth delivering another juicy payload as he said with his mouth full, teeth working around the hunk, "Not just amazing. Fan-fucking-tastic." Calvin took a moment to release some smacking noises accompanied by some more NC-17 rated moans. "I mean, if you can cook like this, why the hell are you working a DOD job, man?"

"Why, indeed?" Guy found himself thinking.

"Man! You need to try some yourself," Calvin said as he enthusiastically stuffed some more of the white meat in his mouth.

Looking down at the slabs still frying on the grill, Guy managed a quiet, "Na. I am a vegetarian."

"Too bad, brother. This stuff is great." Then as if he had given it some further consideration he added some more insight, "I don't know if it is just because I haven't eaten for two days, but this stuff is working something powerful on me."

"How so?"

"It's like…" Calvin stopped eating long enough to look intently off in the distance as if he were concentrating on the mysteries of the universe, "It's like, I am really alive all of a sudden. My mind is like racing, man. Everything is so electric, so now."

"You mean 'in the moment'?"

"Yeah. In the moment. That's it. It's like the best I have felt in weeks. Weeks, hell – years!"

"Cool." Guy was not sharing in Calvin's euphoria. At the present he was tending to the remaining slabs of meat. He decided to pull them off the fry and place them on the platter. From there it seemed right to freeze them. Sometimes fried foods do well to freeze and then fry to re-heat them before serving. This is particularly true if you don't over-cook them the first time. So Guy took care to pull them off maybe before they were completely done.

Of course it was hard to tell with alien.

Eating the last of the serving on his plate, Calvin concluded, "I feel this exhilaration. It's like everything is going to be OK, now. Do you feel it?"

"Yeah," Guy lied as he turned the grill off to conserve the gas.

"I mean, it is really amazing stuff. I have this confidence that I can do anything. I think tomorrow I will try to get a job with that construction site they started up to protect those rich homes up on Monte Sano. I mean, it is probably a useless effort. Those aliens will tear down anything. But who really cares. I mean, hell – free beer! Who needs money, eh sport?"

Guy was noticing that Calvin was a little more than chatty tonight. He was a virtual motor-mouth. But the change was nice. It seemed pleasant to have someone around that had a cheerful disposition for a change. There had been so much doom and gloom.

With Calvin close in tow behind him, Guy opened the sliding glass door with his elbow and began to step across the threshold when he spied the alien's hoof sticking out from the kitchen into the hall floor. Thinking quickly, he spun around and faced Calvin with the platter and said, "You know, Calvin – I think it's getting late and I have a massive headache coming on. I think I will turn in early. Do you mind if we carry on this conversation tomorrow?"

Looking into Calvin's eyes at close range, he noticed that they were black basketballs. Calvin's pupils took up nearly his entire irises. Any more dilated and they would have been solid black. Calvin stopped as if deep in thought. Tugging at the crotch of his jeans with his free hand, he took a swig from his beer with the other and said, "Actually I was thinking of paying a visit to my old lady. Seems something has just," and looking down at his pants, "come up. If you know what I mean."

Guy knew. Good for Calvin. He supposed somebody might as well get some their last night on Earth. "Good luck with that," Guy said as he closed the door. Calvin was already skipping off to his apartment through the backyards.

He took special care to wrap the meat tightly in freezer-safe plastic and stored it in the back of the icebox near the vent. Turning around he faced the carnage again in his floor. "And what am I going to do with you, big fella?"

The alien's lifeless eyes stared back from their shoulder stocks. It did not answer.

After a lazy-man's pickup of the mess, Guy showered the scum off his body, climbed into bed, and fell into a deep, deep sleep.

10.

"What are you talking about, Kallie?" Guy asked as he dangled his right leg off the bed, rocking it back and forth a little. He was twisting the long, white, curly cord of his bedroom phone around his middle finger as a nervous habit.

"I'm saying that you should move down to Amory with me," Kallie's soft voice came down the phone line from the improbable location.

"I thought you were in Tupelo."

"I was. But my Aunt Irene thought that Tupelo was just too big of a city. She had heard that the aliens were attacking larger cities first and she wanted me and Agnes to move down with her. We are actually pretty far outside of town, across the tracks to the west."

Guy wondered what constituted *"pretty far"* for people in small towns. He believed he remembered her once telling him that Irene's place was about 12 miles from the town square. Where that was a huge distance to a country mouse, it was a mere jaunt to a city mouse.

"You should come down and join us. You would be safer. Besides, I have been introduced to the great group of people that rescue animals and stuff. They are extremely sweet and kindhearted."

"Gee, I don't know, Kallie," Guy said absently as he watched a lone fly buzzing around the patterned ceiling of his apartment bedroom. The walls were that lovely shade of Renter's Beige and the ceiling was a stark white. But it had been built in the days when some craftsmanship was still alive and so the painters had taken time to cut swooping grooved patterns into the ceiling freehand to give it some texture. It was only in later generations when the lazy-man's flat ceiling was sold to the hungry masses as the *"new look that everyone wanted"*.

Good to know the Emperor's Wardrobe is still alive and well as a metaphor.

"I was kinda hoping for you guys to come up. I was even thinking about taking little Agnes out to Big Spring's park for a picnic."

There was a long pause. Kallie was clearly thinking about her response. Then, "Guy, I like you and all…"

"Like?"

"Ok, I love you and all. But I am worried about you."

"How so?" Guy asked. The fly buzzed a question mark shape on the swoops of the ceiling. Guy noticed this and smiled.

"I'm afraid that you're having a difficult time with reality like all the others we are hearing about on the radio."

Guy's speech was calm and measured, almost slow and disengaged while he watched the fly joined by a playmate as they danced, bumping into the ceiling again and again, "No. I'm fine. I just have some things I want to take care of here." Then he added as if he was a little more interested, "But I really would love it if you guys came up here for a while."

Another long pause. Then, "Guy." Here she took a moment as if to think again how to continue, "Guy, I am too scared to come up there with Agnes. I mean, have there been any aliens up there?"

Guy was watching the two flies bump into each other now. He was trying to see if there was a pattern to it. Bump, bump, dit-dit, bump. The question seemed to reach him from some faraway place. It was almost a nuisance at first like the buzzing of a fly. But then he realized that it was someone or something that he found even more interesting than the fly variety show. He asked again, "I'm sorry. I was distracted. What did you say?"

With more assertiveness Kallie asked, "Have there been any aliens up there? In Huntsville."

"Oh, right." Guy said as the question now shaped in his reality beyond the fog of his disinterest. "Umm…" Guy looked down, out the door and down the hall. From his vantage point he could just see into the bathroom at the end of the hall – the aliens hoof and what was left of its right leg was dangling over the edge of the tub. Guy noticed with comic curiosity that it was the same leg dangling as his was now. Of course, his was still moving. The alien's wasn't.

Guy wondered if the alien had a name. He decided it was Fred.

Fred was dead.

Again, Guy almost laughed. But finally he said, "Nope. No alien worth mentioning here." It wasn't *exactly* a lie. But at this point, Guy really didn't care about morals or ethics. He really just wanted to entertain the desire of the moment. He was like the flies, he would just buzz through life and bump into things and say, *"Oh, hey, this is cool. I think I will be interested in this thing I just bumped into for a while. At least until I bump into something else that I find more interesting."*

For now, that interest was getting laid, frankly. He had bumped into some magazines as he was rummaging through his underwear drawer for a clean set. And now he simply wanted to get his rocks off. But it wasn't something so interesting that he would drop his life here and drive to Parts-Unknown Mississippi. But it was something interesting enough to cause him to burn the energy of picking up a receiver, dialing in a number (is it dial with touchtone?), and ordering delivery from Kallie's Diner.

For now, he didn't really care about the safety of Kallie or that of her precious little daughter. All he was thinking about was the last thing he bumped into.

Guy the fly and Fred was dead.

"So come on up. We can have some fun."

There was another space in the conversation. Guy was worried they had been disconnected. "Kallie?"

"Guy, please come down to Amory. We will be safe here for a while and we can have a good time here. Besides, you lost your job there and I have a small job working with Animal Rescue – it pays a little. I am worried that you don't really have any way to support us all there. Here we can rely on my family at least. And that is something pretty great. Family is everything in times of trouble. I can even get you in at the shelter. They need two more workers."

Guy was swirling his right finger to mix up the ice in the glass holding his drink on the nightstand. He was pondering the offer. There was a slight bite on his soul somewhere off in the white noise of his foggy haze. He remembered having family once – a mom and a dad. For a moment he wondered if he should be concerned for their wellbeing. It seemed like it ought to be something about which he might-should be concerned. The realization that he indeed didn't even have a drink to mix stirred him from his restless daydream. The sight of his completely dry finger swirling in the air over his bedside table made him want to giggle – that is if giggling had been something he might consider even doing at this moment.

For now he just smiled and replied, "Nah. I think that I have a shot at a job in the morning."

"Really? Where?" came the more excited voice on the other end of the phone. Guy imagined that at the other end of the phone was a place called reality. He used to like it there. But lately he had decided that it was a nice place to visit, but...

"B&E Development. A good friend of mine told me in the strictest of confidence that there would be a job offered at 8:30 AM tomorrow – sharp. He said it would go to the first qualified applicant and that since he had scored one of the local contracts his boss gave him first dibs on inviting someone. All I have to do is just show up at Mr. Brown's desk."

"That's ninety percent of it," Kallie cheerfully chimed.

"What?"

"Woody Hays once said that 'Ninety percent of success is just showing up.'"

"Eighty-five," Guy corrected.

"What?"

"It was eighty-five and it was Paul Allen that said it — 'Eighty-five percent of *life* is just showing up.'"

"Are you sure about that?" she quizzed.

"Positive."

"I could have sworn it was Woody."

"Nope. It was Allen."

There was an awkward silence. Could this be their first fight? It seemed both were afraid to attack or defend and yet at the same time neither wanted to admit they were wrong. But that's the way it is in a quarrel between two people – one has to be right and the other has to be wrong.

Right?

It was Kallie that finally broke what the French would call *un ange passe*, "Well, regardless of who said what, I am happy that you will be in the eighty-five or ninety percent category."

"Yeah, I s'pose."

This seemed to be the end of the conversation. It was becoming apparent to Guy that neither one was going to get what they want. Guy had no intention of moving to Amory and it didn't appear that Kallie was going to sally her way up to Huntsville any time soon.

Sally Kallie, fly Guy, dead Fred.

Guy snorted a little and went back to stirring his non-existent drink.

"Well, I guess that is good." Kallie's voice had the ring of winding down the conversation to it.

"I think it will be. Look, I need to take care of a few things before the evening draws to a close."

"I understand, Guy. I hope that you will come down to visit us real soon."

"Well, let me see how things go tomorrow and I will be in touch."

Be in touch. Has there ever been a better line for keeping one's distance? Guy figured the only other one that came close was *Luv ya*. But that was just for year books. Guy realized that the words meant to push Kallie back a little (hurting her for hurting him) tasted strange in his mouth. He felt like he was making some sort of decision without really understanding its finality.

"Ok, Guy. Good luck."

And before he had a chance to protest or decide to go with the flow, there was a click followed by silence, followed by dial-tone.

Can it really still be called *dial*-tone?

Before Guy could ponder any more about the telephony universal questions, there was a sharp knock at the door. Guy got up and as he made his way, stopping to pay his respects to Dead Fred.

The smell was now becoming a slight bother to his ability to remain detached. It was a good thing his apathy was so strong – stronger than the odor. He figured he should pull the door to. We wouldn't want any Nosy Nates asking too many noisome questions.

The puns were becoming pungent in his mind.

Guy grabbed the door knob and began to pull the door to, when the side of it hit the hoof and made a hollow-core thud. Looking down at the nuisance, Guy tugged harder. Again came the thud.

"Holy shit. Do I have to do everything myself?" he fussed at the decaying leg.

Leaning down, he pulled the hoof up and swung it over the edge of the tub. There was a loud crack as another tendon snapped and the bottom half of the leg broke off and fell, rocking to a stop on the bottom of the tub. "Well that's just sick. How do you shit-heals think you are going to rule the world if you keep snapping apart like some sort of crazy rubber band toy?"

Fred didn't answer. It just laid there in the tub, staring off into space from its shoulder stalks.

"Shit. Not much of a conversationalist even when you were alive."

Guy pulled the door closed and was pleased with the immediately fresher air now that the slight salty aroma was trapped in the hall bathroom.

The knock came at the door – this time accompanied by the voice of Calvin, "Guy, man, open up."

"Ah for shit's sake," Guy said with disgust as he shuffled off to the front door. He was just closing the door on one embarrassing intrusion to open his front door to yet another.

"Hi Calvin. What's new?"

Calvin stood at Guy's front door with the solemn look of patronage one would expect from the hat-in-hand desolates of the great depression as they went from door to door begging for a dime to buy some lunch. Beside him stood the particularly fetching frame of his girlfriend Jolene. She was the kind of well-built blond that looked as sturdy as a champion Clydesdale even though she was only just over five-foot-four. Some women just have the ability to look voluptuous even though they are petite. This particular stereotype would not be complete without the ever-present hole in each leg of her jeans that showed off the roundness of her thighs. And even though she would be considered slender by all, her neck had a subtle thickness to it that made the black velvet chocker the perfect accent.

"Hi, Cal. Hi, Jo. What can I do you for?" Guy asked in a mildly disinterested and yet irritated way.

"I told Jo about your meal last night…" Calvin led, as if expecting Guy to connect the dots and invite them in for a second helping.

"Yeah that was a lot of fun," Guy said in a voice dripping with betrayal that it was not the complete truth.

"And I told her what a dynamite chef you are…" Now Guy's attention perked. Flattery will get you everywhere. Seeing the now somewhat welcoming look on his face, Calvin felt invited to drive on. "… and she was wondering if she might be able to sample the country-fried steak you made for me last night."

This was boosting his ego and all, but Guy had not really planned on entertaining company tonight. He had actually planned to… to… well, he really had no plans at all, to be honest. There comes a time in life when company intrudes, and we look around for something, anything, to present itself as a reason that would gracefully allow us to say "no". Every so often there just isn't really any such alibi lying around in handy reach. But if we are all really honest with ourselves, it is those exact visits that we usually end up enjoying the most.

Jolene was rocking back and forth with a fetching look and smile that asked, *"Pretty please with sugar on it?"*

Still not completely sold, Guy said, "I don't know, Cal. I would love to cook and everything, but I…" Now he was in the middle of a sentence and really didn't know how to finish it. Here Calvin swooped in and saved him before he stumbled.

"Guy, I have always known how much you admire my jet-ski. And I have been thinking about selling it lately, with the shit hitting the proverbial fan. So tell you what, I will trade you my jet-ski for the steak."

Wow. Guy was impressed and intrigued, not to mention flattered. He twisted his mouth into the slight pucker of contemplation as his eyebrows rounded off the expression that communicated, *"Let me think about it."* Then after a few moments he followed with the verbal, "Done deal. Come on in."

As they all made their way into the apartment, Guy headed to the kitchen with the sudden realization that he had placed the meat in the freezer. It would take hours to thaw out. Hours talking to Jolene and tracing her lines with his eyes wouldn't be all that bad. But then again, it could actually be a kind of torture.

Guy made with polite chit-chat as the couple leaned through a large opening from the small dining room into the kitchen; their elbows on the counter as he began his work. First he filled the large sink with warm water as an agent to help speed up the thawing process and then he crossed to the freezer to pull out the meat. Guy reached in and grabbed the smaller of the wrapped flanks – the one from which he had cut the portion off for Calvin the previous night.

As he placed it on the counter, he didn't hear the expected hard thud that a brick of frozen meat traditionally makes. Instead there was the sound of a wet slab wrapped in plastic. *"That's interesting,"* he thought as he continued to talk to the couple about his plans to take the jet-ski out on the river this weekend and how much he appreciated the trade.

Guy came to the conclusion that his freezer must be on the blink. With concern he crossed to it, opened the door and checked the other flank. It too was springy to the touch, not frozen. But then as he went from item to item he found that all the rest of the products were frozen solid. It was then that he realized that the meat from another world and the liquid that sustained it, must have a lower freezing temperature than the water and blood of Earth.

Guy made his best Spock face and thought, *"Fascinating, Jim,"* to himself. Once again, he thought this information might have some particular interest to somebody. But for the life of him, he couldn't think of whom – nor did this bear particularly care.

Care bear, Sally Kallie, fly Guy, dead Fred.

Guy laughed.

"What's so funny?" asked Jolene in a way that suggested she really wanted to know the answer and was looking for a good laugh herself.

"Oh, nothing. Just had a little ditty pop into my noodle," Guy answered as he closed the freezer door and crossed back over to the counter. Of course he wondered that if their flesh and go-juice didn't freeze at 32°, then what about their diseases, microbes, or parasites. Then again, there was the jet-ski to be considered.

Funny how morality is subjective, isn't it?

Guy sliced off two servings from the end and carefully wrapped the remainder up, placing it back into the freezer with care. Then took the two portions out onto the patio and began the preparation, being careful to follow the exact process he used the night before. As with all alien meat, one would *never* use something as common as a microwave oven to reheat. Oh no. One would use the original cooking surface to restore heat. It was the only way a refined chef would prepare left-over alien.

As the stars came out on their little soirée, the conversation was pleasant, the smells sumptuous, the vision (of Jo) delightful, and the evening divine. But the fireworks were the couple's faces as they ate the alien meat.

"Oh man! This is even better than last night!" Calvin exclaimed while Jolene was experiencing her own taste bud orgasm.

"You're just saying that," Guy said half with a feigned modesty and half with a professional curiosity.

"No, no. I mean really! I mean this stuff is fabulous. Much better than last night."

Guy remembered in culinary that some food tasted better after being prepared and then being chilled for a day or two. He supposed this could be true with the alien meat as well.

"You should try this stuff," Jolene said as she offered up a bite on the end of her fork to Guy. Her eyes were big and full, and inviting.

"No thanks," Guy said flatly. "I'm a vegetarian."

Stuffing the bite in her mouth instead, she said working her words around the meat as she chewed, "Cool. That is what they call irony, right?"

"I s'pose," Guy answered.

It was all a fun time watching the couple get off on his cooking. But the real corker for Guy was the way that Calvin and Jolene seemed to become affected; as if they were experiencing some sort of intoxication. They weren't loopy or drugged. But they began to speak of feelings of euphoria, exhilaration and confidence. Guy also noticed that the speed of the banter and chit-chat had increased dramatically. Their words were revving up like a jet-ski on the Tennessee River after a few cold ones.

Eventually, Calvin and Jolene's eyes met and the fireworks were clearly no longer just on their faces. After a few polite farewells, the couple excused themselves to go back over to Calvin's place and do what couples do best.

Guy flipped off the grill and cleaned everything up. Then to cap off his night, he went out front to the parking lot and moved the jet-ski from in front of Calvin's place to the space in front of his. Possession is nine-tenths, you know.

Then content with his evening, he walked towards his bedroom taking a moment to knock on the door to the hall bathroom and shout, "Hey, keep it down in there tonight, you squid!"

Guy climbed into his bed. He was too tired to fantasize and chose instead to set his clock to wake him early enough for the job opportunity the next morning. He would have to be an early birdie to catch Hermie-wormy the next morning.

Guy drifted off as rhyming couplets sounded themselves off in his mind – the last of which was *"Dead Fred"*.

11.

The morning came all too early for Guy and the snooze button felt all too comfortable to the tips of his fingers as he groggily groped to kill the buzzer. It was a little too comfortable and that was the problem. He could find it way too easy to surrender to the sleep that had allowed him a temporary pass so that he could shut off the noisemaker. The warden had let him go for a little bit if he promised to make like a nice boy and return.

But now that he was on the outside, the daytime consciousness that brought with it the compelling reasons to forsake his jailer and stay on the lamb for a while, he became reluctant to slide back to the warm seclusion of his cell of sleep and dreams. For here on the outside came the reminders of just why he needed to be about the opposite of snoozing all day long (though there were very few to be certain). Guy was just doing his best impersonation of the Ancient Mariner, contemplating the balance between daylight and darkness, good and evil, old night and old day, when the snooze buzzer went off yet again.

Very few people really grasp the idea that time is relative. So many people think of it as some fixed Truth upon which they can charge their customers, pay their bills, catch a good movie, or be judged upon whether or not they are a good lover. But all it would take to instantly make disbelievers of them all would be to have them observe the ten minutes between snooze button presses and the ten minutes they have to wait for the IRS auditor to review their tax forms.

Believe me. It is completely subjective and variable.

Guy was now pondering just this factoid when the snooze alarm went off for a third time. Thirty minutes had passed since he was supposed to get up and yet he still fought between the warring factions. Sleep was just about to win when he realized that any hope of scoring a babe would depend either upon his ability to get that job that was opening up or his untapped talent for cave drawings. And since he had never been one much for the visual arts, he figured he had better get up and make for the shower.

Freud would have been proud.

And so without another thought, our hero went to the master bath connected to his room and did the 5 S's once more (Shit, Shower, Shampoo, Shave, and Brush – Guy was still working on a synonym for Brush that started with an S). By the time he reached twenty or so, the mechanics of hygiene had become so routine that he flew mostly on autopilot. This of course gave him time to contemplate life's deeper subjects which for him were relatively few, relatively trivial, and relatively boring. In these thoughts time would move even slower than IRS time, which gave it a whole new classification in physics.

But this particular morning presented Guy with a whole new cud upon which he could chew. He was going for a job interview which meant he had a critical circumstance to ponder – whether to wear the mauve dress shirt or the blue one. He spent the majority of his time wondering what wardrobe decisions the great men of history had faced before ultimately settling on the blue one. He figured it was the color that George Washington would have picked had he shared Guy's current existence in space-time.

Within no time at all, Guy was finished with the morning ritual and was opening up the door into the morning sunshine. There was a brightness to the world and a spring in his step. It was one of those great mornings where you wake up feeling good, everything goes on right, and you feel at ease with your own skin. And then just to top everything off, you discover a jet-ski in your parking space and realize that you own that as well. Guy was tickled beyond the tickle. This was going to be his day. It all had so much promise; so much potentiality to it.

On the way to the job (just a short drive through Research Park to the new buildings out closer to Madison – all the swank companies were building out closer to Madison) Guy purposefully didn't listen to the radio in the car. Radio had become crap since *their* arrival. The alien invasion had killed radio. It was all volunteer now and mostly the same old news droning on and on about some important thing or another. Why would anyone bring themselves down with the facts when they still have their lives to live out, jobs to go to, hobbies to explore?

It was beyond him, really.

On the way, Guy kept looking at his watch and the clock on the dash. By all indications, he was going to make it there with an hour to spare. Even though he really didn't have to worry about it – his friend had given him the exclusive on the position – Guy wanted to be there early just to make sure he got it. Better safe than sorry.

As he pulled up in the parking lot he was a bit moved to see the tale-tell signs that corporate life still existed in some rare corners of the planet. There was not before him a sea of empty pavement. Instead as far as the eye could see were rows and rows of cars, shiny and new. The sun glinted off of chrome and glass dancing across his windshield in a dazzling array.

Guy navigated through the channels and up to the building where he found an entire row of visitor parking spaces. All of the spaces were full. As far as the eye could see: cars. He drove down row after row until he finally found an empty slot around the building. Carefully pulling into a spot, he shut his motor down.

Looking into the rear-view mirror, Guy noticed the little grooming errors and defects that are only brought to our attention by the light of day and close-up scrutiny. Wetting the end of his middle finger, he slicked the hair of his eyebrows down and out from the bridge of his nose.

It's funny how the silly details tend to catch our attention even beyond the important things like education and experience as we sit in our cars for that last moment before we go in for a job interview. Guy spent a good five minutes on his face, the fold of his shirt collar, the buckle of his belt, the fuzz on his pants, and lastly as he stood beside the car using the window as a giant mirror he made sure that the button platen of his shirt lined up with the fly of his pants – what the military call making sure your gate is straight.

When he was completely confident that his appearance was as perfect as it was going to get, Guy turned and made his way to the front door. The building was new and the four stories looked more like eight as the windows were subdivided into false stories by the architect. It was all as welcoming as his day had been and he could not wait for the big moment.

Opening the door gave way to a huge entrance foyer terminating at a round guard desk made of shiny black marble. Everything was marble, glass, and chrome. The lady at the guard desk (one of four guards) asked, "How may I help you?"

Guy made sure to project warmth. After all, these guards would be seeing a lot of him in the near future. Might as well get things started off right! "I am here to see Mr. Brown."

Guy was halfway expecting to explain further. After all, any old hootenanny could come in here and say that. But she said, "Certainly. Just fill out this form and I will need to see some ID."

Guy obliged and the security guard provided him with a temporary pass to clip on his lapel. Then turning the clipboard around to face her she studied it and his driver's license. She handed the license back to him and said, "You can come around the desk to your right and follow the hallway back behind me to your left, Mr. Sayonara. Mr. Brown will see you in about forty-five minutes. Until then, you can wait in the meeting room with the rest of the applicants."

There was a drop in room temperature to Guy as the words registered in his mind. "Rest of the applicants?"

"Yes. You can wait with the rest. Mr. Brown will be in shortly. Until then, make sure that you take a number in the meeting room. It will be first come, first served."

Not wanting this to be real, Guy asked in a stammer, "Are you sure there were other applicants? I mean, I was told…"

"There are some others, yes. But not that many. You will be fine. And good luck."

This last was issued more as a dismissal than a blessing. Guy walked around the guard desk with somewhat diminished enthusiasm. But his curiosity was still driving his steps. As he walked into what turned out to be a rather large auditorium (much like you would see as a high school theater) the rest of his wind left him as the number stub hanging from the machine was seventeen and there were sixteen friendly, well dressed, and professional-looking people in various modes of sitting, standing, and leaning around the room – all of which were wearing mauve shirts.

Well, at least he had gotten the color right.

As he walked in feeling a little overwhelmed by the unexpected turn of events, the day took on an edgier bite as from behind him entered person after person pulling down and tearing off the numbers after his. In a daze and a little bit numb, Guy found a vacant seat and plunked his enigmatic frame down, resume folder in his lap. Eventually his stupor was interrupted by a chipper voice coming from the nicely dressed man now sitting next to him. A hand was thrust into his face in a friendly gesture of introduction begging for a returned hand shake as the perky voice intoned, "Hi there. I'm Fritz Bunwaller. Otherwise known as Mr. Sixteen. How are you doing today," here Fritz craned his neck a little to make out the number on Guy's ticket, "Mr. Seventeen? Hey! How 'bout that! We are ticket buddies!"

The cheerfulness served as a stark contrast to Guy's new mood. "Yeah. How 'bout that." Guy agreed with more than a little sarcasm.

"You have to like our chances! Sixteen and Seventeen. We should have an excellent chance at the spot. Wouldn't you say, uh…"

Fritz was fishing for a name. Guy didn't really want to prolong this so he decided to get the introduction over. "Guy," he said plainly still shaking Mr. Bunwaller's hand.

"Yes?"

It took Guy a moment to understand the question. But growing up with the name Guy had gotten him used to this kind of ignorance. He decided to take the fast route. Still shaking Fritz's hand he explained, "See, you thought I said guy, the word. But I said Guy the name. My name is Guy. I was telling you my name."

Now somewhat embarrassed but still overwhelmingly cheerful as he shook Guy's hand with even more vigor, "Oh I see, right. Nice to meet you, Guy."

Guy pulled his hand back and asked, "You seem to be a bit old for your first interview."

Fritz was a nerdish sort of forty-something with premature balding and a thin physique. He was the type that would forever be pushing his horn-rimmed glasses up the bridge of his nose and folding his hands over his briefcase. "Oh, it's not my first. I guess I am a bit nervous with the news this morning from downtown."

A man sitting in front of them turned around in his chair and asked, "Oh you heard that too? Dreadful isn't it?"

"What?" Guy asked. "What's dreadful?"

Fritz continued, "Why the whole town is abuzz with the news. Haven't you been listening?"

"Dreadful. Simply dreadful," the man in front chimed in.

"What is it? What happened?"

Both men looked shocked – like it was completely impossible that someone had *not* heard the news. Fritz spoke as if telling someone that Kennedy had just been shot, "One of those alien thingies landed in downtown just this morning at the crack of dawn. According to reports many more just appeared out of nowhere as the police tried to stop them."

Guy knew that was incorrect. Guy knew there was probably only one. Guy had Mrs. Owens for fourth grade and that was all it took to put all the pieces together for him.

But was there really any incumbency upon him to actually *do* anything about it? There were more important things at play here. For one, he had a job to win and these ignorant fools were now his competition. And all of it was leading to a more secure future so that he could once again pitch some woo.

Getting up to excuse himself from the conversation, "I'm sorry guys, but I need to run to the bathroom for a bit. Excuse me."

"No problem," the stranger in front said and then he and Fritz went to talking like two gossips at the backyard fence.

Guy walked the long corridor back to where he had seen the Gent's on his way in; a steady stream of eager people clutching resumes passing him the whole way. Once in the bathroom, he became surrounded by a sort of mental fog. He just stood there at the sink and stared at the spot between his eyes in the mirror. Voices of applicants and employees faded behind him as they passed by making last minute corrections to their eyebrows, the folds of their collars, their belt buckles, pant-lint, and of course their gate – mustn't have an uneven gate!

The whole while Guy watched the dot on his forehead become a grey vortex that eventually swallowed up the world around him like the aliens that had returned to his town. It was his internal clock that eventually jarred him from his stupor. Looking down he realized that he didn't have a watch on, but he felt that it was well past 8:30 AM. They would have started the process by now.

Heart now beating a little faster than the melancholy trot it had come accustomed to over the past week or so, Guy walked swiftly back down the hall to the auditorium being mindful not to break his stride into a full run. We wouldn't want the hall monitor to come out and ask for a pass now, would we?

Stepping back into the auditorium, Guy nearly gasped at the site of the now completely full facility. There had to be hundreds of applicants crammed in there - hundreds of them except for his two friends from earlier. They were noticeably absent in the fracas. Guy looked around and found the first person that didn't look like a total gimboid to him (one that looked like he could be trusted with a simple question) and asked, "What number are they on?"

"What?" the gimboid asked.

"The numbers," Guy explained while holding his up in the gimboid's face as an example, "what number are they on? Have they called a number yet?"

The gimboid's reaction was slow, but the look of almost nearly confused recognition crawled across his face. "Oh. Yes. I see. Yes. They have called a number."

Gathering his calm like a hurricane gathering its fuel from the sea, "Great. Do you know the *last* number that they called?"

The gimboid said with yet another sludgy revelation, "Oh, right. Um... yes. They called sixteen last I think. Yes, that's it. Sixteen."

"Good, I'm not too late."

Looking down at his ticket the gimboid said, "Ah yes. I can see that. Seventeen." Then the gimboid thought about it for a moment and asked, "Say, you wouldn't want to sell that ticket would you?"

From deep inside Guy a voice of sanity, you know the one – the little voice that Guy tied up two days ago and keeps locked in his hallway bathroom with Fred, that voice called, screamed as if from miles away and faintly heard, *"Hell no! I will not give up my place in line for the next interview!"* But for some inexplicable reason that Guy could no more explain than you and I could ever possibly explain how DNA gives orders to RNA which in turn makes up the proteins that combine to somehow make it possible for me to write this and you to read it, Guy said, "What do you have in mind?"

"Well..." the gimboid spoke first without thinking. Guy figured at least one *"um"* was coming. "Um..." There it was. Guy smiled with satisfaction at the predictability of it all. "Well..."

"We covered that one," Guy prodded.

The gimboid looked down at his own watch. It was a very nice one. It was an Oakley from their platinum series. It was the one that looked like the front end of the submarine on *"Voyage to the Bottom of the Sea"*, the Irwin Allen science fiction production from the sixties. Guy couldn't tell for sure if it reminded him more of the Seaview or the Mini-sub that dueled as a flying saucer. "I could trade you my watch?"

Guy feigned disinterest, "I don't know… Number seventeen is next."

The gimboid said, "Ah come on Mac. You don't really look like you have the wherewithal to get this job and it *is* an awfully nice watch. Why not give the number to someone that actually has a shot."

Guy was standing there wondering if he should be offended or laugh. It was all sort of amusing in an odd way. Beyond his own vague insanity he saw a manger type with a clip board walk in at the stage area. With a bizarre calmness about him he said, "Let me see the watch. I just might do it."

The gimboid took the watch off and gave it to Guy who immediately started admiring it. As the gimboid went on and on about its distinct qualities, Guy heard the manager type announce that they had found their perfect candidate and though they appreciated everyone turning up, the interview process was now complete and all could go home. But the idiot was still droning on and on about the watch.

Looking at the man that had just insulted him beyond measure, Guy said, "Ok, pal. It's a deal." And giving him the seventeenth ticket, he slipped the watch on and headed down the hall never looking back at the mayhem that was just now beginning to echo from the auditorium as the hundreds of applicants began to clamor for their fair shot at the job that was at this time well and truly filled.

Getting in his car and pulling out on the road ahead of the traffic jam that would soon ensue, Guy drove back through the west side of town admiring his watch the whole way.

Maybe some days you really do get the bear.

The grey dot came back and swallowed him whole. Guy just drove and drove. At one point in his fog he thought he remembered seeing some aliens back behind him. They were in the section of town that was now host to the ever-growing number of illegal aliens (mostly Mexican) that were filling all the menial jobs being left behind by the upwardly mobile society around them. Guy figured that would be ironic – alien on alien crime. Wow.

It was mid-afternoon when his energy as well as his gasoline began to wane. So looking down at his new watch and not really remembering that the time was 3:30 PM even after looking, he headed back to his apartment. The whole time he searched for a radio station that was broadcasting anything other than the shrill terror of eye-witness reporting of all the carnage that was forming a circle around most of the city and working its way out in several directions. Guy figured that at least one station would be doing society a favor and would be playing Iron Butterfly or something. He was really in the mood for some Iron Butterfly about right now.

Don'tcha know that I'll always be true?

The cold metal guitar riff was going through his mind as he pulled into the parking lot of his apartment. You gotta love that psychedelic metal, baby. But the cool ease that befell him with the music in his mind evaporated into the ether when he spied what was waiting for him at his front door.

There at his pad was Calvin, Jolene, and now three others – one guy and two girls. All of them looked to be in their twenties; strange disciples for the much older and nastier Calvin. Guy got out of his car and did his best to silo off his experience of sight and sound as he pressed through the mini-crowd doing his best to ignore their salutations and pleas for dinner. He opened the front door and then unceremoniously slammed the door behind him, locking it once safely inside.

But peace was short-lived as the knocking started almost instantly. "Guy, man. Open up, dude. We want to talk," came Calvin's imploring.

Guy gave in maybe too quickly. He realized that they would not leave and he just couldn't tolerate the noise. After unlocking the door, he snatched it open. "Yeah, Cal. What's up?"

He looked over the petitioners there at his threshold. All three girls were very pretty. The other guy was rather skuzzy. But Guy imagined that they threw some wild parties given a case or two of cheap beer or whatever else they consumed to cop a buzz.

Oh won'tcha come with me, and take my hand?

"Hey, Guy-type dude. We told Van, Glenda, and Robin here about your wicked awesome steaks and we were wanting to know if we could trade you again for some more."

"I don't know, Cal," Guy said in an equally imploring tone, more of a whine than anything else, "Its kinda late, and it's been a pretty rough day. I think I just want to crash."

"Oh come on man, we'll make it worth your while."

Guy thought about it for a moment. Actually, he didn't really think about anything. He just *looked* like he was thinking about it. He wanted to make it look good – like he wasn't really a pushover.

"Well, what do you have to offer? I mean, I already have a jet-ski."

"Ah but you need some gasoline to make that go. Van has two five-gallon cans in his trunk - all yours for cooking for us again."

"Gee, Cal. I don't know." Guy was milking it for all it was worth. This was a new side to him. But looking down at the watch he was now wearing seemed to empower him in some new crazy way.

This time Jolene piped up, "Well what else do you want, Guy?"

All of them were smiling. All of them were waiting.

"Well…" more milking, "I don't know," Guy said making eye contact with the girls. "What else do you have to offer *with* the gas?"

Van started to protest but Calvin was fast to cut him off, "The stuff is *that* good, man." Then Calvin looked directly into Guy's eyes and said, "We were thinking that Robin could sort of be your date tonight, Guy."

Guy remained cool. He was going for broke. This new game was fun – let them twist in the fucking wind a little. Life certainly had done that to him a time or two; this morning being a good example. After a long, deliberate pause, and as the faces of the five began to break into smiles as they could feel him buckling, Guy announced his quiet, confident surprise, "Robin *and* Jolene."

Two things happened at once. Jolene's cheeks blushed and Calvin's cheeks flushed. Blood was flowing to both of their faces but for entirely different reasons. Calvin was the first to speak and it was in blustered anger, "Guy, man! That is…"

But that was all Guy really heard. The rest of the sentence was cut off by the sudden slam of his door as he shut it solidly ending the conversation. Guy waited. He knew it wouldn't take long. For a private thrill he measured the time on his ill-gotten watch. To be honest, he couldn't have told Ripley how much time actually counted off before the knock repeated at his door. But between you and me, it was only twenty seconds. For Guy, the real thrill was that he was watching the second-hand on a watch he had basically stolen tick down to a decision that he knew was inevitably in his favor.

And so it was probably immoral. Who the fuck cares? Aliens were munching on the remains of cops. How could anyone possibly be bound to morals in a time like this?

There was a sheepish knock on the door. Guy didn't answer it. He was perfectly content making Calvin knock again, and louder this time. A few seconds later the promised knock came. This time it was louder.

Guy smiled.

He waited a few more moments. He allowed himself to wonder how many people would remain. Opening the door he was privately thrilled to see all five patrons still awaiting a table at Chez Guy – the hottest new eats in town.

Calvin looked humiliated and beat. Looking down at his shoes he said simply, "Deal: the gas and Jolene."

"The gas, Jolene *and* Robin," Guy corrected.

"The gas, Jolene and Robin," Calvin concurred.

Jolene was smiling. Calvin looked defeated. For a fleeting moment Guy wondered if he could go through with it. Could he actually stab his friend in the back and take his woman for the night? Forever? How far would people go to get his steaks?

Guy intended to find out.

They were all out back while Guy re-heated the steaks. All kinds of conversation abounded. But there was a quiet, private and passionate tension between Guy, Robin and Jolene. From time to time Guy stole glimpses of the two when they were unaware. They were clearly sending private signals to one another. Guy wasn't sure if they had slept together before, but he guessed not by the naïve playfulness and flirtation he saw in these fleeting glimpses.

At one point Guy suggested that Calvin go get some beer. He began to understand the power of the evening when Calvin went out to find some and actually returned with two cold cases. He figured it was stolen, but didn't need to know the truth to enjoy the moment even more.

Hot, cold beer. More irony.

As the steaks reached the perfect temperature, one of his guests (looking back on it later, Guy would think it was Jolene – but he couldn't be sure) suggested, "Hey, Guy. You are becoming so popular, maybe you should open a restaurant.

DING!

The heavens opened up and a voice spoke to Guy. He now realized what had to be done; what must be done. This was his first, best destiny.

The steak was served, dinner was consumed, the buzz was on. In-A-Gadda-Da-Vida, baby.

Then all the guests save two departed. Guy expected Calvin to be particularly moody. But the opposite was the case. He was chatty, happy, and at one with the world. The two boys and one girl left, singing songs and having the time of their lives. In that perfect moment when all was well with the world, Guy could actually believe that he was ministering to a weary public. Maybe there was some moral good he was doing here. He was helping a population go easily into that gentle night. He was helping them slip their surly bonds and shuffle off this mortal coil in peace. They were happy and fulfilled and would go out with a smile as the new visitors snapped off their heads and drank their brains.

Guy pictured himself as a saint. They would one day name churches after him – Saint Guy. There might even be cities in southern California named San Guy or Las Sayonara. His visions of holy delusion persisted until he turned around from the now locked front door and he spied Robin and Jolene, now facing each other in the candle-light of the living room.

Their silhouettes danced in the flickering light as their frames came dangerously close to one another. They were admiring one another while they touched each other's hair and cheeks. As they drew closer to kiss, the frame of their hips began to rub.

It was in this vision that Guy had his one and only temptation to actually try the meat. The wanton pleasure of it all was calling to him. He could so easily slip down that street and join the teaming masses willing to give it all away for just a taste. But all it took was a glance at the watch. For in that watch was power – real power. For here in his living room was the manifestation of all his labors. Here in his living room was the beginning of his rise to power – ultimate power. He joined in as he once again reaped the whirlwind.

12.

The next morning found Guy waking up from a murky haze between two slumbering, satisfied vixens. He sat up a little, resting most of his weight against the headboard. One of the girls had a pack of smokes she left on the nightstand and although it was not his usual custom, Guy pulled a cigarette out and lit up; the smoke filtering the light presented a fitting visualization to how he felt.

Thinking back, pushing back the curtains of the haze to the night before (for he wanted to remember it completely) Guy began remembering the series of events that occurred just after the other three left. It was everything he had dreamed it would be and more – and yet, somehow less. He had seen a French movie when he was twelve, *L'Homme qui Aimait les Femmes*. The hero experienced every joy of the flesh. But when it came to the hot ménage à trois scene, he lamented that he had thought having sex with two women would make him twice the man, and yet after having experienced it first-hand, he realized that it only divided him in two.

Guy had felt that way a little.

Even now he was realizing that the two girls may have been a little more into each other than into him. They needed him for his steak. He had gotten off once, and while he recovered, the two girls seemed to have no trouble going on without him. After as much as he could take, he seemed to remember on the threshold of passing out that they were still quite active and nowhere near ready for the fun to end.

But for what it was worth, he did have the faintest memory of a short time later being awakened to both of them cuddling in on either side and cooing in either ear as they in turn fell asleep.

Maybe it was the steaks that pushed them to go on longer rather than his own ineptness as a lover that pushed him to quit earlier. That thought brought him some comfort. But for a man, doubt about his own ineptitude is perhaps a worse nightmare than the monster in the bathtub.

We all just want to be ept.

Thinking through his options, and being driven by the new demon of power that was growing inside, Guy decided it was time to get his day a-movin'.

"Ok, bitches. Wake up."

The two girls moved a little and moaned. Jolene was squinting as if to keep the morning light out by using eyelid pressure.

"I said, get up!"

This time Guy followed the loud command with a swift kick, pushing both of them violently out of the bed and onto the floor on either side. The girls got up with shocked indignation. Both of them started raising their voices a little in protest as they both began trying to cover up their nakedness with a sheet and a comforter. But really Guy expected more. He expected angry fire to erupt out of them. He expected brimstone to blast his ears. But instead, they were saying things like, "What's wrong, baby?" and "What did I do wrong?"

Now these words were spoken with a certain amount of terseness to them, but still it was not what he had expected. So Guy decided to push the envelope even further. "You two bitches need to pick up your shit and get the hell out of here."

They both just stood there not saying a word but exchanging glances to each other and back to Guy. Eventually Robin said in a sulking voice, "We kinda thought you would want us to stay."

Jolene was fast to agree with a nod and worried, "uh-huh."

Guy waited. He felt he really didn't need to say anything else. He was not going to be the first to blink. At length, Robin began to pick up her clothes and slip them on while she began to cry.

"Don't bother putting your clothes on. Just do what I said."

They dutifully gathered up their clothes and began to make their way out the door. Jolene stopped at the threshold and looked back at Guy with doe eyes saying, "Can we come back again tonight, Chef?"

Guy could make out the curve of her hips around the bundle of clothes she obediently held in her hands. His heart felt the thaw of the moment. But the glacier of reality was pushing ever forward. "We'll see."

Dejected, she and Robin turned back to leave. They had made it halfway down the hall when Guy called after them, "But if you do come back," with this statement the pair stopped and turned with hopeful expressions as he continued, "But if you do come back, you must bring me gifts and a certain willingness. That is important."

They both seemed to gain a little hope as they both agreed in no uncertain terms to meet his wishes to the letter. Standing right there in the hallway and now emboldened by his new attention, slight though it may be, Robin said, "I just need to use the powder room real quick."

The terror in Guy rose as swiftly as her hand reached for the doorknob and opened the bathroom. The girls were still screaming even after Guy had jumped up, ran across the bedroom and down the hall. He pulled the door closed behind him and turned to face them both. Nothing is worse than when the cat gets out of the bag – damn hard to shove it back in.

Guy looked at both of them, terror full in their face. Robin now had her hands (full of clothes and all) up to her mouth and both of them were crying with hysterics. Guy spoke in a soothing lilt, "That wasn't all that bad now was it."

Both were still wailing, but were now looking at his eyes rather than through him to the terror they had both witnessed in the bathroom. Guy continued, "Listen to me, both of you. You want us to all have a good time again, right?" Both ladies were still moaning but they both dutifully nodded. "And you both appreciate me for what I can do for you – for the food, right?"

They were both now quiet except for a softer sobbing. Robin was having the crying hick-ups like a child gets when they cry to hard. Guy reached out and placed a hand on the outside shoulder of each of them. He spun them around as he walked between them both, guiding them to the front door with his arms wrapped around their shoulders. Pulling them in close for emphasis he said, "Now you will forget what you saw here today. You will think about how you will get back into my good graces tonight, and you will speak of this little intrusion of yours to no one. Are we all clear?"

Both of them turned to him. The look of "fuck you pal," was strongest on Robin's face, but even that was being smothered by the yet-undocumented effects of the alien meat. The fire was completely gone from Jolene's eyes. She was looking more thankful now just that Guy would hold her; would take time out of his day for her.

They both said in unison, "Yes, Chef." It just seemed like the right thing to say. To Guy, it seemed like the right thing to hear. They both seemed pleased at the expression on his face at the hearing.

He opened the door and shepherding them out with a little playful spank to their bare bottoms, Guy said, "Now you two ladies run along and don't let me see you around my place until later this evening." Robin and Jolene turned left and headed down the hallway towards Calvin's apartment.

Closing the door, Guy took a moment to compose his thoughts. He had *wanted* to get in trouble. He had pushed them to see them push back. From the far reaches of his once sane and sober mind came the wild notion that if he had just gotten his comeuppance then all would be right with the world. It wasn't his lot to get away with murder. And yet murder he had, and butchery, and sexual molestation, and demeaning women, and the list goes on. Through it all, no one had stopped him; no one had scolded.

And so his slippery grip on reality lost even more traction as he decided to continue with the flow. None of it made sense anyway. There's an old saying in the south, "If it's grits that fit, swing with it." Guy really wasn't sure what it meant. But it seemed to fit the current situation.

As he stood there, hand on the door that had just closed on an impossible scene where he seemed to be becoming a god, his thought returned to a plan that hit him the night before. When he was cooking for the five, someone had said that he should open his own restaurant. The idea that had dawned on him in that very moment was sweet in its simplicity – not much to it, actually. Guy got himself ready and using the newly-gotten gas, headed out on the road to his destiny – Three Caves.

In the early days of the alien invasion when it became apparent that its reach was going to be global, the rich people in most every town began selling off everything liquid and began buying gold by the case. Then they took to the hills for safety. For Huntsville, the "hills" were *not* the Monte Sano mountain ridge which forms the north-south vertical line separating the city from the farm planes that fold out like a quilt to the east. They were far too obvious and well developed to provide any seclusion or safety. No, for Huntsville the "hills" that the wealthy would "head to" are actually the caves *under* Monte Sano, or Three Caves to be exact.

Three Caves was not made by Mother Nature. Back in the 1940s and 1950s, a limestone company dug out a large portion of rock under Monte Sano mountain, creating a cave area with three large openings (hence the name). But the mine closed in 1952, and nature had started to reclaim the caves. By the time shortly after the invasion, Three Caves had become home to about 20 species of bat, several types of salamander, a small flock of pigeons, and about 150 families of Huntsville's rich and famous that had lawlessly outcast the non-profit land grant organization entrusted with its care.

The three mammoth openings stand some thirty feet high and slowly shrink down to endless paths that stretch back some ninety acres and form smaller trails that reach as far as four miles into the mountains. For decades they had been host to a handful of weekend warriors that would spelunk or repel their way to self-proclaimed glory ending in a round of beers at the local TGIFs at the end of a semi-hard, partially dangerous day. To be honest, it really wasn't all that adventurous, but there had been the odd lost soul or injured explorer that helped the local site maintain its mystique over the years.

But now, as Guy drove up to the fence that surrounded the parking lot, he began to question his grand scheme. There were abandoned cars that lined the street, rotting corpses beside them in the grass, and armed guards up ahead. They were not there to fight off the aliens. They wouldn't stand a chance against them. They were there to fight off the Guys of the world, of which he was one. And from the looks of the organized carnage, they were very good at their craft.

"Stop!" came the command of the one that looked to possess the most intelligence, which wasn't saying much.

Guy slowed and obeyed. He rolled his window down to speak to the Neanderthal, "Hello."

"You need to turn your vehicle around and go back the other way now," was the guard's simple command. No further explanation was proffered save for the pointing of several weapons in his general direction.

"I must speak to Mr. Avarice. It is an urgent matter of profit."

This seemed to affect the man somewhat. Instead of asking for water or shelter or food, this nutcase in the car in front of him had looked unerringly up the barrel of several lethal weapons and stated that it was a matter of profit. The guard decided to, without lowering his gun or his posture, lift the wireless device in his off hand and use some of the precious battery life that was worth more than gold to call down to the cave, "Get Avarice. Over."

"Wait one. Over," came the reply.

Guy sat there and smiled. He didn't have to try not to look nervous for he wasn't nervous. If he died here it was just as good as dying downtown in the clutches of the Cajun Creatures that would suck his head just like a crawdad's. Six of one...

Besides, if he died here these goons would have a right mess to clean up and a car to move. He figured they would at least wait until he moved out of the path of the driveway before offing him.

"Yes, what is it?" crackled a familiar voice over the wireless.

"Mr. Avarice, you have a visitor."

"I'm not expecting anyone. Shoot it."

The guard looked at Guy and smiled. Guy continued to smile right back. Without breaking the smiling eye-contact, "He says it's an urgent matter of profit."

There was a short pause. Guy was not afraid. Guy was confident of what would be waiting at the end of that pause.

"Send him down."

The guns relaxed and the guards waved him through. Guy drove into the parking area and shut his engine down. Getting out, he made his way down to the mouth of the caves looking back over his shoulders as the guards were consoling themselves with smokes and awkward looks. Perhaps they would be able to get their kicks with the next visitor.

As he approached the three openings, Guy could make out shapes of humans just inside obscured by shadow. There was one man outside the entrance that was clearly not one of the small army of guards with weapons. This loan sentinel of civility stepped forward to greet him.

"I remember you. You interviewed with me a while back. Jack, wasn't it?" Mr. Avarice said stretching out his hand.

"Guy. Guy Sayonara," Guy said as he shook. "But as I told you before, you can call me Guy."

"And as I told you before, you can call me Wayne. I mean, the world has changed hasn't it? No need for formalities here."

Guy looked around at the forty men holding automatic weapons pointed in the general direction of the ground around him and thought to himself, *"Hell no. Why would anyone feel like being formal in such a casual place?"* but he said, "Thanks. So how have you been?"

"Never mind that. You have an urgent matter of profit? Let's cut to the chase. I'm a busy man."

"Yeah, busy how? Gotta get back to your cave drawings? Grinding the limestone into talc so your wife's thighs don't chafe?" but Guy said, "Can we step out a little bit? This is confidential."

"Not too far," then to one of the guards, "Brian, keep us in your sites."

"Man, this guy is freaked," Guy thought.

Stepping out about 20 yards, just out of earshot but very much still in range, "Ok, young man. You have my attention."

"I've created a new signature dish."

Wayne stood in stunned silence for a moment and then burst out in a belly laugh. The guards seemed to relax a little. Wayne slapped Guy on the back and said, "You have some pair of balls, kid. You risked your life and disturbed me from my safety to tell me *that?* Well that's just wonderful. Make sure to drop by the office on Monday and maybe we can try to whip it up in the test kitchen."

Wayne was turning around to say, "Shoot him," to the guards. But before he had the chance to form the words, Guy said, "People have paid anything to get it once they try it."

Wayne stopped short in his tracks, turned his burly frame around and asked, "What do you mean *anything?*"

"I mean within the last two days I have netted a jet ski, ten gallons of gas, two cases of cold beer, and a ménage à trois."

"Well, good for you. Is that all?"

Guy thought fast and lied, "And a case of batteries."

This seemed to interest Wayne, "Gas and batteries. Hmm…"

Adding quickly while taking a bold step towards Wayne, "Gas and Batteries, and anything else I request. They will do anything to get this dish." He stopped short when he saw the guards raise their weapons in alarm.

"But they are all just animals after any food," Wayne reasoned.

"They could have had any food they wanted when they robbed the store of the cold beer. Why put themselves at additional risk when they had all the food they could eat right there?"

Wayne was visibly looking for another objection with which to challenge Guy when Guy spoke again, "And they are coming back night after night for it." Now Guy took an additional chance and leaned as much as he dared towards Wayne in a show of secrecy as he whispered loudly, "And I think they are addicted to it."

Wayne had several looks at once. In the old world where ethics and morals meant that you could network a young talent out of a dream just because all the old farts wanted to demonstrate their idea of absolute power and yet one would never think of profiteering on a known addiction (after all, that was the purview of the pharmaceutical companies and medical industry and was completely beneath the moral fiber of restaurateurs) this was after all a new dawn, a new era of man. Perhaps for the sake of profit, he might be able to stomach a small piece of their action. His face was a stage and the expressions were the actors working out this dilemma in real-time.

Guy decided to strike while the iron was hot.

"Come back to my place tonight and I'll show you what can be gained from this new dish. I am confident in my product."

"If you had had this much confidence when I interviewed you, I would have hired you on the spot," Wayne said with an admiring smile on his face.

"Good. I'll drive you."

"Oh no. You might just be out for a little revenge." Wayne thought but said, "How about we take my ride and Brian can come along to keep us both safe. The Hummer is fully fueled and ready to go."

Guy thought about it for a moment and then realized he was mortgaged to the hilt already. He was not in a position to make any more demands. "Sounds like a plan. When do we start?"

"There is never a better time for profit than the present, Guy." And waving to Brian he started walking toward the car park. Guy looked down at his ill-gotten watch. It felt nice and reassuring around his wrist. He mulled Wayne's words over in his mind: Never a better time for profit than the present.

Guy and Brian fell in tow behind him making uncomfortable glances at one another. It was with this feeling of unease that they climbed into the car; Wayne driving, Guy in the passenger seat and Brian sitting directly behind him holding the barrel of his weapon directly at Guy's head.

So much for the comfort of confidence.

As they drove back through the northern core of Huntsville, they could see the carnage to the north and south in either direction as they passed the larger thoroughfares. "We know that they have moved to the east. Three Caves avoided any battles because they used the roads and easier valleys to the north and south to press east around Monte Sano Mountain. Some of our scouts have reported them as far east as Scottsboro already. And as you can see," Wayne said pointing at the smoke columns to the north and south at

Memorial Parkway, "They have already begun spreading out from the center of town." Sitting back a little in his driver's seat and accelerating a little once they cleared some smashed and burned cars blocking one intersection, "If my guess is correct, they will leave a small core in downtown and fan out in all directions from here to conquer the Eastern United States."

Conquer. There it is - the word that had not really registered with Guy. These aliens were out to conquer his world, his planet. The thought of this almost sent him spiraling out of control. It almost robbed him of the finger-tip grasp he still held on reality. But there was profit to be made and dishes to be cooked. This was, after all, *his* dream. Now was the moment. Now was *his* time.

Guy would follow right behind the aliens and conquer the culinary world. He would be the Great Chef Guy!

As they turned into his apartment complex, there was a large crowd forming outside his front door. There at the front of it was Calvin, Jolene, Van, Glenda, and Robin sitting in a little quintet on the stairs smoking cigarettes.

"Holy shit," Wayne said under his breath.

"Yeah, I should have enough for this meal. Maybe a little leftover," Guy said. Then he added in his own mind, *"But not enough for tomorrow."*

13.

They parted the crowd like Moses and the Sea. Everyone was fairly calm and passive, not boisterous or violent. As they went inside, just the three of them, Guy began his prep as he spoke plainly, "The dish seems to have a calming effect. They will not get out of hand or pushy. If anything, they will become extremely compliant and malleable."

After turning on the grill out back to pre-heat it a little, Guy came back inside and pulled the larger slab out of the freezer and plopped it on the counter.

"Sort of like this meat here. I have figured out a way to keep it pliable even fresh out of a freezer." To make his point, Guy slapped it down on the counter as it made the spongy slap demonstrating that is was not frozen stiff.

"Remarkable," Wayne said, noticeably impressed.

Brian was making his way around the apartment checking for security issues. Guy saw this and asked Wayne, "Could you keep the brute out of the bedroom area? Personal space of an artist if you follow."

Wayne had seen enough to let the leash loose a little. This kid wasn't bullshitting about much. There *was* a crowd. They had treated him like some sort of hero. And he was preparing the most unusual flank of meat he had ever seen in his life. "Brian, why don't you stay in here with us a little while? I'm sure the place is fine." The guard looked a bit perturbed behind the aviator sunglasses, but obediently dropped off the hunt and took his station behind Wayne.

"So what is it?" Wayne asked.

"Well, that is one of my little secrets – along with the rub."

"Ah yes. I remember you told me about that during our little interview."

"Tried to," Guy corrected as he massaged the meat a little making sure it was still suitable for heating up.

As if he didn't understand, Wayne asked, "Pardon?"

"I *tried* to tell you. You cut me off."

There was an awkward silence. Guy wondered if he had pushed a little too hard against the perimeter. After all, he now needed Wayne more than Wayne needed Guy. Or at least that was what Wayne *thought* for the moment.

Guy rescued the conversation by changing course a little. Picking up the slab of meat he said as he passed Wayne and Brian, "Follow me."

They went out back and Guy placed the meat on the grill – the whole slab.

"It looks cooked already," Wayne noticed.

"It is. I cooked it up initially two days ago. It holds its flavor well and can be re-heated fairly quickly."

"That *is* amazing," Wayne thought as visions of processing centers, freezer trucks, radiating hubs and delivery schemes danced in his head. "The rub must be quite unique."

Deciding not to rub in the fact that Wayne had already passed up his chance once before, Guy said, "I think there is much yet to be learned about it. But yes, it offers some interesting potential."

"Have you ever tried the dish yourself?"

"No. I'm a vegetarian," Guy answered as he flipped the flank.

After a little culinary chitchat and talk about what they had both done since the initial interview all those months ago, Guy pulled the meat off the grill and divided it up into roughly enough servings to go around to the forty or fifty people outside. Then he lead Wayne and Brian to the front door.

Guy emerged into the happy greetings and stepping up on the stairs next to Jolene and Robin, he spoke, "Hi everyone."

The crowd answered back in happy hellos.

"Thank you all for coming here tonight. Hopefully by tomorrow we will have a better place for us all to meet. But for tonight, I will pass out plates here at the front door. Now as far as compensation for my work, can I hear some offers for trade?"

People started shouting out immediately. Guy took a moment to look at Wayne who was now looking dutifully impressed. Then Guy raised his hands to gain a moment of quiet.

"Calvin, what do you have?"

Calvin looked down sheepishly at first but then looking up at Guy from his seated position below and squinting in the afternoon sun he said, "I've got ten more gallons of gasoline and another case of cold beer."

Looking at Jolene and Robin, Guy asked, "And you two dears? What do you have to offer?"

Robin and Jolene exchanged glances and then Jolene said in front of Calvin and without any shame, "We would offer you another night like last night. Would that be enough?"

"And what was the last thing I told you this morning?"

The two girls looked down at the ground. Robin mumbled, "You said that we must bring you gifts and a certain willingness."

"That's right. And you have the willingness but what about the gifts?"

Jolene said with a complaining tone, "We tried to think of something to get you all day, but we couldn't think of anything at all."

Guy looked back at Wayne and asked, "Well Wayne? What would you like? I'll make my first profit tonight a gift to you for your troubles."

Wayne took a moment to think about it and said, "How about a case of one hundred D size batteries? All have to be fresh." He had actually thought this would be impossible, a ridiculous request.

Guy unabatedly turned to Jolene and Robin and said, "Well girls? How about it? One hundred D size batteries."

Looking at each other, they both nodded as Robin said, "I think we can find those."

"And…" Guy continued. This time he looked at Wayne first to make sure he was paying attention and then he looked to Van as he spoke, "Van, Glenda is your girlfriend, right?"

"Been together three years," Van answered cheerfully enough.

Then speaking to the first two girls Guy said, "Jolene and Robin, you will have to entertain me tonight *with* Glenda and you will have to get Van's permission first."

Wayne placed a hand on Guy's shoulder and said, "Guy, that won't be necessary to prove your point."

Guy turned around to Wayne and now grew in stature and confidence. It was time to peel back that envelope whose edges he had been so afraid to push just a moment or two earlier. He spoke directly and with vibrato, "But it will be necessary if any of these are going to enjoy my cooking tonight!"

"Yes, yes. We will do that," came Robin's fast reply and then she turned to Van, "Please Van. Please let Glenda sleep with us tonight."

Van looked at Glenda and said, "What do you want baby?"

Glenda hugged into Van and said, "I want what you want, Van."

Van looked up at Guy and asked, "Will that be enough for us all to have some steak tonight?"

Guy looked smugly over his shoulder at Wayne and said, "That will be enough for the ladies. The one hundred D batteries and the three of them entertaining me tonight, But Van will need to do *something* for his meal."

"Just name it."

At this, Guy asked for a little recess and took Wayne and Brian back into his apartment. After closing the door, Wayne said, "Ok, what do you need?"

"I need an agreement. I will supply you with tonight's take beyond my own personal needs, but you will supply me with a place, provisions, staff, and a hunter by tomorrow night. From there, we will split the profits 50/50 above whatever it costs us to form partnerships and alliances."

"Hunter? Partnerships? Alliances? What do you have in mind? This is just a restaurant you're talking about."

Guy walked towards the back hall. Wayne and Brian following closely behind, "This is not just a restaurant I am talking about." Then opening the door to the hall bathroom he proclaimed, "This is the world!"

Wayne and Brian stared at the mutilated mass in the bottom of the tub for a full minute stunned to silence. The weight of it all hit them in waves. It was finally Wayne that spoke first, "I'm not sure we can do it all in one day, Guy."

"Then we will have to try our best and if we do not succeed, then we will need to do something to keep the customer base until we can."

Looking up from the grizzle to Guy, Wayne asked, "But how?"

"I think there's a way to kill them. It takes two distinct strikes in two distinct places at the same time. If you know a good hunter I think I can help him."

"I may know just the right person. I also think there's a good space we can use not far from here on University Drive. What will you need for your rub? What ingredients?"

Guy started to answer. He could feel himself getting caught up in the excitement of the moment. It looked like his dream was going to come true. But just as the words were forming in his mouth, he realized the fatal flaw that was waiting upon the hearing. Brian had a gun, Wayne would have the secret, and Guy would be un-Guy. Wayne now knew enough of the truth that the rub was the only thing standing in his way to owning it all.

"I will take care of the rub for now. Let's just get things moving."

Wayne relented and the two of them spent twenty minutes creating a list of things Wayne would need from the group as trade for tonight's meal: fresh water, batteries, sleeping bags, sweaters (the caves stayed a constant 53 degrees year-round), food supplies, medical supplies, etc. Guy threw in a few items for himself: shampoo, soap, some food (vegetables), new clothes, and a big screen TV.

Lastly, Guy requested that Wayne send over some of his people to clean up Dead Fred. He agreed but said that the hunter would need to see the corpse first. He would try to arrange that for later this very evening. Wayne left with the promise to return in a couple of hours asking Brian to stay there to manage the gathering of supplies. Brian objected a little, but Guy said they could get him a few things as well if he wanted.

The rest of the evening was an orderly process of bid and award. Supplies were delivered, alien was consumed, and Guy had one wild time. In the end, he sent the girls away opting for a rain check on the promised evening. *"After all,"* he thought looking down at his watch, *"I have pressing business with which to attend."*

Not very much longer after that, just as he was cleaning up the kitchen, a knock befell his door. Guy used the dish towel to wipe his hands as he walked towards the front door, "Just a minute." Brian got up from the sofa in the living room and walked over, weapon drawn and loaded.

Guy opened the door to a broad smiling Wayne with four other men behind him. Guy could see from the start that these were no ordinary city-dwellers. They looked rough, and rugged, and well-proven by the elements.

"Guy, I want you to meet Archer Thornwall. Archer, this is Guy, the bright young chef that is going to save the world for us."

Before Guy knew what was happening, he was ascended upon by four expert woodsmen, shaking hands with one and all as they introduced themselves. There was Archer, older but still with red hair mixed in with the silver, Ted, Logan, and Jorge (pronounced Horehay). Jorge looked like he really didn't fit in with the bunch, slight and diminutive he was from the Dominican Republic where he had helped the rich hunt exotic, dangerous and often illegal prey. If that meant an unauthorized trip to Cuba, then that meant an unauthorized trip to Cuba. The boys knew him as Blackie (although not in front of their Politically Correct customers, oh no).

"Archer owns a place up in Ardmore where he helps the local so-called sportsman hunt wild boar."

"Actually, I help them lighten their wallets a little more than anything else."

Everyone laughed - even Guy, although he was not quite sure why he was laughing. These were the types that would have white circles in the jean hip pockets from the round cases of dip they would carry. They would meet out at the back stoop behind school between driver's ed and football practice dipping snuff while making fun of the hippies smoking cigarettes over in the smoking court. They would get drunk to the point of violence on the weekends, take lightly their literary education, screw as many cheerleaders as their headboards had room for notches, and never, ever seem to fail.

Guy was always the one they would ignore because he saw the hypocrisy in being bad and yet sighting the evil in others, he didn't want to treat women as inferiors, and he didn't mind copping a buzz but didn't want to damage the property of others to get his kicks. Guy saw himself as the good guy in the movie of life and just knew that karma or God or something would balance the world by making fools out of these rednecks. But if there was ever proof positive that karma didn't exist or that God was dead, it was in that these guys were heroes and he was considered a loser. In the end, guys like this make as much money as they want to be happy and they go on spoiling the landscape of the world until they procreate and began passing on all their bad habits to their spawn – little tadpoles with cans of Skoal in their hip pockets.

But here he was among them. Glancing at his watch he realized that he had somehow changed. They could actually see him now. He was no longer invisible. He thought about the three girls he had manipulated earlier and was almost convinced that he could hear the old Guy calling from some distant mountain to stop the madness before it was too late.

That was when Archer walked up and pulled out a tin of snuff and offered a dip to everyone. Holding the can out for Guy he asked, "Care for a dip young chef?"

Looking at the can and at the company in his living room, at the focus that was now on him, and at how he felt about his new position in life, Guy reached out and took a pinch and pressed it hard between cheek and gum.

"Now tell us more about how you bested the beast," Archer instructed.

As he spent several hours talking over the details of the creature and what he had learned from his butchering, Archer and the boys took mental notes on every detail. Sometimes they would interject an "I see," or an "Oh, I get it." Mostly they just listened. At one point, Archer asked to see the fence out back and all four men took careful measurements of the poniards including their thickness. All of them agreed that a wide bore arrow shaft from a crossbow just might do the trick.

Guy used Fred to show them the details. Fred was remarkably preserved, though still quite dead. There was however some sign of deterioration and Archer agreed to have the boys haul him away in the dark of night after they were through here.

The whole time he was talking, the nicotine from the dip was easing its way through Guy's veins just as the new way of life was now easing its way through his psyche. He was no longer questioning the right and the wrong. He was just making sure that he moved as far away from that old voice as he could get. These guys were drawing him into their circle – the circle of success. And he no longer cared for anything else but to prove to them that he was one of the boys.

In the end, it was agreed that Archer and the boys would go out and hunt one of the varmints the next day and bring it over to the restaurant for cleaning and cooking. Guy looked at Wayne and asked, "What restaurant?"

"Guy, you are going to be the new Executive Chef for our new restaurant, Southern Flair. I already have Jean Louis," this name he said with a French accent – Schzawn Lewie, "working on pulling together a staff for you. The first night will be pretty straight forward, just the alien meat. We are going to call it Country Fried Steak. It will be our signature dish. But within a week or so, we will offer a full menu."

Guy didn't really question the motives. All he heard was Executive Chef. All the rest was just so much babble.

It was Archer's turn to speak, "I think we have enough to go on here. Me and the boys will head into town at sun-up. I think there are a few of the critters still left there. We'll try to pull one off and take it out. If we are all armed with cross bows, then we should be able to pull off the critical hits needed. Of course, after we get one kill in for sure, then we will need to create some custom gear. I'm thinkin' we might be able to rig a double-shot crossbow that will let us hunt these beasties with just one man."

It was amazing how quickly a rich man could amass his forces and get a large-scale project started. So many details to be covered. So much work to be done. Wayne made sure Guy knew where the place was and clasping his shoulders he said, "I will need you at the restaurant tomorrow at seven o'clock sharp. Can you make that?"

Guy realized that the new world was waiting for him to answer. He pulled up his Styrofoam cup, spat some dip juice into it, and said, "I'll be there."

14.

Theodore Thornwall felt the sharp pain in his ribs as the monster brushed him aside like a rag-doll. Things were going decidedly bad for them at the moment. The first alien had gone down fast enough, but no one had expected the second one. Apparently Sun Tzu is taught and appreciated on planets other than Earth – the element of surprise was well… surprising.

Falling to the ground he saw the hulking creature grab Blackie by the head, its reticulated coils wrapping around his dreadlocks like Slinkies meshed in Slinkies. How had this gone so very wrong so very fast? The day had started out so much simpler.

Lying on the pavement of the three story parking deck in downtown Huntsville, feeling the soft place that once was three ribs on his right side, he remembered that those were the exact same ribs that had been his wake-up call just a handful of hours earlier. Placing his left hand on them, he was relieved to see there was no blood. He wished he could feel the same relief as he saw the menacing alien pull his old friend several feet off the ground and rare back with its huge claw as it prepared to pull a Cajun and slurp out Blackie's thought center.

All he could do was prepare for the enormous snap. He was going to see the violence close-up and personal. This wasn't the evening news, and they weren't in Trinidad or some such place. This was Huntsville, Ala-fucking-bama, and what he was witnessing was larger than the 26" color set back at the farm house.

This was High Definition, baby! Full Surround Sound. 5.1 and all!

The first thud had come swiftly to his ribs earlier that morning. He had been asleep and then whack! He was awake. "Shit, Dad. What was that for?"

"Time to rise and shine Sleeping Beauty," came the all-too-familiar voice; that belonging to Archer Thornwall, his father for nearly twenty-seven years. "Get the lead out. You're burning daylight."

Looking up from the rocky shelf in one of Three Caves smaller branches, he saw his father's silhouette in the bare harsh light of the Coleman lantern. Cold immediately gripped his muscles reminding him that his box-springs had been nothing more than limestone for the four scant hours he had been able to sleep. The shadow of the man that had taught him everything from womanizing to dipping snuff didn't tarry long. Once assured that his one and only son was well and truly up, Archer went back to the butane stovetop where he was cooking real eggs and bacon, a family tradition before a particularly dangerous hunt. The rich smell of it brought the warmth of their hunting club back to him. For a moment he was no longer in Three Caves at all but up in Ardmore preparing to take another group of doctors, lawyers or Indian chiefs out for the day.

Blackie was there sitting Indian-style at the portable cooking device along with Logan, the fearless bass fisherman from Guntersville. All of them were laughing at the lazy-bones still lying in his bag. "I tink your faudder be teaching you a lesson, bwa," came the thick Rastafarian accent through the dark.

"And what would that be, Blackie?"

"You snooze, you bruise mahn."

Everyone burst into laughter. Ted's feelings were more bruised than his ribs were – at least for the time being, that was.

"Very funny. Hey Blackie, smile so I can see you."

There was a fast movement from the fire like a cheetah, almost too fast to follow with the human eye. The form of Blackie-Jorge was at one moment sitting by the warmth of the stove, then it was in motion, and then it was full on top of him, straddled and raring back for a severe pummeling.

"Cut the crap, both of you!" came the immediate charge of the great and powerful Archer Thornwall. Blackie instantly stopped. They both recoiled from their threatened melee as they did every morning about this time.

"Me tinks da bwa will not always have ya der to protect him, Faudder."

"Well, while I still draw breath, I'll protect both of you heathens – even if it is from each other," Archer grumbled as he scooped out the steaming scrambled eggs from the flat pan that came in his mess kit onto dull silver plates that made a thick, heavy sound when they collided.

Both young men said, "Yes sir," obediently at the same time. Their war was over for the moment, and breakfast now held their attention in a firm aromatic grasp. Faudder-Archer was now serving out the sizzling bacon with a scraping sound that was all too familiar from his hunter's spatula. The mix of smoky aromatic bacon and buttery scrambled eggs was enough to bring Lazarus back for yet another curtain-call from the dead.

As their mess-kit utensils with the fastener studs halfway up the handle to lock them together clanked against the dull and well-worn plates, they all slipped into another time and place in their minds as tasty morsels were greedily consumed. They were on the hunt again, and the world was a different place. Archer looked wistfully over his tin cup of camp-brewed coffee and speculated, "I wonder what all the other morons are doing today."

Across town, Guy was standing in front of a mirror. The uniform was more than a few years old now. It was bought in a time when dreams could really come true, or so he had thought then. In overly proud blue cursive letters it stated for all the world to see, *"Chef Guy"*. He hadn't managed to pull his pants on over the red and white striped boxers that looked a little like a barber's pole that had been unwound. From the waist up he was the vision of his dream. From the waist down, he was a comic figure of hairy apathy and bad taste in underwear.

The black socks and polished black shoes at the end of the trouser-less legs really set the image off.

The sun wasn't even up yet, and he didn't have to be at the restaurant until 7:00 AM, but that hadn't stopped him from putting on the whites (or at least half of them) since 3:00 AM and daydream (or would that be night-dream?) in front of the mirror for hours on end. Looking up, he now saw the pinkening sky to the east over the apartments across the yard and realized it was time to begin his prep work.

Guy had wisely concealed his secret ingredients for his rub from the rest of the world. He knew that he would now have to prepare enough for a larger crowd and wanted to do it in the seclusion of his own kitchen. So he turned and marched from his worship of Narcissus and headed towards the day ahead.

The light switch of the old apartment kitchen clicked as it sparked to life the garish brightness of the overhead fluorescents. Light always seemed too bright to Guy this early in the morning. It was as if you could hear a soft roar from it as it washed the kitchen with its over-zealous illumination. Little imperfections in his surroundings seemed to stand out more in its rude shower. Roaches scurried from their nightly antics to the safety of the darkened cracks in cabinets.

Guy stood there in his partially clothed state and basked in the glory - he was about to make his rub for the buying masses. His public awaited and he had no intention of disappointing them. For just a moment he felt the unerring creep of paranoia. The dark western sky outside the kitchen window could conceal a number of prying eyes watching his every move. Pulling the blind down over the kitchen sink helped some, but it was only when he crossed all the way through the living room and pulled the vertical blinds shielding the now orange sherbet pre-dawn from the privacy of his inner sanctum, his holy of holies, that he felt better.

The uneasiness seemed to be shut out along with the breaking dawn.

Even though times had been tough, he had absentmindedly continued to purchase the ingredients for his rub over the years. It may have been a subconscious plea for help from a trained therapist. At any rate, he had done it quite without his own knowledge. And now as he made his way back to the kitchen to mix up a batch, his initial concern for his own preparedness was dispelled as he found rather large containers of each herb and spice.

"How the hell did all these get here?" he thought.

Not that it ultimately really mattered. He was quite mad with his newfound happiness and this was just more goodwill and blessings falling on his head from above. When things are going right, he had learned to not ask questions – knock wood. He didn't give it a second thought as he mixed up enough fresh rub to work into eight large flanks. The dill was the last of the ingredients to make it in.

Over the years since college, he had wondered if the spaced-out stirring of the mixture for hours was really necessary. Of course, once a chef encounters perfection, they rarely ask questions. They simply repeat the exact same behavior over and over again. Some famous chefs yell at their food, others dance on one leg, and still others beat up the kitchen staff calling them morons because that is what they had done that one time the soufflé came out perfect.

And so Guy stood without slacks in front of the counter that was too-brightly lit for this time of morning, stirring the concoction that would soon change the world. He stirred until the sun was well and truly up.

The four hunters had climbed into the dusty, green Jeep Ranger, top down of course, and were presently flying down a street named Hermitage, the wind sweeping through with the cool reminder of the early day. But this trip there were only small guns to be found and these were simply to fend off any unwanted humans that might attempt to interfere. All three boys suspected like Archer that they would not be necessary. And they were right.

So instead of the usual fare of long barrels sticking out of the open Jeep like so many masts and yard arms, turning their darkening green vehicle into a mini-spinnaker of old, there were instead crossbows; really, really big crossbows jutting out at awkward angles making the squat four-person Jeep look more like some ancient siege weapon or machine of yore than a modern-day vehicle.

They weren't speechless due to fear, for none of them were rendered incapable of speech. They were quiet because this was tradition. They had begun their hunt when the last items were packed into the Jeep and the high-fives and handshakes had been doled out all around. Once each one of them climbed in and belted down, the rest of the world passed away. There was only the prey.

That is why all four really hated the very job that kept them fed and kept a tin roof over their heads. Fee-paying weekend warriors wanted to jaw too much, flapping their gums about how important their work was, or how amazingly beautiful their latest affair was. It was as if the strangers were trying to prove their manhood (for most of them were men) more by convincing the guides than by their actions on the hunt. They found that women customers spent less time talking and more time seriously wanting to learn the craft. Blackie had rightfully postulated that women had little if any need to demonstrate their masculinity and were more interested in experiencing a new facet of life. There seemed to be an amazing symbiosis or connection with the hunters, as if some more basic natural instinct were at play. But with most of their customers it was the proof of the gab.

It only took a little while for the guides to figure this out, so they became forest shrinks accepting the hourly fees of civilians ridiculously dressed in impossible combinations of brand new hunter oranges and camo. Usually by the end of the day, the skill of the four would find at least a grouse to shoot to save the ego of the paying customer. Only the dumbest of animals were ignorant to the collective lust of a hunting party unless the hunters had learned to shield even their thoughts and work as a team more from instinct. But that didn't really matter; the customer had felt certain that the guide was duly impressed with both who and what they were in the real world.

Thus the silence fell over them now like the morning dew. For to them, the hunt was where they proved themselves as men. They were sober and serious about this one thing. If they indeed faced their impending death, they did so fully alive and aware of their surroundings.

That is why the natural hunter can drive down the road spotting and pointing out hawks, deer, owls, and the like to non-hunters. Once a person has tapped into the thin layer of consciousness that exists, that has always existed just beyond the ether of our blinkered and tunnel-visioned existence, they are incapable of unplugging, as it were.

And so now these hunters four were plugged in, quietly aware of their existence as well as that of their prey. Archer turned onto California as they moved through the abandoned streets ever steadily toward their target downtown. Logan and Blackie were swaying a bit, each to the unique ethnomusicology playing in their minds, one of grass roots country and the other of rich reggae. Ironically, the inner tempo was remarkably the same and if there had been anyone there to witness it, they would have sworn that they were sharing some private musical device.

Archer and Ted, father and son, were riding up front; Archer with the seriousness of purpose and Theodore with the Cheshire grin of confidence in the moment. To them, all was right with the world as Faudder-Archer turned onto McClung angling more toward Big Springs Park downtown. The sun was cutting through the early morning fog that was common there at Maple Hill Cemetery. The granite sentinels of tombstones and markers forged row upon eclectic row at the juncture of eternal artistry and history.

Maple Hill was one of those increasingly rare civic cemeteries in the modern world of low maintenance, eternal rest parks. This place was proud to make caretakers laboriously toil to trim weeds and grass between impossible angles and infinitely small spaces. It was clearly not designed with ease of maintenance in mind. It was rather from the bygone era where form and function could yield to monolithic statements of the permanence of death. The handcrafted markers, some towering twelve feet or more over the viewer begged to be touched, appreciated, and revisited. The maple and oak titans lined the purposefully non-symmetrical lanes that meandered through the resting places like spaghetti noodles thrown by Jackson Pollock.

There were no restless or menacing spirits in this place of true peace. Even the gates were left open at night for the odd romantic couple to drive in and attempt to spy the gothic white angle that would adorn the huge doors of one of several sepulchers, visible only by the headlights of a car positioned just right. The heavenly vision is simply not there in the light of day and even local police will allow a short direct trip if the trespassers do not tarry. But rather than fright or cheap thrill, the occasional traveler experiences a rushing calmness that is unique to this quiet, ornate place.

Looking now over the southwest corner of Maple Hill from the speeding Jeep, Logan looked with fond memories; tossing a Frisbee in that very corner in the magical summers of his early teenage years when the world was washed anew with budding adolescence. He now wondered if any of them, or all of them would find that peacefulness again in this place by nightfall. For the hunter feels life and death, and the beautiful balance between them when the moment of truth is so very near. And as they passed the antebellum houses and businesses aligning the streets in either direction, that moment of truth was indeed nearly upon them.

Archer began to decelerate as McClung Avenue begat Williams Avenue at a slight fork to the left. The smiles were gone, the inner music had stopped. They all four became aware of the wind, the smells, and the stupefying silence that was almost a character in and of itself. It took only a moment for all of them to register it, but even the birds had departed from this place. All around them pressing in from all sides were evidences of cataclysmic death and destruction. But the area was presently quieter than a tomb. Even the shafts of light through the quaking and ancient trees seemed somehow dull and pale with exhaustion.

With a growing uneasiness (or was that adrenaline?) the hunters turned north onto Church Street and started the last one-block crawl to the parking deck next to the large body of water that was the Big Spring. The fountain in the middle had been shut off and the water was made unquiet only by the restless and grey wind that blew across it in choppy strokes reflecting the scattered and black sky. Up ahead on the left, they could see some movement between the floors of the short parking garage.

Blackie silently pointed, but all had already seen. There seemed to be but just one of the creatures milling about the cars that had been left behind. All wondered if the monsters could be so confident or arrogant to leave only one unguarded troop behind to watch over what remained of the Rocket City. If so, these hunters knew it to be a fatal flaw and the moment would have to be the present to take advantage of this tactical mistake.

Archer gunned the Jeep realizing that if these creatures could hear at all, it would have been alerted to their approach long before now. So speed would be the only advantage of surprise that they would be able to maintain. Riding the Jeep up on two wheels as they made the left-hand turn into the deck caused all the passengers to grab their proverbial "Oh-Shit Handles" and brace as Archer dropped the track of the Jeep down hard on the ramp leading into the level they had spied the alien from the road.

The Jeep fishtailed to the right and stopped halfway across the lot from the wickedly dark figure giving the quartet ample time to jump out and steady their shots as planned. Archer and Logan were using the Jeep, Ted and Blackie moved rapidly to the right to gain a flanking spot upon the wheels of an overturned Cutlass Supreme.

The alien wasted little time as it began bounding toward them. Its aggressive path of attack was somewhat hindered by its height which was already tight in the sixteen foot space of the level. It had to take smaller steps to prevent smashing its triangular appendage against the ceiling. But even with this deterrent, the speed was frightening in its momentum.

Archer and Logan drew first strike duty. Poised and ready, they waited for the right moment. Archer had instructed them all to wait if possible for some pause the creature might make. Guy had told him about the delay right before attack where the creature seemed to be proud of its impending kill. That would be the moment if it came. But they were all to remain acutely attuned to his voice. He alone would call the shot.

But the beast showed no sign of slowing. It was charging upon them like the behemoth from the book of Job. Archer remembered the passage upon the seeing: the strength of its loins, the power in the muscles of its belly, the sinews of its thighs are close-knit, the bones are tubes of bronze, the limbs like rods of iron. Every hunter in the Bible-Belt had read that passage. Most had thought the Good Book had been talking about a hippo or an elephant. Oh how amazingly this described the creature that now approached him like a charging freight train. Lacking the patience of Job, his finger itched nervously for the trigger of the crossbow. In that moment Archer began to worry, really worry, for the first time in his life.

This was not going to go well.

It was on his second trip to the car that morning that he noticed it. It wasn't there on the first – the trip where he had taken the large container of dill and two or three spices that had absolutely nothing to do with his rub out to his car. He had stacked them in the bottom of an overnight bag and filled up the rest of the space with a change of clothes and a towel.

But on the second trip he thought for a moment that there was something just to his left as he pulled the door behind. Initially he thought he would describe it as a shuffling sound as the form ducked behind a nearby shrub. But ultimately he decided that a scutter was a better description.

No 'bout a-doubt it, it was definitely a scutter. Nothing more, and nothing less.

The feeling of being watched immediately returned. But Guy dusted it off like so much dandruff. What did he care? He had his rub in a Tupperware® container and his sign was under his arm with the roll of Scotch® tape along for the ride. With his one free arm, he locked the door and pulled out the paper he had hurriedly torn from a spiral notebook after scribbling a short note directing all of his would-be patrons to the address listed (replete with map – hand drawn!). At the bottom was scrawled a plea to not remove this particular sign but to make a copy if needed.

Guy manipulated the note as best he could, holding the roll of tape fast with one elbow. He looked for all purposes like a partygoer attempting some crazy and embarrassing stunt to win a party favor – balance a container between your knees, hold this tape role under your arm, and place the sign on the front door with your left thumb – then hold it there while you break off a strip of tape to stick it there.

Well, Guy was not the brightest candle on the cake. But he did finally manage to hang the piece of paper; its rough fringe ruffling in the wind.

Hopping in the car and pulling out to his first day at his new job, Guy was blissfully unaware of many things – like the spy he had earlier foiled, the squad of break-in artists that would soon be ransacking his kitchen, and most importantly the fact that he still did not have a proper pair of britches on to cover up his hairy legs.

It was at about this moment, the one where Guy thought he was approaching his first day on a job that he hoped would be his lifelong passion, that Archer was having the thought that he was approaching the last day of his.

The behemoth was charging too hard and showed no sign of breaking. He wondered if he would be able to maintain the patience of Job. Seeing the huge claw opening and snapping releasing two great shock waves, he began to doubt it. This was a hurricane of madness and he had brought his team, his son! to the very eye of the storm. This was no wild boar or charging she-bear. This was a fucking alien and no cavalry was coming up from behind with laser-swords to save them.

Feeling the vibration of the footfalls shaking the concrete structure and hearing the screaming battle cry that sounded like a thousand conch shells all being blown at once, Archer Thornwall wondered in awe at the sheer ferocity of their prey.

Prey. Hah! The thought of it made him feel like an arrogant fool. And like Job, they too were being humbled in this moment. Archer now realized how foolhardy confidence had been – what a trickster bravery was. He was reminded of the rest of the passage from chapter 40. Job was instructed to "… look on every one that is proud, and bring (them) low; and tread down the wicked in their place. Then will I also confess unto thee that thine own right hand can save thee."

Archer looked at his right hand. It was shaking pitifully. It was not the thundering vibration of the hoofs, but his own fear that was the blame for this newly developed palsy. The creature was just too fast and just too close, and closing even faster, twisting and torquing for all the world to see like some wild windmill shaped into a fearsome minotaur with a savage lust for blood. He could feel the hot breath of its roars as it came closer and closer still.

But then the instincts kicked in. How many bears had he stopped with a last-second shot? How many lions had been slain by the aim tried and true? Surely the God that had saved him from the paw of the bear and the paw of the lion would now deliver him from this philistine!

In that moment the shaking weathered hand stilled, and the grey-stubbled jaw, slack-skinned with age drew taught with renewed determination, and the glaucomic milk in the pupils cleared with a dazzling blueness to their rings. The mammoth alien stopped just feet shy as if noticing the glint of light that suggested the indigenous food knew something it didn't.

Of course this simply couldn't be and killing the four of these in their pathetic band was almost too trivial for a Ggelvring of its rank and stature. But then again, if this was the whole of the army sent to avenge their masses, so be it. Pride filled its being as it knew the time had come to demonstrate the superior skills of their higher race. Trel took a moment to revel in the glory as it flexed its form before the kill. It did not understand the sound the food uttered in that moment, but frankly it did not really care.

"Now!" shouted Archer and two appointed arrows, his and Logan's sang in the early morning air.

There is a moment, and it may be one of the few true psychic experiences we have as humans. It is akin to the feeling a baseball player feels when a homerun-angled swing connects with a fastball and the batter can tell by the feel of it that they are about to make an uncontested run around four bases and into glory. It is the very last push of a mother long-troubled by labor that knows before knowing that it is all over and that the baby is fine and all is right with the world. And it is the feeling of a solid click, metal trigger on hardwood, when a hunter knows that the prey will fall.

But the ball doesn't always clear the fence, and the baby doesn't always pass the Apgar, and the hunted sometimes becomes the hunter.

This shot was one of those moments. It just felt right to Archer. The large-bore arrow exploded with velocity, the grip smooth, confident with season. Its path told no lie but stayed true to the story, finding its appointed mark in the triangular head of the fell-creature.

But for all that was right, there was but one small thing wrong – Logan's arrow flew high with the swinging torso. It lacerated tissue in what might have been a mortal wound to any other quarry - but not to the behemoth, and not today.

The alien stopped as Archer prepared for the fall and the rejoicing that was so rightfully theirs. They would succeed where so many others had failed. And yet the fall didn't come. The creature just stood there agape at them, its orifice opening and closing in a shocked mockery of cry. The eyes on the eye-stalks now clearly visible at close range appeared to be lolling to and fro.

"Shit," Logan allowed.

Archer was about to ask what was wrong when there was a loud crack that filled the silence of anticipation. The alien appeared to split in two with the savage fury of a hundred-year-old oak touched by the finger of Thor. The two halves looking for all the world like twinner M's.

"Fuck," Archer now conceded to Logan's point as he backed up and crossed behind Logan. "Be ready," he called to Ted.

"Check," Ted confidently called back. But he was not feeling altogether confident in this present moment.

The alien on the left formed first, righting itself and charging. Archer had a moment to wonder at the simplicity of it all. They would become the ultimate irony of their own existence. Then he corrected his own thinking. It probably wasn't the *ultimate* irony. That would be more like being hunted down by feminists in some twisted game where they were forced to do chores around the house while the women-folk scratched themselves and chewed tobacco, spitting on their freshly mopped floors.

This was simply a mediocre or passing irony that would be suitable for instruction in a junior high English class on the subject.

Archer's thoughts were as interrupted as the morning air was by the zing of two more arrows following the confident command of his progeny. There was no drama in the fall as the alien on the left immediately crumpled to the ground and expired with a pleasing thud that engendered confidence that it was not only merely dead, it was really most sincerely dead!

But the second mocked this understanding. Without hesitation it now turned towards these two new and mortal threats and charged.

The alien roared as it effortlessly crossed the short distance to the overturned Cutlass Supreme, its claw raising up behind like a polo player preparing for a full gallop swing. The claw was brought down with impossible force, spinning the car like a bottle situated in the middle of six anxious middle-schoolers hoping for that stolen kiss. The roof gave off a shower of sparks as the whirling vehicle knocked Ted towards the monster and Blackie hurtling to the ground in a limp thud.

Ted was actually in the air sailing towards their foe when the alien unwound and delivered a backhand that would have easily won any tennis tournament. The blunt side of the enormous claw made contact with three of Ted's ribs sending him flying in the other direction. His body fell like a rag-doll to the parking deck floor.

Then the alien turned toward Blackie. Bellowing its rage at the corpse of its bitter half now laying inconceivably dead not ten feet away, it charged toward the form of the food that was trying to pick itself up from the recent game of spin-the-Oldsmobile.

Blackie was barely up in a standing position when he felt the tightly-wound coils clasp his head. He was shocked that it was not at all an unpleasant sensation. The long careful fingers wrapped completely up and down his head in an almost comforting surety. If he was doomed to die, then at least it was in the grip of gentle confidence. There was only a slight pinch at the base of his neck as the weight of his body was lifted fully off the ground by the raptured pull of the soft coils. There was a slight click as his spine aligned itself as if adjusted.

Fully aware of his surroundings, Blackie could see through the coils wrapped down his face and was only a foot or two away from the mouth-like flap with its adjacent eye-stalks. But something wasn't quite right. There was shouting and a lot of noise and blood rushed through his eardrums. And he couldn't quite be sure if all of this was real as the strain on his neck was ever-increasing from the dead weight of his body. But there was still weight from his body.

What was the alien waiting for?

It was then that the upward roll of the creature's eyes first led his own graying gaze to the shiny shaft now sticking directly out of the front and back of the thing's head. Then Blackie noticed another arrow protruding from its left chest-pipe. Then there was a euphoric feeling of falling; floating actually. And then there was darkness.

Darkness and warmth.

Followed by a rushing sound and pain. Severe pain. A shocking pain to his left cheek. And then again. He saw shadowy shapes in his returning vision as he heard voices dimly down a long corridor.

"Blackie, come on damnit!"

Then the pain again. This time to his chest. There was definitely a burning sensation in his chest. The air tasted all wrong. There was no oxygen to it. Then the pain returned and the blurry visions snapped into view.

Blackie drew in breath upon frantic breath as Archer and Logan lifted him to a sitting up position. He sat there a moment, legs all splayed out and head dangling as he took in more and more of the precious oxygen. There would be time enough later to determine how bunged up he really was. For now it was enough to just sit and breathe.

If he was breathing... he was alive! And looking across at the splayed out corpse, it was apparent that the alien was morally, ethically, spiritually, physically, positively, absolutely, undeniably and reliably dead.

It was 11:00 AM before the foursome had cleaned themselves up enough to clean and field dress their kill, and then clean themselves up yet again. There had been a landscaping hose along the lake side of the old folk's recreational facility next door and they were able to extract four rather large flanks in the manner Guy had shown Archer with Fred. And it was noon before the fearless foursome had pulled up in the back parking lot of the new restaurant, delivering the meat to a helpful and waiting kitchen staff.

Guy was there himself, seen through the open back door, giving directions for menu, lighting, preparation work, you name it! And to Archer and the boys he looked to be a real pro. There was no doubt the boy was in his element.

Wayne Avarice was there as well and passing out the cold beers to all around while they stood beside the Jeep parked by the back door. There was something about that man that made others just simply want to please him.

"You all did an outstanding job!"

"Thanks, Wayne. It was a bit more difficult than we had planned."

Logan added, "It was the fastest Archer and I had ever reloaded crossbows in our lives."

Then Archer quietly added, "I hate to think what would have happened if it hadn't been," looking at Blackie with careful concern as he said it.

Wayne glanced at Ted's ribs. His flannel hunting shirt lay open in the midday breeze exposing the white dressing of wrapped bandages that had been applied as best as they could in the garage. "And how will Ted be?"

"Oh he'll be fine," Archer answered for the boy, taking great pride in his son's resilience.

"Well, to be on the safe side, take him back to the caves. Doctor Riley will have a look at him and I will make sure he gets the very best care."

"No need," Archer said plainly. "We can do that later. We're heading up to Ardmore. I have some tools there and I think I know a way to make this hunting business twice as productive as it was today."

Wayne Avarice was never a man to snub productivity, even if it was at the possible risk to one in his employ. "Sounds great. When will we see you four again? We may need to go back out tomorrow, maybe the next day depending on our opening night crowd."

"We'll be back by morning."

At that point Guy came bursting out the back door yelling something over his shoulder to the maitre de. There was a muffled yell with a slight French accent trailing behind. Guy turned around and yelled back, "I don't care if that is the way they do it in France, this isn't bloody France, it's my room and what I say goes!"

The concession was made in a stream of words that should have been prefaced by the phrase "pardon my French." But it was a concession none the less.

Guy turned to the hunters and shook each one's hand, looking them dead in the eye and thanking them. Then he added, "I guess in a way, the five of us have joined some sort of brotherhood."

They all just stared at him, waiting a further explanation.

Guy awkwardly continued, "Well… we are the only ones that have killed one of them."

The four gave a half-smiling snort of consent. Indeed his words were *basically* accurate, but they would be polite and not point out that they would *never* really be in a brotherhood with the likes of poof-boy chef.

"Don't mention it," Archer said with a gravelly voice.

Guy turned and went back inside. After the door closed Archer asked Wayne "Does that boy always run around without pants?"

Wayne just looked at the door pensively and said, "We think it's just his way. You know how it is with these creative types. They can be eccentric."

"I reckon so."

15.

Guy Sayonara lived in a dream for the rest of the day and well into the night. Even the occasional spats with the snooty maitre de were part and parcel for his joy. He slipped into the role like a child into a set of warm jammies – the kind with little footies when they fit just right.

"Only one vegetable dish?" Maximilian Hornbuckle, the Sous Chef asked.

"Only one for now. We can expand the menu over the next week. We simply have too much to do in order to become operational by tonight."

"Joe, Theresa, Alex!" shouted Max at the prep staff who were presently wandering around various parts of the kitchen becoming familiar with their new surroundings.

"Yes, Chef!" they all immediately and obediently snapped. As they lined up along the food prep counters in the middle of the kitchen area, Guy was privately delighted to see that one of them was Joe Calamari, the chef that had beat him out of a job what seemed like centuries ago. He had hoped that all his old nemeses had become alien lunch. But falling short of that, now working for him as an underling was just desserts enough for the time being he imagined.

"We need to begin on the vegetable medley for tonight. Joe…"

"Yes, Chef?" came the singular reply.

"Joe I want you to…"

Just then Guy stepped in and cut Max off in mid-sentence, "Max, a moment please."

"Sure, Guy. What do you need?"

Guy took a moment to gather his storm. He wanted the pause to have weight in the eyes of the staff. Then at just the right moment he asked the leading question, "I am the executive chef, am I not?"

"Sure…" Max conceded, however irreverently.

"And as such, I can hire whoever I like to be in my kitchen staff?"

Max looked a bit unsure of this upstart. But ultimately gave in with some reluctance, "I suppose that is true. But we already have a full kitchen staff."

Guy chopped in on his last word to show that he was taking control of this conversation, "And… I can fire whoever I like. Is that not also correct?"

"But certainly you are not thinking about letting any of these people go now? We have only just gotten started."

"Which of these three have the most experience?" Guy demanded of Max.

"I have worked with all three. They were my staff as I was the most successful chef in the Southeast." Then Max added as almost a snobby defense, "We did win two Michelin Stars."

Guy let this last statement hang in the air, completely unaffected by its intentional posturing. He raised his right eyebrow as if to communicate that Max had still unfinished business in answering his original question.

"Theresa. Theresa has the most experience. She studied in Europe and has run the kitchen in my absence as my Sous."

"Very good. And which of these three has the least amount of experience?"

"Alex. Alex has only worked with this crew for about a year."

Guy stepped over to Alex. The three staff cooks were standing in a row, now doing their best to at least give the impression that they were standing at attention while being reviewed by a ranking officer. "Tell me your story, Alex."

"I've always loved cooking. I used to make breakfast for my mother as a child. I guess her delight was my muse. I went to MSU for two years and then left college to learn as much as I could in NOLA. My last two places were in the 'Quarter'. I wasn't very high up, just doing prep. But I learned a great deal."

Guy smiled. This young man was exactly what he was looking for. He turned swiftly around and said with the staff behind him while looking Maximilian Hornbuckle dead in the eyes, "Around this kitchen, I am the executive chef. Is that clear?"

After a moment's hesitation, all three snapped, "Yes, chef."

"And as such, I am the only person that shall be honored with the title "chef" when you reply that you understand an order."

He waited. He was not going to ask for it. Eventually it came.

"Yes, chef." Even Max moved his mouth, though Guy could not really hear the words.

"As the executive, my first action is to fire you, Max."

There was a stunned silence. But Guy confidently kept his back turned to the troops and maintained the eye contact of a hawk with Max.

"I'm sorry, but I don't think you understand…"

"I understand perfectly. That is why I am letting you go. Collect anything that is yours and leave now."

Max stood there as if weighing his options. Anger was furling in his brow like the battle banners of an approaching army. At length he huffed, "This is bullshit."

"Sorry you feel that way. Take it up with management. But on your own time and on your own property. Leave mine now, or I shall have you bodily removed."

Seriously wounded in ego only, Max turned and left in a flurry of cuss words and promises that Wayne was going to hear about this. Guy kept his back to the team until the back door slammed and the bright light of day that had invaded his kitchen upon Max's departure was now once again shut out, kept at bay in the afternoon by the heavy metal kitchen exit.

After a nice basking pause Guy turned around to the remaining three. "Alexander."

Now came a much faster and aggressively obedient, "Yes, chef!"

"Alex, you are to be my Sous."

Looking around at the others in humility and smiles that were either feigned or genuine, Alex answered with a growingly pleased surprise in his voice, "Yes, chef."

If the other two were disgruntled at all, it didn't show on their faces. No protests were issued.

"Let's start on the vegetable medley. And since I am a vegetarian, I want to make sure that it sings. It should stand on its own and could serve as its own entrée."

"Yes, chef." The three said, already moving to their stations and preparing.

"I want the customers to taste the veggies and cry out to the heavens, 'My God, but that's an amazing thing!'"

The three were smiling this time as they said, "Yes, chef."

"And I want the Father to look down on your work as people consume it and say, "This is my Veggie dish, in whom I am well pleased." This last, Guy delivered in his best movie voice, thundering the base as best he could.

"Yes, chef."

"I want mothers to weep and fathers to mourn that this ecstasy can only be found in our restaurant. And anything short of that will mean that I will fire the lot of you and hire a new staff tomorrow. Is that clear?"

The smiles left as the sobriety returned. "Yes, chef," they said as they visually doubled their efforts and speed.

Guy watched for a moment and then announced, "I will be taking care of the main tonight." Then he added as almost an afterthought, "Where is the head moron?"

Alex looked up from his chopping of fresh greens, "Pardon, chef?"

"I saw four or five morons out front. They were setting up the tables."

"Oh, you mean the wait-staff?"

"Right, the morons. And there is a head moron, the one that spoke with a fake French accent – probably from Decatur judging by the redneck twang just behind it."

The three smiled in a guarded way as Alex answered, "Ah, you mean Jean Louis."

Guy just stood there and looked amused for a moment. What else could it be but Jean Louis? He said in a trailing sigh of sarcasm, "Right."

Then turning around and going through the double doors to the wait-staff area, where they prepare drinks, place the orders to the kitchen and pick up finished dishes in the hot plate staging area, Guy raised his voice enough to where the staff could continue to hear, "John-Claude, come here for a moment."

A moment later the three heard the maitre de answer quite near the doors, "Pardon, I am Jean Louis."

"Right. Listen, John. I need a few things to be just so for the evening."

Alex, Joe and Theresa traded smiles as the maitre de was directed in a list of orders from Guy. They had known Jean Louis for quite some time and not even Max had the balls to stand up to him. And yet, here was this unknown issuing orders without regard, even getting his name wrong on several occasions through the diatribe.

Within a few hours, everyone in the entire establishment had met and submitted to Executive Chef Sayonara. Part of it was Guy's unusual confidence, almost as if he was insane and just didn't really know any better. And part of it was the fact that Wayne had instructed everyone that they were to keep up the pretense and illusion that Guy was really in charge.

Wayne had assured them that the situation was temporary and that in the near future things would be back to normal for all of them. "Just roll with the punches and do as he says for now. He has to *believe* that he is in control for a bit. But soon, we will be all wealthier than imagination."

That night, the place was packed. At first it was the crowd that had gathered at Guy's apartment the night before, now transplanted to the new environs of a posh restaurant. Wayne had selected this particular spot with purpose. Firstly it was one of his prime locations that he owned outright, but secondly and more importantly, it fronted a personal storage location with rows and rows of lockable storage garages. Wayne had crews working all day exercising article 7 of countless contracts – that, missed payments would be tantamount and equal to abandonment granting the leasor rights to remove and possess personal belongings.

There had been some items that were of value, but most of it was personal rubbish. The endless stacks of photo albums, hope chests, hatboxes of correspondence, and sticks of inherited furniture all burned on the giant bonfire. The hopes and dreams of generations floated up into the starlit night with the ash and smoke of the consumed material.

In an organized stream of workers protected by a massive security force all looking like a train of busy ants, the briefly empty storage spaces were filled to brimming with the gold of the day: fuel, batteries, ammunition, food stuffs, clean water, filtration systems, generators, and the like. Pretty much anything Wayne could think of that would be needed to begin the arduous task of rebuilding a small civilization was on the list posted on a power pole out in front of the restaurant. People were more than happy to go scavenge an item on the list and bring it back, bartering for a seat and a taste of the dream that was waiting for them in each tasty morsel of the Country Fried Steak.

By halfway through the evening, the repeat patrons from Guy's apartment were slowly being replaced by a new crowd. These were not required to pay or barter. Wayne had set it up so that their first visit was complimentary. It was, after all, their opening night.

The battle-weary masses, the remnant of a once great Rocket City that had in a dream turned their eyes to the stars and had reached the moon, now cautiously left their various hidey-holes and braved the darkened streets driven by curiosity, hunger or some mixture of the two. They showed up in different stages of deterioration. Some looked for all the world like nothing had happened and their middle-class existence had been uninterrupted. Still others looked as if they were fully prepped to shoot a scene in the latest zombie movie complete with ashy complexions and holey clothing.

One and all were treated as royalty. One and all were granted one night of civility in the midst of chaos. And each and every one lived the dream of the alien meat. For them, the world came alive and they felt every wrinkle of the universe. They owned that universe and fully knew who they were. Confidence swelled with their burgeoning existence and yet their inner peace was total and complete.

In fact, pretty much all they really wanted to do was live and apart from that they wanted to make Guy and Wayne as happy as they had made them. Pleasing those two with their actions may be the only unsatisfied gap in their souls.

The restaurant staff watched in amazement as the patrons left in pairs, quartets or odd combinations, giggling into the night as they tried unsuccessfully to contain their groping enthusiasm. Their passions spilling ultimately over into lust for it was the only direction such a force could travel within them. Every other nook and cranny of their existence was filled to capacity.

For a moment, the wait-staff, cooks, security, and workers watched from the pickup area as the effects of their labors drifted off into the brave new world. None of them had ever felt that they had contributed more to the better good than they did right now. All those people had drifted in like flotsam and jetsam and had left as restored human beings.

Alex was the first to reach over to an un-served flank and ask as he picked up a fork, "What's in that stuff?"

His wrist was immediately cuffed by the unforgiving grip of Wayne Avarice. With stern authority he announced, "You can all eat what you like of any food that is left. But none of you shall eat the steak. If you do, you will be terminated immediately."

Everyone conceded to the owner and assured him they understood the rules.

16.

As the crew broke up and went about the work of cleaning up and closing down, Wayne pulled Guy aside. "Fantastic first night."

"Thank you."

"You really did show us that you had the right stuff to run a kitchen."

"Thank you."

"I especially liked the victory lap. Going out and personally thanking the customers one by one was a great touch."

Guy feigned modesty and bowed his head slightly.

"We might not always have time for that sort of thing."

Softly now, "I understand."

"But we were sort of light tonight, nowhere near capacity. So it was ok, I guess."

Guy reeled. Nowhere near capacity? This place was a madhouse and he was only barely able to keep up with demand. It had required him working harder than he had ever worked, or imagined he could work. "That was light?"

"Don't worry about it. Do that sort of thing when you can. It was a great first evening – many more to come!" He slapped Guy on the shoulder and rubbed a little. The physical praise felt good, reassuring. "Now, I have a special treat for you this evening. Follow me."

Guy followed Wayne out through the staging area, the kitchen, and grabbing up his overnight bag now stuffed additionally with the rub mixture, they went out through the exit into the night air and into the parking lot. The horizon was still orange by the multiple bon fires burning down, exhausting the remnants of so many personal existences like flickering candles in the sky of pitch. Most of the owners were dead and those that remained probably wouldn't give a rat's ass about trying to remember the world that was now gone. In Wayne's eyes, he was doing society a favor.

It was always a wonderful thing, thinking upon the good of the public and turning a buck or two while you did it. It was one of the reasons he so enjoyed being an environmentalist.

Years before, restaurants had dumped waste products freely. Some of it they sold to farmers, but congress had put an end to that in the sixties. But they didn't really care. They just boosted their prices to make up for the small lost revenue stream and happily arranged to dump whatever was leftover. In those days, corporate America had no soul.

But in the late eighties and early nineties, socially conscious groups began to rail and brawl against corporate America for all sorts of things including illegally dumping waste products like oil and grease, along with the more toxic dumping of chemical plants. The first flyer that was given to Wayne that his chains were going to be targeted by the Clamshell Alliance, a local no-nukes group that was expanding their scope to increase their donation base (their CEO needed a new Mercedes for his wife – another funny irony leftover from that time-period), he immediately began thinking of how to turn a dime from this latest development.

The answer was so amazingly clear he was surprised that no one else had ever thought of it. He purchased an old oil truck and had it fitted with the gear necessary to pump out the grease traps of his restaurants. Then he found a location just west of Madison near the river, and more importantly the kibble and pellet plants of Decatur that turned milled grain remnants into dog and cat food (real meat byproducts, Holmes!). There in the perfect nexus between the source and the customer he set up a tallow furnace that would cook the grease down with other fat byproducts from butchered meat, and began supplying the pet food companies with the liquid concoction that they would mix with their grain to make dogs smile and cats do the cha-cha on all those commercials.

It became almost as big of a money maker as his restaurants. Eventually it even dwarfed that income when he would go around to all the other restaurants and charge them for the removal service. Imagine – a business where your suppliers pay *you* to take the product off their hands and the customers pay you to take the product off *your* hands. Money was coming in from both directions!

With so little cost and such a huge return on investment, Wayne joined local and state conservation groups and began underwriting flyer campaigns against restaurant chains that were still dumping their waste. He felt so good when he went to sleep at night knowing he was doing the environment and the society good.

And now this evening when he stepped out into the eerie orange glow and artificial warmth of the cold and callous act, he saw his deeds as preventing so much heartache for the remnants of society that would no longer have to look upon painful reminders of their past and at the same time freed up valuable protected real-estate that provided safe haven for the growing foundation for his empire.

Indeed all was right with the world.

All Guy saw was the excessively large military troop vehicle now painted shiny black and decked out with chrome. It was as if someone had taken an armored carrier and fitted it out with decoration to turn it into a limousine of sorts. A driver was standing at the ready.

"Guy, your carriage awaits."

"My carriage? To go where?"

Wayne belly laughed at the young naïve. "Why to your new home, of course!"

"My *new* home?"

"Yes. I've taken possession of the old Sally Carter estate."

Sally Carter was a local icon and fodder for the legend urban. She had been murdered at the tender age of 16 and buried not in the Maple Hill cemetery but directly behind the antebellum mansion occupying the rather large estate on the corner of Drake and Whitesburg nearly a century earlier. Her ghost was said to still wonder the woods, toppling her tombstone from time to time, and appearing at the end of a complicated teenage séance, the steps of which are still handed down generation to generation.

During the financial expansion of the eighties, the estate sold to a land-developer and the prized corner acreage was turned into a substantial, gated community complete with guard shack. The ominously large wall only under-girded and fostered the feel that something dark and sinister could happen inside its concealed space.

But no one called it by its new cheery and serene community name. It was still Sally Carter's place. And the massive wall was still not enough to stop her ghost from taking the odd stroll through the woods behind and up to the parking lot of the gothic Presbyterian Church at its perimeter on the mountain. There is no doubt that Huntsville has its dark side and like New Orleans or Savannah is not in any hurry to bury it in the past.

The gated community had some rather nice homes for millionaires. Granted, the yards between each were a scant ten feet or so, but the one-time owners saw it as more of a "low-maintenance" thing than being cheated out of an acre or two. But the close community of thirty or so homes with their high medieval walls and single entrance protected with the guard shack would make the perfect staging ground for Wayne's vision of a returning civilization. He would let Guy live in one of the houses until his plan to steal the formula was complete.

Once the ransacking of his apartment was finished they felt they had everything they needed to replicate the rub. But there was no reason in dispensing with the young whippersnapper chef just yet. Time was squarely on his side at this point and Judge Greenhouge could spend a few more nights in Three Caves. He did just barely make the list of the new society, after all.

"The place at Whitesburg and Drake?" Guy asked.

"The very same. We have a most excellent house already picked out and prepared for you. It's time that you stepped up into the primetime, Guy, and grab the brass ring and all that comes with it."

"The brass ring," Guy said in an absentminded awe as he ascended the step into the carrier.

"And all that comes with it," Avarice echoed as he slammed the door shut behind him. Patting the vehicle twice in a visible gesture to the now mounted driver, the hulking vehicle roared to life and made its departure from the restaurant.

The house was amazing. Guy stepped across the threshold with his overnight bag and was instantly mesmerized by his new surroundings. The blond hardwood sparkled highlights from the dazzling overhead chandeliers. The overwhelming front foyer unwound into a showcase stair that climbed to the heavenly bedroom suites above; the swirling handcrafted banister gliding playfully down the hardwood steps.

To the right, the formal dining room overflowed into the bay windows that extended the house virtually out into the yards, front and side. And to the left was an old-time parlor made opulent with the baby grand ready for the evening entertainment at his next soiree. Finally straight back, Guy could make out the glimpses through a large lead-crystal door the frame of stainless steel and brick that was the hallmark of the dream kitchen.

Thanking the driver, he made his way back there first. The entire place was filled to the brim with supplies. And he noted that there was an entire cupboard exclusively for spices and herbs – some of which looked to be the exact containers from his old apartment. Upon closer examination he realized that they were indeed from his old kitchen. "They must have moved all my shit during my shift at the restaurant," he mused out loud.

Thinking twice about it, he decided to leave the rub and the dill in his overnight bag and trundle off to the bedroom upstairs. But not before discovering a den with home theatre, a study, and a mudroom all leading off from the kitchen in the back like spokes from an axel. The mudroom passed through to a large three car garage. His GMC Pacer was parked next to a brand new sedan.

Upstairs was even more resplendent than below. Guy counted at least three bedroom suites. One looked as if it may have had multiple bedrooms off it, but he would save that investigation for a later time. For now he had one last chore to take care of before crashing into a well-deserved slumber.

He pulled the large double French doors closed to his main suite and then drew all the shades locking in the precious light. There was a rather nice stereo system and since there were really no radio stations on this time of day (if they were even on any more) he started a CD that was handy. Paul Anka may not have been his personal favorite, but it would suffice for his needs.

Guy wandered the long corridor that led past a walk-in closet and large double vanity and into the bathroom suite. Backing up to the walk-in closet he flipped the switch. There on the ceiling was the thing for which he sought - a push-up trap door to a storage attic. It took a moment to find a set of small boxes, like small commode tables actually, that he could stack up in the corner of the closet. They provided just enough height for the clumsy attempt.

Guy stretching up from his precarious perch, pushed the trap door open a little with his fingertips, and then carefully slid into the space on the corner the two herbs he had packed from his apartment that had nothing to do with his rub. Then he took special pains to slide the trap door back into place, leaving only the slightest gap to suggest it had been disturbed.

Then hoping down, he approached the double vanity. First he turned on the water. He thought it was silly, but it was a trick he had learned from watching one of the old Cold War movies where two spies needed to speak without being heard. Pulling out the dill and the Scotch® tape from earlier that morning, he climbed under the vanity and using dozens of long strips of tape he secured the large container of dill behind the vanity drawer. It was positioned between the two sinks. Even if someone completely pulled the drawer out, they would be hard-pressed to actually see the container.

Climbing back out, he took a moment to listen to Anka. He had never really noticed it before but he supposed that if you took "Times of Your Life" and blended it with "If You Could Read My Mind" by Gordon Lightfoot, you would end up with "The Greatest Love of All" by Whitney Houston. It was a private hobby for Guy, discovering un-credited origins of popular songs. Hip Hop artists would call it sampling. Motley Crew would call it plagiarism. But he just thought of it as inspiration.

The song by Paul Anka came to an end and he shut off the stereo at the power source. Confident that his secret was safe for the evening, he rested easily in the opulence. Sally Carter did not haunt his sleep. Neither did the scores of people that provided him endless praise at the expense of becoming addicted to the alien meat. For Guy, the ends justified the means. He had finally arrived.

This was indeed the high life.

The days that followed scored out the steps of a huge chess game. Wayne was ever after the elusive but essential rub, Guy always seeming to scheme one step ahead. They played out the delicate tango, never allowing the other to know they were on to the first.

What was of particular interest to Wayne was that the alien steaks appeared to be toxic, lethal. People would show up to the restaurant during the day, junkies. They would need a fix and would not be able to hang on until that evening. They were Jonesing for a meat-fix, baby! Wayne would quietly have them taken to another location and fed the steaks with various concoctions that Maximilian Hornbuckle created in vain attempts to duplicate Guy's success.

But ever the misfire caused the pyres to continue as they stoked the burning; so many storage compartments to clear out. The combinations should have been easy. There were the bottles and boxes from the kitchen of Guy's old apartment, and the two they found in his attic. Some could be easily discounted – there was clearly no trace of cinnamon or brown sugar, nutmeg or allspice. By a process of elimination, Max had the possibilities down to 12 different root ingredients.

"You have to eliminate more," Wayne had told Max in the test kitchen they had set up at a restaurant across town.

"Why? 12 is not a very high number of ingredients to begin with. We can just try different combinations until we get it right."

"Permutations."

"What?"

"Permutation calculations. Didn't they ever teach you any math where you were educated?" Wayne asked.

"Of course they did. What does that have to do with anything."

"Calculate the permutations, the different number of possible combinations that you can make with 12 separate ingredients. The number is damn near 500 million."

"So?" Max asked incredulously.

"So?" Wayne parroted with astonishment. "So? Max, think. We have already killed five junkies with mistakes. Where are you going to find 499,999,995 more volunteers? And if you could find them, even if you could prepare one steak every ten minutes, it would take thousands of years before you had time to test every one."

Max slammed his utensils down and glared at Wayne with frustration. "Then what do you suggest?"

"We simply need to catch him in the act. We have the house bugged and pen video cameras are all over the place. Same is true with the restaurant. Besides, his supply is bound to run out soon. We will simply capture it all, test it a few times to make sure, and then add his body to the clearing fires down the street."

Max smiled. The thought of that novice heading his staff was enough to make his blood boil. But the thought of Guy smoldering in leftover chunks of ash from armoires and steamer trunks brought a cooling delight. Who would notice one more body roasting now that so many others were being cleared out for sanitation's sake?

During this time, Guy would take occasional trips around Huntsville. It seemed that a new ragtag civilization was trying to pull itself together. But it seemed quite different than the one he remembered from before the invasion. This one looked more like bands of ravagers from some poorly made seventies apocalyptic B movie than the wholesome streets of a fifties family sitcom.

Most of the time he was tailed by security, but there were the odd times when he was allowed to travel alone. In these solo jaunts, usually short in duration, Guy began contacting the friends and co-workers that were left. Most died in attacks or fled to the high country. But when he found someone he knew from his DOD days, he would quickly conscript them into his plan using medical supplies, food, or other such items in trade.

When that didn't work though, he would carry some of his steak. It bothered Guy a little at first — feeding a substance that would force old friends and coworkers to do his every bidding or whim. But these were drastic times, and the saying does state that the measures can be the same.

The ends justified the means and Guy slept well at night.

Ultimately, Guy was exercising a skill he had learned and mastered in the DOD. He was breaking down his recipe for the rub into random combinations that changed on a daily basis. Some of the sub-components were red herrings, thrown away and never included in the final rub. Still others would contain the odd inert ingredient that did not seem to change the overall effect.

Lastly he would stir. He would stir for hours. On several instances, Wayne's security crew would swear that there had been a technical malfunction. Guy would mix three or four ingredients from baggies and then just stir. It almost looked as if the video cameras had been placed in an endless loop of Guy stirring and then repeating back from the beginning. He always had the same blank look on his face.

Archer and the boys returned from Ardmore Tennessee with an impressive device. It was a branched crossbow on sliding angle joints. The butt would rest against the shoulder and allow the hunter to independently slide the laser scopes in a controlled way. There were two triggers, one that would lock the angle joint into position and the other that would fire both shafts simultaneously. With a little practice, the four had become quite skilled with the new weapon.

So skilled in fact that upon their return, they had eight flanks from four kills they had encountered along the way. One of the aliens had been a lefty and Logan had needed to come in as backup when Blackie's shots had not felled the great creature. But even that harrowing experience had paled in comparison to their battle in the parking deck downtown. It was so much easier with the new weapons.

They pulled up in the open Jeep, smiling like jackasses eating briars.

"You fellas look happy!" Wayne shouted as he banged the kitchen door open and crossed the parking lot to them.

"You know it," Archer answered spitting tobacco juice on the pavement. "Boys and I killed four more on the way back. Got you eight more of those flanks. Two of them were even from a leftie!"

"Wow. No shit! That should hold us over 'till at least the end of the week."

Ted and Blackie were pulling the ice chest out of the back and opening it like proud fishermen showing off their latest catch. Wayne looked down into the chest and whistled. "Fuckin' A, boys. You're really coming through with the goods."

Wayne Avarice looked as if he were going to burst with pride. Then he sobered a little, "What can I get you boys for your trouble this time? Name it – it's yours."

"Well," Archer said pensively, spitting again to make it look extra good. "We were kinda thinking a proper shower, shit and shave would do us all nicely. And a good night's sleep, seein's how we provided proper for you through the rest of the week."

"You got it. First class accommodations. What else?" Wayne asked.

"Well, we need replacement gear: more bows like these, dozens if we can get 'em. And we need arrows."

"Done," assured Wayne. "I know a shop, metal works place out old 72. I'll get them on working up some molds. I think they even have one of those CADCAM machines. They should be able to crank out thousands."

Archer's eyebrows went up with surprise and his face was consumed with modesty, "Thousands? Ah shucks. We don't need thousands."

"Nope," conceded Wayne, "But I will. And what else, boys? Name it."

The three younger men looked around at each other for a moment and then Ted said, "We could use a little leg."

Mr. Avarice smiled knowingly. "Go to your place. Clean up and rest up. Then come back down here any night this week – hell! come down here *every* night this week. You can have your pick. I guarantee a good time."

The boys broke out into elbows and exclamation as they poked each other in the ribs and laughed at the thought. Life was indeed good. Then Wayne transitioned back into business mode, "I will need your services again soon; maybe as soon as Friday."

"You'll have it," assured Archer.

"Good. The good times will keep rolling as long as you fellas help me out with a few favors when you come back for more work." Then to Archer he said, "Any plans on your next hunting ground?"

"I thought we would head west to Decatur. I figured the beasts probably stopped off at the Jetplex outside town. And I-65 runs north and south just past there. Should be some easy hunting between the two." Then Archer turned all pensive again and after another obligatory spit, "But I imagine that after a few more hunting trips, we might start thinning out the local heard a little. We haven't seen that many left behind on our ride up to Ardmore and back."

"You fellas don't worry one wit about that. I have a plan and will take care of the rest. You just rest up and come back on Friday ready for action."

"We figured you would say something like that."

There was, on that very evening, an unexpected and unwelcome shock. Several of the patrons died while eating the steak. Mr. Avarice was brought in and the bodies were carried out through the side door. Everyone worked hard to keep this from Guy. "No need worrying the chef with this," Wayne instructed.

He was afraid it had something to do with the rub. He suspected that Guy had gotten something wrong with the recipe and *that* difference might expose the true recipe if they were clever. But as he was pondering this, Jean Louis pointed out the flaw in the logic, "Not everyone is dying. He uses one container of the spice, the same for every patron, but not everyone is dying."

After some careful observations and theories, Wayne finally realized what the problem was. One of the aliens had its large claw on the left side – a leftie, Archer had called it. Upon investigation, they discovered that all the dead patrons had eaten cuts from two of the eight steaks.

Wayne quickly collected up any of the plates waiting on the hot-plate staging area and the two remains of the steaks on the prep counter. He then summarily threw them away.

"Hey!" Guy shouted as he watched one quarter of his night's inventory slide into the dust bin. "What do you think you are doing?"

Wayne looked up at the chef like a child that had just been caught watching the naughty channel while mom and dad slept. With a sheepish grin he said, "Health inspector. There was a hair."

Wayne waited a moment to see what the reaction was going to be and Guy starred at him with an equally deadpanned expression. Then after a few slow blinks Guy said, "Oh. Ok," and went back to his work on another flank.

Over the coming weeks, Wayne remained true to his word, at least to the hunters. The metal shop to the northeast of town sprang to life again, grinding out models and prototypes. Although the shop manager had been in the business since the days when the local machine shops required apprenticeships, he had never quite come across a device as clever or well-crafted as the angle joint that held the two stocks of the compound crossbows together. It was amazingly strong and yet surprisingly easy to manipulate quickly.

It took them dozens of dry-runs before they got the programming of the Computer Aided Design/Computer Aided Machining device to duplicate the handcrafted pieces of the old mountain-man from Tennessee. But once they got it just right, they were pressing, lathing, and assembling a hundred units per hour. Wayne would have his requested thousand units within a week or two — easy.

Meanwhile, Wayne also began to build the nexus of a new empire. Like any spider that is building a new web, he required runners first, the long strings that radiate out in all directions from the center. He assembled a core of managers he could trust and began sending them out in all directions. Their orders were clear: go out and recon, bringing back intelligence on nearby towns. Specifically he was interested in availability of utilities, locations of nice restaurants with all the required equipment, some sense of the local factions or remnant governments, and an idea of approachability or difficulty they may encounter moving into the area.

If they ran into any trouble from the locals, they were to evaluate what bribes or trade would woo them into an easier trial period. Once they had them eating the steak, the rest would be easy.

Oh, and one last thing — hunters. The managers were to scout out hunters, preferably with bow experience. That was a plus! And Archer and the boys were to train them.

In most cases, the work went smoothly. There was the rare instance where a manager didn't return. The stumbled-upon alien nest would do unto the manager before Wayne could do unto the aliens. But all in all it went decidedly well for the home team. They would just send in a hunting squad and clear them out, providing steaks for the restaurants along the way.

17.

Things were going a little too well and within a handful of weeks Wayne had 12 restaurants operating in eight cities and townships, nearly thirty managers growing the business, an ever increasing stockpile of essential rebuilding supplies, and one very *big* problem. He had anticipated it to some degree and was in the process of working it out when it finally came up.

"What do you mean 'all hunted out'?"

Wayne was standing in the back parking lot looking sternly upon the now sheepish Archer Thornwall.

"It's like I told you. The valley is gettin' dry. We're killing them as fast as we find them but there's competition out there."

"What the hell are you talking about?"

"Some of the folks that have survived have seen us hunting. They apparently figured out the secret and have replicated it to some degree of success. But they aren't interested in the meat. They have formed ragtag bands to take back the planet. They are out for vengeance. Call themselves the Eagles of Freedom or the Tide of Freedom. I reckon it's a football thing."

"You think?"

"Yep. And that could present a small problem over time. Some Southerners will hunt for hunting's sake just to get a trophy. I can't imagine how much they will slaughter out of revenge. And there's another thing. The aliens don't seem to be sending replacements."

"Replacements?"

"You remember how there had been no reported attacks in the eastern US? And then our young friend, Guy, killed that first one?"

"Right…" Wayne answered with a leading tone telling Archer to continue.

"Well, according to his account and what we know to be the next attack, the aliens waited a day or two and then sent down a replacement. But now that attack has fanned out across the eastern US and we are killing all the aliens left behind, which ain't that many. And still, there haven't been any additional landings."

"What are you trying to get at Archer? What's the point?"

"Well," Archer said like the seasoned countryman who knows something the city slicker doesn't, and further, he knows that he knows it. Now he was going to let him in on it, "The way I sees it, them alien dudes have hit the dusty trail. This is their modus operandi. They drop a few aliens off, right? Then they attack. Each time they get injured they multiply. So anyone that's raised rabbits knows what that means. Pretty soon the whole planet is filled with them. They just keep splittin' till the whole damned planet is full."

"So what does that have to do with the expanding ring and our problem?"

"Well, I was just gettin' to that part. They sent a replacement to a lost seed, right? But once that second seed took and they started spreadin' there was no sense to send more. Most of the planet is dominated already. They have never encountered a loss before or we would have seen a replacement by now."

"So you think they have moved on?"

"Sure, why not? It will take a while to clean everything up. If their goal is to own the planet, then I figure that is what they do all the time. They just hop from planet to planet. They're probably already gone," Archer said thoughtfully and then added, "the ship I mean."

"So that shouldn't be a problem for us. That is a great thing!" Wayne concluded knowing full well there was probably still more in Archer's head to be communicated.

"Not really. We now have two more problems. With no replacements comin' we have to drive hard to reach the expanding ring. Transporting the meat back here will take longer and longer until they hit the other forces to the west and maybe the north. That could mean driving to Canada to catch up to the front by the end of the week."

"What's the other problem?"

"How mad is the mother ship going to be when it gets back? You ever been around when a mama bear comes back to the den to find all the cubs are dead?"

Wayne had given some thought already to the first problem. He had not really thought about the second. His silence told the old grizzled hunter that the city slicker still had a few things he could learn from mountain savvy. But Wayne never liked to lose – even when the contest was an unspoken battle of wits with a hunter from Tennessee. With the wry smile of a chess champion he looked up at Archer and said, "Come inside. I would like to introduce you to someone."

Archer fell in tow as the two left the parking lot and passed through the frenetic kitchen that was already busy with preparation for the evening's junkies. Then walking through the waiter prep area they came out into the dining room proper. At one of the larger tables, Archer saw a group of three gentlemen leaning over what looked to be blueprints. "Archer Thornwall, I would like to introduce you to the senior partners of Emerald Valley Engineering. Gentlemen, this is the legendary Archer Thornwall."

Everyone shook hands and exchanged names. Archer noticed that only one of them actually looked old enough to be a legitimate senior partner. That one introduced himself as Randal Jones. Archer knew him to be a descendent branch of the Joneses that settled the large track of valley land southeast of Huntsville, known now for perpetuity as Jones Valley.

Old money for certain.

Even in his casual clothes, he gave off the sage maturity of an engineer of the world. The other two were little more than boys. Archer figured that these three were all that was actually left of the now mostly eaten Emerald Valley Engineering. Archer looked down at the drawings as Randal explained, "These corrals are made out of a new polymer that was developed here in Huntsville for the next generation line of passenger jets. The material is extremely lightweight, strong, and mostly transparent. When used on the jets, the material creates a natural skylight that brightens up the entire cabin saving on power costs for lighting during the daytime.

"For our purposes, the material will allow us to use those sheets, manufactured out past Research Park, as panels that can quickly be assembled into one of these corrals. We believe that if we ship them in their full uncut size that two sheets mounted side-by-side will be higher than the creatures can leap. And as long as there are no objects to hurl within the corral, we think it will be strong enough to withstand any attempt to pierce or break."

Archer asked incredulously, "You're gonna stop one of their beast claws with plastic cups? I don't think so."

Randal was unflappable. With the calm patience of a former CEO to a worldwide marketplace of skeptics he confidently explained, "This is a new polymer - a new material. It was designed to flex and stretch under stress. When the creatures hit the material it will give, but it will not break. It is strong enough to withstand torque on a fuselage that is 186 feet long with a wingspan of 197 feet flying at over 650 miles per hour against cross wind shear - most of the material being one continuous sheet."

Then for effect he looked up from the drawings at the hunter, staring directly in his eyes he added, "I think it will be strong enough to hold your beasties."

Wayne stepped in, "And best of all, the site is local and has already been made operational by his crew." Having won at least one of the two chess games, Wayne slapped Archer on the back and cheerfully added, "All we need is for you boys to drive one back down to us and we will have the pen waiting for you when you get back."

Archer shot back, "Drive? You mean like cattle?"

Laughing, Wayne said, "Ok, lead. Lead at least one back. We will have the site fully erected out at the university campus. There are some good, wide open spaces there and it will be easier to fix any problems out in the open like that."

"Any particular part of the campus? That place spreads out pretty far." Archer asked.

"Randal, you guys are setting up out beside the arts building, right?"

"That's right. We have the gate fully constructed and operational." Pointing back to the blueprints for Archer's sake, "You and the boys enter in the large gate off North Loop Road – here. Then move quickly to the smaller gate on the south side of the holding corral – here. The double locking mechanism should provide adequate escape through that portal and the translucent nature of the walls should lead to very little suspicion. If anything, the alien might think it a weak attempt of an inferior race to capture it. Obviously the first thing it will do is attempt to smash its way out. After that fails, it will try to scale the surfaces or jump out. That will be when we know if the design works or not."

"I would feel better if you have a backup team of trained hunters there in case this plan doesn't work," Archer added.

"Already taken care of friend," Wayne concluded.

The rest was idle chitchat and details of the planning session were well covered. The irony was that to preserve the fledgling culinary business they would now need to *protect* the aliens instead of hunt them in the wild. They would now willingly befriend their mortal enemy, preserving their number like so many cattle from those humans that would seek revenge for their overwhelming loss. But t'was Profit that brought them safe thus far and Profit will lead them home.

In all the success inherent with the plans as they spiraled out in front of him, becoming real on the razor's edge of the continuing present, Wayne had become a man divided. While his plan had met with finally skeptical acceptance from his old friend, he could not help being nagged by the now new thought: What will happen when the mother ship comes back?

While this all continued to develop, Guy was growing in stature and strength. There's power in the rub, wonder working power. For Profit begat Power and Power their fears relieved.

In the cool morning light, streaming through the glass walls of his newly discovered arboretum (it was amazing to Guy what all he found in his house once he started exploring) he reclined in a chaise lounge and casually dialed a number. There was no expectation of an answer; the aliens had probably eaten Atlanta by now. But then there it was, the old familiar click followed by the long delay of conquered shock and apathy.

Then at the end of a patient wait, "Yeah?"

"I need a lawyer."

"Guy?" the voice of Dexter Stavro seemed to be emerging from the end of a depression tunnel into the light of temporary hope even as the word was being spoken. It started with the G of sullenness and ended with the Y of elation. Guy was amazed at the transubstantiation that occurred within the utterance of such a short word.

"In the flesh. And I need a lawyer. Can you move to Huntsville?"

"What the fuck are you talking about, Sayonara? The world is over. The waves moved through Atlanta last night. Rednecks with shotguns litter the streets and most people are dead."

"I guess the words of the bumper sticker prophets have finally been fulfilled."

"How so?" Dex asked.

"You can have my gun when you pry it from my cold dead fingers."

Both laughed. It was sick to ponder. So much culture, so much history, all just blown away in a single wave. It would be a long time before cars could be left to rust in front yards or appliances to stagnate on front porches again – if ever.

"So why would you need an attorney?"

"Look, life is over there, right?"

"Toast."

"Then you need to get your shiny lawyer hiney up to Huntsville."

"I think it is much more dangerous to be out traveling – safer in here, my little catacomb."

"They travel by the main thoroughfares. Take the back roads to 41, then cut through to Rome. You can cross over to Alabama two different routes that way, both end up at the Tennessee River Bridge that crosses over to Scottsboro, Then just head west from there. Highway 72 is clear now."

"I know the way. But the aliens are all over the place."

"Trust me. I know for a fact you will not run into any interference once you get west of Rome."

"Guy, this is stupid. I can't go anywhere."

"Why the hell not? I need you!"

There was a long pause. Guy's frustration was beginning to mount. It had been a long time since anyone had denied him anything he wanted – and damnit, he was spoiled. He repeated, "Why not, Dex? Why can't you come up to Huntsville?"

Another long pause was followed by a defeated voice dripping with failure and despair. Guy could almost not hear it; the sound of it was so small. "I'm dying."

"What? How? I mean, were you hurt in the attack?" Fear was beginning to creep into Guy's voice replacing the earlier confidence.

"No. Nothing like that. It started before the alien attacks."

"What started, Dex?"

"The bleeding."

Another pause.

"What?" in disbelief and confusion.

"Look, I've been shitting blood for quite a while. I think I have cancer. I feel it eating away at my insides."

"Shit."

Yet another pause.

"Well, maybe it's not that bad."

"Guy, its bright red blood and it comes out when I shit. How can that be not that bad?"

Guy was at a loss. What could he do? Then he remembered just *what* he could do. He was the king of the fucking world after all. Dex just didn't realize it yet.

"Can you drive?"

"Of course I can drive. I shit blood. I'm not a paraplegic."

"Ok. Get your ass up here and we will fix everything."

"Guy, there is no more world. There is no more 'fixing' things."

"There is and there is. What is your alternative? Stay in Atlanta and rot from the inside out?"

"I had thought about joining the militia and fighting the aliens. At least then the death would be quick. But I chickened out last night. Now I am just a sniveling attorney in a closed off condo waiting for the patrols of aliens to find me and suck my head."

"Not much of a meal there, mate. They would starve on you."

"Thank you very much. Remind me to throw rocks at the steps of your nursing home when you retire."

"Now you're talking like the old Dex I know. You just need a good fight. And I have one for you. I am going to take over the world and I need a good lawyer – there is a ton of profit to be made here. Know where I can find one?"

"Alright. Alright. I know you are out of your head and this makes no sense whatsoever. But if I am going to die, it might as well be doing something less futile than joining the militia or rotting in my condo."

"Trust me Dex. It will be a blast."

"I suppose I have a few weeks or months left. I might as well live in your delusion instead of my own."

How precious did that Profit appear the hour they first believed.

The wind was blowing the grass, too tall from lack of mowing, like waves on a green ocean between the arts building and the west parking lot. The grey sky over the uneasy flat field seemed to portend ominous shadows over the day's events as the group of four hunters, all armed with the newly manufactured crossbows stood behind Blackie. He being the lone sentinel, left behind as the other three trekked to Scottsboro had spent the better part of the day engaging in nervous but friendly discourse with these four new hunters from the west.

All the while he did his best to hide his worry. He was unconvincing, however, and the other four seemed to pick up on his anxious vibe, their conversation turning tinnier in his ear; always looking to the north and east for the approaching Jeep.

Jorge Castillo had seen firsthand how fast one of those creatures could cover distances in a crowded garage. He could not imagine how fast they must move in the open. Faudder Archer had promised him that the Jeep could keep pace, but he was not so sure. The old hunter was going to need every trick in the book to make it the forty-five minute trip back with head and torso still intact. He wondered if any of the three that had come to know him as Blackie would ever be around to pick on him again.

He looked out past the other four hunters and over the grassy sea to the massive containment area erected by the Emerald Valley Engineering group. Blackie thought about young Ted insulting him and remembered the sting as he told him to smile in the dark so that he could see him. His face washed warm with embarrassment as he felt the jibe anew. The sky seemed in that moment to get a little greyer and the wind felt a little sharper to the skin.

But then the fear melted away as he heard a distant horn sound across the open space to University Drive. There coming around the curve of the North Loop was the old familiar Jeep. Thundering up the drive not fifty yards behind was one of the aliens. It appeared to be gaining on them – its claw slashing in the wind in an effort to assist a leap every third step.

With each leap, the alien seemed to shorten the distance to the Jeep and Logan would have to gun the accelerator to regain his lead. "Holy shit, boys! This is it. Get into positions now!"

The four hunters dispersed with Blackie's order to their appointed positions around the corral, running as fast as they could. They just barely made it as the Jeep came crashing over the curb and up into the open field. Here the alien made up a little ground as it cut off the corner. It was now a mere ten scant yards away from the Jeep.

The three hunters drove fast and furious through the large open gates as the alien took another pin-wheeling leap. This time its claw came down hard on the back corner of the Jeep, throwing it for a roll as they all cleared the main gate inside the corral. Blackie watched helplessly as his three best friends, his only friends left in this world, tumbled out of the Jeep pell-mell onto the grassy floor of the containment area.

"Oh shit!" he cried as he realized that they had not planned for this eventuality. With the large gate slamming shut behind them and the double safety portal to the south being closed on the exterior door side, there was no way he could level a clean shot at the beast. Precious seconds were ticking by as he looked around for a solution. The large double sections of polymer material sloped inward like the top half of a shaded arena. There were rather large arms made of small triangle and geodesic shapes that strengthened the arch-based architecture to ensure rigidity around its perimeter.

These lattice towers protruded up from bases in the waving grass every fifty yards or so completely around the outside and were cut short of the very top by about three feet. This would prevent the creatures from being able to leap up and grasp the tops of the towers from the inside. But Blackie knew that he was taller than three feet and if he could scale one fast enough, he could stand on top of the tower and possibly reach across the top edge of the polymer sheet. Without giving it a second thought, he ran for the nearest tower and started climbing with all his might.

Inside, the threesome had all finished their unexpected flights through the air with cartwheels, summersaults, or rolls. All three stopped short, dazed and confused. The alien had batted the Jeep to the side and remarkably it had landed back on all four wheels, not much worse for the wear. The creature now towered over the three bellowing louder and deeper than any lion they had ever heard. Archer was genuinely afraid.

They scrambled to their feet to see it making up its mind on which to attack first. Without giving it time to choose from the dinner cart, the three turned and sprinted for the exit portal now standing wide enough to accommodate their Jeep. Unfortunately it was also wide enough for the monster as well. They didn't have much of a head-start and even if they did make it, the creature would surely be so close that the portal would not have time to save them.

Archer realized that not all three of them were going to make it. At least two needed one to remain as a diversion. It was obvious what needed to be done. Archer stopped as the beast ran past his flank still chasing the other two. He began to flap his arms and scream profanities at the monster.

The alien stopped in its tracks. Turning left it looked straight at Archer. "Oh shit," Archer allowed as he began to run.

It was then that he realized that he had forgotten something. That Randall fellow had mentioned that the cage would be secure, providing that the alien didn't have anything to use as a projectile. And as Archer turned to run he found himself facing nearly 2,000 pounds of scrap projectiles in the making – the Jeep! Someone would have to get that hunk of shit out of here or all this work would be for nothing.

Archer doubled his pace. He was no longer running to become the willing martyr to save his own son and fishing buddy. He was now running to save possibly everyone here. He didn't even look back when he heard the thundering footfalls that were sounding an obvious pursuit close behind.

Archer threw himself with reckless abandon at the Jeep, perhaps one step before he should have. His right leg caught the dip in the side next to the driver's seat and his tibia and his fibula snapped cleanly in two like a wishbone on Thanksgiving Day. He fell awkwardly in the seat and pulled himself around just in time to see the beast not three feet away from him, raising its claw in the air like it just didn't care.

In that moment he saw his son and friend Logan enter the portal and the door slam shut behind them. As the outside door swung open, he could see Ted inside the portal area screaming "No!" at the scene inside. He hated that it was going to end like this. He hated that his own son was going to witness his demise.

He had never really given it much thought actually. To him, his own death was a deeply personal thing. He had always held to the silly fantasy that Ted would one day settle down and make little Archers that could climb up in his lap and play Ride a Little Pony. Then one day he would know the time was coming and quietly slip away to an old hunting lodge he knew in the Appalachian and there ring down the curtain and join the choir invisible in privacy.

But now as the claw came singing out of the sky, he was going to go in a most public and flamboyant way – and right in front of his own son. The thought of that and the thought of screwing everything up for everyone else in the bargain made him sick to his stomach. He would go with bile in his throat instead of a smile on his face.

Just then an arrow hit his seat beside his ear. An arrow! A fucking arrow hit his fucking seat right by his fucking ear! Archer barely had time to register the spray of alien blood across his cheek and see the frozen stun in the posture of the monster beside him before he heard the sudden and unexpected crack.

The alien split in two as Archer heard Blackie's voice like an angel from above, "You don't have much time Faudder. Get the hell outta der!"

Archer reached down, fumbling with the keys. In the desperation of a second chance, he turned the keys still in the ignition. But the Jeep would not do much more than turn over and over. It was not getting enough gas. He commanded his right foot to stomp on the gas pedal as he continued to turn the key but stubbornly it refused. Looking down he saw the spray of his own blood jetting into that of the alien's on his face and seat as two white sticks of broken bone protruded from his ankle lolling to one side like a worthless mannequin's foot in a shoe store display case.

Looking to his side, he saw the all-too-familiar M brothers springing new appendages. He didn't have much time. Archer reached across his own mutilated right shin and placed his left foot on the accelerator. Stomping hard the still-turning ignition roared to life and lurched forward as he shoved it into first.

Without a clutch foot, it would be hopeless to try to change gears. So Archer floored it and began burning up the transmission at thirty-five miles an hour, The Jeep making a high pitched scream from underneath. The inside portal door was open now and the two creatures were bounding towards him from behind.

It was then that the real horror hit him. Ted had not left the portal area. The outside door had opened and the fool had stayed behind screaming at his father. There was no time to do anything but hope the boy could move quickly to the side. The Jeep came flying into the portal area at a severe thirty-eight miles per hour and that was when it slammed into the outer door. And that was when Archer Thornwall lost consciousness.

18.

The ancient Hebrews that documented their understanding of God, the Earth, and all that stuff were perhaps the first of the monotheists. That is to say that they believed in only one God and further that they were perhaps the first to feel that way – on this planet at least.

The Ggelvring were singular in race and as such had a limited capacity for theology. Since there were no sexes or races, there were no internal struggles of any kind. There were no battle of the sexes and certainly no wars, civil or otherwise. In fact, they would probably find the oxymoron 'civil war' to be amusing if they were in any way able to translate it into their tongue.

This limited exposure to diversity is probably the singular reason that only one religion sprang forth on their planet. Ggel-Ta was the only point of origin. Everything began there. But unlike the human concept for continuation, Ggelvring were completely content in the idea that this consciousness, this 'life' was unique and finite. One's understanding of all things bright and beautiful simply stopped when one ceased to exist.

In this they were ironically connected to the Jews of the Old Testament for the Jews before the expansion of Greece during the inter-Biblical period of the Apocrypha ascribed the after death experience to a place called Sheol. Loosely translated this meant 'place of the dead' or 'in the ground'. When you died you went into the ground. That's it. Nothing more.

But unlike the Jews of the Old Testament, whose God constantly subjected them to loss after loss in an effort to bring them to repentance for things like worshipping more than one God, the Ggelvring had never suffered defeat. They had little concept of life hereafter because there was precious little need.

Perhaps a greater argument could be made here – that the eternal reward promised by a certain religion may be somehow scaled based upon how severely and regularly that group of people is defeated on a continuing basis. For example, the Hindi who arguably have never really been conquered at all (although they have been occupied for a time) believe we just keep coming back again and again until we get it right and then we move on to something else. While the Muslims, who have been so busy being defeated by every other country that when they are not being ruled by outsiders they take turns conquering each other, get 70 virgins and a mule.

This concept seems to hold water until it fails in its final application to the Mormon men that never really suffer much at all (as long as you don't count those two years on bikes around twenty years of age) and they get an entire planet inhabited by good women and get to become little gods themselves. It still has not been determined what the women did to piss their god off so much, but that is fodder for a later debate.

The main point here is that there seems to be difficulty in establishing absolutes of any sort in this universe. For before the current circumstances, if one were asked to find an example of a race or culture that had discovered any clean absolutes, they would be hard-pressed not to point to the Ggelvring. They had one race, one sex, one religion, one purpose, and had never suffered defeat. In this absolute state, they had thrived. They had thrived that is until they met those that inhabit a tiny blue marble spinning gracefully in the black space of our solar system.

This was their introduction to a universe seemingly devoid of absolutes. And without conspicuous absolutes, all that is left one is faith.

It took the humans here on Earth literally centuries to come to the conclusion that absolutes were probably a bad idea. The only way one could keep them was through faith. This is probably why all those that had Near Death Experiences had interpreted the random collision of chemicals in the brain shutting down as tunnels of light, floating over their bodies, hearing familiar voices, or the warm comfort of home. It was their faith superimposing upon physiological events like a lithograph at a boring Wednesday afternoon business meeting.

Perhaps there is a heaven. Perhaps there is a God. Perhaps those pesky Christians have had it all right all along.

An atheist once approached a sage old pastor and in front of the entire church had a desire to humiliate him. He asked the old pastor, "Can you prove to me now that everything in that book is true and accurate using scientific measures and tests?"

The old preacher smiled. He wondered why God had chosen this moment to allow this test to fall upon his shoulders. The old pastor knew that his answer was more important to his own congregation than it was to this non-believer. But further still he knew it was even more important to himself and the state of his own soul than to even this congregation – for in the end he would only be held accountable for a reckoning of but one soul.

With the patience and charm and warmth that only comes from season, he asked a question rather than give an answer, "If everything in this book," he said patting his own well-worn volume with his own well-worn hand, "if *everything* in this book were true..." Here he stopped to measure the preparedness of the young upstart. Continuing after he breathed in through his nose and out through his mouth, "would you have to change?"

The young atheist thought for a moment. Of course he would have to change. He lived his own life. No one told him what to do or when to do it. He lived to make himself big by making others small. He proved his own intelligence by stripping others of theirs. Thinking carefully through the possible rebuttals that could come from a concession he realized that he would be in a better position to prove this old codger a doddering old fool by conceding this one point and then hammering home his inability to scientifically prove his own religion. He had used this technique hundreds of times in the past and always felt better about himself when he could call into question the faith of another human being. "Alright. Yes. If everything in that book were true, then I would have to change."

Here the old man shot faster than a trained fencer – the rapier words cutting deep into the soul exposing the ultimate fraud from within, "Then the question is not whether or not everything in this book is true. The question is: Are you willing to change?"

Willingness to change. It is the stumbling block to progress. Did we really start out trying to be good? Or did we start out to blame and hurt everyone that doesn't believe as we do?

Regardless of the conclusion, Archer Thornwall found no answer from his own experience after he rammed the Jeep into the outside portal gate at the translucent holding pen erected to capture and defeat a species that had never known defeat before. All he knew was that one minute he was conscious and the next he was not. For all he knew, he was in Sheol, the place of the dead.

There were no bright lights. There were no angels singing. There was just emptiness and space without comprehension. In that void, there were no emotions, no family members from before, no imagination, and no life. There was just time and unconsciousness.

But then something odd happened. In the middle of the dark empty space came a blurry light. It moved closer, or at least it appeared to move closer. Archer was not entirely sure if it was moving towards him or simply growing where it was. And all he could make out of it was that it was blurry and that it was white.

Then he began to register some discomfort. The light bothered his eyes and seemed painful in a dull sort of way. Just as he began to feel the floating sensation take over he realized that he was now lying on his back and was turned slightly to one side. Archer began to feel the weight of his own body pressing into some sort of soft surface and the light began to take on the shape of another creature beside him.

This new image seemed to be a human, male and was turned sideways beside him. The other was also dressed in what looked to be white cloth wrapped around him. The face was not familiar to him but it was not at all unfriendly.

Archer desired to talk to him. He had so many questions. As he began to speak, he first coughed. The man floating beside him shared a compassionate look of concern for a moment but then relief as Archer caught his wind and finally cleared his dry throat. He croaked, "Are you an angel?"

The man looked with stunned shock and answered, "Fuck no. I'm a lawyer."

Archer Thornwall rolled over on his back as best he could and sighed as he said, "Shit. Then that means I went to hell."

The laughter from the lawyer caused him to look around. As his vision continued to improve he began to realize that there was no fire and brimstone. There were only the common fixtures you might see in a hospital.

"Glad to see your anesthesia has worn off, Dex," a new voice said as it entered the room. Archer looked back over and saw the young chef, Guy, as he approached the bed closest to the door. "I told you it wasn't going to take long."

Guy looked over and saw Archer Thornwall looking back. "Ah, Mr. Thornwall. Good to have you back in the land of the living."

Everything came back to Archer: The Jeep, the alien, the crash, his son, "Oh shit!" he said as he struggled to sit up, "My son. Ted. Where is Ted?"

Guy came running over to Archer's bed trying to calm him down and hold him still until he could explain. He didn't want the old man to pull all the pins out or tear down the gear holding his right foot up. "Easy, old man. Everything is fine. Ted will be here soon."

"The Jeep. I was going to hit him."

"From what I understand, you did. But you only barely grazed him. He had a few stitches and was released by Doctor Riley three days ago."

"Three days?" Here the old hunter made another effort to free himself from the bindings and traction.

"Easy, easy. Everything is fine now."

"And the beasts?"

"The two aliens are still in the pen. I'm sure Wayne will be around soon to catch you up on all that you have missed. But in the meantime, your three friends are healthy and fine."

Archer relaxed. His head was swimming a little. He raised his hand and felt a bandage. There was a shooting pain when he pressed a little too hard and he nearly blacked out again. Guy pulled his arms down and asked him to lie still until he had some more energy. Archer complied.

During the conversations that followed, Archer gleaned a few things. First, this young man was a friend of Guy's and had been afraid he was eaten up with cancer. The doctor had pulled together what resources he could and performed a colonoscopy. In the end (no pun intended) it had turned out to be a benign growth sort of like a mole. The doctor had zapped it and Dex would be fine.

Second, Archer found out from Guy's accounts that there was something wrong with the two creatures in the pen. After the Jeep crashed, the door to the inside slammed shut. It had taken over an hour for the engineers to break open the now mangled outer door tangled in all the wreckage from the collision. Archer had lost a great deal of blood and had nearly not survived the trip to the hospital and the surgery. But in the end, he would be mobile again and may even be able to keep the leg if all goes well.

But the two creatures, once captured, did something rather odd. First they tested the material just as Randal had thought they would. They attempted to pierce it with their massive claws. They tried to scale it. They even tried to stand on the other alien and jump (something no one had foreseen but fortunately the form was still tall enough to contain them). But after several failed attempts, the brutal beasts of destruction did something completely odd. They sat down.

They sat down on the grass and started picking at it with their claw.

"You have got to be kidding me. Those murdering bastards just sat down?"

"That's right. They sat down and started aimlessly picking at the grass."

Archer sat back on his bed. After a moment he asked, "How many times have they tried to escape since then?"

"None. They have stayed there in that position since that afternoon."

Archer was dumbfounded, "No shit?"

"No shit," Guy confirmed.

As this awakening was occurring at the minimally operational surgical center, across town Wayne was nonplussed. "What do you mean you hit it?"

He was shouting up to one of the guards standing on a makeshift stand atop the tower poll that Blackie had climbed to save Archer Thornwall. The hunter looked down and shouted, "I hit it cleanly in the shoulder."

"That's impossible. There are still only two of them. If we are going to reach anywhere close to demand, we'll need to get these two to multiply."

"Look, all I can tell you is that I shot it cleanly through its shoulder. Both of them are just sitting there like nothing has happened."

Wayne looked around at his small entourage with whom he now traveled and said, "Dammit. If you want something done right, you have to do it yourself." Then up to the hunter on the stand he said, "Come on down. I need to have a look."

The hunter climbed down streaming profanities at the futility of it all. He had done exactly like the man had asked more than five times and still he was pissed off. Sometimes you just can't please the boss no matter how hard you try.

He had no sooner hit the ground than he felt Wayne Avarice clamor over the top of him on his way up the tower – streaming profanities all the way up. Once he reached the perch, Wayne pulled out his field glasses and focused in on the beasts. From up here he could see clearly what was only a mere blur through the polymer sheets.

The two aliens were facing each other and sitting in what could generally be described as Indian-Style. Both of them had liquid traces of alien blood oozing down their respective bodies from the large bore holes that had been made by the hunter's weapons.

Pulling out his own revolver, Wayne took dead aim for the head of the one on the right. He squeezed the trigger with the patient pressure of a practiced marksman until the pistol sounded the report that signaled him to relax. The alien rocked to the side from the shot and blood issued forth from the entrance and exit wound. But still there was no crack, no split into two creatures. All that was there was the gentle bleating from the mournful creature expressing an almost apathetic sense of pain.

Wayne just stood there and pondered. "What the fuck am I going to do now?"

Climbing back down the tower, he decided to go to the Restaurant. The early seating would begin soon and seeing all the profits come rolling in like a whelming flood had a calming effect on his jangled nerves. There would be enough meat from their recent hunts to sustain them for the next few evenings. But Wayne knew that he would have to figure out a way to automate his supply chain or the world would be stuck in this neo-Iron Age for a very long time.

Pulling into the drive to the back parking lot he was pleased to see that his thoughts were not misleading. Wayne began to feel better almost immediately. Walking in the kitchen door he was greeted by a swell of salutations.

"Good evening everybody. Looks like another packed house!"

Jean Louis approached him and smugly asked, "Ah, perhaps Monsieur Avarice," this he pronounced 'Ahforeece', "you have forgotten that today is Thursday?"

Wayne thought for a moment. He looked over at Guy and nodded. Guy looked back from his hectic pace and smiled. For the life of him, he could not fathom why the fact that this was Thursday was important. Then it dawned on him like a flash and his smile doubled, "Thursday! Right." Then looking over to Guy he asked, "Guy, what other entrees have you perfected beyond Country Fried Steak and the Vegetarian plate?"

With pride Guy answered, "We can prepare lamb, pork tenderloin, or a chicken entree. But no one really orders anything other than the steak."

"Excellent. I think you will get a chance to try out some of your other dishes tonight. We have some special guests joining us." Then Wayne said as an aside to Jean Louis, "Hmm... Lamb, pork, and chicken. That gives me an idea."

Jean Louis looked a little like he didn't follow this last statement but at the same time he was too snotty to admit it. So he just smiled and said, "That's good."

Wayne waved that idea off as if to say it was not really for the Maitre De. Then he grabbed Jean Louis by the shoulder and leading him into the dining area he began to speak as if he were conveying a confidence, "Jean Louis, when Rothschild gets here, make sure that he gets the large corner booth."

"Very good, Monsieur."

"And when Senator Applegate gets here, let me speak to him before their table orders."

"Of course, Monsieur."

"I think we are going to have a little fun tonight."

Wayne stepped out back, across the small 12 feet of un-landscaped dirt between the restaurant and the self-storage center behind it, and found one of his security guards. "Brian, I want you to run out to the University. Find one of the hunters at a large containment area beside the Arts Building. Do you know where that is?"

"Yes, sir."

"Good. Find one of them and tell them that I said to bring down a couple of sheep, pigs, and chickens to the pen. I want to see if we can get the aliens to eat. I'm worried that they will die in captivity. Then tell them that if they begin to fight to shoot the weaker looking of the two with one shot."

"Yes, sir."

"That's one shot only," Wayne emphasized.

"Yes, sir. I've got it."

"Good."

Wayne spent the next hour or so going over the assets with one of his managers. They had already implemented a scheme to begin moving the existing stockpile to a centralized warehouse which was now operational not too far away on the northwest side of downtown. Further they had begun to modify slightly the list of goods that they were requesting in barter for an evening's meal. There were things that the growing satellite townships needed beyond the basics and Huntsville had been affluent and diverse enough before the invasion to be able to stockpile some of these.

The list of new items included such things as replacement auto parts, computers, welding gear, pneumatic compressors, and a wide variety of other components. All of these things and more were needed beyond the basic necessities in order to move a re-colonization of the United States forward to the next stage. Pretty soon some facsimile of law and order would need to be restored beyond brute force. They were approaching a time when a recognized body like Congress (at a state or even national level) would begin to come in handy. And Wayne Avarice did not want to miss his opportunity to be ahead of the power curve.

Stepping back inside, he was pleased to see that his expected guests had arrived. He went back to the kitchen and grabbed Guy. "Follow me, chef. Your public awaits."

"But Wayne," Guy protested sharply, "I have orders to oversee."

"Let your Sous handle it. This is your moment to shine," he said with all the enthusiasm of a used car salesman whose customer has just asked if they could acquire an extended warranty with their purchase.

Wiping his hands and removing his cover apron, Guy agreed and joined Wayne as he walked out into the dining area. They approached two tables that had been moved close together for a party of ten. Wayne led with a jovial, "Senator Applegate, how very good to see you."

"Good to be alive, Wayne. Thanks for having us tonight," the Senator said. His grey hair was a little unkempt and his suit a little disheveled. But still he seemed not entirely worse for the wear.

"And Abigail," Wayne said moving towards the senator's wife, "How very delightful to see you again."

Mrs. Applegate held out her hand in such a manner as to suggest that Wayne kiss it as she said, "The feeling is always mutual, Mr. Avarice."

Wayne dutifully pressed his lips to the back of her hand and added, "The place seems to sparkle with your smile. You are welcome any time you can slip away from this old bloviator."

"Oh Wayne, do stop," she said with a fake laugh and a slight slap to his lapel.

Then back to the Senator he asked, "And who are your charming guests?"

"These are Senators Valorem and Crotchet, Representative Parsons, and you know Speaker Hagglepoint. And of course their lovely wives."

Everyone exchanged pleasantries as Wayne took turns to welcome each couple at length. Then he said, "Allow me to introduce our new Executive Chef, Guy Sayonara."

Guy bowed and Senator Applegate asked, "What's on the menu this evening chef?"

Guy humbly replied, "We have a very nice lamb with mint sauce, a pork tenderloin in a reduced cherry sauce, a very tender chicken fricassee, and of course our signature dish – a country fried steak."

Mrs. Applegate was the first to speak, "It all sounds so lovely. I think I will have the pork."

At that moment the senator's demeanor changed slightly as he cut in, "Dear, we are being rude to our host." Then to Wayne he asked, "Wayne, what would you recommend?"

"Well, I know that you all love rich food very much." They all agreed. "And I know that for two of you, Senator Applegate and Representative Parsons, that rich food doesn't particularly love you back very much." There was some mild laughter as everyone knew that both of these men had survived bypass surgeries over the years. "So I would, at the risk of making you two feel left out," here Wayne played for sympathy from the wives and got it with visible pats on the hands and arms of their spouses, "I would recommend the steak for everyone and the Chicken for our two light-hearted friends."

They all agreed and Wayne was about to make his excuses and dismiss Guy back to the kitchen when Jean Louis approached from his flank, "Pardon, Monsieur."

"Yes, Jean Louis?"

"Mr. Rothschild is in the corner booth."

"Excellent." Then to the party of ten, "Thank you all for joining us this evening and bon appétit."

Wayne escorted Guy over to the corner booth. On the way Guy attempted to ask about the last table order. He felt that Wayne could not possibly have been serious giving all but two the steak. But he wasn't able to complete the sentence before they were standing in front of a fairly portly fellow leaning back in the fullness of the corner booth and wearing the most pompous and smarmy smirk Guy had ever seen. His narrow-lipped mouth drew up tight like a bow stretched between two over-sized earlobes and highlighted with impossibly red circles for cheeks. The overall effect of the large slit that served as his mouth was accented further by the fact that his eyes were unusually tiny and his multiple chins were unusually large.

To Guy it almost looked like the face of a person looking in a carnival mirror.

Brief introductions were made and an order for one steak was suggested by Wayne and accepted by Mr. Rothschild.

Back in the privacy of the kitchen Guy confronted Wayne, "What in the hell was that all about?"

"Well, the party of ten is going to be putting together a provisional government for North America soon. And I am going to help them."

Guy whispered in surprise, "But you are going to feed them all the steak! What kind of government could you possibly shape with junkies?"

Wayne said back sternly and without apology, "One that is friendly towards restaurateurs, of course."

Guy stood there and thought for a moment and then added, "But you steaked the Speaker and Chickened the Rep. Isn't that backward?"

"Not if I am assisting in a coup d'état it isn't."

"Oh," Guy said as if he understood. And then he actually *did* understand and added a much more affected, "Oh." Then after he thought for a moment longer he asked, "Is that fat man in on it?"

"What fat man?"

"The razorback in the corner booth."

"Oh, Rothschild," Wayne said as he started to laugh. "No, he is not in on it."

"Then what is his story?"

Wayne took a moment to collect himself from his jocularity and then answered, "He's the local food critic for the newspaper. Bastard hasn't given one of my places a good review in twenty years. The way I see it, I have some payback coming."

The next morning, Wayne went back out to the corral where he was dismayed to see the sheep, pigs, and chickens just walking around the aliens who were still sitting there – crisscross-applesauce. Nothing looked to be changed, not even as the occasional barnyard buddy unfeelingly stepped on the odd leg or hoof of one of the caged and wounded beasts.

Talking to one of the guards he learned that the animals had been placed in the pen right away after being delivered. Then everyone had waited for some sort of interest. But the aliens had paid the new guests no-never-mind. They simply refused to budge from their defeated posture. Several guards now joining the conversation tried to make suggestions but none of them seemed to ring true with Wayne. That's when one hunter by the name of Bob said, "Perhaps they need violence in the hunt."

There was a moment where no one said a word. They were all simply stunned at the simplicity of the man's observation. "Shooting at them from up on top doesn't seem to give *them* a sporting chance to hunt. And pigs and sheep ain't gonna attack them none. Maybe they need to be hunting something else and then get attacked or hurt."

A rueful smile absent of mirth slid across Wayne's face like the shadow of an eclipsing moon. Through the tight expression he graveled, "I have a cunning plan."

19.

"We simply must have one of the houses, Wayne. That is my position and I am sticking to it."

"Judge, be reasonable. We have a house all set aside for you and soon you will be in it with your whole family."

The eternal trickle of water dripped from the cave wall down into the first pool of hundreds creating underground tributaries that ultimately fed the larger lake in the back of Three Caves. The limestone floor was slick and reflective from the constant spattering and the overall effect made Wayne Avarice desperately need to pee; the pressure so great he had a hard time focusing on the present conversation.

"I *am* being reasonable, I have *been* reasonable, and I am *fed up* with being reasonable!" The judge stated in a crescendo stirring echoes like eddies through the endless chasms.

Wayne took a minute to let the ensuing silence heal and sooth. As his eardrums slowly retracted from their guarded positions, their hammers momentarily stunned by the outburst, the unwelcome trickling softly returned replacing the muffled hum. This made his compulsion to urinate even greater. Wayne shifted his weight from one foot to another hoping to momentarily appease his burgeoning bladder.

"You know that we have a little… umm problem with your house. I have a plan in place and the space will be available soon. That is - if you help me." Then for leverage he added, "You scratch my back…"

"There has been a Greenhouge in this valley since Hunt discovered the spring. By sheer rights I should…"

Here Wayne took control of the conversation by cutting the plump judge off in mid stutter, "By sheer rights your brain matter should be providing one of our extraterrestrial friends a fine case of acid reflux. May I remind you that

174

our provisions here in this cave were the highest and best accommodations in the world? Whole countries are dead. Huntsville was ground zero for the third landing for Pete's sake! We are all beyond lucky just to be alive. I don't want to hear any more of your whining."

The judge recoiled some. This was a different world and at the present Wayne did hold all the cards. Seeing that Greenhouge had acquiesced he continued in a softer voice.

"Let's just get our little supply chain problem solved first. All right?"

"What do you have in mind?"

"You were telling me about a serious problem last week."

The judge now given a moment to re-present his case to the seat of power regained a bit of pride to his stature as he recounted, "It's the prisons actually. When the aliens attacked, Madison County facilities were loaded to beyond capacity."

"Sounds like the same problem the whole country faced."

"Indeed. Overcrowding in nearly every system across the country. And when most of the population is being mutilated or fleeing, no one thinks to open the jails and release the prisoners."

"Which means…" Wayne led.

"Which means that the prisons are probably now overfilled morgues. But if the inmates could get to some food, and in most cases you have classes of low risk inmates that do have certain extended access rights, then most or all could still be alive but probably nearing the complete exhaustion of their supplies. It seems the only humane thing would be to at least free them and let them have the same chance as the rest of the general population."

Wayne thought a moment and then asked, "But if a new civilization were to rise up?"

"Well, then the released inmates would constitute a considerable risk to that civilization. The chance for reform *before* the attack was slim to none with most of the vermin, but now that there is virtual anarchy, they would wreak havoc on what's left of us."

"And so your dilemma is what, judge?"

"My dilemma is to weigh the risks of first traveling to the various jails and prisons not knowing what we will find there, and then choosing to either sentence those inmates to a long, drawn out and painful death of starvation and disease or to free them and suffer possibly even worse results with the remnants of the population of Earth."

Wayne tapped his chin thoughtfully and said, "No. Your real dilemma is that your family is living in a cave and you need a house in a safe zone guarded from roaming gangs and thugs. And to get that, you need to do me a simple but effective favor that will take care of all of the before mentioned problems."

A week had gone by since his rude violation proved his worst fears to be but minor worries. Dex was consumed with the story he had just heard, been waiting to hear for some time now from his old college friend.

"No shit? They become addicted to the stuff and do whatever you suggest?"

"Pretty much. You take my rub from college and add the meat from our clawed-friends and boomo! They are hooked for life and become compliant puppets."

"Damn."

Guy was a bit concerned. Dex was not speaking much. What he didn't understand was that lawyers go through a special class in law school where they are jabbed in the stomach with a cattle prod every time they say anything superfluous to a card-board cut-out of a client. Eventually their conversations become non-conjuncted closed-ended questions for the most part.

Guy asked, "Are you ok buddy?"

"Don't I look ok?"

"You seem quiet. Is there a question of ethics here?"

Dex laughed. "I'm a fucking lawyer," and he shot him a look that said, *"Does that answer your question?"*

Guy smiled, "Then why the sullenness?"

"You have invented a rub that provides for ultimate power. You have entrusted this information to an unscrupulous entrepreneur. There is no more law. And if there is any law at all, it is *his* law. And yet you have not given him the formula for the rub." Then with full sobriety he said to his old roommate, "You, my friend, are a dead man walking."

"I know."

"As soon as he has the formula, you will be history."

Guy opened the refrigerator door and grabbed two more beers. Then tossing one to his friend he said, "Let's walk."

He led Dex out the side door and out into the middle of the picturesque drive that made a pretty good pass at looking like an old Twickenham street from the historic district. The large antebellum replica houses stood shoulder to shoulder pressing in toward them as they walked but kept better than arm's length by their twelve-foot excuses for front yards.

"The place is bugged."

"I know. I could see the lenses through the vents. They may be smart enough to attempt to cover all the bases but they really do it in an amateur way."

"I have a cunning plan."

Laughing a little, Dex looked at Guy and, for just a moment, they were college freshmen again. That old familiar feeling of excitement in new vistas returned. This was, after all, a new world they were living in.

"We are getting to the point where half the world is addicted and the other half is pushers. Wayne has already used his power to open up key airports with enough staff to have his managers fly to ever expanding numbers of locations. In just one week he has opened three new restaurants.

"I hear enough from the kitchen, pretending to be completely ign'ant, to know that the Congress will be reconvening next month and will begin to work on a new constitution for North America."

"Well that should take years," Dex said as a given.

"Not really. They will need food and Washington D.C. is one of the three new restaurants that Wayne opened. It was good timing too. The wave had recently moved through there. The remnants of the U.S. army made it their Little Bighorn."

They walked in silence for a while. Neither one was really mourning the passing of the once great nation. They were both far too stupid with insanity by this point. And yet there was enough soul left between them to cause a momentary pause in the dialog.

Then Guy stopped and turned to his old friend and said, "I have found three Project Managers from my old DOD days that I trust implicitly. I have set up a way to manufacture the rub so that no one will ever be able to figure out the exact recipe. Congress will be meeting next month. I will use my influence to make sure you are there."

"Me? Why?"

"Because I need representation if I ever hope to live through this mess. And because you always wanted to get into politics and shape the world's future, remember? I can't think of a better opportunity than this."

There was a pensive pause as Dex thought things through. "This is a very dangerous game you are playing, Sayonara. There is a very high chance we won't live through this mess. If I do agree to this ign'ant plan, what is my interest in it?"

"You know, if I were a salesman, I could assume the sale based on that question. The deal is done. All I have to do is find your price."

Dex chuckled a little and said, "I think we have both become a bit cynical over the years."

"Your cut would be running the Chef Guy Sayonara Spicing Company."

Dex said with a little bit too much breath in it, "Run? You would want me to be CEO and President?"

"Pick one. I'll be the other."

"Guy, you are making a play at being the most powerful person in the new world and you are not wanting to run it all?"

"I have no real intentions. I have always had one dream in life – to be a chef. Now I have but two goals in life – to *live* and to be a chef. Your running CGS Spicing Company will make both of those dreams come true. I don't really need any more than that."

"CGS? You're an acronym now?"

"All the hotshots eventually become acronyms."

"You know, before I got into law, I thought an acronym was a small person from Ohio."

The two old buddies laughed and jabbed at each other and began plotting how they were going to take over the world.

The gun shook a little in his hand. The sky was a little grey but was made to seem darker and more ominous looking out through the translucent walls of his new containment area. But it was the gun that really gave this setting the feeling of other world to him. It was weighty and felt too heavy as he gripped the handle, not quite sure what was going to happen next.

Of course guns felt all wrong to Stanley Crookshaft. He had been on death row for seven years now as appeal after appeal unfolded. His public attorney had assured him that he would not face lethal injection for another decade or two. After all, a death sentence in the US was really little more than life without parole. And death row was so much more civil than the rest of prison. For one thing there was a lot less overcrowding. And for the other, all the inmates faced a greater thing than internal politics or finding out what tossed salad in the showers was all about.

But Stanley had been unique. It wasn't that he hadn't done it. He had. But a pickaxe feels a lot different when used as a tool of death than a pistol does. When Stanley went over the edge, when his mother-in-law pointed that boney finger at him one time too many and reminded him just how worthless he was and how foolish her daughter had ever been in throwing her life away on him, he wanted to feel the jolts of life transmit through to his hands via a wooden handle. He wanted to feel the object of his obsession jerk and bob as her head tried to reflexively extricate itself from the unwelcome and unexpected violation.

But in the end, he had been really let down. Sneaking up behind his soon to be ex-mother-in-law who was sitting on the couch watching yet another soap opera, he swung the pickaxe like a great baseball player, feeling the heavy end slice through the air gaining momentum as it arced. Then he felt with fleeting satisfaction the tip crack the bone of her skull just in front of the ear where it swiftly penetrated deep into her thought center and out the other side.

But there had not been any jolts. There were no bobs or spasms – not even a gurgle. The bitch had simply passed from this life into the next without regard for his feelings or his needs. It had been so like her. Stanley believed to this present day that she had done it on purpose; denied him any satisfaction in knowing her at all. In the end, she had simply been a sponge or a parasite living off him while feeding her need for ridicule like an obese person feeds on coconut cream pie.

Having been left so unsatisfied, Stanley decided to go up and down his street finding all the neighbors that had offended him over the years looking for just one to do him the polite courtesy and decency of jerking at the end of his pickaxe like a lively largemouth bass at the end of his line on the first good fishing day of the new season. But in the fourteen attempts he got in before the police came and rudely interrupted his experiment, not a single one was decent enough to twitch a single time.

To Stanley it had been one of the great social injustices in world history.

In the end, it was the boot print on the side of his mother-in-law's face that had tipped the blind scales of justice against him. He had explained that the pick was stuck and he had to stand on her head to finally free the tool with the leverage of his weight. He tried to explain that he had not had to use that trick on any of the other fourteen, but the jury had been unsympathetic by that point.

He blamed his free counsel for his plight. Some of those lawyers on TV would have been able to get him off. After all, she fucking had it coming, pointing that damn finger around like she was God's gift to pointing or something.

But now he stood in an unfamiliar place with an unfamiliar weapon, all alone not really understanding why. They had pulled him out of his cell, marched him between two men that looked like they could be plainclothes but he didn't know. Then they had driven him out here to the university, opened up the door on a small containment area, and unceremoniously thrown him in. He had found the small pistol on the ground in front of him. It looked like it had at least three bullets in it.

Just as he was about to turn around and bang on the entrance to be let out (he had grown tired of the little field trip) the door on the other side of the holding area slid open. Stanley naturally crossed to it and walked through. Once you have spent five or more years in the pokey, you tend to become somewhat institutionalized. And when one door closes and another one opens, you just sort of walk through it without questioning.

As Stanley emerged into a much larger area, the door slid closed behind him. He could make out two large forms sitting on the ground out in the middle of the large holding area. They were grey and hulking with yellow splotches up and down their skin. Looking up, he saw four different makeshift guard stands at the tops of support towers. Men stood there with rifles drawn on him and the creatures. All of a sudden, Stanley did not have such a good feeling about this little excursion.

"Hey, man. I don't want any harm here."

The men in the towers were stoic and silent.

Holding the gun out in front of him clearly not fingering the trigger and showing that he was going to drop it sideways if instructed to do so he cried out, "I found this in that other area. I'll drop it if you want me to. Just let me out of here."

The men in the stand remained silent - their silhouettes still with focus and aim.

"Hey man! I mean it. I want to talk to my lawyer!" Stanley shouted, his voice shrill with growing anxiety.

The guards watched and waited. None of them moved.

"This is bullshit! I didn't do anything wrong! Let me out!" His screams reached a new high level of desperation and panic.

One of the aliens moved a little. It turned its shoulder to square off in Stanley's direction. The eyes showing the first sign of life in days as it murmured something to its partner.

Stanley continued to scream his pleas for release and even fired one shot at a guard. The shot went harmlessly off to one side. The shadowy figure held up a hand in the universal sign to the others to halt. Nobody moved. Nobody fired.

The silence was getting to Stanley. He started spurting out profanity like a severed artery spurts blood and looked around the walls for anyone that would listen to him. He was so intent on communicating his dissatisfaction with the present circumstances that he didn't notice that first one alien and then the other had stood up and were presently moving towards him one behind the other.

"Look you assholes. You got the wrong person. Take me back to the row! I have another appeal coming up next month!"

Turning around in his natural course, Stanley saw for the first time the huge beast advancing towards him. Without thinking about it and guided purely by instinct he raised the gun and fired another shot, this time at the alien. The shot went wide to the right.

"Shit."

He pulled the trigger again and this time grazed the creature's shoulder.

"Shit."

But then something happened that Stanley Crookshaft didn't expect. There was a loud crack and the alien split in two and fell to the ground. The other one was clearly visible now behind the two halves squirming around on the ground and changing somehow.

The second creature began bounding toward him, leaping through the two halves like a stag through a tree split by lightning. Stanley fired again but the pistol sounded an impotent and terrifying click. He heard a cartoon character's voice in his head say, "What do you know about that… no bullets left." The last three words sounding like "no buwwets weft."

The short-lived comedy relinquished the moment back to terror as the trigger continued to make the hollow click, click, click sound. Stanley was not even aware that his right finger was still hard at work. And still the beast continued to rampage.

Wayne watched from the guard-stand, still holding up his hand in a sign for all to hold their fire. He watched as the creature wrapped its coiley fingers around the inmate's head and drew back its claw.

The slice down and through Stanley Crookshaft's neck was an ironic parody. A moment later Stanley's thought center was being sucked out by the alien's hungry and perfectly formed lips. Not a drop was wasted on the grass.

But there was time for one more irony. After the sudden slice, Stanley's body twitched and jolted. The other two aliens, now completely formed and mobile descended on his remains like ravenous hyenas. One of the creatures lifted his body while the other one neatly severed Stanley's legs from his torso. Then grabbing up a half each, they began to suck out what they could from the piece of Stanley they got.

This task was not so neatly performed for their mouths were not quite large enough. By the time they were done, they looked like two toddlers that had consumed large plates of spaghetti without the benefits of silverware or bibs.

They definitely needed a moist towelette. But they didn't seem to mind.

Wayne spoke to his chief of security. "Kill the third one and send it to slaughter."

"Yes sir."

Then he began climbing down. Stopping as if he remembered something he turned back to the guard and said, "Oh, and make sure the next gun has four bullets."

"Yes sir."

"We want a higher production out of this."

Wayne Avarice made his way down and across the grass to an on-looking Judge Greenhouge.

"I take it that met with your satisfaction and approval?"

The judge looked like he was about to cum in his pants with twisted excitement and delight. "Yes. Very. I think it is amazingly efficient and humane." Then as almost an afterthought he added, "And stimulating."

Wayne was about to continue in his normal discourse of business but this last observation caught him a little off guard and he allowed the rare smile of amusement. Then back to business he said, "Good. I want you to meet with Senator Applegate and the new Speaker of the House Parsons. Write all of this into the new code and make sure the new constitution allows for it. They owe me a little favor for helping them with a little marriage difficulty."

The judge looked a little like a child in a candy store as he said, "Yes, Wayne. I will take care of it."

"Good. Let's begin protecting our society by carrying out the sentences on all the death row inmates." Then looking at the judge with perhaps a little too much impishness in his eyes he added, "Oh, and let's make sure that the rest of the inmates get some nice hot meals. I'm sure that if we improve their dietary plans that moral will improve dramatically."

The judge caught his drift and smiled at the thought of prisons filled to the brim with complacent junkies. "I will make it so."

Wayne was already turning to walk back to his chauffeured car that was waiting for him at the curb when he turned and said, "And what the hell, see if there is some way to fit the place out with bleachers and charge for an audience. The new republic will need some entertainment after all."

20.

Like hot cakes, like popcorn, like pipe bombs in Jenin, regardless of the euphemism used before the invasion, they were all replaced with the phrase "Selling like Chef Guy's Country Fried Steak".

Over the coming months the world opened up to them like the preverbal oyster and while they devoured opulence on the half shell, they had to keep pausing to pick out the perfectly formed pearls that kept getting in the way. It seemed like they couldn't swing a dead cat without hitting a grand slam. Half the world was addicted and the other half was entering the fast-paced and exciting life of the culinary business. You were either consuming or you were supplying. One way or the other everyone was dancing around the steak.

There was no reason to find it odd really. It was simply the way the world was playing out in its new paradigm. If one stops and thinks about it, there is little more than random chance involved in the way it was before the invasions, little more than chaos theory at its best before Guy's rub caused a new era to begin. Who said it was fair before the invasion anyway?

Oh it seemed fair. That was the intended perception. The masses of the population were treated unfairly every day. It was just unfairness in economy. That is to say, it was a modest unfairness. Of course there was the occasional malpractice or class action lawsuit that would do little more than provide for the odd lottery bonanza for some lucky and more than likely horribly disfigured or handicapped person due to incompetence. But even though they knew better, the general public would allow this medicine show hoopla to pacify their own personal need for equality and fair treatment. The yahoo getting six bazillion dollars for a lost left lung would somehow make them feel better when the doctor left them in their underwear for an hour while he or she played Tickle-Me Elmo with the office manager.

Somehow the human race had allowed a system to evolve where the government took part of what you made, part of what you spent, part of what you saved, part of what you invested, and part of what you left behind and thought of it as normal and fair. And when the government wasn't taking its 65% from each and every person regardless of tax bracket, people were busy giving the rest away to inflated utilities, energy costs, hidden fees, surcharges, franchise costs, licenses, teller charges, transfer rates, escrow, insurance, interest, late fees, over-limit fees, postage, tolls, SPLOST, margin, commissions, retainers, tips, shipping and handling, import fees, undercoating, titles, deeds, closing costs, and rent. And after all of that, they had the gall to call it Social Security?

Now *there's* hyperbole!

People were lucky to get $3,000 of real value out of every $30,000 that was earned. By the time a young adult was twenty years of age, they were so heavily leveraged into the system that they would be its slave for the rest of their lives – driven forward by the false and misleading glimmer that there would be a life of relaxation waiting for them at the end if they just were good little troopers and worked their asses off for about forty-five more years.

And yet somehow, that whole kooky world was looked upon by most of its inhabitants as normal. To Guy, the new way of doing things made more sense. So what if half of humanity was being manipulated for the benefit of the other half? That was a hell of a lot more equitable than it had been before. Before it was more like 90% working to support the select 10%. To Guy there was still a part of humanity that was little more than cattle. It was just a lot smaller part than it had been before and they were a lot more content in being so thanks to his little contribution to the race.

"We have three major networks to create your rub now. They are geographically distributed as you outlined in your original plans. It was a little difficult to incorporate what used to be Canada and Central America into the nexus of it all, but that is what the new congress wanted."

"Imagine, Dex - a world without boundaries. One united continent. They used to sing songs about it, you know? They sang about us, Dex. They dreamt of a generation that would bring it all about."

"Peace and Love, man."

"Freedom and Profit," Guy added.

Guy was looking out of his office window. He had taken over the corner office in one of the more posh locations in Huntsville. It had required a little more involvement to help Dex set up the encrypted manufacturing process for his rub than he had originally thought it would. But still he had been able to maintain his post as head chef of Southern Flair.

The discussion with Wayne had not been received very well three months earlier. Guy and Dex had preempted any chance Wayne had at controlling their plans for owning the rub industry. But in the end, Guy had gotten

Wayne to confess that Maxwell had been unsuccessful at duplicating the recipe (to the tune of over 250 deaths – but who's counting?).

In this particular game, Guy had the upper hand. You see, there had been a stool pigeon – a certain prep chef in Max's kitchen, had been bullied by Max, and just so happened to be the roommate of one Alex, Sous Chef. Pretty soon Guy was getting daily updates on the secret plans of Wayne Avarice to replace him and bring an end to his culinary bliss.

Dex had been a master at crafting an agreement too. With all the inside information, Guy and Dex worked out a deal on paper that would be protected by the new cannon of global law in such a way as to be non-threatening to Wayne's empire. Wayne needed the rub, but what he really wanted was the power, fortune, and glory. Guy and Dex simply wanted enough power to provide for their security and riches beyond their imagination.

Both could be entertained. The world was big enough for the both of them. One hand would wash the other. In the end, it was their uncontested agreement that the name for the planet would be changed from Terra or Earth to Avarice.

Everyone agreed that it was fitting.

With the private agreement, it became a breeze to have Dex represent the Spicing Company's interest at the new Constitutional Congress. Now in one of his increasingly rare visits to Huntsville, Dex was briefing Guy on all the latest news. "Our expanding radius of managed sites has finally reached beyond the counter-front."

"Counter-front?" Guy asked. He had purposefully kept his distance from the day-to-day engagement and strategy. After all, he had just perfected his new dessert - a peach cobbler with vanilla bean ice cream. Someone had to keep the overall integrity of the place going. Their recipes were now being replicated across the land. It was a hell of a responsibility to get it all right.

"The aliens attacked by dropping a single creature in a lone place. Then as they replicated, they expanded in a ring until they encountered a natural termination point like a coastline. Along the way they left a lot more people behind than was originally thought. Now we understand why.

"The front would then start to move in the opposite direction like an echo. The aliens would slowly disperse their population along the way feeding on those that were left on the initial wave. Most of the people by that point gave little resistance so each creature was rewarded for its battle pay with herds and herds of easy feeding. It was like buffet night – all you can eat.

"As our efforts started out in Huntsville and grew out in a ring, we ended up chasing the front across the country. But at a certain point, their front ran into a coast, like at the tip of Florida, and while some small attaché might be sent to neighboring islands like Cuba, the majority of the front would echo back and spread out. Eventually our front of setting up restaurants and building containment areas would meet the counter-front."

"Sounds like it makes for a fun day," Guy said.

"Clearly you aren't getting this."

"Nor do I really want to, Dex."

"Look, as our front met with the counter-front, there are typically large battles. We don't always win at first. We have lost a lot of hunters when this occurs."

"Any chance of a counter-front reaching Huntsville?"

Dex was visibly a little miffed at his friend. He had expected maybe a little more compassion. But then again, it didn't really surprise him. Nothing surprised him anymore. "No, Guy. I don't think one will reach here."

"Good. Then I really need to be getting to work. I have a new dessert I am introducing and I want to…"

At that moment there was a loud explosion from outside. Guy looked at Dex in stunned silence. Then Dex asked, "What in the hell was that?"

He had no sooner gotten the words out of his mouth than there was another explosion - this one louder and shriller than the one before. Both of them jumped up and ran to the window.

The visage of twisted metal and human debris spanned out from the corner of the building across the parking lot. Wayne had selected these buildings because they were close together and provided pretty good security for his worldwide operations. Dex and Guy were using the adjacent Building 2 just to cut down on travel time. But Building 1 now looked like a rectangular block of cheese after a large rat had bitten off the base of one corner. Beneath the impossibly balanced and teetering remains of floors three through six were strewn typewriters, arms, computers components, legs, filing cabinets, and heads. They fanned out across the parking lot and side yard. People were streaming out of the main entrance in panicked globules.

"Shit!" Dex cried and Guy was already moving rapidly towards his own exit.

In a matter of moments, the pandemonium was in their face. Injured and yet mobile employees from Wayne's corporate headquarters were running hysterically around in circles, often colliding into each other. Meanwhile, not-so-mobile survivors were screaming and braying from the pabulum that was the exposed guts of Building 1.

Four solid hours everyone worked to wrench those that could live beyond their pain out of the twisted rubble. They saved the ones they could. No firemen would be coming. No ambulances would arrive with sirens blaring. Not even a staff doctor would be made available. The world was simply too immature for society to afford such luxuries.

By evening, the sanitation department (one of the few recovered albeit altered civic functions from the past) had ignited the pyres to clear out those that were not fortunate enough to have been spared. The flames were licking up as the ashen remains were scattered over the roof of Building 1 and carried by the winds out over the Parkway.

"Well, I'm numb," Dex said after pitching in as much as he could.

"I'm not numb enough," Guy measured. "Let's go tie one on."

"Can we cruise the main dining hall?" This was a newly developed euphemism used by Dex when he wanted female company for the night. There were still plenty of women in the world that were not addicted to the steaks. But the boys would not be looking for commitment or intelligent conversation tonight.

"Yeah, sure. We can pick up a nice Claret too.

The two best friends turned to head out when Dex stopped short. Guy kept on walking a few steps as he pontificated on the qualities of a fine Bordeaux when he suddenly realized he was walking alone. Turning around he saw the look of stunned shock on Dex's face. Dex's mouth was working but no sound was issuing forth until he finally formed words as he looked off in the distance behind Guy. "How did we miss that?"

Guy turned around and looked in the general direction Dex was pointing. There on the side entrance of Building 1 not ten feet away from the blast site on the corner were the large yellow spray-painted letters scrawling out the message:

Free them!
ALF

"Alf?" Guy asked.

"Not Alf. A.L.F. It's an acronym. This one I know from some of my pro bono work in Atlanta. The senior partners are always after you to rep some hack job for free to prop up the rancorous reputation of the firm. Usually it is some liberal activist group. ALF was the Animal Liberation Front. I had to defend a chick that caught a pet store on fire because they were caging the animals and not letting them roam free."

"Let me get this straight," Guy said, "They would kill the animals horribly by burning them to death just to teach the humans?"

"Not the animals. In this case they locked the manager and two clerks in the back room and set it on fire from the outside. They disconnected the sprinklers for the back room. Very neat, very sick."

"I bet she got the chair."

"Nope. She got off without so much as probation. It was easy back then to get those types off on technicalities."

"Huh," Guy grunted. He liked the present world much better. It all made so much more sense now. Then he continued, "But what would the Animal Liberation Front be doing bombing Wayne?"

"My bet is that the A doesn't stand for Animal," Dex postulated.

"We have made great strides, Wayne."

"Excellent," Wayne Avarice said puffing on a cigar and gazing out of his luxurious DC office which overlooked the finer monuments on the mall. The news of the bombing in Huntsville had not yet reached him and in his blissful ignorance the heads of government were now briefing him on the latest news from the hill. "How do we stand on the defense, Senator Applegate?"

"Well, we have most of the protection acts passed. Of course there is no opposition or minority party any more. We are all one big machine now, quite content on passing legislation for the better good of all humanity. We should be able to have the remaining restaurant liability matters closed to your favor within the quarter."

"Wonderful!" Wayne nearly shouted with pomp and arrogance as he spun around the corner of his desk, allowing the trail of his cigar to swirl. He walked past the congressmen in their chairs as he asked without looking, "And what of the offence, Speaker Parsons?"

The Speaker of the House looked over the clipboard in his lap, a satisfied puff to his smile, "Well, as we expand the franchises to new regions we are seeing a nice natural balance being struck. About half the population have become patrons and the other half are now associates. Further, the Judge's Judicial Reformation Act has decreased prison population for certain segments by as much as thirty percent."

"Thirty percent?" Wayne asked around his cigar butt, a mocking surprise dripped from his southern drawl.

"Thirty percent." Speaker Parsons answered with emphatic confidence.

Looking out a different window, Wayne Avarice stuck his thumbs in the small coin pockets of his tailored suit and said in a smaller voice as if to himself, "Thirty percent. Can you imagine that?"

"There is one small problem with that success though," Senator Applegate interrupted. "With such a decline of death row inmates, we fear there may be a shortage."

Wayne looked unconcerned. He suggested, "Just lower the bar a little. Let's make the minimum crime for being introduced to the containment areas Felony One."

Here Parsons chimed in adjusting his body in the rich crimson leather chair, "We already have that measure in the works. But even that will not be enough."

"How so?" Wayne asked incredulously.

"Well, the number of Felony One criminals and up *is* a high number," Parsons conceded, "But it is still finite in nature. So eventually we will run out. And our criminal justice system isn't what one would call completely intact. And then lastly, the steak does have a calming impact on our patrons.

No crimes of any kind have been reported by any of those that consume the steak. So your supply for more criminals has all but been cut off."

Wayne was tired of thinking. "Ok, so what do you suggest?"

"Well, it makes sense to us that those who consume need to maybe give a little something back to the society that lives to supply for their happiness."

"Sounds reasonable. But how can they help?"

"We will begin social programs to help with controlling population growth in the new world. We don't want to grow too quickly. That would jeopardize their ability to attain the steak. And no one wants that."

"Not at all," Wayne agreed.

"So a certain percentage, and we are still working on the exact amount, but a certain percentage of new births will go into the young hunter's club. The state will raise them up and prepare them for the one day when they will sacrifice themselves for the greater good of society."

"You mean kind of like the terrorist organizations used to do with some of their children?"

"Why not? It made sense to them. It will supply our needs now. We will just promise them paradise in the afterlife."

"As long as we can keep profitable. Ultimately every organization has to make the occasional sacrifice in order to remain profitable. Hell, even Microsoft had to give in some to the feds in order to maintain what we could never describe legally as a monopoly – wink, wink."

The two congressmen laughed at the obvious jest. They were both relieved that the worst of their plans had been revealed and that it had been apparently accepted and even green-lighted by the boss. Wayne finished up by asking, "Is that the full report?"

"Well, there is one more thing," Parsons stated from the bottom of his check list.

Wayne turned, cigar smoke twisting around his glowing face, "Well tell me. I want to hear it all."

"We have set up the rights and ownership laws to license the franchise overseas. You will naturally get a cut as will our continental treasury for North America."

Wayne heard the word. He didn't really believe it, but there it was in green and white for all to hear. "Did you say treasury?"

"I did."

"Then you guys have been busy. What is it based on? What is the solid commodity you selected?"

"The supporting base is gold, naturally. We have been getting plenty as we added it to the bartering menus for all the restaurants. People are more than happy to donate their wedding jewelry, family heirlooms, even coins and ingots in some rare cases – all of it for the cause of liberty and freedom."

"How very patriotic. Makes me proud that the common man would be so willing to sacrifice for our unified visions for Avarice."

"The planet will be in good shape, no doubt."

"But if gold is supporting, what is the prime?"

A curl formed at the corner of the Speaker's smile. He sardonically intoned, "Why, the rub of course."

Wayne's face became flush with anger as he ripped the cigar from his lips squeezing it in the vice of his two fingers as he growled, "What?"

Parsons looked shocked, taken aback. He gasped at the air like a largemouth bass half out of the water, "But we, I, I mean, er…"

"You based our currency on a product we don't own outright in the clear?"

The Senator stepped in as a calming force. Parsons was still relatively young and this delicate situation needed the practiced persuasion of a more senior partner. "Wayne, calm down a moment and let me explain."

Wayne took a deep breath and stubbed his cigar back in his mouth, chomping down hard in a sign that he would listen. He wasn't going to like it much, but he would listen.

"We can't barter forever. But to the rest of the world, your six more market expansions, gold just doesn't hold much value. The aliens have rampaged completely and the counter-fronts are now surging back across the landscape like the mouth of a river at high tide. We need to act fast while there is still market viability."

"Yes I see."

"And if we approach the future franchises with gold, they will laugh at us. But once we send in our advance teams of hunters and chefs, it will just take one look. Just one look at the potential will have them eating out of your hands. During that age of expansion, the single most prized element on the planet Avarice will be our dear friend Chef Guy's spices. It will be the single standard *at first*."

Still not happy about it, Wayne grumped, "Yes I see."

"Then, since we are backing it with gold, when we reach expansion saturation we will drop it back and swap them. By that point the expansion will be waning and you will have stockpiled the majority of the gold."

"Yes I see."

"Of course, it will be important to leave sufficient coffers of gold in the possession of the other six continents. But only enough to arrange for market stability."

Wayne allowed a moment to pass. He liked the sense of power that he got from anger. These two were arguably the most powerful men in the world and they were groveling at his feet just because he started to bust a gasket. This was power. This was gravitas.

"I still don't like it. We are basically making Chef Guy the most powerful man in the world."

"For a season. What is the old Latin expression? Gloria brevis?

Wayne pulled his cigar out of his mouth. He watched the stump burning down and imagined it to be Guy Sayonara's lifeline. He smiled as he translated the Latin, "Glory is fleeting."

He turned back around and walked quickly back to his desk as he asked, "What does the law state will happen to the Rub Rights should Chef Guy meet with an untimely demise?"

"They would go to the CEO."

"Dex," Wayne said under his breath.

"And then to you," Parsons added. "As the majority shareholder in the Spicing Company, that honor would revert to you should anything ever happen to the President *and* the CEO."

"Then all I have to do is decipher the recipe and find myself a really big…"

"Bomb." A different voice finished his sentence as a strange man with a bad toupee walked into the office and right across to the bar. Much to the shock of the two congressmen, the stranger began pouring a drink without invite. The looks of indignation could cut like knives had the stranger cared.

Wayne smiled. He saw the way this newcomer affected his company and liked it. "Gentlemen, allow me to introduce James Navarone."

21.

The two congressmen stared at the intruder and then traded uneasy glances. Senator Applegate stammered, "Wayne, if you will excuse us a moment, I need to verify that a tiny detail made it into the latest legislation while you and Mr. umm, ah…"

"Navarone, James Navarone," the newcomer reminded as he thrust his hand out to shake. The two congressmen introduced themselves and then excused themselves. In a flash they were out in the rich dark hardwood halls illuminated by golden incandescent light from the ornate sconces that adorned the panels. These kinds of surroundings have been taken for granted by these kinds of men for centuries.

"What in the hell is that little pipsqueak doing here?" Applegate demanded.

"I'm not sure," answered Parsons. "I had heard that he was back in town, but for the life of me I can't figure the angle."

"Look, James Navarone is only the most crooked and sinister arms salesmen on Earth…"

"Avarice," Parsons correctly.

"Avarice, right," Applegate allowed. "All of the foreign governments around the globe have bloody well collapsed. We have no allies. We have no enemies. If we wanted to, we could just take over the whole damned shoot-and-match. How could the likes of Navarone fit in around here?"

Parsons thought for a moment, finger to his lips in a pensive state of shhh. "Well, one thing we know – if *you* don't know, and *I* don't know, we sure as hell won't find out if we stay out here while he meets with our boss."

"A good point, my dear man. Shall we ingress?"

"Let us."

The two went back into Wayne's office where they found Mr. Navarone now sitting in one of the two chairs they vacated. Neither he nor Wayne gave any appearance that they were getting up any time soon. By seniority, the Senator took the remaining open seat forcing Parsons to find another, smaller chair nearby and pull it to the side of the power circle.

Navarone smiled at this.

"So we will have our nukes in place and operational by year's end?" Wayne was asking.

"Probably sooner, but that is a safe bet."

"Nukes? What nukes?" demanded Senator Applegate.

"Why our own nukes, our old ones of course," patronized Navarone.

"We are buying our own nukes from ourselves?" questioned Parsons.

"No, you are buying your new nukes from me. I possess them after the old planetary governments fell."

"Possess them?" decried Applegate, "You can't possess something that isn't yours! What impudence."

"Possession is nine-tenths Senator. And I will be happy to concede ownership back to you if you can either come up with a receipt or a set of control panels. You see, I have the motherboards. And unless you can get IBM or General Dynamics on the horn and order some more of those puppies, then what you own is a bunch of metal and worthless components."

"Gentlemen, there is no need for heated debate or posturing. We are all one big happy family." Wayne first scolded and then encouraged – which was his way.

"But what part could a weapon's salesman possibly play in the new republic?" Parsons asked.

Wayne sat back in his chair and spun a bit to the side. In a reflective tone he spoke, "We are expanding into new markets, right? And when you make a global move, you have to consider security. Protecting ourselves becomes a priority.

"But we can't just stop there. New markets must *feel* safe in order to invest and expand. We will teach them how to conquer and control the alien threat. And they will be motivated by profit potential. That much of the world is universal and unchanged. Man conquers his own fears and possesses them, controls them, only when he sees the ability for profit in it. That has been our story down through the ages.

"So our customers, our green-fields must in and of themselves feel secure from their neighbors." Here Wayne stood and began pacing around the room as he sermonized, "There was once a sociological experiment performed in Colorado I think it was - out in the planes east of Denver, wide open spaces and all that. They purchased dozens, hundreds of toys that were the most popular of the day and placed them in a field with no trees, nothing on the horizon but wide open grassland. Then they introduced a class of thirty bright young children to the environment. After about ten minutes they all settled down and began talking quietly as they pushed and poked lethargically at a few of the toys.

"Then the test team erected a fence around the play area. A secure containment area that was highly visible and tangible. They then introduced the control set of another group of children equal in demographic in every way. This time, the children understood their boundaries and that they were secure, spent hours ripping and running and playing and most importantly being contented little children.

"What we learn from that exercise is that man needs boundaries, whether real or imagined, and that man needs to feel secure, whether real or imagined in order to thrive and grow.

"Therefore, our friend Navarone will supply us with working, and *real* nukes to make us secure. And then he will supply each of our franchise continents with nukes that appear to be working and real so that they can imagine that they are secure."

There was a moment where the two congressmen were still skeptics, scowling and waiting for all this to make sense. But then as the last of Wayne's words landed like seed on fertile ground they began to see the perspicuity of it all. Their growing smiles were echoed and amplified by those of Wayne and Navarone.

"And in conclusion, for every sale, real or imagined, that Mr. Navarone makes, we will all get a nice, juicy, generous cut. And that, gentlemen, I assure you will *not* be imagined."

Just then the door slammed open. One of Wayne Avarice's managers came barging in. Excitedly he virtually screamed, "Sir, there's a problem in Huntsville. Your headquarters has been bombed."

It's funny how the reception of sudden and stunning news has a tendency to have the same temporal effect as a physical bomb. The explosion is fueled by emotions. The fragments and shrapnel are nerves and stress. The residual effect is a wave of shock and awe and exhaustion. In the following moments, the four men lived through such an explosion, full of sound and fury as if the blast had taken place in that very spot. As Wayne, the Senator, and the Speaker each went through the five stages of acceptance nobody noticed that James Navarone had been smiling through the entire thing.

Over the coming weeks, the explosions continued. Five of the six remaining continents were contacted with emissaries, teams known as F.A.s (Franchise Ambassadors). Wayne held off on Antarctica. He doubted anyone was left alive there. All the population lived in little clusters like small nomadic villages – he had seen that on a science special once. If the aliens had even attacked there, the few people in each remote camp would have probably supplied just enough sustenance to subsist. They would leave no survivors.

Therefore, franchises were begun in Europe, Asia, Africa, Australia, and South America. As they continued to perfect their craft, the re-colonization of restaurants along with the construction of the containment areas expanded rapidly. And right along with this growth came the ever increasing incidents from the Alien Liberation Front.

Alfred Foreman sat in the makeshift office that used to be the utility room off of his carport. Vera had just poured him a fresh cup of morning coffee as he studied over the new contracts that lay before him. Stamped across the top of the papers was the now all-to-familiar logo of the "New Republic of North America" and then below that was the secondary title of "Avarice Food Corps Services".

By a simple twist of fate, he and Vera had left town just a matter of days before the aliens arrived. They had taken what was left in their savings out of the bank, converted some of it into gold, and then headed out to a lake cabin in the middle of Southwest Bumblefuck. It was a getaway, one they had shared since their crooning days.

Alfred had unplugged the TV so that his wife would not worry so and the two of them spent their days walking on the shore, sharing old memories, and making love. The manager of the lake stopped coming around to collect rent on the secluded cabin. They later found out that an alien had eaten him.

Sometime after that local supplies started dwindling and they needed to go home or die there. They weren't sure what would be waiting for them back Ft. Wayne. They were both surprised to see how relatively intact the city was. Typically in the movies all of the buildings are reduced to burning rubble as bands of friends and foes dash back and forth to hide from crossfire and explosions. But not in Ft. Wayne. The city looked normal save for the thousands of rotting corpses. The traffic lights were even still working – winking harmlessly at the headless multitude lining the streets as if to tell them it's OK to walk now.

Since theirs appeared to be the only vehicle moving on that particular day, it was easy for Krista of the FA team to spot them. The blond woman approached with a group of five or so in tow and after introducing herself as the representative of the new government explained that they were looking for wealthy businessmen in the area. Alfred Foreman did something for maybe the first time in his life.

He lied.

Reaching back into his car, he pulled out the small satchel of gold from the back seat and said, "This is my driving around spending money." He pulled out one of the three ingots that represented his entire life's savings without any hope for pension or insurance and gave it to Krista asking, "Is this enough to prove my intentions in earnest?"

Krista took the gold, wrote out a receipt for what she called an initial investment, and handed Alfred a stack of papers. "Please go over these. We will be contacting you soon as we make our way back through. It should only be a week to ten days, but if you onboard with us, then we can help you get your first franchise up and running and from there the sky's the limits!"

Alfred was smiling ear to ear as he took the papers. To seal the deal, he grasped her petite little hand in his massive paw and shook. The warmth of the years communicated his sincerity. Krista smiled and waved goodbye to him and Vera, who was standing on the other side of the car.

Vera had been upset at first. "I don't understand why you just gave away one third of our life's work to that carpetbagger. You might as well kiss that money goodbye."

But she had calmed down some when Alfred re-assured her, "Honey, we were coming back home to lay down and die. There was no hope left in it for us. Look around at all the dead. And then here is this lady, all shiny and spiffy, walking up to me asking for local businessmen. You know how my bosses got to be bosses in the first place? They had to have the balls to do what I just done. And for some of them it paid off. If she takes us, and robs my money, all it did was give my last few days on this here Earth a little less despair and a little more hope. Even false hope is better than none at all. But if'n she's true, then you are looking at Mr. Ground-floor, baby!"

And with this he clapped his hands and did a little spin before getting back into the car.

Now a good ten days later, Alfred Foreman was reading through the well-worn contracts for the fifteenth time. Some of the pages were dog-eared and others scratched up with highlighter marks and penciled words in the margins. It all had made sense to him. He would have to see what the advance team could do to bolster his trust. He would have to see a bonafied kill and see for himself the effects of the steak. But he had seen enough in the documents to risk another ingot or two.

He would just play his cards real close to the vest and see how long he could run them until they discovered that it was all he had left in the world to his name. Krista had already contacted them two days earlier by an advance person and Alfred expected her to knock at any moment.

As if on cue with his thoughts, there was a knock at the door. Alfred shot an excited look across the kitchen to Vera and she smiled as she quickly waved for him to scoot. He got up from his makeshift desk of ten days and walked with purpose to the front door. He opened it to find a different young lady there. She was just as pretty and about the same age as Krista, but different nonetheless. His heart sank a bit. He guessed there had been a delay, or worse, they had found him out to be a liar.

"Mr. Foreman?"

"Yes?"

"I am Kallie Sayonara of the Alien Liberation Front. We understand that you are considering becoming a franchise holder."

"I suppose so. Did you say Alien Libation…"

"Alien Liberation Front. We fight for the rights of all captured and mistreated creatures around the planet. Do you realize that Mr. Avarice's scheme includes the rounding up, capturing and torturing of God's creatures Mr. Foreman?"

Alfred looked up and down the street at the remains of his neighbors – most had had the decency to fight the aliens in the streets. At least the yards were relatively tidy. He said, "Considering the carnage that God's creatures unleashed on me and mine, I would say that they have it coming a little."

"Mr. Foreman, we have to turn the other cheek. If we seek retribution or even worse, exploitation of them, then we are no better than they."

"Well, as long as I recuperate my pension and then a little, I guess I don't really care much for how the universe will look upon my actions. If you want to lecture me on karma little girl, then you need to realize that I am the instrument for paying *back* right now. Someone else is reaping what has already been sowed on to me. That merry-go-round comes back on you too, you know. Sometimes your actions of selfishness might just be paying someone else back for some wrong they have done. Who am I to argue with universal justice?"

Kallie looked a little miffed. She had that look like the young bicycle missionaries do when they come to a Southern Baptist preacher's house by mistake and try to tell him what is wrong with the condition of his soul. Often times they end up leaving a little less certain of their own condition. "But Mr. Foreman," she said, re-gathering her fortitude, "we are adamant about our position. We have seen the containment areas and what they are doing to humans there…"

"Humans? You mean convicted murderers and felons. Rapists and thugs," he corrected.

"Humans. Humans that can be easily reformed and help us rebuild the Earth."

"You mean Avarice, right?"

With an even more severe determination she gritted her teeth and speaking through the clinch restated, "The Earth. I said exactly what I meant." At this she looked down the street. Krista's convoy of shiny black military vehicles was approaching. Looking back at Alfred she continued, "And here comes the proof. You want to see how committed we are to our cause? Well here," she said as she raised her right hand. There was a black device with a switch in her palm and her thumb was reaching over it. "Here is your proof Mr. Foreman."

She waited a few more seconds – time enough for the caravan to pull right up in front of the house, time enough for Alfred to figure out what was about to happen. He shouted "No!" and before the word was half stated, the switch on the device went click and the lead car went boom just as Krista was climbing out. The explosion was intense and the shock nearly knocked him backward. But the young petite lady holding the trigger was standing firm, watching the fireball consuming all the people in the car with a wide smile and a blank dazed look in her eyes.

People started filing out of the cars behind the lead and that is when Alfred saw them for the first time. There were a dozen or so young activists in his side yard and driveway now having sprung out from behind hedges and trees. Their automatic weapons started firing and the rest of the people in the convoy fell to the ground as soon as the leveraging force of the riddling bullets could no longer hold their jerking corpses aloft. When the tiny clicks and rapid pops were finished, nearly sixteen people lay strewn across his once tidy front yard.

Kallie turned back around to Alfred and asked, "Do we have a deal?"

"Leave my property. You will get no more trouble from me."

Contented Kallie called for her troops and left.

Alfred waited until they were gone as best as he could tell. Then he went out front and put out the remaining fire with his garden hose. It was just contained to the lead and second vehicle and he smothered the flames before the second one could explode. Then he went back to the third vehicle and found what he was looking for. It looked like a cell phone only a little more substantial.

He took the heavy portable phone back into his house and pushed the only speed dial number programmed in. The voice on the other side answered, "Avarice headquarters, how may I direct your call?"

He recalled the name from the contracts, a Mr. Tim Parsons, director of franchise development and first cousin to the Speaker of the House. He replied, "Mr. Tim Parsons, please."

"Certainly, one moment."

About a minute later there was a click followed with a "Tim Parsons."

"Mr. Parsons, this is Alfred Foreman of Ft. Wayne."

"Yes, I remember your name from the advance prospect list. How are you Mr. Foreman?"

"Well, I am pretty upset at the moment. Is this the way you run a business?" His voice was beginning to expose a certain anger in the edge. Vera came up from behind asking him to calm down and remember his blood pressure. He waved her off in frustration and hoped that she would understand that he was playing poker here - high stakes poker.

"Why what do you mean, Mr. Parsons?"

"Well, Krista showed up a while ago. We finished the deal and she said that everything was in order. She would process the paperwork tonight and order in Phase One development with a standard detail of hunters, chefs, and security right away. We even picked the perfect spot downtown, not far from my house."

"Excellent! Welcome aboard. So it sounds like it went well for you and that you measured up to all of our basic minimum requirements."

"Yes, we handled all of the business-side of things and her team was packing up to leave when these crazy people claiming to be from the Alien Lusitanian Forum or something came bursting out from out of nowhere and killed everyone from your company. The whole damn lot of them."

"Holy shit!" proclaimed Mr. Parsons. "Were there any survivors?"

"No. And then the ALF people ransacked all the vehicles and stole everything. Even the funds they were carrying from previous deals. But especially mine."

Alfred waited a moment for effect and then added, "I don't intend to pay those funds again. I expect that me and all the other franchise owners will expect you to keep your end of the bargain."

"Oh, don't you worry about a thing. We will guarantee your satisfaction. Don't give the down-payment a second thought. We will have you in business within a week or two. But is everyone else ok on your end?"

"Sure. Everyone is fine. I look forward to seeing your Phase One team soon. Thank you."

"Thank you Mr. Foreman. We will send extra security your way, but the ALF doesn't usually double back. They are traveling bands and usually make only one hit and run in an area such as yours."

"Get them here soon. My company will be nervous about this."

"Yes sir. Consider it done."

He hung up the phone and breathed a sigh of relief. Vera hit him over the head with a dish rag, "Company? What company? Alfred you ain't got no company."

"I do now. You are looking at the first franchise owner in all of Indiana. And you are my first employee. As long as we have a boss," he pointed at himself, "and an employee," he pointed at her, "Then we's gots a company."

She hit him with the rag again and as he recoiled she said, "There's something wrong with your finger. It must have gotten broke in the explosion. It's pointing all wrong."

They both laughed and hugged, and then began cleaning up the mess around their house as best they could.

By the end of the month, the ALF's influence had become so disruptive that congress voted through legislation making membership, assistance, or participation in ALF in any form a Class One felony. For the first time since the alien invasion there was work to be done for the criminal justice branch of the government.

By the end of the quarter, ALF members were starting to appear in the containment areas with a gun and four bullets. Many of them refused to fire choosing to spare the aliens and becoming a sacrificial lamb for them. Some however chose to fire in self-defense creating more aliens for slaughter and then ironically finding the same fate.

22.

"… and *that* is how it is done, ladies and gentlemen."

There was a smattering of applause as yet another group of chefs in various styles of white outfits and silly hats watched on as the one and only Chef Guy finished frying up another flank of alien steak. Guy had learned to hate these sessions. Wayne had called them "Train the Trainers" classes. Franchises from around the globe were merging, forming conglomerates. They would then send one or two of their very best chefs to Huntsville, Alabama – the new culinary Mecca of the universe, to study from the one and only Father of Modern Cookery.

These trainers would then return to their countries of origin to take on the mantle of a Disciple of Guy and in turn train all of the other chefs in that particular syndicate. In some cases the systems were so large that the returning disciples would then hold their own Train the Trainer sessions. But regardless of their constituency base size, these that actually got to spend an evening with the great Guy Sayonara in his own kitchen became little more than groupies for the experience.

"Have you ever tried varying the heat during the cooking process?" one chef asked. Guy looked at his nametag. He recognized the name from college. It was a world renowned chef from France. For a moment Guy thought through all the complexities of answers he could have provided. This man was a legend after all. If this had been four years earlier he would have loved just sitting over a cup of Earl Grey and debating the finer points of temperature control with this legend.

But as the world stood at this moment in time he was the greatest chef in the all of everything. His mind turned over the word, *"France"*. What did France know about cooking? After all, they were basically a bunch of conflicted, neurotic, paranoid elitists that would bicker and fight for hours with one another internally about the correct degree to poach an egg. But let one person from any other country step into the mix and they would band together instantly to denounce the foreigner as an ignorant ponce, a dimwitted neophyte twit that would not know the difference between sweetmeats and their asshole. Then after the intruder left, they would reach the near point of violence over the definition of the word *"twit"*.

It was like the Arab Muslims say, "Me and my brother against our cousin. Us and our cousins against a stranger."

"French — fah!" Guys thoughts spun. *"What do they know other than snobbery and infighting?"* He realized that this was his moment. In front of the most influential cooks in the world, he could once and for all settle the score that the French did not have the market cornered where it came to preparing fine food. If his retort was sharp and his aim was true, he could bring down this paragon to the monolithic emblem that was French Cuisine. And why not? He had brought down bigger and badder before hadn't he?

Guy began shaping his reply into a wrought iron fence with poniards sticking up. He realized that the French chef's questions had been the pebbles on the patio. His own question would be the slippery stones that would bring about his demise. In the seconds that ensued, Guy finished formulating the perfect stinging and rapier retort (or would that be re-torte?). At last he had the perfect answer. Summoning all his strength and drawing in his breath as he constituted his mental stance, he unleashed his reply.

"No."

Ok, so Guy was still pretty much a numb-nutted twonk.

To be honest, he really didn't see himself as much more than a paper tiger. He had lucked into killing an alien — watching it have a mortal accident is more like it. He had lucked into finding the flanks, little more than the insane butchery by a man half out of his mind with apathy (ok, actually probably more like full out of his mind with apathy. He might have been able to get a better measurement had he cared a little more about it). He had lucked into using some failed concoction from his failed college days. And he had lucked into the fact that the alien meat had an addictive quality to it and created for the consumer a pleasant and desired euphoria.

Maybe it was all luck. Maybe he didn't deserve becoming the most powerful man in all of Avarice. He now waited for the French chef to parry his lame excuse for a lunge and riposte back with a fatal lash. He imagined he had it coming. Here he had been given the perfect opportunity to level the culinary score on a global scale and the best come back he had been able to muster was "no". Guy braced himself as he now fully expected the great chef to rip his mask off and expose him as the fraud that he was to the whole world.

The French chef looked measured in his thoughts and at long last spoke. The room was silent and taut with anticipation. "No. I don't imagine you would need to vary the temperature. I mean, why monkey with perfection?"

The room agreed in quiet nods and smiles.

Guy guessed that the French chef for all his fame and fortune, deep down may have been a loser as well. Maybe he had lucked into an old cookbook and had simply followed the recipes on the boxes of instant mixes himself. The damned cheesecake chimmichangas taste a whole lot better when you thought they were the masterful and imaginative original work of the folks in white behind the swinging door. It is always such a letdown when you learned that they come by the carton from a mass-marketing food company every morning via cooler truck.

"Have you tried variations in your spice?" another chef asked. This one had the halted, slightly altered English accent that one would expect from some parts India.

"We avoid such variations. I believe others have tried it and the meat has proven to be fatal if consumed. We stick to the safe, tried and true here in our kitchen."

All the chefs smiled.

"Were you frightened when you faced the first kill alone?" This time the question had come from the spunky blonde that had been leaning into the brunette next to her the entire presentation, whispering and sharing smiles as Guy worked on the entrée.

He had seen their kind before. He had actually enjoyed it the first few times. He and Dex would troll for junkies, cruising the main dining hall as it were. It was good for sexual relief and the junkies worked exceptionally hard at making sure they both had a wild and satisfying time. But after a few months the meaningless, passionless eruptions worked actually to heighten their sense of being unfulfilled rather than to bring any warmth to their lives.

They had money. They had power. And they had an endless supply of pleasure. But after months and months of it, the ability to be slaked became the elusive brass ring – always just out of reach.

Then the Train the Trainers began. In every class there would be about half women. They were exotic and furtive women, always intelligent and coming across as genuine. Here Guy and Dex thought that they had found it. Here were women not controlled by the rub. They thought that seducing such would be a greater challenge and thereby bring with it the greater satisfaction. Having sex with someone with an equal interest and desire, and more importantly freedom of choice was expected to fill the growing emptiness in both of them.

Dex thought it was interesting that they were even aware of the void. He asked, "Could that mean that in some remote way, we may actually be starting to care?"

Guy had quickly dismissed this notion and the two of them continued with the orgy of that particular night. But the women in the Train the Trainers meetings had the propensity to be different. In free will they hoped to find their hope.

In the end though, it just turned out to be a cruel joke by an even crueler universe. The brass ring, just on the tips of their fingers, moved impossibly further out of reach as they realized that the visiting chefs were nothing more than groupies looking for a one-night stand. They wanted nothing more than to return home with a notch in their purse strap – but most importantly they wanted to return home. There were boyfriends, husbands and even girlfriends waiting there. For them, that was *their* brass ring. They had compassion and passion waiting there for them. For them, Guy and Dex were the excursion.

And their sex was not nearly as driven as the junkies. With the exuberance of the stolen forbidden fruit they could go maybe longer than the average afternoon delight. But in the end they had nowhere near the staying power as someone hopped up on the meat. So to Guy and Dex, they were twice as bad. Oh it was novel at first – having intercourse with someone alert and fully conscious. But when all was said and done, the word propensity is far too close to the word potential.

"No. I was not frightened," Guy answered the blond.

"Veronica and I think that you are ever so brave." This of course was followed by giggles from the two of them. Guy was not surprised. They always giggled.

"Thank you. Are there any more questions?"

Guy had learned in one of his management courses while working for the DOD that asking this question is a mistake. Peer pressure is a real thing. At the end of a meeting, all everyone really wants to do is leave and get on with their work or their lives or whatever it is that they want to get on with. The main point is that they desire to *get on*. When the leader of such a meeting asks if there are any more questions, what they are really perceived as saying is, "If anyone asks a question it will prevent the rest of us from leaving – and you don't really want to do that now, do you?"

So managers, good managers are taught to ask the question in this way, "Ok, we will end the meeting and get on with our own stuff as soon as I get three really good questions." This then uses peer pressure in a reverse way to accomplish what the leader really wants, which is good questions.

But tonight Guy did not want to be a good leader. He did not want to get any good questions. He wanted to draw the session to a close as quickly as possible and get on with his own stuff, which for him was to wallow in an ever increasing pool of self-pity and doubt.

No one asked any questions. And so the sociological construct proved accurate once again. The class dispersed and everyone began the arduous task of getting on with their own stuff. As the kitchen cleared, Guy began to pack up his case. Dex was watching from the shadows just past the staging area. He occasionally dropped by, particularly when he was in the mood for trolling.

It had been a gift from Wayne Avarice, the kit, when they formally moved into Europe. The case was somewhere between the size of a briefcase and a proper suitcase and housed custom utensils: spatulas, knives, graters, peelers, etc. All were gold, all were perfectly balanced, and all fit neatly in their own custom space inside the case.

Guy would rarely use them, opting instead for the regular set in his kitchen most of the time. It was a chore to hand-clean and dry the show utensils after every use before they went back into the case. But he would bring them out for the training sessions.

Chicks dig a gold spatula.

Usually the process of putting the kit back together would allow those students that actually did have a question but were driven to social submission by peer pressure not to ask it, a chance to ask their question without keeping everyone else from getting on. Tonight was no exception. The blond and Veronica came up to the prep table where Guy was putting up his now clean tools.

"Nice spatula."

"Thank you."

"Is it gold?"

Guy held up the spatula while wiping it dry with a dish rag. Looking as if he were inspecting it more closely he said, "Yes. I believe it is."

"Wow. A gold spatula."

With some degree of disappointment that this was yet another groupie, Guy's returning apathy was readily apparent as he said, "Yeah. Wow."

"I'm Penny. This is Veronica."

"So I gathered," Guy said looking at her nametag.

"Do you ever do anything after the training session? I mean, what are the hot spots in Huntsville?"

Guy just stood there enjoying the built-in comedy of the question. Even before the alien invasion, Huntsville was not really known as a great place for nightlife. There had been the odd nightclub. Some had live music but others were known as little more than meat markets. A curl formed at the corner of his smile as he now thought about the irony.

"I would imagine the hottest spot in Huntsville might be in your hotel room this evening."

Both girls giggled a little.

"I know I will probably be envious while I am at home. But I am sure that you two will find something to get on with."

Immediately the two girls looked crest-fallen. Guy packed up his case and excused himself as he left them befuddled and dumbstruck with his rejection.

The kitchen door to the outside world swung wide, exposing the ink beyond. And then, just as quickly, it shut. The girls turned to Dex, the only one remaining other than the kitchen staff. He shrugged and smiled. Then he bolted for the door leaving them to whatever lay in store for the both of them.

As his eyes adjusted to the darkness and his skin to the cool autumn air, he walked up to Guy who was placing his case in the passenger seat of his Mercedes. "Wow. That was sharp."

"Harsh?"

"Maybe a little," Dex said.

"Well, I just didn't feel like company."

"Well, I did."

Guy laughed a little. Looking back up from his case, he slammed the door on the passenger side and began walking around the front of his car and to the driver's side. Opening the door there he looked back at his old friend and said, "Well, I would say that the buffet has two different choices for your dining pleasure tonight, Fried Junkie, or a Chef Sandwich. Both come with or without sauce."

"Very funny. Ha ha." Dex said sardonically.

"Look Dex. I'm tired. If you want to have fun, go have fun."

"Alright, alright," Dex said in an apologetic tone, "I get your drift. Take off and swim in your own juices."

"What's that supposed to mean?" Guy's temper flaring a little as his words spoke plumes of moisture vapor into the chilling air.

"Nothing," Dex dismissed.

Closing his door as a visible cue that the conversation was *not* over Guy said, "It's not nothing. What's eating you?"

"What's eating me? What's eating you?"

Guy stood without speaking.

"I mean, you are this great guy. You are the most famous chef in the world. You are the most powerful man in all of Avarice, all that shit. And you're what? Afraid of living it up a little?"

"A little? Dex, you and I have been partying like we were sophomores for nearly half a year now. Straight! No breaks!"

"So?"

"So?!" Guy shouted. "So what are we supposed to do? Carry on with meaningless sex and drinking, snorting, popping and toking until when, Dex? Until they perfect the replication of my rub? Until they come and kill us both?" Now walking over to his friend he placed his hands on Dex's shoulders and asked, "What are you hoping for Dex? Are you hoping they at least wait for you to cum before they blow your brains out?"

"*If* they kill us, then they kill us. And that is a pretty big if. But what else is there Guy? This is a new era. What else is there to live for?"

"Are you trying to tell me that sex is the meaning of life?"

"And what if I am? What if hedonism is the only purpose we have left? It's a damn site better than not having a purpose at all. Not having a purpose in life may be the biggest, scariest monster living under your bed, Guy."

Guy was momentarily stunned. His arms dropped to his side. He had never really thought of that before. He started to reel a little as he began to contemplate that what he had mistaken for purpose may in fact actually be a string of unrelated and lucky events. Was the root of his emptiness really simply a lack of purpose?

His mind began combing through all the things that made up Guy Sayonara, testing each one, holding it up in the light of discovery and asking the question, is this a purpose? While it continued on this track he said, "Look. I'm tired. That's all. I need a night off to recharge."

Dex looked a little less worried at this. All Dex wanted to do was to ride out the end of the universe without slipping off the crest of the wave. He was hanging ten and didn't want to wipe, let alone slip off the back in the impotence of a night off. For Dex it had been balls to the wall as long as his buddy was along for the ride. But now he was seeing that Guy would not apply guilt if he went on surfing solo for the night. And now his own internal turmoil was giving him permission to fly alone knowing that Guy would be ok. He was just taking the night off.

"I will be fine, Dex. You go back in and make sure that Penny and Veronica have a good evening."

"Fuck the foreigners," Dex said dryly.

"I thought that was the idea," Guy chided.

Dex shot him a perturbed look. "No, I mean I think I want some junkie ass tonight."

"Suit yourself," Guy said as he got into his Mercedes and drove away.

He drove up Monte Sano Mountain where he now lived. The mountain had remained relatively pristine for eons and millennia. In the antebellum days, a rich surgeon had built a single mansion at the very top. It eventually became a museum. Erecting a cross was his one penance for defacing the small speck of land nestled in the mammoth green giant that watched over the quiet little town from the east like a comforting sentinel of the sunrise. The amazingly tall and blazingly white Christian symbol was erected in a time ignorant of political correctness. Throughout the fifties, sixties, and seventies the city woke up in its shadow – an emblem that there was something permanent, something fixed in this life.

But the eighties brought with its greed and decadence two important changes. One was an encroaching canopy of growth from neighboring trees hiding all but the very top of the three story cross from view by the town's people below. The other was the profit to be gained by developing the side of the mountain which far outweighed any feeling of environmental or civic responsibility. There was enough gold to be made from them-there hills to easily compensate for the huge hassle of taking on the then maturing hippies who were busy themselves building the framework of their own big chill as they now enjoined the very machine they had railed and brawled against for nearly two decades just so they could drive their SUVs to their children's soccer matches. Their bumper stickers, yard signs, and occasional letters to the editor were little more than lip service to their ideals and were easily mowed over by the bulldozers on their way up Governor's Drive to the surveyed lots hungry for the upper class.

Now pulling into the huge mansion overlooking the twinkling lights of the valley city that stretched out below, he passed the sign he kept in the yard so that he could at least maintain a firm grip on the ironic. The green sign was adorned with white printed letters that said, "Save our Slopes".

He pulled into the archway that separated the front yard from the auto yard and the six car garage. The limestone and brick manor door glided open as he slid inside, the silver body of the Mercedes reflecting the brilliant light from within. In a matter of an hour or so he was showered and changed.

He spent a couple of hours at his communication center. He had insisted that it be built here in his home. Guy could have better control over the access here. But even then he did not fool himself into believing that every communication to and from this location was not carefully watched and recorded. So all of the recipes he sent out were feints within feints. Some were bogus and some were correct. Even the correct ones had non-required and inert ingredients in them that constantly rotated out. The permutations had now grown to the point that it was highly unlikely that Wayne would ever be able to duplicate the rub. Every time he played with the formula though, Guy stayed extremely vigilant.

The food industry had changed a great deal over the preceding months. Gone were the days of the advanced slaughter, cooking, freezing, thawing and reheating. The containment areas and franchises had grown to the point that fresh meat and spices were possible on a global level. The upside was that the junkies who were growing in their pickiness (they swore they could tell the difference between a fresh and thawed high) were getting the very freshest of fixes. The downside was that the total time from start to finish was in most cases below 48 hours which didn't leave a lot of time for quality control. Guy realized that one slip up in the rub recipe had the propensity to, in a matter of a day or two, kill the entire addicted half of the planet.

On top of his own morose he did not need to add guilt – at least not *that* much guilt. Too many ingredients spoil the sauce.

After completing and checking twice his nightly updates to all the processing plants for the batches that would be made tonight and shipped immediately worldwide, Guy moved out of the communication center and into the large central gathering room. Sitting in front of the massive stone hearth fireplace he began drinking a scotch and smoking a fine cigar.

In the perfect loneliness of the moment he sat. The fire crackled and popped its hickory demise as the scotch swirled softly in the crystal tumbler. The smoke from his stogy drifted in streams to the rough-hewn rafters high overhead. Not for the first time, Guy Sayonara sighed.

Purpose. There was none. His fear increased.

Reaching over to the phone on the stand, he picked up the receiver and dialed in a number. As he heard the relays click and the tone simulating a ring (for phones had not actually rung in the literal sense for decades) he thought once again about the whole dialing thing and smiled.

"Hello?"

Guy allowed the question to hang in the air with his cigar smoke. He looked up at the rafters and measured the weight of the moment. The voice on the other end repeated the question.

"Hello? Is anyone there?"

"Hi Kallie."

A moment passed. And then Kallie asked, "Guy?"

"One in the same."

"The greatest chef in all the world?" she asked with a little too much sarcasm.

Guy waved off the chance to debate and asked instead, "How are things there?"

"They are fine, Guy. They are just fine."

Guy watched the smoke drift alone now – no words remained there to keep it company.

"How is Aunt Irene?"

"She is fine, Guy. Aunt Irene is fine. Agnes is fine. We are all fine here."

Guy waited again. This conversation was not going well. Sitting up a little he took a sip from his glass. Then returned to the conversation, "So everything is fine there then."

"Look Guy. We loved you. You and I had some fun together. Agnes adored you. But now we all have moved on, right?"

"Why all the past tense?" Guy asked.

"Because everything *is* past tense now, Guy. The world is past tense. All I have now is my rescue work."

"Oh yeah, the volunteer stuff with the animals. How is that going?"

"If you are interested, it is going fine. It keeps me busy. Aunt Irene watches Agnes while I lend a hand where I can."

"Sounds fun. I suppose it is very fulfilling pitching in and helping out a team when you can."

"I don't pitch in. I lead. I am a team leader now. And yes, it is very fulfilling."

"Wow. A team leader. That is cool."

Another pause in the conversation. This time it was Kallie that spoke first. "And what about you? I see your picture on the money. I suppose you have done alright for yourself."

"Well it is just on the one. Wayne and others are on the more important bills."

"More important?" There was a growing frustration in her voice that belied a deeper anger just below the surface, "Guy, the one *is* the most important bill. And we all know what you have done to get there. You turned your back on me and Agnes when we needed you most."

Guy came back calmly, "If I had come down to Amory when you asked, none of us would be here right now. I did what I did to give you and Agnes a chance."

"Oh thank you for the favor," she dripped.

"Look, I don't like the direction of this conversation."

"And I don't like the direction of your planet."

"And what direction would you like me to take?"

Guy expected this conversation, this argument to end badly and end soon. The one thing he did not expect was her next sentence.

"Why not come down and see us. See the good work we are doing here."

That was an interesting twist, Guy thought. "Come down to Amory, Mississippi?"

"Sure silly boy," Kallie giggled, "Don't they give the head honcho a vacation up there?"

Guy was nonplussed. The thought of a vacation had never occurred to him. But the thought did have a certain charm to it. Aunt Irene was supposed to be an amazing cook. That would be nice – some fresh southern veggies! And there was a new processing plant just west of Decatur he was having fixed up to be one of the prep locations for his rub. He could swing by and check on the renovation effort on the way. All in all, a week or two away from the kitchen may be just the thing he needed.

As if reading his thoughts, Kallie picked back up the invitation, "I want the old Guy. I want to see the man I loved. Can you find that man and bring him down to Amory?"

Guy thought a moment longer and then said, "What the hell. Why not? Ok. The most powerful man in the world will pay you a visit. I will have the office arrange it."

"No Guy. You are not listening to me."

"What?"

"I don't want the most powerful man in the world. I want Guy. That's all. No entourage. No autocade. No official state visits to all the little peoples. Is there any way we can just see you?"

Guy got up and walked through the huge kitchen to the parking bay. "Just me? No one else?" Opening the door he flipped on the light switch. There in bay one, before the Mercedes and other even more rare and exotic cars, was an ancient but still functioning GMC Pacer. Guy looked at it and the feelings from a bygone era pulsed just below the event horizon of emotion as he said, "Yeah. I think I might be able to manage that."

23.

"Well it just sounds dangerous to me," Vera said to Alfred as he lit a fire to fend off the autumnal chill in the place. He was still not used to the high life.

Over the months their franchise had grown out from Ft. Wayne in all directions with surprising rapidity. By the time of the October moon, he controlled all the restaurants to the north all the way to Detroit, the west all the way to Michigan City, to the east well into Ohio, and to the south all the way to Indianapolis. By the new laws and constitution, he bridged into three states which gave him as much clout as those that covered three states entirely.

His position near two borders had helped him gain the same power as people with far more difficulties. Usually a single franchise owner with multiple states had to support populations in many large metropolitan areas and that could prove to be tricky. In Alfred's case, the only large city he had to deal with was Ft. Wayne but he got to claim ownership in three different states.

State boundaries carried little meaning except in estimating how many votes one got in the new congress. There was only one government over the entire continent of North America, so statehood became nothing more than convenient lines on a map. There were some that argued it should be more of a grid and that idea had been given a lot of serious consideration as of late.

"You know how it's getting out there Vera. We have grown in all directions until we hit the established restaurants of other franchise holders. The law clearly states that we cannot encroach. But the meat seems to have made our customers somewhat sterile. The doctors are looking into it, but for now there seems to be little population growth in consumers. That means there is no growth potential for us."

Vera looked at him with sincerity and echoed the words she had heard him say a thousand times, "And in business, if you ain't growing, you're dieing."

"You know that's right," he nodded.

"But a syndicate? And at your own expense? It just doesn't sound right to me."

The mansion they now lived in was huge and it was difficult to knock the chill out of the air. Alfred actually wished at times that they lived in their little ranch once again. They had worked to pay it off most of their lives. Living in this place was so unlike them that he constantly worried the owners would return and call the police – if the owners hadn't been eaten that is, and if the police hadn't been eaten.

But irrespective of the facts and the dispensation of the ex-owners and the ex-police, he still didn't feel quite right living here.

"Vera, we are business people now. We have dozens of successful places, but if we quit growing we could lose our entire investment."

"Well I told you that we were investing too heavily. Do we have any savings to speak of yet?"

Alfred didn't want to answer. He knew what was coming at the end. At long length he finally reluctantly replied, "No. All of our funds are tied up into capital expenditures to grow the business."

The dish towel popped him on the head. "You spent all of it?"

"More than spent. I borrowed."

The look on her face made Alfred Foreman ashamed. He had hocked them beyond their ability to immediately compensate and he had known it was a bad idea when he did it. "But the potential is overwhelming. I now have three votes instead of one. That makes me the senior partner in the proposed four-way merger."

"Mergers. Partners," Vera grunted. "It all don't mean more than a tinker's dam if the government exercises its right of eminent domain."

Alfred felt the heat of embarrassment flush in his cheeks. "How do you know about that?"

"I know enough to do some reading myself when my husband has lost his mind and is squandering away a second chance at a retirement. I know enough to know that the same problem plaguing you and those other three no-accounts you run with is staring our government in the face."

"Vera, that day will not come for a long, long time. The best chance right now…"

Whack! The dishrag hit him again. "The best chance you have of living past tonight is to start listening to your wife and pray you don't fall asleep before I do."

Alfred laughed and grabbed Vera, slinging her over the sofa and falling on top of her. He kissed her on the cheek and said, "Alright Mrs. Foreman. I will look for opportunities to start streaming some of our income off as dividends."

"Gold ones. I don't want to see none of that paper crap come through my door. I want something we can take out to our old home and bury in the basement."

Alfred laughed again. "I got your gold in the basement," he said and the two of them began to remember what it was like to be frisky honeymooners all over again.

"Let me just plug the video tape in and away we go," Kallie said. Guy watched from his seat on the ancient sofa. Everything was ancient in Amory. The house was ancient, the giant oak tree in the front yard was ancient, the furniture on the handmade hardwood floors was ancient, even Aunt Irene was ancient.

Guy had enjoyed the lunch of pole beans, turnip greens, lima and squash. People in Mississippi don't mind vegetarians all that much. All they have to do is not put any pork on the plate and substitute pepper sauce for fatback in the veggies while they infuse in the pressure cooker, the metal top spinning and clattering as the steamed aroma is released into the kitchen. You know dinner is cooking when you here that rattle-pop from the stove. The top dances for hours in its own harvest celebration.

He could still smell the yeastiness in the air of the house from the dinner rolls, its light dusty smell mixing with that of clothesline fresh linen placed on the bed in the parlor bedroom behind two large interior French doors, made special for company. All of the smells and tastes swirled with the sounds of Jo-ree and Jay birds, the rustling from hoary pecan and hickory trees as they yielded their dying leaves to the autumnal breeze. Then add in a dash of blue October sky streaming through crafted window sheers and let soak for an hour or two and the yield is a Guy Sayonara that is so relaxed that he felt he could virtually melt into the sofa, becoming one with the horsehair tapestry adorning its back.

"Right. Video tape. Whatever you want Kallie," Guy practically babbled from his environment-induced stupor.

Aunt Irene had taken Agnes down the street to play while Kallie spent time with Guy. She had said at lunch that she didn't think it was a good idea to let her watch those dreadful tapes, the ones from the rescue work Kallie was so fond of. In Guy's mind, watching thirty minutes or so of kittens being saved from trees or little doggies being pulled out of junkyards was tediously boring, but a small price to pay for the nirvana he was now enjoying.

He guessed that he really did need a vacation after all.

Guy daydreamed hazily as his eyes followed the curves of Kallie's body. She really was a pretty thing. He had always enjoyed his time with her. And now as she stooped over the video tape player and fussed with a tape he allowed himself the momentary and unnoticed lusting. Of course his eyes snapped to the window as he realized she was beginning to turn around.

"Ok. I got it. Are you ready?"

"Ready for what?" Guy dreamily asked.

"To see my work, silly." she giggled.

"Sure. Let her rip."

"Funny you should say that. Ok. Here it goes."

The tape began. The title stated simply "A.L.F. Recruiting Tape 1". Guy jolted. The dream was over, the peace destroyed. "Kallie, that's an…"

"An ALF tape. Yes."

"But you will… *I* will…"

She finished his sentence for him, "…be arrested and thrown in with the beasts should anyone catch us. Yes."

"Thrown in with the beasts?" Guy asked. "You mean in prison?"

She paused the tape. "Guy, do you know how they harvest the creatures you cook? Do you understand what is involved?"

"Not really. The truck arrives every morning from the ranches and then a second one from my spicing companies. That is basically all I know. That is all I really care to know."

"But you figured out how to kill them."

"Well, that was really kind of a fluke. And besides, Archer Thornwall took over those duties since the second kill."

"Yes, we all have learned the history. He is on the fifty dollar bill and all - brave man that he is," she goaded.

"Look, Archer is a good friend of mine," Guy protested.

Again she interrupted him. "Guy you don't have any good friends. Archer Thornwall is a ruthless killer and would kill you as well in a New York second if there was any profit in it for him. Hell, he might just do it for shits and giggles. Would friends keep this from you?" she asked as she hit the play button on the remote.

Guy watched in growing horror as scene after scene played out in front of him. He saw the aliens kept in pairs or in sets of threes sitting on the ground in a containment area. He saw the eerie guard towers watching on as the creatures murmured softly to each other. Kallie gave voice over explanations describing the scientific experiments being carried out every day. Aliens being tortured and mutilated as businessmen spent untold resources trying to extract a use for every aspect of their bodies. Their skins were being tested for application in processing plants, their eyes for adding texture to milkshakes, their bones for medicines and cosmetics, their claws for weapons and construction devices. The goal is that not one ounce of alien matter will go to waste.

The video jumped from one graphic scene to another forcing Guy to move ever closer to the thin membrane that separates apathy from caring. It was as if he had been deep under water for years and was now approaching the shimmering surface, about to emerge out into the open air for the first time in a long, long while. He could feel something stirring deep within.

"Do you know how they actually kill the poor creatures?" she asked.

Guy shook his head, now totally incapable of taking his eyes off the carnage on the screen. As much as he wanted to look away, he could not.

"Then watch this next scene."

A large truck pulled up to the containment area and a woman in an orange jumpsuit was pulled out. There were two officers on either side of her and they unlocked her handcuffs while a third man present in a black robe and wig read from a three-ring binder, "Sarah Adams, you have been found guilty of the high crime of treason against the great republic of North America by participating in the terroristic activities against one of its restaurant franchises. Do you have any last words before we execute the perfect justice of Avarice?"

The woman in orange started to scream incomprehensibly.

The men threw her in a small clear holding cell and the door closed behind her. She knowingly went to the center of the cell, picked up a revolver and immediately shot in the direction of the men. They jumped reflexively but the bullet froze in midair, suspended next to the many others trapped in the clear wall of the containment area.

After this futile stunt the door behind her opened up. She was screaming and crying in hysterics. Guy could make out the occasional, "I'm not going to do it!" and "You can't make me!" At that point, one of the guards reached over to a control panel and pressed a button. The floor of the containment area sparked with blue arcs of electricity and Guy now noticed for the first time that the prisoner was barefooted.

The woman howled as she ran reflexively to the area past the open door where the ground was grassy and dirt. There she was met by two charging aliens. She raised her gun and fired in self-defense. First the aliens split, and then she was split – the aliens greedily fighting with each other over bits of her. They were no longer restrained by any sense and sensibilities that their original manners may have provided. The aliens had devolved to little more than pit bulls ripping and growling as they gorged on their latest kill.

A divider came up from the floor separating the newly created aliens from the originals. Then the divider pushed the new ones, squeezing them into ever decreasing amounts of space as the rest of the containment area opened back up to its original size. Once trapped to the point of immobility, spikes shot out from holes in the walls piercing their bodies and killing them instantly.

Here Guy saw that the smaller areas had floors that were actually conveyer mechanisms and the alien corpses were moved, shunted to an awaiting truck to be hauled to a nearby processing plant.

The camera swung in jerky chops back to the prisoner truck as another prisoner was brought out wearing an orange jumpsuit. The video paused.

Guy looked up at Kallie who was now standing beside him. The look of ghastly terror was white upon his face. Looking up at her with disbelieving eyes he tried to speak but couldn't.

Kallie said, "Wash, rinse, repeat. Any questions?"

"But the hunters… the hunters are supposed to hunt them in the wild." Guy stammered.

"The hunters are now a thing of myth and legend. The processing of alien meat holds little more adventure than the meatpacking plants of Chicago. No sport there."

"And they kill a person each time?"

"Every steak you prepare at night came at the end of a human's life."

Guy sat back and ran his fingers through his hair as his brain tried to process all the horror. More thoughts were starting to flow, "But at that rate…"

"At that rate, they will go through all the prisoners in about five to ten more years. There will be none left."

Guy's eyebrows furled. "But that doesn't make any sense. If the junkies are complacent, then only those who have not eaten the meat would join ALF. And that is a finite number of people. The system would eventually fail and that is not a good business plan."

Kallie didn't say anything. Her face just filled with an honest concern and sorrow as she pressed the play button again.

This time, Guy saw a much different scene. This was a baby nursery. It was a huge baby nursery; rows upon rows of babies being cared for by a staff that moved through them with the vacant daze of junkies. Then the camera panned out to a fenced-in yard filled with little toddlers, hard at play. Lastly it moved into the adjacent dormitory like structure with what had to be hundreds of beds.

"They are junkie children," she said plainly.

Guy couldn't comprehend what he was seeing. "But junkies don't have children. They are barren," he reminded her.

"That is what your precious government *tells* everyone anyway."

Kallie waited for a moment to let this last sink in a little. Then she continued, "What you are watching are scenes from a baby farm – a junkie baby farm. The government is ordering junkies to make babies. Some are siphoned off and raised to replace older junkies that eventually die so that the attrition is stable and they will have a perpetual marketplace.

"Within the next five to ten years, the excess children will be moved to a training area where they will be taught to commit minor offenses against the state by joining up with ALF groups or making their own. Then they will be easily captured, tried, convicted, and executed."

Looking down at Guy through quiet tears rolling down her cheeks, the video showing happy children playing on swing sets, she plainly said, "At least that is the plan, anyway."

"I would kindly appreciate it if you would stop referring to them as puppy farms," Avarice growled. Tim Parsons knew that he was serious by the way his cheeks scorched with a tinge of redness.

"Alright, market growth farms."

"That's better," Wayne said.

"The market growth farms are pretty much in place in our market. But the other continents are lagging behind a little."

"That is fine. That is most excellent."

"But if they lag behind, they will face a prisoner shortage in the next five to ten years," Parsons warned.

"Beringer." Wayne called to his new junkie accountant standing across the room at idle.

"Yes sir?"

"If we increased production at Parsons' puppy farms, can we meet enough numbers to contemplate export?"

Beringer scribbled some numbers on a pad for a moment and said, "I believe that is possible. It may be close in year five, but that would only help to promote demand over supply. And as everyone clearly knows, that would play only to your favor, Mr. Avarice."

Wayne looked back at Parsons, the cigar butt in the corner of his mouth had gone out on its own nearly a half hour before, but he liked the feeling of power it gave him to chaw on it, ever switching it from side to side to speak around it. "Junkie accountants. Everyone should own one."

Parsons sheepishly asked, "Are you really considering going into the business of exporting farmed children on a global scale?"

"And why the hell not, Parsons? This is a fucking business and we are in the business to make profit. What is our alternative here? World collapse? I refuse to go down in history as the man that drove the global markets into chaos." Now standing up and walking around the office, using its entire space to make his point, "Can't you see it Parsons? We are doing what we are doing for the benefit of mankind. We are exploring profit potential while bringing stability to foreign markets. To even consider not doing so would be to consider causing human suffering on scale beyond measure."

Parsons conceded, "Well, you do have a point there."

"Besides, these little ones are rogues. They are second generation junkies. If we don't control them, who's to say they won't develop some immunity or insanity, and end up controlling us?"

Parsons shuddered at the thought.

"Now, to more important matters. Beringer, have you got the most recent growth numbers?"

"I do, sir."

Now in front of the window overlooking the D.C. renovation and cleanup work going on by junkies in the mall, Wayne Avarice stood with his back on the room full of advisers and managers and commanded, "Then report."

Beringer cleared his throat and stated, "The market has become super-saturated. Power-grabbing now runs the growth market. The franchises are turning on their own. Chains are buying out or leveraging other chains, what used to be countries are now merging or taking over neighbors. The Risk Board, as you put it, boils down to six of the seven continents (Antarctica was never really in the mix). As it stands the world is in the beginning throes of tottering towards global war. We have already seen skirmishes between the old China, India and Pakistan as Asia begins to align itself against what they see as an early first merger with Australia.

"Should that merger take place, then our contacts and emissaries feel that Asia will move towards franchise realignment globally. This will of course ultimately threaten us. As the other continents consider fighting or yielding to each other in an effort to either join Asia or thwart them in favor of their own growth plans, the old DOD initiatives are starting to be dusted off. Nukes are being restored. You are now considered powerful if you have old warfare knowledge."

Wayne continued to look out the window. The cigar butt was tasting cold and slimy and stale, but now was not the time for him to lose his stomach for the game. "How long before we see the first merger attempts?"

"I would predict twelve to eighteen months - longer if it becomes a hostile takeover."

"Longer if it becomes a hostile takeover," Wayne echoed. "Parsons, you have a good feel for this thing. Will it become hostile?"

"It will have to. The junkies in India, Pakistan, and China are complacent enough. But the franchise holders have long memories. Old feelings die hard."

"Die hard," Wayne again echoed as he thought. Then turning around he looked at the roomful of the best business minds in the world and proposed, "And what if we move on eminent domain? What if we strike first and takeover China?"

The new chief of defense was the first to speak, "China is not simply going to yield to a clause in a contract. If that were the case, then Microsoft would have been even more powerful before the invasion. They have a proven track record of conceding to legalese only to ignore it in the application. If you want China, it will have to be tactical and it will have to be soon."

"So we attack with a show of force? A nuclear shock and awe?" Wayne questioned for clarification.

The defense chief answered, "If you strike now, they will retaliate. But as everyone in this room knows, their nukes are actually impotent. Isn't that right James?"

James Navarone smiled from his leather wingback chair. He answered a cool, "That is correct," as he secretly made plans to travel to old Chile for the winter. He should be able to watch the fireworks safely from there. The idea of actually getting to orchestrate Armageddon brought the kind of chills to his spine that were difficult to hide from the rest of the room.

But he managed.

Just then the phone rang. Wayne reached over and answered it. Those in the room witnessed him go through a series of monosyllabic grunts rounding out the call with a final, "Excellent." Hanging up he looked at the rest of the room and said with a grin that started at one earlobe and continued all the way across to the other earlobe, "Maximilian Hornbuckle has just perfected the rub recipe."

Wayne Avarice took the slimy stump of a stogy out of his mouth and as he threw it into the bottom of a waste basket he proclaimed, "It is time that we rid ourselves of this meddlesome chef!"

24.

Guy sat at his computer terminal in his communication center and watched the cursor blink. He thought, "It would be so easy, wouldn't it? Just to push the Enter key and start the chain of events that would bring an end to all the madness?"

The path had seemed so clear on the way home from Amory. It all had made so much sense in his little GMC Pacer putting along the back highways and byways. It was no wonder to him that nobody had been able to find him or follow him. He knew the way there like the back of his hand. And there was at least three ways to get there, all of them rife with unexpected twists and turns.

He had lost the last of his pursuers in Hamilton but he realized they probably knew where he was going anyway – all the phones were surely tapped.

And on that long, introspective drive back from Amory, the scenes from the ALF video played in an endless loop in his mind. The madness would continue and even worsen as long as there was profit to be made. As long as there was a market for insanity, there would be people like Wayne Avarice to stand at the end of the assembly line of human suffering and collect the money in large baskets as it poured off the conveyer belts.

But he wondered if it could really be as simple as that? Cut off the marketplace and the conveyer belt would be shut down. If there was no market, then there would be no madness. Supply has no purpose without demand. And Chef Guy Sayonara was an expert at having no purpose.

So he followed the string of logic to its ultimate conclusion. If you want to free the children, take away the need for replicating the aliens. If you want to free the aliens, take away the demand. If you want to stop the demand...

Here is where the cursor flashed at him. Was he really ready to give the order?

Just then Guy saw headlights strum across the window frames of the great room like fingers across the strings of a harp. Someone was coming but he didn't really worry about it. He was safe as long as he remained the only person with the real recipe for the rub. Even if it was Wayne or some of his thugs, they couldn't do much to him. He was the one and only Chef Guy.

He heard the car door slam followed shortly after that with the side door to his kitchen. "Guy? Are you here?"

It was Dex. Guy looked at the cursor awaiting his decision. It blinked at him optimistically, even hopefully.

"In here Dex. In the great room." Guy got up from his computer and made his way into the hall. Dex entered from the kitchen side. He looked like an old time newsy about ready to shout, "Extra, extra, read all about it!"

"I'm glad I found you home. We were worried when you just wandered off the reservation like that."

"Sorry Dex. I guess I should have at least told you. I just needed some time away – to think things through a little." Walking across to his bar he asked, "Pour you a drink, sailor?"

"I might need one after I tell you the news."

Guy stopped in his tracks. Could they have figured him out? Could they have guessed or even known somehow that he had met with ALF and now knew their darkest plans?

"What news, Dex?"

"They are going to bomb Asia."

There are moments when someone tells you a string of words that defy making sense. It is like when someone says, "Oh, John Kennedy was just shot," or "Terrorist just flew plains into the Twin Towers." They are simple words. Each one in turn is used many times by all of us every day but never in that particular string and sequence. *Going* is just a word as is *bomb*. *Asia* is a location and *they* are a group of people. Each and every word is relatively benign in and of itself.

But string them all together and state them plainly to a friend that is in the middle of his own crisis and they come across as, "They are going to bomb Asia."

Before it really made complete sense to him Guy asked, "What? Why would they bomb Asia?"

"Wayne sees it as an early move for a merger. He wants the restaurants to share a single franchise and sees it as a positive move towards synergy. The two conglomerates will be able to remove duplicate resources and focus on their individual strengths with less overhead. As far as unions go, it makes a hell of a lot of business sense."

"But won't Asia just bomb us back?"

"It will never happen. Navarone sold them blanks."

This was all too much for Guy's head. "Avarice is about to kill millions of people and he thinks it all makes good business sense?"

"Of course."

Guy stood and stared at his old friend. He could not believe these words were still coming out of his mouth. He walked over to Dex and spoke in hushed tones. "Dex, Wayne is insane. He is about to do something very foolish and the violence will not stop there. Even if he does win Asia, there will be more killing. The world is no longer the peaceful bastion for restaurateurs that we originally envisioned. It has slipped back declining rapidly to where we started the whole thing. Nation against nation. Continent against continent. And for what? So someone can make more money? So businesses can live with the delusion that their markets will continue to expand?

"And once the strongest has finally won, if that could ever be accomplished in the first place, we what, Dex? We begin growing babies in farms to feed to the machine? What we have become is sick and twisted and almost beyond the point of no return."

Dex looked at him with the shock of betrayal. "They got to you, didn't they." This last was more of a statement than a question.

"Who Dex, who has gotten to me?"

"The ALF. They have brainwashed you into believing their bullshit lies."

"No one has brainwashed me, Dex. The madness has to end and I intend to do something about it." Guy walked back over to his communication console. The cursor was still there winking its anticipation for Guy to press the Enter key.

"How Guy? How are you going to stop a powerful and great man like Wayne Avarice?"

Guy stopped at the keyboard and turned around to his old friend. "I am in over my head. I started to realize a long time ago that I don't actually have any real power. The people that surround me have been cutting deals and making decisions behind my back for a long time." With this he noticed a flash of guilt on Dex's face. Up until that moment he had suspected but was not entirely sure.

"Dex, I am really just a figure-head – nothing more. However, that means I am the one that is actually in danger. My time is limited as it is. So I have decided to try to stop the whole thing."

"How?"

"It is simple actually. I have devised a way to end it all. I will give the command tonight to change the formula worldwide. Within forty-eight hours, all of the junkies around the globe will be dead."

Now a look of shock and anger was replacing the guilt on Dex's face.

Guy continued, "Of course it would mean killing off half the world population but by my own reckoning at least that many are going to die anyway if a global war breaks out."

Dex began crossing over to him, "I can't let you do that, Guy."

"Why not? I am President of the company. I get to make the rules. Besides, we can find something else to do with our time, Dex."

"No, I mean I can't let you do that – period. Not because of our company but because *my* boss has paid me to stop you should you ever try to do something stupid."

The words immediately stung Guy. He flashed back in anger, "You have never changed, have you old chum?"

Dex continued his advance. It was clear from his body language that this was about to get physical. "What do you mean?"

"I mean you sold me out to my own mother in college and you sold me out to Wayne Avarice now."

"Guy, I didn't sell you out. I am a lawyer. I accepted a retainer to represent the certain interests of my clients. This is purely business."

Dex had no sooner gotten within arm's length of Guy than something totally unexpected happened. Guy hauled off and decked Dex hard. It was the first time he had ever inflicted brute force on anyone else. But the punch was solid and Dex fell backward over one of the large couches landing hard on the floor on the other side.

Guy turned around and without giving his cursor the satisfaction of blinking one more time, he pressed the Enter key as hard as he could. Looking at the screen which now spelled out the message that the order had been received he quoted Admiral David Glasgow Farragut, "Damn the torpedoes! Full speed ahead!"

When Dex came to, he was alone in the house. He staggered to the communications console and stared unbelievingly at the confirmation message still on the screen. Picking up the phone he shakily punched in the direct number to his real employer. A few moments later Mr. Parsons answered.

"Tim Parsons."

"Tim, this is Dex."

"Yes, Dex. We are quite busy here. What can I help you with?" His voice was filled with the obvious contempt. Dex did not care that he was viewed as an underling. Lawyers never really care about what others think. That is trained out of them early on. All that really matters is billable hours.

"Look, Guy has flown the coop. He thinks he is on some crusade or something."

"Dex, we have solved the problem. Everything is fine. Maxwell has duplicated the recipe, no thanks to your efforts I might add."

"Look, I did everything I could to deliver the formula to you. But Guy was extremely stubborn."

"Don't worry about it. You will get your fee and eternal thanks from your government. Guy Sayonara is no longer a priority for us. Mr. Thornwall will take care of things from here on. Now if you will excuse me, Dex, we have more important matters to attend to."

"More important than the deaths of half the population of the planet?" Dex asked. But there was no response. Tim Parsons had already hung up the phone.

"Shit," Dex swore. Then he dialed the number again. This time a different man answered.

"I am sorry but Mr. Parsons is otherwise occupied at this time. Please submit any more requests to him in writing through his office."

"Otherwise occupied? Well you get him unoccupied this instant! Half the world is about to…"

Click.

"Fucking hell, you morons!" Dex screamed at the already dead receiver.

From the moment Guy pulled out of his driveway, the green Jeep Ranger turned on its lights and pulled out behind him. Archer Thornwall had lived the life of a mighty hunter. He had shot a charging rhino. His nerves of steel had no equal as he faced bears and lions. Even the aliens had fallen at his boots after seeing the determined grit in his eyes. But there was one prey, of all the dangerous creatures he had slain, that still eluded his experience in the hunt.

From the first time he killed a small bird in his backyard with his first BB gun, he had desired to hunt the one creature at the top of the food chain. He wanted to hunt man.

But the laws had been a little picky on that subject. And although he had been approached with more than one contract to kill a human, he had always thought that the risk of long-term jail time was greater than the reward of finally bagging the one creature on Avarice that he had not before hunted.

But times had changed, hadn't they.

Now as he pulled out behind the silver Mercedes he was finally on the hunt to end all hunts – and with the government's blessing! The headlights of the jeep kept the prey on the run as they drove down the mountain on the winding curves of Governors Drive at ever increasing speeds.

"Good. The hunt is always so much more enjoyable when it involves a chase," Archer said out loud.

The age-old hunter picked up a cell phone from the passenger seat. He was not one to really use these new-fangled contraptions. But as a hunter he was always happy to use any device no matter how advanced to make the hunt better. He pressed the speed dial for the number in memory slot seven and waited as the phone on the other end began to ring.

Guy had hated to punch his old college chum. He was certain that deep down inside Dex was just confused about things. They would be able to work it all out after this madness was over.

After he had pressed the Enter key and began the chain of events that could not be undone, he stepped past his old friend that was out cold and then to the parking area beyond the kitchen. His original intention was to drive his old GMC Pacer to Amory and go into hiding using the ALF if he could. But when he opened the bay door he saw that Dex's car was blocking that exit.

He cursed softly and went to the second bay and jumped into the Mercedes. The case of gold utensils were still in the passenger seat from the Train the Trainers session. Looking at it now, Guy could not believe that the class had only been two nights earlier. He felt that it had been ages ago. So much had happened in the interim. So much of his life had changed. For the first time in a very long while, he actually felt something. And from that moment on, the rest of it, the fame and fortune, the power and wealth had all been just a crazy dream. He was now awake and all the rest had been forever ago.

Looking at the case he realized that it was tangible and it was real. He had not really escaped without consequence or penalty. The only way out of the nightmare he had helped create was to now euthanize those he had used to his own gain and glory. He wondered if he would ever be whole again. The order to kill the junkies was the right one. He still knew in his heart of hearts that that much was true. The planet would recover somehow. It always did.

Guy just wondered if *he* would ever recover.

Maybe after the restaurant chains collapse, there would be no reason to upkeep the holding areas and maybe the aliens would escape. Perhaps after all is said and done, maybe the human race really didn't have a reason to be persisted. Maybe they really should just become a footnote in galactic history. "Don't let this planet happen to you."

He drove past the sign in his yard, "Save our Slopes", and began to cry for the first time in memory out of time.

So intent was he on experiencing this newfound emotional freedom that he didn't even notice the headlights of the jeep pulling out behind him as he left. It was as he pulled out on Governors that he finally did spy his pursuer. It was here that Guy Sayonara experienced his own rebirth. Instead of being apathetic, instead of sighing at the newfound trouble and ignoring it, he became scared. He had just ordered the largest extermination of human life in the history of man, he was being tailed, and he was very, very scared.

Guy stepped on the accelerator and tested the scene unfolding in his rearview mirror. The lights from behind matched him, speed for speed. This was not a test or coincidence. He was being followed and there could only be one reason. He would either escape or he would die this very night.

Just then the phone on the seat beside him twirped and lit up. Guy picked up the phone and answered it, "Hello?"

"Hi there college boy. Kind of fun isn't it? Playing a little game of cat and mouse."

All of a sudden Guy wondered if it was worse to live life without a purpose or to die *with* one.

Archer watched as the Mercedes sped up suddenly. It was easy to match the speed on the curves. He was a little worried that the jeep might not be able to keep up once they hit the long straight-aways that waited for them at the bottom of the hill. But for now he was happy with the chase.

Guy had hung up on him. But that didn't deter him. He pressed seven again and waited. After a moment the call was switched over to voicemail. Still determined he hung up and pressed seven again, enjoying the torment he was inflicting on the fleeing prey. It was then that he saw the sunroof of the Mercedes open up and a small cell phone, still ringing, fly out and back towards him. By reflex he swerved to the right but it was too late. The cell phone hit his hood and exploded into a thousand useless pieces.

No elephant had ever done *that* before. This was indeed going to be a unique hunting experience.

As they leveled out onto the flatter plane of the valley, the prey did something quite unexpected. The Mercedes took a sharp turn to the left on California. The jeep had a hard time matching the turning circle and speed and went up on two wheels landing hard once the turn was complete.

The silver car in front of him accelerated sharply up the small hill on California and went completely out of sight as the road crested and leveled off. Archer stepped all the way down on the gas and the jeep virtually took off as it zoomed up the small hill. As he broke the horizon on the top of the hill he was pleased to see the tail lights of the Mercedes still on the road in front of him. It was a short distance at these speeds before they came to the five-way intersection of Whitesburg and Bob Wallace. Here the prey took a sudden hard turn right onto Bob Wallace.

This was a bad turn for Archer. Bob Wallace was a long straight road that would lead to all the major arteries through town – not to mention it had dozens of small side roads that would lead through windy neighborhoods to the north and south. All of these had their own exits out to even larger thoroughfares.

Several seconds later as he matched the hard turn right his heart sank as the Mercedes was nowhere to be found. Slowing down he lowered his windows on both sides in order to give his ears a better chance of picking up on the tale-tell motor noises. There were none.

There on the short road that connected all the major streets he stopped between the little shops that crowded in on both sides. Killing his engine he sat in the patient silence. He could see nearly all the way to the Parkway a mile to the west. There was no sign of the car and even if it had been going at its top speed it would not have made it that far in such a short time.

No, the prey would be close. He would just wait for it to make a mistake.

In the complete quiet of the hunt, Archer Thornwall slowed his breathing and heart rate. He allowed his body to become completely still. There was no one out on the roads this time of night and the city was ghostly silent.

Archer sat there for untold seconds. Just listening and breathing. The only sound he could make out was the ticking of the jeep's motor as it cooled from the hot pursuit. He was just about to give up and move on down Bob Wallace, looking down the side streets, when a voice came at him out of the still of the night.

"Archer Thornwall!" the voice cried to his left in a boom that startled him from his patient hide. He snapped his head to the left and there from the shadows he spied a flickering of gold that was spinning. He was not able to really make out what it was before he lost consciousness.

Guy had turned onto California from Governors drive. The jeep was still in hot pursuit behind him. Tossing the cell phone at the hunter was a good idea. It had almost caused the bastard to crash. Emboldened by the idea, Guy began looking around the car for anything else that he could use as a projectile. He was disappointed to find that he had been a relatively neat person during his years in a delusional state. There was precious little debris at all in the Mercedes.

About the only thing he had was the gold utensil set that Wayne had given him. It was at this moment that the plan popped into his head.

Up ahead and coming at him fast was the intersection of Bob Wallace and Whitesburg. There were some little shops that pressed in close on either side there. Judging the seconds after he crested the hill on California to the time the jeep's lights reappeared in his rearview mirror he felt he had just enough time.

He knew that the longer this chase continued the better chance Archer Thornwall would have of wearing him down.

Pulling hard into the right-hand turn Guy allowed the inertia to continue the curve of the Mercedes into a controlled fishtail. Pulling into the shops on the right he doubled back around behind a small stand-alone building that would block the Mercedes from sight.

Grabbing up the case, he made a mad dash running as hard as he could across the street to the shop on the other side. He tumbled into the dark shadows not far from the street and opened the case just as the jeep approached and turned the corner.

The plan was simple. If Archer kept driving, then it would all be over. If he doubled back and found the car, Guy would have the element of surprise. And at least that was something.

But the wise old hunter did something unexpected as well. He did neither. Instead of driving on or doubling back, the old fart just simply stopped in the middle of the road – precisely in the same place as Guy.

"Holy shit!" Guy thought to himself.

He had played Jail Break and Kick the Can enough as a child to know that in moments like this, you can't let "It" even hear you breath. Guy began trying to calm himself. It was no good. His heart was about to pound clear out of his chest.

Then to his horror, the engine shut off and the windows rolled down. He could hear the old man breathing. He was certain that at any moment the ancient hunter would hear him and shoot him where he stood.

Guy could see the hunter breathing slowly. He could hear the engine ticking down as it cooled. That may have been the only reason that his own breathing didn't give him away. He wasn't going to wait and find out. If he was going to move, it had to be now.

Picking up the sharpened gold spatula, he noticed that it felt heavy in his hand – weightier than normal. He turned it in his palm so that the blade's surface was perpendicular to the ground like an Indian's throwing hatchet.

Summoning all of his strength he unleashed a battle cry, "Archer Thornwall!" and he released the spatula with all of his might. It spun end-over-end from the shadows and out into the light of the nearby streetlamp. Guy saw the old man turn his head toward him, turn his face toward the rapidly spinning blade. And with the dumbstruck look of a deer in headlights he saw the old hunter take the point of the spatula directly into the forehead.

There was a satisfying sound that it made. To Guy it rather sounded like the round side of an egg as it cracks on the edge of a skillet when you hit it just right.

Not wanting to give the hunter a second chance, Guy scooped up a set of large butcher knives. He would take the moment of surprise for what it was worth and finish the job properly. But as he neared the now silent jeep, he could make out in the hollow grey light of the streetlamp that no more work would be necessary. The job was done and the goose was well and truly cooked for Archer Thornwall.

The spatula had hit the mark and driven at least a good two inches into Archer's forehead. His blank eyes were looking cross-eyed at the handle sticking comically out and still quivering a little like an arrow that had landed a solid hit.

Guy reached up and pulled the spatula out. It made a subtle scraping sound as it was released from the wedging sides of bone that held it in place. Feeling a little like the boy King Arthur, he pulled Excalibur from the stone that was Archer Thornwall's skull. The hunter slumped forward on the horn of the jeep and the sound pealed the night air announcing the end of the hunt.

No more bulls would die tonight.

Guy thought about pushing the corpse back to mercifully stop the blaring of the horn. But in the end decided it was more poetic to just let it blare on. It would only be a matter of time before the whole of the North American defense would be upon him and he didn't want to give them any more chances than they already had by tarrying for some false sense of honor.

Guy Sayonara jumped back into the Mercedes with his utensil kit and sped away into the night towards Amory, Mississippi.

25.

The trip wound through the night like Guy's life through the world, sometimes seemingly without direction, sometimes feeling lost, and never a really clear look at the road ahead. All in all it took the better part of the rest of the night for Guy's little silver Mercedes to find its way to 3rd street in Amory, Mississippi, to the house just behind the small bank annex.

The sun turned the corner of the globe at about the same time that Guy turned the corner at the bank and slid up silently to the curb. He stopped the car, killed the engine and just sat there for a while as the sky played out all the best flavors of sherbet above: raspberry, orange, peach, and finally lemon. All of them swirled in their transitions playing out a visual opera while he contemplated his own lot in life.

To be honest, he thought of very little at all except for a momentary flashback to the flies in his old apartment living out their short existence bumping into each other. Bump, bump, dit-dit, bump. There hadn't been a pattern after all. Perhaps life was truly random and the concept of sequence only a theory used to keep humans sane while they learned new math.

But beyond this, there was no thought – only observation of sky and flies, trees and shadows, sidewalks and porches. It was here, at this last that he first spied her. On the porch sitting in an old metal glider there she was - the object of his affection and his recent awakening. She, the mother of Agnes and niece of Irene glided back and forth, to and fro echoing out the eddies and wakes of his thoughts, patiently watching him. She was waiting quietly – waiting for Guy to come to his own conclusions, his own solutions to the puzzles that plagued him so.

At first he wanted to jump from the Mercedes and shout, wave, run, embrace. He wanted to do anything that would immediately entwine him in the arms of the one that had set him free. She, the liberator of his soul sat on the glider gliding. And in that perfect moment, that was enough – just to watch her and desire her touch.

Sometimes the thing that heals us the most is that perfect moment. It is the instant we see someone for the first time. It is the color of morning, the autumnal chill in the air, the grey giving birth to the new life of color. It is the giant oak protecting us with their blazing canopy from the dew forming all around, but not touching us.

Here in this perfect moment, Guy Sayonara realized that he had, after all is said and done, followed the only course that he could. He would set one half of the population free by setting the other half of the population free. And he realized that in this perfect opera, those pour trapped souls, those addicted, would find their ultimate peace at the point of a steak knife in little more than twelve hours from now.

And it was good.

He opened the door and stood between it and the car's interior. There was no need to run. There was no need to hasten the moment. He saw her, and she smiled. That was enough for now. Sometimes it is better to just drink in the moment and remember. There would come hard times in the future when such a memory will feed the soul on its nourishment like a nut stored away by the squirrel against the winter's cold.

He held up his hand and waved. She waved, her hand mostly hidden by the cuff of the oversized sweatshirt. It was then that he realized that he was truly bugnuts in love. Bugnuts. It's a technical word. Look it up.

Regardless of the validity or erroneousness of the word, it was enough of a distraction to prevent either one of them from perceiving the military convoy that was now rapidly approaching them from two different directions until it was too late. The black and shiny vehicles sped to an ominous rendezvous between them.

The spell of the moment was cut short as all of the doors swung open and armed defense guards quickly took their posts in a semi-circle separating the two of them in potential and threatening violence. Guy realized what was coming. He had sinned and this would be his sentence, a flash of rounds and then no more.

The front door on a troop carrier to the left opened and out stepped Wayne Avarice, himself. He walked to the sidewalk behind the arc of soldiers and not so very far from Kallie. He had a pistol in his gloved hand.

"Hello, Guy."

"Hi Wayne," Guy calmly stated. The apathy returned to his voice for the moment.

"You have been a naughty boy, Mr. Sayonara."

"I *feel* naughty, Wayne."

By this point, Guy had at least fifty automatic weapons pointed at his heart and head. He realized that he was not long for this world. But that was ok. He was ok, just ok. It was so-so. Not too bad, actually – well, not really. He would end this thing in the same way he had begun it. Perhaps mediocrity was enough for the likes of him.

"It is ok if we kill you today. You know that, don't you Guy?"

"If you want half the world's population to die with me, that is, Wayne. Do these thugs know that? You kill me and half the world dies with me."

Wayne un-holstered his pearl-handled revolver and waved it limply in the palm of his hand at the arc of soldiers in front of him, "You mean these well trained and loyal men and women of the ultimate franchise? Do they know that killing you will bring about the loss of untold humanity?"

"Yes, Wayne. Do they get it? Do they know what is riding on this?"

"Of course they do, Guy. They know, as I know, that Maximilian Hornbuckle has perfected the replication of your rub. And as soon as your stockpiled spices are exhausted, the new production of his masterful work will take over. There will be no loss of life, no great ransom held by our good and dearly departed friend, Guy Sayonara."

It took a moment to register. Actually for Guy it was the shit-eating grin on Kallie's face that ultimately spelled it all out for him. What was it about Wayne's words that made her so abundantly happy? His mind slowly put it all together.

If Wayne had said that Guy was about to be killed because Max had duplicated his rub, then that meant that Wayne didn't know about his own orders to change the existing rub. Dex had not been able to warn them and production of his ultimate plot continued unabated.

Looking now to Kallie for confirmation he noticed that her smile was unwavering. She awaited the firing squad with the certain secret knowledge that trucks were now carrying the ill-fated cargo to countless millions around the globe. There was nothing that Wayne's ignorance, or the death of her and Guy for that matter, could do to prevent that from happening now.

It was all too perfect. In the end, Guy would snatch victory from the jaws of the grave. In his death and that of his beloved, he would free the world from the bonds of Avarice.

Guy began to lie. He had become quite good at it in recent years. He imagined that it felt so natural because the person he had lied to the most was himself. "I guess you have me, Wayne. You have caught the great Chef Guy Sayonara."

Wayne spat on the ground in front of him. "You little pipsqueak. You fancy yourself the greatest chef. Let me tell you something. The lowliest prep cook in the most run-down of all of my kitchens shits better chefs in the nuggets of corn that pass through them then you will ever be."

"A little harsh aren't we, Wayne?"

"Not even remotely. You have been the thorn in my flesh from day one. I loathed you when I interviewed you. I hated you when I needed you. And I detested you when you killed one of my best friends."

"With your spatula that you gave me I might add, Wayne. Thank you. I think the words you used were that it might come in handy someday. I have to admit you are always right."

Wayne's complexion flushed. It was obvious now that he intended to kill Guy himself. The muscle of the guards was just there to hold him still while he squeezed off a few rounds in case he missed. Wayne leveled the gun at his heart.

"Your cooking sucks you know."

"I guess that is why half the world is addicted to it. Think about it Wayne. You are about to kill the man that put you on the map."

Wayne screamed, probably loosing what was left of his mind, "I put me on the map boy! I am the master of my own domain! I was the one that crafted this new planetary order and franchise!"

Guy said calmly and with smiling patronage, "And do tell these brave men and women of your armed forces where you were when I found you."

"Shut up!" The hammer on Wayne's pistol cocked.

"I found him cowering in a cave in Huntsville, Alabama. Cowering in fear and waiting for the awesome aliens to come and suck his brains out."

"Shut up!" Wayne screamed. This time his voice carried with it the frayed edge of ripped vocal chords.

"He was standing behind his hired security, his wife and children, hoping that the monsters would take them first."

"Shut up you bastard!" came the final retching and vile scream as the shot from his revolver reported in echoes off the neighboring houses and bank annex.

Guy flinched.

There was no pain really. He only registered the shock of having heard the shot from the pistol. He saw the smoke from the end of Wayne's barrel at about the same moment he lost the hearing in his left ear. But as he tried to hold on to the moment, he still felt no pain.

Guy figured this is what it was like to finally face death. The moment had come so quickly that he almost was not completely prepared for it. The first thing he actually felt was the sudden numbness of adrenaline coursing through his veins. His blood pressure was immediately constricted and driven up to the point that he could actually hear his own pulse in his right ear. Everything seemed calm enough as he looked around at the arc of soldiers, their rifles at the ready pointing at his vitals should Wayne give the order.

But the only thing that seemed to be coming from Wayne Avarice's mouth was not orders to kill, but an apparent string of profanities. Guy focused all of his remaining mental acuity at the words forming on the lips of his ex-boss. After all, he presumed he had at least been fired. Wayne seemed to be saying the words, "fuck", and "I", and "missed", over and over again.

Guy looked to his left and saw the entrance wound to the silver Mercedes just beside him. Now in an otherworld and out-of-body way he found himself saying the words, "fuck", and "he", and "missed", over and over again.

Then as time seemed to restore itself he saw Wayne level the pistol again. This time he held it in both hands. He was using the grip Guy had seen on so many police shows on TV over the years. This time there would be no string of words repeated over and over again. This time he would be D.E.D., dead.

"This time Sayonara I will not miss."

If it were possible to see a finger squeeze a trigger, if it were possible to hear leather gloves creak, if it were possible to smell the sweat of anticipation, Guy Sayonara did so now. For it was in this very moment, this defining second, that the event that would echo through history took place.

It was the moment that the world literally stood still.

Sunlight is made up of all the colors of the rainbow: red, orange, yellow, green, blue, and violet. The gas molecules in the atmosphere interact with the sunlight before it reaches our eyes. The gas molecules in the atmosphere scatter the higher-energy (high frequency) blue portion of the sunlight more than they scatter the lower-energy red portion of the sunlight. And therefore the sky is blue.

Or at least it normally is.

But in that precious moment as Guy awaited his final breath, the sky instantly erupted into a brilliant purple overhead. Years later, scientist would deduce that the molecules of the atmosphere were literally rearranged by the introduction of large plasma energy fields from multiple locations at once. The upshot was that the combination of impurities trapped within the water vapor increased the frequency of light momentarily trapped by these molecules and then scattered them as they were used to amplify an audio message to the entire planet.

The whole atmosphere became a resonating frequency producing sharp and crisp sound so stunning in clarity that hi fidelity systems were subsequently looked upon as tinker toys by those who witnessed the event.

As the words virtually sizzled in the ears of the hearers, every person heard the message without ambiguity in their own native tongue – even those standing within feet of each other.

Of course, scientists to this day have not been able to explain that one.

"Attention people of Earth."

Wayne had wanted to correct them, but the overall effect, the purple sky and sound so juicy it rattled his fillings, had his mind a bit preoccupied with just listening at the moment. He lowered his weapon and looked up at the purple haze. The arc of soldiers were likewise checking their weapons as they looked quickly around and up in near panic.

Guy and Kallie just continued to smile.

"This is Prel of the planet..."

Here the translation paused a moment to catch up. A sound that was incomprehensible came across as clicks, pops, and sputters, and then was neatly followed by the translated words, "from a planet that would be extremely difficult to pronounce in any human dialect because our aural communication is derived from a flap of open skin on what you might call a neck. But for the sake of argument, you may call us Ggelvring."

Guy found this to be slightly amusing but an understandable assumption necessary in order to get on with the conversation. And that was what everyone was interested in at the moment – getting on.

"We have returned in order to be updated on planetary management and to enjoy a concert or two of rhythmic enunciation by some of our more talented rhythmic enunciators. Imagine our surprise when our scouts found our Ggelvring comrades captured and being abused. This was a state and condition that we simply could not tolerate."

By this point, Wayne Avarice was quite near mental meltdown. The horror of the forewarned and imminent return of the mother-ship had been set aside in everyone's mind while they pursued their dreams of wealth and power. This new frightful realization was waging war with the more aggressive feeling of being horribly wronged as this unwelcome intrusion seemed to be robbing him the moment of ultimate conquest. He didn't know whether to run for his life or file a very serious complaint with management.

"We regret to inform you that we have transported all of our siblings to safety aboard our ship."

At this point Wayne lost it, screaming at the sky he shook his fists as he literally hopped in his anger, "That's it! I'm definitely filing a complaint with your management!"

The Ggelvring announcement continued as if they had not heard Wayne's impudent cry – which of course they had not.

"We clearly underestimated the ruthlessness and savage violence of your species. We correctly identified you as food. But we certainly missed that you were also poisonous."

Here the alien's tone shifted slightly for those people with languages that would support such a shift in tone. "Well, I suppose that is what happens when an advanced race such as ours speeds through the galaxy settling worlds such as yours with seeds such as ours. Eventually, you find a rotten apple in the barrel."

For some inexplicable reason, this last was translated into a rare dialect spoken only on Buckle Island as a sentence slightly similar to "At a certain point, you find a Buick in Love Canal." Linguists still wrestle with this translation to this day. But since the only people that spoke that dialect were leading expeditions on the mainland of Antarctica and were only now coming out of their shelters for what would be their early spring, they really did not understand the context. The restaurants had never really caught on there, after all.

"We will leave your quadrant. Your race is a sufficient distance away from any civilized planets and will not be able to spread your uncouth arrogance and violence upon truly gentile environs like the plague that you truly represent in your hearts.

"We had entertained the idea of punishing you; bring justice on your heads from above. But then we realized that probably the only true justice, our greatest punishment, would be to leave you unto yourselves. We figure within a short amount of time that you will be robbing, hurting, murdering, hating, incarcerating, and warring against each other anyway. What on Earth could we possibly do to you that would be any more horrifying than what you probably already do to each other on a minute by minute, second by second basis?

"Once we have traveled a sufficient distance from your world, we will place devices far enough out to prevent you from tampering. These will be quarantine buoys that will warn any other spacecraft that may otherwise stumble upon your quaint but surprisingly lethal little orb to stay the hell away. And short of that, if they must visit your planet, to at least leave crop circles or some such in order to really fuck with your heads."

"You may be doomed to your own lusts and greed, but we certainly do not intend to stick around and subject ourselves to any more of your vitriol."

A moment later, the sky returned to blue and everyone was very, very quiet for a really long, long time.

26.

Wayne came to the realization that all was lost. All the meat was gone.
Guy came to the realization that all was saved. All the meat was gone.

Kallie came to the realization that all was well. Guy was still alive.
Wayne came to the further realization that all was not well. Guy was still alive.

He raised his gun at Guy and yelled, "Sayonara!"

Guy had never really been sure when someone called, if it was his last name or if they were trying to be cute. He guessed at the demeanor of Wayne, now seemingly ready to continue with his little execution, that he was not trying to be cute.

He was wrong.

Oh, Wayne intended to kill Guy. That was calculated fact. But he also intended to be as cute as his now fully coup-flown mind would allow him to be.

"Wayne, let's think things through. We can work all of this out."

By this point the so-called defensive units had realized that everything they had followed before the remarkable events of late was probably pretty well history. Many of them began wondering what they would do with their now-pretty-much worthless money. Many of them just began wandering away and gathering in little groups of three or four trying to determine where to go from here. This was a pattern repeated in all corners of the globe. People just gathered, wondering where to go from here.

It was actually a remarkable time to be alive. So much potential. So many propensities.

"Work all of this out?" Wayne cried. "Work all of this out?" he repeated. He began stepping towards Guy and the line of remaining guards. He remembered what the sum of the long distance and his crap-aim had netted him the last time he shot at Guy – bupkiss. "And how, Guy? How are we going to work all of this out?"

"Well, we could start by putting the gun down."

"Putting the gun down?" Wayne asked, clearly slipping his buttery noodle. He stepped even closer to the line of soldiers. Most of them were now raising the rifles at *him*. Several of them were yelling for him to drop his weapon. Others were trying to order him to drop to the ground. There were even still others that were arguing that Wayne was still in control and what he said goes.

In the mass confusion and tension several of the alert guards reached out and with relative ease wrestled the gun from Wayne without a shot and took him into custody. It would later be said that the great Wayne Avarice just didn't seem to have any fight left in him. They were not quite certain about it but several of them felt that he would need to face some sort of criminal charges.

"What about him?" one of them asked of Guy who was still standing beside his car grinning wide at the spectacle.

"Who the chef?" another one asked.

"Yeah! Wouldn't he be just as guilty as Mr. Avarice?"

"Of what? Crimes against the pallet?"

Several of them laughed. One of the commanders said, "Nah. We can let him go. He was just the cook. Besides, if we need him, he won't be hard to find. He's on the One for crying out loud!"

This was followed by more laughter, jocularity, and jokes at Guy's expense.

The armored vehicles began pulling out from in front of Aunt Irene's house one at a time as Guy made his way through the dismissing fray and walked up to the ancient porch where Kallie still waited patiently for him on the ancient glider.

For quite a while they just stopped and smiled. Then Kallie finally broke the silence, "What's the matter Sayonara? Didn't all the culinary cut-downs get you boiling?"

Guy kept the grin as he said, "No. It's hard to take all of this too seriously when the leader of the alien race is named after a tube of green shampoo."

Kallie answered without blinking, "Actually… I don't think it was."

"Why do you say that?"

"The shampoo is spelled with two 'L's."

Guy sat there and nodded. Then asking with a quizzed look, "And how do you know its name wasn't spelled with two 'L's?"

"Let's just say it was a feeling I got from the purple sky. I guess I *saw* its words more than heard them – in my mind."

"I guess that makes as much sense as anything else," he concluded.

For the most part, the world pretty much freaked out at the message from the Ggelvring. Many well-known psychologists postulated that the eerie form of communication, coupled with the seriously mean-spirited content, combined with the brilliantly purple sky culminated in a sensory overload for most. For others it simply caused an overabundance of stating the obvious. This symptom was found most prevalently in the psychological community in general.

For some it was a somber and rather rude awakening from a depraved dream that slipped continually downhill into degradation and devolution. These found it very difficult to cope as the heavy burden of guilt was increased knowing that the junkies would soon begin to suffer from withdrawal symptoms and possibly even face death. The realization that this pain and suffering would be as a direct result of their own greed and will to power only increased this growing sense of doomed responsibility.

Sigmund Freud popularized a notion in psychology that was already pervasive in the field at the time, that the entirety of the human race was motivated by the will to have sex. This single motif became the seed for modern psychological thought well through the twentieth century and further proved that psychologists largely stated the obvious.

But in the latter twentieth century, several thought leaders such as Willard Waller and Tony Campolo had the bold insight to suggest that Freud was only partially correct. Yes, humans were driven by a will to something. It is just that the something was not necessarily sex. In their mind, sex was just a subset of a much larger something. And that larger something was power. All of the human race, they postulated, were driven in all of their actions every day by a will to power. This was certainly not stating the obvious, but that is ok. As it turns out, Waller and Campolo are sociologists and not psychologists after all.

But now looking back on the events of the recent months and the hungry, even ravenous desire to gobble up with gluttony as much power as was humanly possible made even the sociologists of the time realize that this too was pretty much just stating the obvious – which is probably why the psychologists were talking about it.

One thing that was especially novel in all of this was that while at the same time the majority of the world's population was feeling shame and remorse at the words of their alien adjudicators, there were at least two of the continents involved that took their message as a blasphemous diatribe intended to provoke the human race into action. As a response to this lecherous message, these two continents immediately sent a reply via radio to the aliens that they were gearing up their research for interstellar travel (and potential conquest) and that the Ggelvring actions of stealing the meat supply was tantamount to an act of war. The aliens were in for a really good old fashioned earth-style ass-kicking – quite oblivious of the howling irony they had committed.

Over time, the common glue of the continental government system and now-defunct franchises was simply not strong enough to maintain integrity. In a matter of weeks, the unities had broken down along old boundaries and border lines had been redrawn in the sand. As pretty much a complete planet, nation upon nation voted to re-adopt their old constitutions and concepts of law and order. Rebuilding work-projects began as economies slowly righted themselves. Pretty soon it became difficult to determine that anything had ever really happened and the whole event became a faded memory.

Even the two continents that declared war on the Ggelvring gave up their silly tirades and chose instead to begin beating the shit out of each other – once again totally oblivious to the howling irony they had committed.

And what about the addiction? What of the terrible withdrawal, anguish and perhaps even death that all the junkies faced? To be honest, it really wasn't all that bad. It was rather akin to giving up caffeine after drinking it daily for the majority of one's life. There was general crankiness accompanied with nagging headaches. Don't think too lightly of it. The world is a piss-poor place to be in when half the population is cranky and have nagging headaches. Quite a few marriages and reading clubs were ended during that time – everyone arguing about the latest empowerment book to come along, "What I Learned from the Ggelvring about Eating" by the Parsons wives.

But for Guy and Kallie on that day, the day of the purple sky, the day when the world got its old name back, for them it was bliss.

"Tell me what's on your mind, Guy?" Kallie asked as they moved nearly effortlessly to and fro on the metal glider.

The sun was high now and the beams dappled light through warm colored leaves and on the browning lawn that stretched out in front of them. Guy smiled yet again and sighed heavily, breathing in through his nose and out through his mouth.

"For the first time that I can remember in a long while I can actually feel concern. And yet, I have absolutely nothing to be concerned about."

Kallie shared his smile and looked back at the yard in front of them; a leaf fell playfully to the ground in loops and turns. "How do you figure that, Sayonara?"

"Well, I didn't kill half the world today. And I suppose any day that you can say that, is a pretty good day." Kallie nodded, still watching the leaf as it tried without success to take flight again in the gentle autumn breeze.

"There are no more frozen steaks since we were all on the fresh system now. The batches always begin with my orders going to the Eastern Time zone of North America first. That means the bad batch of rub will not arrive to any of the prep centers or restaurants until later today at the earliest. If there was any frozen meat it would have been fully prepared and cooked with good spices from before my change.

"So I guess no one will be hurt. No reason to be concerned there. And I don't have a job to get fired from; prob'ly don't need to report to work today."

"There is that," she conceded.

"And you and I are officially out of the terrorism business."

"I guess that's a shame," she admitted.

"A shame?" Guy asked, surprised.

"Well, you'd be amazed at how empowering it is, breaking all the rules, ruining people's lives just to gain control over them."

Guy felt the weight of her words in perhaps a way she did not intend. He kept this particular pain private, to himself. "I s'pose," he allowed.

Kallie sat up a little and playfully poking him in the ribs she confessed, "I used your name, you know."

Guy rocked in the glider. This last surprised him enough to lift his left eyebrow, "Did you, now?"

"Yup," she grinned, "You should have seen the effect it had on others. Your name was synonymous with power, Guy."

Guy didn't like the way that sounded. But he let the words stand without challenge. Kallie sat back and retuned to leaf watching.

"What are you going to do now?" Kallie asked.

"I don't know." The glider swung another two times while Guy thought about it. Then he concluded, "I think I'll have some lunch. I'm hungry. Got anything good to eat?"

THE END

EPILOGUE

Dr. Maria Isabella Consuelo Aufvedersane, Frank and Dottie Sayonara, and Dr. Misanthrope died in the initial alien attack. Guy never found out what happened to his parents. This was probably for the best. They had been surprisingly cruel in their will and rather unforgiving in the fact that their son had abandoned the promise of fortune and power in Aerospace Physics or Industrial Real-estate Law. They never lived to see him become the most powerful man in the world.

Benvolio was really named Jake, a forty-seven year old plumber from Michigan who moved to the panhandle of Florida to get away from the dreadful mosquitoes. He had been horribly misinformed by an Industrial Real-estate Lawyer and believed that there was no problem with the pests at all. He ended up marrying Belladona27, who was nearly half his age (the 27 was a slight exaggeration of some three years). When she first saw him after getting off the little commuter flight in Pensacola, she almost faked being someone else to wait for the next flight out. He was rather large and not the handsomest man. She on the other hand was a serious knockout. She decided though that his face was honest and his words had always been warm. She is extremely happy now and models swimsuits in nearby Panama City when she is in between squirting out babies. They have three happy and healthy children, all of whom come up with goofy ideas of their own to stir the pot.

Much to everyone's dismay, Junglejim, Jennfer19, and Shivagit were all killed by aliens. But much to everyone's non-dismay, Tarkus was also killed by the aliens so the new internet was spared a little l33t spe4k for a while.

Tinkerhell (Gina) survived, drifting from relationship to relationship, flirtation to flirtation. After the trip to Florida with Dex, nothing really quite satisfied her. She ended up as a nun in the St. Bartholomew convent and enjoys making macramé and seashell art to sell in the gift-shop to support the sisterhood.

Mrs. Owens is still teaching fourth grade. If the aliens ever come back, they won't stand a chance against her math students. They will undoubtedly change the world in the decades to come.

Daniel Guedbye was memorialized as the first human to have been killed by the invasion. Most importantly, the South African government insisted that his legacy of survival and endurance would be an inspiration for all the people for generations to come. They took the money donated for a monument and decided instead to invest it into a trust. This fund now pays for five college students a year to attend the college of their choice on a scholarship that bears his name.

Krel was equally memorialized. Its parents had been rather unforgiving in the fact that their spawn had abandoned the promise of fortune and power in planetary management or rhythmic enunciation. They demonstrated their surprising cruelty by boycotting the dedication to the first Ggelvring to have ever been slain in battle opting instead to rip the head off some poor creature imported from another planet and drink to more civilized life choices. But Krel's monument stands to this day as an inspirational epitaph to those Ggelvring that would pursue their dream regardless of their own frailties or shortcomings. "It is better to chase your vision with mediocrity than to die never having chased it at all."

Alfred and Vera Foreman finally retired in style. Alfred managed to convert a large percentage of his power from two of his three votes into real liquid assets like gold and gems. They moved out to their lake house and acquired all the other property around it to rent out for a continual source of income. Vera keeps the books straight with a keen eye for business and keeps Alfred straight with a keen use of a dishrag.

Calvin, Jolene, and Robin spend their weekdays rebuilding Huntsville, their weekends jet-skiing on the Tennessee River, and their nights having three-way sex. As it turns out, Jolene and Robin really enjoy it and Calvin has never seen *L'Homme qui Aimait les Femmes*.

Van and Glenda bought a doublewide on Sand Mountain southeast of Huntsville and attempted to start a chapter of the Aryan Nation. But since most of the population of gun-toting rednecks had been killed off by the invading aliens, there was not a strong enough base left to make it worth the trouble. So they ended up selling Amway to people that did not understand what pyramid schemes were.

Brian (the security guard at Three Caves) opened up the first strip club in North Alabama after the rapture of the trapped aliens in order to have a place that he and the other bouncers could actually get jobs.

Blackie, Ted, and Logan returned to their hunting farm and lived out their days hunting and fishing. Occasionally one of them would craft a dummy out of straw and scrap material, place a chef's hat on top, and take turns at target practice with their double cross-bows.

Jean Louis (John-Claude), really named Bubba Hickman gave up the whiny maitre de act and got a job at a local Jiffy Lube in Decatur. He spent the better part of his days fixing up the abandoned automobiles for a growing population. He made extra money on the side by selling air fresheners that hang from rearview mirrors.

Maximilian Hornbuckle committed suicide after having spent months killing untold hundreds of people in order to perfect Guy's rub recipe, only to have his opportunity to become the most famous chef in all the world yanked out from underneath him by those meddling Ggelvring – just desserts.

Joe Calamari, Theresa, and Alex opened the first post-steak restaurant in Huntsville. It was a huge success as people were still recovering and needed a nightly place to congregate and plan. They named it the Town-Meeting and they even had a dish or two of Guy's on the menu. All in all, they enjoyed him as a boss. He was a damned site nicer than Max to work for.

Speaker of the House Parsons and Tim Parsons took cyanide. There was no hope for them in the political or business world. Both Parsons wives developed a self-improving and empowering program that would help ex-addicted wives cope with the memory of the all-shocking things their husbands made them do while they were under the influence. They were the first to have an afternoon, nationally syndicated talk show on TV.

Senator Applegate and his wife recovered nicely. The Senator waited until the Parsons boys committed suicide and then framed them for the whole damned thing. His office spearheaded the investigation to get to the bottom of just how it all happened. After a solid year of due diligence, they came out with the evidence pointing to the Speaker and his manager brother. The good

Senator and his wife are regular guests on the Parsons Wives TV show. Those are usually the highest rated episodes.

Rothschild died of a sudden heart-attack while eating a giant bowl of Alfredo Sauce at a fine restaurant in New Orleans. They say that when they finally pulled his face out of the bottom of the bowl and wiped it off, he was still smiling.

Judge Greenhouge was found guilty on a series of indictments that kept the local courts busy for a solid five years. In the end, death was considered too good for him. It was an inspired bit of judicial magic that led to a sentence that all felt to be fitting. Judge Greenhouge is now the administrator of the complaint box at the maximum security penitentiary for the criminally insane west of the tri-cities. It is his responsibility to daily come up with creative solutions to reform prisoners while he is held accountable by the inmates to improve their own condition to their satisfaction or face their choice of punishments from a controlled list.

Randal Jones (engineer) retired to the family property east of Huntsville after coming up with a quick, efficient and cheap way for the world's governments to dismantle their containment areas while reclaiming as much of the material as possible for reuse in other projects.

It would be nice to say that James Navarone met with a bitter end. But as long as humans continue to prove the Ggelvring parting observations correct, there will be room for his kind of scum to prosper. Mr. Navarone retired to a country that had loose laws in the areas of his particular interests and the rest of the world was better served on that day. It is a pity there were more like him to take his place.

Irene Hawkins knitted and sewed, baked and stewed, and gardened and mended her way into all of the hearts that came to know her during those hard days of recovery that followed. The world misses her kind more and more every day as generations are born and raised ignorant of the precious miracle that is a pressure cooker.

Wayne Avarice's trial was a worldwide spectacle. He was found guilty on all charges and sentenced to death more times than a country full of attorneys could possibly appeal in a lifetime. In the end it was decided to deny appeal and Mr. Avarice was stoned to death the following April by over two hundred volunteers – they had to cut it off at that number to have room to fit them all into the quarry. The execution was the only globally televised event in the two years that followed the alien invasion and their subsequent rapture.

Dexter Stavro continued his law practice. He and Guy kept in touch for a long time, but as in all long-distance relationships their calls became more and more infrequent until they eventually stopped altogether. Dex will occasionally do pro bono work, typically for chefs or proctologists. He just has a soft spot for both, really.

The GMC Pacer was recovered from the mansion Guy abandoned on Monte Sano by a local garage that won a county contract to help in the cleanup effort. After sitting unused on a massive lot for years, it was eventually purchased by a broke college student for $25.00 New American. It has served him to this day without fail.

Kallie(Lambie22) Hawkins married the man of her dreams. She works to this day as a volunteer for a whole plethora of animal support and rescue groups. The former terrorist is now seen from time to time rescuing the odd kitten out of a tree or puppy from the local junkyard. But every now and then, just every now and then mind you, she will leave for a short vacation to somewhere. Guy never pries. He doesn't need to pry. But he is never surprised to see a news story or read an article about how a certain furrier was destroyed by explosions. No one is ever hurt though – that is their unspoken agreement.

Guy Sayonara changed his last name to Sandolls. He liked the way it sounded. He also started saying his first name with the Italian pronunciation of Gee (with a hard G). This was partly because he thought it was cool, but mostly to cut down on the Broadway musical jokes. After some time off to recover, spending days at the lakes and rivers, forests and fields, or just sitting on Irene's front porch glider, he eventually got a job at a small but respectable restaurant in Tupelo. He started as a prep cook, at the bottom. But he believed that if a dream was really worth it, then it would be worth paying some dues as well. When all was said and done, Guy chased his dream irrespective of his own mediocrity. He stopped playing it safe. He risked more, he reflected more on what he was doing while he was doing it, and he did more that would live on after he was gone.

ABOUT THE AUTHOR

Mr. Glasgow is an eclectic visionary whose day-job might best be described as "inventing the future".

In the arts, he writes original stories that entertain, composes music that reflects our times, and enjoys photography.

Mr. Glasgow makes his home in Atlanta, and for fun travels the world, plays trumpet, runs marathons, supports education, and has a passion for Habitat for Humanity.